Armine W. Mountain

A Memoir of George Jehoshaphat Mountain, D.D.

late bishop of Quebec

Armine W. Mountain

A Memoir of George Jehoshaphat Mountain, D.D.
late bishop of Quebec

ISBN/EAN: 9783337288204

Printed in Europe, USA, Canada, Australia, Japan

Cover: Foto ©Raphael Reischuk / pixelio.de

More available books at **www.hansebooks.com**

A MEMOIR

OF

GEORGE JEHOSHAPHAT MOUNTAIN, D.D., D.C.L.,

Late Bishop of Quebec,

COMPILED (AT THE DESIRE OF THE SYNOD OF THAT DIOCESE)

BY HIS SON,

ARMINE W. MOUNTAIN, M.A.,

Incumbent of St. Michael's Chapel, Quebec.

Montreal:
JOHN LOVELL, ST. NICHOLAS STREET.
LONDON: SAMPSON LOW, SON & MARSTON.
1866.

Dedicated

To the

Glory of God,

And the

Good of His Church.

ERRATA.

Page 11, line 6 from bottom, for *fluttering* read *fluttering*.
"   61, line 1, for *very* read *every*.
"   64, line 6, for *or* read *for*.
"   lxxxix. line 25, for 18*th* read 16*th*.
"   ccx. lines 11 and 12, for *thirty* read *fifty*.
"   ccxxxvi. line 3 from bottom, for *clergymen* read *clergyman*.
"   cccxxxii. line 22, for *besides* read *beside*.
"   cccxlvii. line 19, for *two thousand* read *one thousand*.
"   ccccvi. line 6, for *with* read *by*.
"   ccccxviii. line 14, dele comma at end of line.

CONTENTS.

PREFACE.

THE resolution* of the SYNOD OF THE DIOCESE OF QUEBEC, in obedience to which I have undertaken the work which is contained in the following pages, seemed to point not only to a personal memoir, but also to a quasi-historical sketch. This double character has rendered its execution peculiarly difficult, as it must necessarily make it fail to interest any one class of readers throughout. Apart from this consideration, there are reasons which have made me of all men the most unfitted for the task. But I have done my best, though too fully conscious of manifold imperfections; and I may truly say that it has not been without prayer that my work may, in some humble measure, advance the glory of God. It is in this hope that I have made public many words and thoughts which may be regarded, in some quarters, as too sacred to be so exposed. If any one person shall be moved, by reading these pages, to strive to follow the ex-

* "*Resolved*, That it is the earnest desire of the members of this synod, that a memoir of our late beloved Bishop, the chief ruler of the Church in Canada for so many eventful years of her history, should be published;

"That it is, also, the wish of the members of the Church generally, to possess some of the eloquent and admirable sermons of that lamented Prelate;

"That, therefore, a committee of three be named by the Chair to convey to the Rev. A. W. Mountain, the unanimous request of this synod, that he will prepare such a memoir, and also publish two or more volumes of the sermons of the late Bishop."

(A single volume of sermons was accordingly published, early in 1865. London: Bell and Daldy.)

ample of faith and patience which they set forth, I shall not have written in vain.

I have omitted much that relates to the more recent history of the diocese (inserting in fact scarcely anything beyond what is of a personal nature), because it is preserved in the records of the different institutions of the Church which sprang into existence during my father's episcopate. Partly for this reason also, as well as because the work grew in my hands to greater proportions than I had desired, the details of the later years of his administration are less full. Besides, as the condition of the diocese assumed a more permanent character, the journals and letters from which I have derived my information exhibit less variety, and the interest attaching to the description of the state of things in a new country diminishes as it grows older. I regret, however, that I have not been able to find room for some interesting notes on the early history of the Canadian Church which I was permitted to make from the records of the Society for the Propagation of the Gospel.

I have thrown into the form of an appendix some prayers and counsels composed for particular persons or occasions, as well as some brief extracts from letters, and some poetical compositions.

I earnestly hope that I have said nothing that will cause pain to any one. I am sure that the fear of doing so has often withheld me from giving what some persons might consider a just description of events in the history of the Church. And if I have incidentally been led, by the circumstances of my narrative, to indicate persons who had merited my father's approval, I trust (as he always did himself) that I shall not be understood as implying any disparagement of others to whose labours or character I had no such occasion to refer. This was a point in which, in all the published accounts of his doings, he was particularly sensitive. I trust I have not unconsciously done injustice to any one.

MEMOIR.

CHAPTER I.

Parentage—Birth—Emigration to Canada—Childhood—Boyhood—College Course.

THE family of Mountain is of French extraction, having emigrated to England on the revocation of the edict of Nantes, and settled in Norfolk, where they became proprietors of a small landed estate, called Thwaite Hall. It remained in their hands till about the middle of the last century. The last occupant, dying young, left two sons, the younger of whom afterwards became the first Bishop of Quebec. The subject of this memoir, the second son of the Bishop, was born on the 27th July, 1789, at the parsonage house of St. Andrews in Norwich, of which parish his father was at that time incumbent. He was baptized, privately, on the 3rd August; for, though a little more than an hour after his birth he was described as " apparently a sturdy fellow," he was a delicate child. While he was still an infant, his father removed to Buckden, in Huntingdonshire, of which place he had become vicar, being also examining chaplain to the Bishop of Lincoln, whose residence was at Buckden. This prelate had been tutor to Mr. Pitt, and when, in 1793, the Government determined on the erection of a see in Canada, his lordship recommended his chaplain for the appointment. Dr. Mountain

B

had himself been known to Mr. Pitt at Cambridge, where he
had been a fellow of Caius College, and the Bishop's recommendation was willingly adopted. Neither of the persons
more directly concerned in this measure appears to have had
reason to regret it, for we find it mentioned in Tomline's life
of Pitt, as a testimony to the wisdom of that statesman's
measures, that the first Bishop of Quebec had presided over
the Canadian Church "with great honour to himself and
advantage to the concerns of his extensive diocese ;" while
Dr. Tomline's own biographer, in his turn, brings forward
this appointment as a proof of the Bishop's good judgment,
displayed in his recommendation of Dr. Mountain.   Dr.
Mountain having been consecrated on the 7th July, 1793,
embarked almost immediately for Quebec, accompanied by
his wife, (Elizabeth Mildred Wale Kentish, co-heiress, with
two sisters, of Little Bardfield Hall in Essex,) and four
children, of whom George was the second. A residence in
Canada in the eighteenth century involved so complete a
separation from English friends, that all the members of the
Bishop's family, and one of his sisters-in-law, the future
Bishop's godmother, resolved to share his exile. His elder
brother, Dr. Jehoshaphat Mountain, rector of Peldon in
Essex, with his wife, son and two daughters, as well as his
own two sisters, accordingly accompanied him, and after a
voyage of thirteen weeks, the thirteen Mountains landed at
Quebec on All Saints' Day. The Bishop proceeded immediately to Woodfield, nearly three miles from Quebec, which
had been secured as his private residence. Here the boyish
days of his sons were spent, and the character of the surrounding scenery tended to form and encourage the power
which they inherited, in a remarkable degree, from their
father, of appreciating the beauties of nature. There is little
recorded of these boyish days, though enough to shew that,
besides the relish for natural scenery, turned, as it always
was, to a means of lifting the heart from nature to nature's

God, a correct classical taste was early engendered, and a natural turn for poetry indulged. In a journal kept by the Bishop in 1796, there is frequent mention of walks "with the children before breakfast," and on the 28th March it is noted that "this day George began his Latin grammar." A youthful effort at composition is in my possession, containing an account of a birthday spent at Powell Place (now called Spencerwood), then, as now, the residence of the Governor of the province. The grounds of Powell Place immediately adjoined those of Woodfield, being separated only by a small brook called Belle Borne, across which it is related in a work recently published on the environs of Quebec that the sons of Sir R. Milnes themselves built a bridge, which they named Pont Bonvoisin, for the purpose of establishing a ready communication between the two houses, and in this work we may presume that their young companions from Woodfield lent their aid. · The events of the birthday are thrown into the form of a drama, the personages of which are Sir Robert and Lady Milnes, with their children, and George Mountain and his brothers. A strong and affectionate friendship began at this early age, and continued through life, between the members of the two families. One of Sir Robert's sons, who was just two years younger than his friend George, was killed in the American war of 1813 : and his father having requested the Bishop of Quebec to write an appropriate epitaph, he transferred the task to his son, then rector of Fredericton, who subjoined to it four stanzas, of which the concluding two are these :—

> O wherefore, but to leave a deeper gloom,
>   Do these brief flashes pass before our eyes ?
> Why do fair Hope, and fluttering Promise bloom,
>   If Hope is early nipt, and Promise dies ?
>
> Forbear ;—these ashes cold, the blessed breath
>   Of Heaven can kindle to eternal light ;
> That Name can ope, which Milnes* invoked in death,
>   Germs of new life, to blow for ever bright.

---

* An allusion to fact.

A " puerile account " of an excursion made in September, 1804, drawn up at the time by one of his brothers, " to see the lake in the mountains called by the inhabitants the Lake of Beauport," is so curious at this distance of time that I am tempted to give an extract from it :—

"The party, consisting of the Bishop, his three sons and their tutor, set out on horseback early in the morning, and breakfasted at Mr. Duchesnay's, where we were received with great kindness and hospitality. Mr. Duchesnay himself then conducted us as far as the house of our guide, a civil, active fellow, named Jean Marie Belanger. We set out from his house on horseback, followed by a cart containing our provisions, and preceded by our guide and his son, a boy of sixteen yet in appearance hardly ten, his growth, as he said, having been interrupted by labour. After proceeding about half a league in the wood, we were obliged to leave the cart behind, as the road would not admit of its proceeding farther. Our guide now informed us that there were three lakes, the two former small, and the other larger, which was the one we were to see ; but on our expressing a desire to see them all, if possible, it was agreed that we should see the two farthest in going, and the nearest, or " Lac des Roches," on our return. About a league from the place where we left the cart, we were obliged to leave also the horses, and proceed on foot ; and very soon after we saw the first lake, which is a pretty little lake in a wood, called " Lac des Chicots," containing a small island. This lake abounds in fish and ducks. We now ascended the first mountain, the guide having nothing to direct him but his general notion of the place, no path, no traces of art. The trees grow to a great height, perhaps some exceeding 100 feet, but of a girth proportionably insignificant. We were in hopes of seeing some bears, as both they and beavers are occasionally found here ; but as we conversed as we went, our guide observed that the sound of our voices would occasion them to retire. The soil of the mountains is very soft, composed chiefly of dead leaves and fallen trees. We soon came to the second mountain, which is much larger, and part of it offers a curious appearance, being composed solely of dead trees heaped over one another, and thickly covered with a great variety of beautiful mosses interwoven with elegant creepers. The trees that grow here are often so loosely rooted as to give way to the hand. After a walk of at least two hours, we arrived at the borders of this charming lake : its noble and majestic beauty baffles the most ample powers of description ; the hills, the woods, and their various tints and shades, offering a variety and contrast hardly to be conceived. Completely repaid for the labour of our walk, we prepared to return, and found the mountains, by having a little changed our route, much steeper than before ; and when we arrived at the foot of the second, we were surprised with a proof that, in a wood, to be lost ten yards is to be lost as certainly as a thousand. We had descended the mountain rather too much to the west, and our guide, we saw, did not at all know where we were, though the path, to which good Providence directed us, was certainly not twenty yards distant. When we arrived at the place where our horses were stationed, we found that we had been gone considerably more than four hours ; but we considered ourselves amply repaid by the exquisite beauty of the lake we had seen. Our guide informs us that there are lakes between every two mountains in this vast range, and that he has been at one which he calls the "Lac des Vermins." As it was late, we did not see the third lake, called "Lac des Roches" we saw, however, as we returned, a bird called here the spruce partridge, but by naturalists the ruffed grouse, and a very beautiful creature it is. Fully satisfied with our day's expedition, we arrived home some time after dark."

A happier home than that of Woodfield (during the Bishop's occupation of which three younger children were born) has seldom been seen. The parents were regarded with unbounded and tender affection, mingled with veneration. Feelings such as these the characters of both were eminently calculated to inspire, and they produced their effect in unwonted brotherly love among their children, which continued, in a most remarkable degree, while they remained on earth, notwithstanding separations of great length both in time and distance. Some proofs of this will appear in the following pages. The Bishop continued to reside at Woodfield (though the winters had been occasionally spent within the walls of Quebec) till 1802, when he finally left it. George was then in his thirteenth year, and he gave vent to his feelings in the following lines, which are here inserted as a specimen of the poetic taste which he exhibited at that early age. They are the first in a small manuscript book filled up in a similar way from 1802 to 1804, which shews a very unusual familiarity with Greek, Latin, French and English authors. I have also some rough notes on the natural history and peculiar customs of Canada, written in 1804-5, with an index of more than one hundred subjects, displaying equally unusual powers of observation, and acquaintance with the points treated of.

O, must I leave thee, Woodfield?—sweet retreat
From the world's busy strife, delightful seat
Of rural beauty, where with bounteous hand
Nature hath lent her charms to grace thy land.
As feels the African when torn away
From friends, from parents, from his country's sway,
From all that's dear, and to a distant shore
Sold barb'rously for price of baleful ore,
By those detested traders—so my heart
Melts into sore regret from thee to part.
Thee must I leave, compelled by fate severe,
Where my sweet hours I spent without a fear
Of being forced from thee—enchanting spot,—
Unwilling forced to burst the tender knot.
But ah! those hopes, those raptures now are flown,
And why did I indulge them? Now are gone
All the delights that then did warm my heart,
And now by cruel fate I'm forced to part.
How can I part? How leave thee, charming place?
How leave the beauties which adorn and grace
Thy bound'ries? thy rich fields, abundant food
To cattle lending, and thy verdant wood;
Thy firs, thy venerable oaks, thy shades,
Thy purling rivulets, thy deep cascades,
Forming a pleasing contrast to the eye?
Thy views, in which no other spot can vie
With thee, extended o'er the country round,
O'er forests wild and cultivated ground,
O'er hills and valleys, o'er the rugged steep
Of the great king* of rivers, Lawrence deep?
Such are thy beauties, such my humble muse
Attempts to sing; yet thou wilt not refuse
This tribute to thy memory; thou wilt deign
To accept a faithful though a feeble strain.
And now by cruel fate severed from thee,
Wherever 'tis my destiny to flee,
Still I'll remember thee, O Woodfield dear!
And still on thee will drop a tender tear!

The education of the sons of the Bishop was conducted at home, for some years, by the Rev. Matthew Feilde, M.A., of

---

* Fluviorum rex Eridanus. Virg. Georg., I, 482.
Κρειων Αχελωιος. Hom. Il. Φ. 194.

the University of Cambridge, who lived in the house as tutor. Between Mr. Feilde and his pupils a strong feeling of attachment grew up, and he never ceased to take an interest and pride in them, or to look back with thankfulness to the happy days he had spent with them in Canada. In a letter addressed to the two elder, on their entering college, he says, "it is unnecessary for me to lay down rules for the profitable employment of your time ; you need no admonition of this nature from me."

When he was just sixteen, George Mountain left Canada with his elder brother, to pursue his studies under the care of the Rev. T. Monro, at Little Easton, in Essex, with whom they remained till their removal to Trinity College, Cambridge. He had received, together with his elder brother, the blessing of confirmation from his father's hands, at Quebec, on the 18th September, 1803. The letters which continually followed him from Canada from his relatives are full of expressions, not of affection only, but of strong and unvarying approbation, and others from companions of his own age, several of whom afterwards rose to eminence at the Canadian bar, exhibit the same proofs of his power of attracting regard and esteem. His regret at leaving Canada was very great, and found expression in some lines in which he says that in England,

> "—'Mid the grandeur of men
> And the wonders of nature and art,
> For the wildness of nature again,
> A sigh shall be felt in the heart."

But a taste for which there was no exercise in Canada, soon grew almost into enthusiasm.* No one who ever travelled

---

* In one of his journals, written in 1830, he mentions taking a note of the name of a place near Montreal, where the remains of a feudal-looking mansion were to be seen, " in order to see it and shew it to my children, if it should be fairly in my way; for although I would not now bestow time and thought upon such objects, I feel that I am not divested of some lurking

with him can fail to have been struck with the wonderful
keenness of his perception of the beauties of nature, enabling
him to see something to admire in combinations or contrasts
which an ordinary observer would have passed without notice ;
and all his letters and journals are full of descriptions into
which many other minds could not fully enter in the same
scenes. Yet to the last he used to say that even the
recollection of architectural remains of antiquity gave him a
pleasure which he described with a zest and a freshness
that carried one back to them as if they were before one's
eyes. None of his own early letters have been preserved,
his contemporaries to whom they were addressed having
all passed away ; but their letters to him speak of the
pleasure they derived from his description of the new scenes
on which he now entered. One of his Canadian friends,
writing from Quebec in February 1806, speaks of the pleasure
" of enjoying such sentiments as you describe to have filled
your mind on beholding the celebrated and venerable cathedral of Canterbury, and to have enraptured it on hearing the
solemn strains during divine service there." Among his
fellow pupils at Easton were some who afterwards became
distinguished in different professions; and among them all a
feeling of kindliness prevailed which manifested itself in after
years, whenever, by any circumstance, any of them were
thrown together. A letter written from Easton soon after
his removal to Cambridge ends with the words, " all the
boys send their *love* to you." One of those boys, who was also
with him at Cambridge, the only one (besides his brother)
of school and college companions, who now, it is believed,
survives, writes of him thus : " My affection for him was
such, that nothing which was cause of gratification in our

---

remains of a fondness for them, which, in my early youth, amounted to a
romantic enthusiasm. My children may, perhaps, contemplate them with
a similar kind of interest, accompanied by an attention to the moral and
religious lessons which are to be read in the changes of this lower world.

early associations seems to have left my memory; and often
as I sit opposite his picture in my drawing room, are scenes
of our dear early days brought vividly before my mind.
Alas! the last time we met, when he was last in England,
he felt our approaching separation so strongly, that as we
were moving about London in a cab, he stopped it, and said,
'Wait here, I must get out.' He said no more, but I lost
sight of him, and waited for a long time. But he never
came back, and I received a note from him next morning to
tell me, 'My dear——I could not say good-bye ; my heart was
too full ; I knew we should never meet again in the flesh ;'
and so we parted. Our first friendship was formed at Easton,
where we were placed for tuition under our kind friend, Mr.
Monro. There were eight of us. Happy days were those.
He was a first-rate classic. From thence he went up to
Trinity, and I to St. Johns, about 1808. He often passed
his vacations at my father's house, and was a great favourite
with everybody. Some years ago he went with me, at the
request of the vicar of ———, to preach a charity sermon,
and when we arrived in the vestry, we found a note addressed
to his lordship, requesting he would on no account read the
Communion-service at the altar. He observed it was a
very extraordinary request, and asked me to account for it.
I told him what I believed was true, that the vicar had a
very weak voice, and could not make himself heard in the
body of the church, and did not like any other person to do
differently from himself. On which he doubled up the note,
and said he should carry it home to Quebec, and have it
framed and glazed, and placed in his study as a direction by
a vicar how a Bishop ought to comport himself in church.
However, we did read the service, of course, in the chancel
and at the altar.

"His mind had always a religious tone and bias, and I
never knew him allow the least approach to irreverence of
any kind in his presence, even at his earliest youth. He

was my earliest, dearest friend, and there never was any
person out of my own immediate family, for whom I entertained so great a regard and affection. All my children
and Mrs. ——— were greatly attached to him."

I have given this extract, though part of it anticipates the
course of my narrative, to shew how lasting was the mutual
influence of his early attachments, as well as because it is
characteristic of him in some other points.

He became a scholar of Trinity College, but as his tastes
were strongly bent towards classical rather than to mathe-
matical studies, he took his degree, in 1810, without honours.
The number of his own books at that time, as exhibited in a
catalogue which has been preserved, would now be considered
surprisingly small, and proves how willingly he must have
had recourse to other means of improvement which were
within his reach. One of the tutors of his college, writing to
his brother, so long afterwards as 1821, says, "I need not
tell you how pleasing to me all my tutorial reminiscences are,
when I think of you and your brother. I have often regretted
that his acquirements and amiable talents should have so
little chance of being known in this country; the examination
which he passed for the scholarship in Trinity College was
certainly that of no ordinary scholar; his copy of Latin verses
and the accuracy of his English translation from the Greek
I remember to have been much commended by the seniors."
But the tutor who knew most of him, and for whom he
entertained a reverent affection to the day of his death, was
the late Rev. J. K. Miller, a man of unaffected piety and
wonderful humility of mind, as well as an accomplished
scholar. In a letter written nearly forty years after he had
left Cambridge, Mr. Miller says, in reference to a charge to
the clergy of the diocese of Quebec, then recently published,
"I have been, indeed, especially pleased with it, and have
not only read it over more than once, but made an object of
reading it to a coterie of special friends, who, I was persuaded,

would hear it with the same gratification as that which it gave me ; that is, the same in kind, but in degree it could not be so, from their want of personal acquaintance with the author. And from hence arose a peculiar accession to *my* pleasure ; because I traced in the charge, throughout, those tokens of identity of mind and feeling, with which I became acquainted early, and which are such interesting and powerful corroborations of truth,—truth in which we are all transcendently interested, and which we are bound to seek and to prove. Every page, every paragraph, almost every sentence, reminded me that I was listening (a curious metaphor as applied to reading, but intelligible,) to the same earnest-hearted, thoughtful, intelligent, discriminating friend whom I was early connected with as a pupil. Our hearts were then lighter than the discipline of life and probation of the world and a sense of the highest things have allowed them to continue, uniformly at least. Yet I hope that even then there was ' a sense of something far more deeply interfused ' than the atmosphere which immediately surrounded us, and that we have still been living for the same end, and had the same love of truth in view, and embraced it as it has more opened itself out to our ken, and ' proving all things ' have endeavoured to ' hold fast that which is good,' and still to ' walk by the same rule, to mind the same thing.' I persuade myself that I trace in this last, as well as in all previous compositions (to me an unsatisfactory word) of yours, successive evidences of this persevering course of mind. And while it is gratifying to do so, as a personal reminiscence, it is also didactic and edifying, as maturing sober convictions of what is true and indestructible. The individuality and identity and originality of mind which I trace in your writings is by no means inefficient as a power of spiritual suasion of the highest order. It is an evidence that you have gone to the root of the matter yourself, that you have not traded on other men's labours, or ' sworn to their words,' while you have had a just respect for the conclusions at which the wise and good of older times have arrived, and in which they have found rest, consolation, and satisfaction. In fact, you have contributed a sensible share to the proving afresh of not new things, but things which have been from the beginning, yet partly over-laid and over-ridden, but which are never to be forgotten and can never be lost. I could willingly go into divers particulars of your lordship's charge, with which I have been cordially delighted, but I fear I shall be led into disproportionate lengths of remark, and indeed never find an end. With regard to * * * * † I only demur to the courteous consideration which you have shewn towards them; yet, probably, you are right there, too, if I could see all. I am sure, however, I do not see enough in this case to entitle them, as of right, to so respectful a mention as you have made of them." Writing on the same subject to the Bishop's brother, Mr. Miller said, "It is so genuinely his *own;* the expression of his thoughtful, discerning, energetic, and yet delicate mind; so authentic, so conscientious, kind, candid, variously good, more than I can well particularly describe, that it has been quite refreshing to me to trace these evidences in it."

He was surrounded at Cambridge by friends whose affection continued unabated during their lives. and whose kindness his children, for his sake, have in many instances experienced. Like his companions at Easton, many of them became afterwards more or less conspicuous in their different callings. Among them was the late Dr. Chambers, whose refreshment in his busiest days was to read Æschylus in his carriage as he moved from house to house in his extensive practice. Their classical tastes were similar to his own, and many proofs of the accuracy and elegance of their scholarship might be produced. He had a wonderful memory for classical

---

† A party which had caused some trouble in the diocese.

literature, and especially for poetry in any language, and in
his old age could quote at great length from **authors whom**
he had not read since his **youth. In the year 1855 he was**
travelling, on one of his shorter visitations, with a distinguished
fellow of **Magd. Coll.**, **Oxford, who** had taken **duty near**
Quebec in a long vacation, and who was **about half his age,**
and to beguile a somewhat **tedious drive, they tried who**
could remember the greater number **of classical** quotations."
He said afterwards, " **I really believe B. began to think me**
quite a learned man, till we **got upon some more modern**
subjects, and then he found me **out.**" **It may not be out of**
place here to record the impression made on his companion
by his intercourse **with him. Writing in 1863, he says,**
" The pleasant **summer I spent under his hospitable roof**
gave me an opportunity **of knowing what a great loss you**
must all feel it to be. **I do not think I have ever come into**
similar contact with any **one for whom I have felt a stronger**
regard and reverence. **I felt always that I was with** a man
of gentle and warm heart, **of singleness and** simplicity **of**
character, of delicately **refined feelings, of high** christian
principle." †

---

* In the account **of one of his journeys as Archdeacon, when he was**
accompanied by **a** brother clergyman, **still labouring in the** diocese, he
says, " I would you had **heard** how my **companion, as we** tolled along,
beguiled the way through the midnight **woods,** by repeating from his
favourite poets, to whose works the conversation chanced to lead, I believe
a hundred lines **at a time,** and favoured by the **darkness,** which removed
some of the **checks upon his confidence, gave their full effect to many**
animated **or touching lines.**"

† I cannot forbear from **recording here** the impression made upon the
mind of another English clergyman, **who,** while an undergraduate, had paid
a long vacation visit to Canada **in 1845 : " The best of** the able account
given in the Quebec Mercury (January 1863,) is, that it is every word true,
and if anything under the truth. I shall never forget the impression which
I received of the beauty of his character during the five happy weeks
which it was my privilege **to** spend under his roof. He has ever since been
my beau-ideal of a Christian Bishop."

After he had taken his degree at Cambridge, he was a candidate for a fellowship at Downing College, which he did not succeed in obtaining; but the manner in which he acquitted himself at the examination was such that more than ten years afterwards, when application had been made to the then Professor of Greek, (Dr. Monk, afterwards Bishop of Gloucester,) to recommend a person to fill the office of Principal of a College in Nova Scotia, he wrote to his brother to enquire whether he thought such a situation would be acceptable, adding, " if you encourage the idea, I shall be delighted to offer my testimony in favour of his classical qualifications, which I well recollect at the examination for a fellowship at Downing College, when I thought that he displayed talent and good scholarship in no ordinary degree, and he would, I am convinced, be a most desirable head of the establishment."   I ought not to pass over the assistance which he derived in the pursuit of his studies from his elder brother, to whom this letter was addressed ; he was a ripe and accurate scholar, and though only eighteen months his senior, was able to give him much valuable advice. He still survives, the only one remaining of the children of the first Bishop of Quebec, is a prebendary of Lincoln Cathedral, (almost the senior prebendary of England,) Rural Dean, Commissary of the Archdeacon of Bedford, and rector of Blunham, Beds, where, in his 79th year, he performs three services, and preaches three times every Sunday of his life.

CHAPTER II.

Ordination—Journeyings with his father—Marriage—Settlement at Fredericton—Removal thence to **Quebec**.

AFTER leaving Cambridge, **the younger of the two brothers**
returned, in 1811, to Canada, where he had the great
advantage of pursuing his studies in preparation for Holy
Orders, to which his mind had been long directed, under the
guidance of his father, whom he aided at the same time, in
the work of his diocese, as his secretary.* He continued
to act in this capacity after his admission to Deacons' Orders,
which were conferred in the cathedral of Quebec, by the
same hands by which he had been baptized and confirmed, on
the 2nd August, 1812. He rendered assistance, during
his diaconate, in the duties of the parish of Quebec, of which
his cousin, the Rev. Salter Mountain, M.A., of Caius Coll.,
Cambridge, and chaplain to the Bishop, was minister. Mr.
Mountain was one of those who had accompanied the Bishop
to Canada in 1793, being then already in Orders.

In 1813, the Rev. G. J. Mountain attended his father on
his triennial visitation of the diocese. He took rough notes
which he designed afterwards to expand into a fuller journal,
but even at that early stage of his ministry, his hands were
always more than full, so that it does not carry us to any great

---

* This preparation was not deemed inconsistent with his obeying the call
made for volunteers in the American war, and though he was never engaged
in any active operations, he served as one of the garrison of Quebec, on the
ramparts of which he was long remembered to have mounted guard.

distance. **It is** sufficiently interesting, however, as affording
a picture of **the means of** conveyance half a century ago.
Their destination was Upper **Canada, and** in order **to** reach
it, the Bishop, with **two sons** and a daughter and two servants,
embarked at Quebec in a *bateau* (after waiting an hour at
the water's edge till it could be got alongside the stairs.)
This vessel was provided by Government, and " over the
middle part of it, a neat wooden awning was built, and
lockers, which also formed seats, were arranged along three
sides of the square apartment under the awning ; the fourth,
towards the front of the boat, being open. The Bishop,
however, sat in the middle, in a great old arm-chair. The
crew consisted of a pilot and four rowers, two before and two
behind the awning. For these men, who were engaged to
convey them to Montreal, fifty pounds of pork and thirty
loaves were provided by agreement, in addition to which, the
pilot was to receive £4, and the men nine dollars each."
It was proposed to proceed to Pointe aux Trembles to sleep,
but having met a gentleman from St. Nicholas, (Mr. Caldwell,)
pulling himself in his own wherry, who invited them, on
account of the threatening appearance of the weather, to
pass **the night at his house, the** Bishop **and** his whole party
availed themselves of his hospitality. It was arranged that
the bateau should go on at daylight, to take advantage of the
tide, to St. Antoine, whither the travellers were to proceed
by land to join it. The next day, however, the Bishop's
daughter became so unwell, that he determined to return to
Quebec on her account, and after sundry delays and difficul-
ties in recalling the bateau, the party reached Quebec, three
days after they had left it, having accomplished just fifteen
miles of their upward journey. " Thus ended this expedition,
which had proved nothing **throughout but a** series of discouragements and distresses. **A delay of two** days, difficulty
of arrangement, and contention with grumbling, unreasonable
people, in the first instance ; inability to reach our destination

the first night; a leaking bateau; a most unaccommodating tide; a continuance of rain unexampled; the illness of my sister; the failure of the bateau's return from St. Antoine, and the consequent necessity of my father's sitting up (for his bed was on board) all night; and the very considerable expense to no purpose, make up the history of this memorable excursion. A —— drew up a string of miseries under eleven different heads, and his account was perfectly just." About a week afterwards, the Bishop made a second and more successful attempt. He left Quebec with his own horses on the morning of the 22d July, and reached Kingston on the 8th September. He had four times before visited Upper Canada, and once had been driven back to Kingston by a storm, when in sight of Niagara. On this occasion, the delay was caused by the necessity of waiting at Montreal for his baggage, which had been entrusted to a schooner. For in the little steamer in which his sons took passage from Quebec, and which had but recently begun to make occasional voyages to Montreal, the passengers were limited to a very small allowance of baggage, and all that the Bishop required for a large party to travel in canoes or bateaux for an indefinite time exceeded the prescribed quantity. The arrangements of the steamer are all minutely described in the journal. Montreal was reached after a voyage of forty-eight hours, and there the Bishop joined his sons on the 27th. After waiting a month for his baggage, he despatched a servant and some men in a bateau, in search of the schooner. They met it twenty miles below Montreal, and the baggage, having been transferred to the bateau, reached Montreal on the 30th August. The minister of Montreal, at this time, was the Bishop's elder brother, and the Church of England was obliged to hire a Scottish kirk to hold service in.* On one

---

* A church had been begun in 1807, in which year Dr. Mountain, writing to the Bishop, complains of the backwardness of the people to pay their subscriptions, adding, "We have paid 500*l* or 600*l*, as a committee, out

C

Sunday it is noted in the journal, that "the Scotch congregation having a sacrament, which occupies a long time, there was no service for our Church." Dr. Mountain was the only clergyman in Montreal, or for many miles around. He carried his ministrations to other places, at a distance, where there was any demand for them. He is described as a man of a "cordial, cheerful, benevolent, active disposition, shining forth under his grey hairs—of a simple, guileless, ingenuous temper, and the most indefatigable attention to the duties of his profession (which fall heavily upon him), united with the capacity, of which it has shut out the habitual exercise, for elegant and tasteful recreations." Mr. Jackson, the rector of Sorel, happening to be in Montreal during their stay, dined with Dr. Mountain one day, when it was observed that nearly half the clergy of Lower Canada were at the table. There were four in all, including the Bishop, so that besides the four who bore the name of Mountain and Mr. Jackson, there were only three in Lower Canada; the Hon. and Rev. C. Stewart, the apostle of the Eastern townships, the Rev. C. C. Cotton, one of the earliest labourers in the same field, and the Rev. R. Short, of Three Rivers, grandfather of one of the S. P. G. missionaries now holding charge in the diocese of Quebec.

During his stay at Montreal, the Bishop held a confirmation on St. Bartholomew's Day, when forty-two "only" were

---

of our own pockets, besides our subscriptions, and the workmen and others are still very importunate for more money. I hope, according to what you mention in your letter, that we may reckon on 500*l* from the Society, 200*l* from the Lord Mayor and Corporation, and 150*l* from the London Merchants,—in all 850*l* sterling. Could we draw for this money we might possibly go on with the building, having confidence in your goodness in endeavouring to use every means of procuring us a sufficiency to finish it." A large grant was made by the Imperial Government, but a great delay took place in the payment of it, from correspondence occasioned by a mistake made in the Colonial office, where it was supposed that Montreal was in Upper Canada.

confirmed. After a detention of five weeks, the party was at last enabled to set off for Lachine, en route for Kingston, on the 30th August. At Lachine they were detained a whole day by an adverse wind, and on the 1st September, embarked in their "old enemy, a bateau" which was provided by the Commissariat at the Bishop's expense.* The voyage was enlivened by the company of other bateaux carrying troops to the seat of war in Upper Canada, which served as a protection where their course lay within reach of the American shore. They proceeded, however, without any symptom of molestation, and it was only the possibility of this that made precautions necessary. The only clergymen stationed between Montreal and Kingston were Mr. Baldwyn, at Cornwall, (afterwards at St. Johns, L. C.,) and Mr. Weageant, of Williamsburgh, who had been a Lutheran minister, but, having joined the Church of England with his congregation, had been ordained by the Bishop. He officiated alternately in German and in English. The Bishop did not stay to perform any episcopal acts at either of these places, but reserved them, apparently, for the downward journey. Kingston was reached on the 8th September, where the Bishop became the guest of Mr. Stuart, the minister of that place. The journal does not go beyond this point, but there are some rough notes of the Bishop's which serve to carry it on to the 17th. He left Kingston on the 14th, in a canoe, with ten Indians and an interpreter, provided by the Governor, Sir G. Prevost, for the Bay of Quinté. The voyage was not prosperous,—the Indians were "lazy, and at last drunk,"—and afterwards became so terrified by reports of Americans being in the neighbourhood, that they refused to go on.

George Mountain was admitted to Priests' Orders by his father, in the cathedral of Quebec, on the 16th January,

---

* I have a memorandum of the expenses of a canoe, paid by the Bishop, from Montreal to Detroit, in 1816, (exclusive of provisions,) which amounted to within a few shillings of £150.

1814, and on the 18th, licensed as evening lecturer of the cathedral. The value of this appointment was £150 a year. Not long afterwards it was rumoured that a clergyman was wanted either at Fredericton or at St. John, in the adjoining province of New Brunswick ; and the Bishop of Quebec, being desirous of providing for his son, wrote to the Bishop of Nova Scotia to recommend him for whichever post might be vacant, if in so doing he "should not interfere with the fair claims of any other person," adding, "in one word, unless you are at a loss for a proper person to fill one or other of these situations, my son would be as unwilling to obtrude himself upon you, as I should be to offer him to your consideration. God forbid that we should attempt to stand in the way of any of your own clergy who wish for and may be suited to the situation in question. I must, in justice, say of my son, that he is a young man of learning and ability, of sound principles and exemplary conduct, and already much considered as a preacher here." The Bishop of Nova Scotia replied, that what he had heard from different sources made him "desirous and even anxious that Mr. Mountain should settle in his diocese." Preparations were made at once for his removal to Fredericton, for he had a step in contemplation which rendered the augmentation of his income, which his appointment to that charge would bring with it, a matter of some importance. On the 2nd August, 1814, he was married, by his father, in the cathedral of Quebec, to Mary Hume, third daughter of Deputy Commissary-General Thomson. They lived together in the tenderest and truest affection for forty-seven years. Immediately after their marriage they embarked in a transport which was conveying troops to Prince Edward's Island ; from thence they crossed to Pictou, and proceeded by land to Halifax. There are some very rough, and scarcely intelligible, notes of this journey, but it appears sufficiently that they left Pictou on the 29th August, going on horseback for the first twenty-five miles, and reached

Halifax in three days. One letter has been preserved, in which the approach to Truro is thus described: " Like all the places in these new countries, it refuses to exhibit anything picturesquely rural; and the eye looks in vain for the village scenery of the mother country,—no hedges, no sunk, shady lanes ; no Gothic church* embosomed in yew; no snug, old-fashioned farm, with casement windows ; no village green, with here and there a pond ; no venerable hall, nor respectable family-mansion, surrounded by its comfortable appendages, screened by a tall rookery, or caught through an old avenue ; nothing that interests the fancy; nothing that excites a pleasing association." The journey from Charlottetown to Halifax cost £17. At Halifax they remained a week, at the end of which they set out for Annapolis, where they were to embark for St. John, N. B. This voyage was easily accomplished. At St. John they were detained another week, making necessary preparations for settling at Fredericton. When they were within ten miles of their future home, the wind proving contrary, they left the little vessel in which they had ascended the river, (having been three days on board,) and " went ashore, opposite a church, having made a small bundle ; no gig or horses at the house. Two black girls put us over ferry, and we walk a mile. There two saddle horses ; arrive at five," on the 27th September. This was the manner of his approach to his first pastoral charge. He had not been idle on the way, for every Sunday it is noted that he preached, generally twice. Besides the rectory of Fredericton, he held the posts of chaplain to the troops, and to the Council. A letter from his predecessor, the Rev. George Pidgeon, Commissary of New Brunswick, who had removed

---

* In this respect, at least, things had improved, some thirty years later, for, in 1843, the people of the inn at Truro used to point out the wooden church, and tell that its spire had been built in *imitation of that of Salisbury Cathedral*, apparently without any consciousness of reserving the rule, *Si parvis liceat, &c.*

to St. John, dated 20th October, 1814, shews that he was not long in throwing himself into his work, and into a department of work not always considered the most agreeable. Mr. Pidgeon acknowledges the receipt of a list of subscribers to the S. P. C. K., to be forwarded to Halifax. His reports to the S. P. G. from Fredericton evince his earnest care for the welfare of his flock and of the destitute settlements in the neighbourhood. He dwells particularly on the means of education. And while he gives, on the whole, an encouraging picture, it appears that he did not shrink, even during his short sojourn, from endeavouring to correct any laxity of practice into which the people had, to some extent, unavoidably fallen. An instance of this is found in his urging upon them the duty of bringing their children to the church for baptism, instead of having the ceremony performed in private houses. In the letter just referred to, Mr. Pidgeon says, " I rejoice to find you are so much pleased with your habitation ; the situation, in summer, is indeed delightful, but I fear you' have brought an old house over your head ; the kitchen was, when we left it, in a deplorable state, and many other places exhibited strong symptoms of decay." In this old house, however, he spent three years very happily and comfortably ; though, if the price of all the necessaries of life was in proportion to that of two bottles of lime-juice which Mr. Pidgeon forwarded by " sloop," valued at eight shillings,— for lime-juice was a luxury not to be procured in Fredericton —the emoluments of the rectory could not have been much too large. Another illustration of the condition of things in this point is found in Mr. Pidgeon's letter, for he speaks of some " common tables" which had been ordered at St. John, but about which there had been some mistake. They were " two pounds a piece ; but, if they have turned legs, round corners and castors, they will be three dollars and a half more per table !"

Another letter, of a very different kind, deserves to be here transcribed, as shewing the influence which helped,

by Divine grace, to make him what he was. It is from his
father, and is dated Quebec, 31st October, 1814. " I think
by this time I may congratulate you upon being settled in
your own house. I am glad to hear that it is so comfortable,
and that its situation so much pleases you. The whole of
your journal has been most interesting to us ; and your letter
to me from Fredericton such as could not but give us the
greatest satisfaction. You now, my dear son, enter upon the
important business of life, and you will not be surprised that
I take this occasion to offer some suggestions as to the conduct to be adopted, to secure its best enjoyments. I need
not recommend to you regularity in the discharge of all your
clerical duties, nor an earnest desire to promote the religious
knowledge and the piety of your people. I am satisfied that
you have these objects seriously at heart. I will, therefore,
only caution you to take care that, from the outset, your
manners and conversation may be such as are best calculated
to secure to you the respect, as well as confidence and kind
regard, of all those of whom you are the pastor ; and that you
will, upon all proper occasions, take care to let them see that
your first object is their spiritual improvement, and that you
are by no means indifferent to their temporal welfare, the
concerns, more especially, of the unfortunate, the sick and
the poor. Make yourself, as far as you can, acquainted with
the situation and circumstances of every person in your parish ; and endeavour to have such personal acquaintance, even
with the lowest, as may afford opportunities of instruction,
comfort, and advice. Accustom your mind to the consideration that you are ' an ambassador for Christ,' and endeavour,
in all things, to conduct your embassy in the spirit of your
Master. Be very watchful over yourself, that no degree of
languor or indifference creep by degrees into your manner of
performing divine service. Impress upon your mind the
fixed recollection, that when you open your lips in the church,
it is to address yourself to the Almighty Lord of heaven and

earth, in behalf of yourself and of all who are assembled
with you. This recollection, faithfully preserved, will make
it impossible for you to pray without deep seriousness, awful
reverence, and devout affections. In the pulpit, always keep
it in mind, that the eternal condition of all, or of many at
least, who hear you may depend upon and date from the
doctrine and the exhortations that you deliver, your animad-
versions upon sin, and instructions in righteousness; and keep
the same things in mind in the composition of your sermons,
never addressing yourself to this part of your duty without
prayer to God for His blessing upon your labours. In private
instruction, (whenever an opportunity offers of conveying it,)
do not be deterred by a fear of the imputation of methodism,
from being warm and earnest in your endeavours. Do not
be discouraged by perverseness or conceit, nor disgusted by
vulgarity and ignorance ; keeping always in mind the infinite
importance of the object, and the reward of those who turn
many to righteousness.

" I will conclude by begging you, in the most earnest manner, to be strictly regular in your application to the studies
proper to your profession. Observe, I say regular. I do not
wish you to be a hard student, I ask you to be a regular one.
Set apart a convenient portion of the day, and let nothing
(but what may be still more necessary and important) divert
you from the observance of it. Remember the parable of the
talents, and cultivate yours with conscientious perseverance.
Believe me, there is no need of heinous crimes, or of notorious misconduct, to fix in the mind the anguish of remorse.
He who, as life advances, is conscious of having neglected
or abused the talents which God was pleased to bestow upon
him, who is conscious that he has done infinitely less good
in the world than he might have done if he had sedulously
cultivated, and properly and steadily applied, those talents,
will need no other consciousness to embitter the maturer
years of life, no other offences to make him fully acquainted

with all the anguish of unavailing regret, and all the apprehensions of a late repentance. God grant that you may duly and in time consider this. I know the excellence of your principles, and the goodness of your heart. **Be resolute, my** dear George, with the grace and help of God."

In another letter, dated 12th February, 1816, his father says, "**All your** doings comfort me greatly."

In this year, the Rev. Salter Mountain became desirous of exchanging his post at Quebec, the duties of which, discharged as they had **been** for twenty years with an unremitting attention, had outgrown his strength, for one demanding less labour and anxiety. It **was** accordingly arranged that he should remove to Cornwall, in Upper Canada, which was then vacant, **where he** continued till the day of his death, and where his memory **still lives,** as that of a guileless **true-** hearted Christian.* **His widow** and some **of** his children still live at Cornwall, where they have been long known as large benefactors **of** the Church, and leaders in every good work. When he had determined on leaving Quebec, it was proposed to the rector of Fredericton that he should become his successor. His father offered it to him, but left the choice entirely **to** himself, saying, "**I** neither advise, **nor** object to your coming." He was unwilling to influence him in any way, although having no son in Canada, and no prospect of seeing any **of** them, and being upwards of threescore years of age, **he** naturally desired to have him at Quebec, particularly with **the** prospect of losing the assistance of Mr. Salter Mountain **in** the capacity of chaplain. In **the** letter in which the change was proposed, (October 7th, 1816,) the Bishop says, "You will be glad to hear, that I got

---

* One of the most liberal and humble-minded churchwomen anywhere to be found traces her systematic and self-denying habit of alms-giving to his instructions, aided by those of his sister, at the time of confirmation, some sixty years ago. She has been under the pastoral care of five members of the family of Mountain, of two different branches, and three generations.

through my long visitation, (three months and four days,) in all respects more satisfactorily than I expected. Travelling in the canoe enabled **me to see** a great deal more of the **country and of the people than** I could otherwise have done. **That part of the upper province which** was new to me,[*] **far exceeded in beauty and fertility all** that I had seen before, **and the climate appeared to be delightful.** A great part of **the new townships in Lower Canada surpassed** in beauty, **and equalled in fertility, all that I had seen in** Upper Canada. **I can scarcely imagine** anything more picturesque or romantic. **The country about** Lake Memphramagog more especially, **I think can hardly be** exceeded anywhere ; but the **climate is not so soft, nor the** colour and form of the woods so **admirable, as in** Upper Canada. From St. Armand to the **river St. Francis, (a sort of zig-zag** diagonal of all these townships,) **we travelled in** waggons, over high mountains, **and through deep valleys and** woods, in roads composed of **rocks and roots, only** exchanged, occasionally, for short, but deep, black, swampy **soil.** Nobody would believe, before I **tried it, that it could be** so accomplished; but, thanks be to **God, it** *was* **so accomplished, although we** sometimes could **not advance more than twelve miles a** day, and though we ourselves frequently thought the obstacles insurmountable. It has been accomplished, too, (through mercy,) not only without injury to my health, (though, for a few days, I had **reason to fear that the old complaint** in my side was alarm**ingly increased by it,) but with a** great improvement of it. **I found myself able to walk seven** or eight miles at a time, through bad roads, and much more through good. **My rest** was perfect ; the coarsest food was acceptable to me. **My strength and activity seemed** almost daily to increase ; and though I was often sensible of fatigue, it was not a fatigue

---

[*] He had coasted Lake Erie in a canoe furnished by the N. W. Company, with twelve voyageurs, and visited the missions at its upper end, which, by the route he took, are scarcely less than 1000 miles from **Quebec.**

followed by languor or debility. I never took cold, though wet through on the water, and sleeping on the shores of the lakes, six times in a tent, and often in strange houses. I preached at every place where I stopped and found it practicable to hold divine service (four times, for instance, in five days,) and made many arrangements for the establishing of future churches. Have I not great reason to be thankful that I have been enabled to do all this, and that, having done it, I yet experience, undiminished, the strength and activity which I have recovered? At my time of life, this cannot last long, but it becomes me gratefully to enjoy it while it does. The reception which I met with on the journey (from Governor Gore downwards) was in the highest degree gratifying, as well as that which I have since met with from Sir J. Sherbrooke. The latter behaved in the most obliging manner, and said the kindest things of what he had heard of you, when I mentioned to him my probable wish for an arrangement that would bring you here. * * * I am delighted, my dear G., with your employments. How, indeed, can I be otherwise? Persevere, my beloved son, in the 'narrow way,' and may the blessing of God rest upon you and yours, now and forever! You have been very good in writing, and your letters are always a cordial to me. Give my blessing, with my tenderest love, to Mary and her little ones. I need not say how truly I am your affectionate father and friend,

J. QUEBEC."

At the date of this letter, the Bishop was on the point of proceeding to England,* in the hope of procuring some relief

---

* I cannot forbear from giving here a description, contained in a letter from his eldest son, of the Bishop's meeting with his family in England in 1817, as shewing the extraordinary affection entertained for him by his children. "Yesterday, as we were looking out of the window, a cry was uttered, 'what's that?' (a carriage approaching)—a tremendous rush of feet

from his episcopal labours, which he had now carried on for
twenty-three years. When his son removed, therefore, in
the following year, from Fredericton to Quebec, he did not
find any of his own immediate family there, nor did they
return from England for some time afterwards. He was most
affectionately welcomed, however, by other relatives and a
large number of friends, among whom he was to exercise

and overturning of furniture followed, and in a moment I found myself in
the garden, in my father's arms with E. and C., the latter of whom declares
that she expected to be killed, and actually was deprived of breath by the
violent compression of agitated embraces. This morning the effects of con-
vulsive and hysterical joy are visible in all our faces, but we are too happy
not to be well. The dear object of our prayers and anxiety is thin, but
looks admirably, and is quite young, lively and active, and so beautiful ! in
his 66th year—wonderful in all things ! We cannot, at least I cannot,
write, nor take my eyes from that face which they have so longed to see,
but we have time to rejoice in your promotion to Quebec, and to offer our
best congratulations on it. How comfortable for my aunt M."

I am tempted to add the testimony of his youngest son, written more than
twenty-five years after his death : " Our father lives in my recollection as
a being of a higher order, and of a different race from the men among whom
my life has been passed. He was not only essentially a gentleman, but I
have never, in all my wanderings, seen a prince who had his bearing. He
was stern when his indignation was justly roused, but who more kind and
gentle, more playful in his own circle, more consoling as a friend and adviser,
more beneficent in private charity? Full of talent and scholarship, whatever
he did was handled with a master's touch : his pencil and his flute he laid aside
in maturer years, and his pen was only employed in the performance of
his duty or for the amusement of his friends; he eschewed authorship, but
whether he wrote a sonnet or a satire, an epitaph or a humorous ditty, an
official paper or a sermon, truth and vigour, keen perception, deep feeling
and exquisite taste were his attributes. His ' Hints' given to R—— and
me on leaving home are the most perfect manual for a young man entering
life, and his sermons were at once the most striking and the most convincing
that I have ever heard or read. And when at the close of the Communion-
service, he advanced from the altar, with the open book upon his hand, to
give glory to God on high, I have never witnessed any thing on earth so
godlike as his figure, his voice, his manner. How often do I think of him !
When I recall his letters and his verbal advice, I feel how wise he was, and
yet withal only too indulgent. When I was escaping from my teens, I was
a somewhat precocious youngster. I had at least the good looks of youth,

his pastoral charge. His farewell sermon* was preached at Fredericton, on St. Peter's Day, from 1 Thess. iv., 1, 2. It is particularly designed to guard his flock against the danger to which they would be soon exposed, in consequence of an unavoidable vacancy which would occur after his departure, from the practices of some irregular teachers of religion. He carried with him, though he had been less than three years among them, the love of all the members of his flock. The President of the province, writing to the Bishop of Nova Scotia respecting the appointment of a successor, speaks of the " salutary effects of his prudent zeal, and indefatigable diligence in the various branches of his pastoral office," as having " already contributed, in no small degree, to confirm the well-disposed, and to conciliate the disaffected;" and the Bishop, in reply, writes thus : " That the intended removal of your excellent pastor should excite great concern in the parish of Fredericton is not to be wondered at. I am truly sensible of the loss we shall all sustain by his departure from the diocese." The letters of the Bishop and his commissary

---

high spirits, and manners formed from having been thrown early into good society. Our father sent me for the first time to the continent; he spoke to me at parting, kindly but seriously : you have, he said, such and such advantages,—enumerating them with a father's partiality,—but do not deceive yourself : you are now well received every where, but unless you exert yourself to obtain solid and useful, as well as elegant, information, you will find, as you grow older, that you cannot maintain the same relative position in society ; and unless you study the Word of God, and make it your rule of life, when the pleasures of this world lose their relish, as they will, you cannot be happy." The character of the Bishop was drawn by his second son, in a brief memoir, in 1825, and he received many testimonies to its faithfulness. I have heard people say it was worth while to go any distance to hear him pronounce the benediction. And since I wrote this note, an aged and very poor man told me that " when he said ' the peace of God,' it went all round the church ; it was like silver."

* He had previously published one (by desire) on Judges viii, 34-35, preached as an appeal on behalf of the Waterloo sufferers, 14th January, 1816.

(who was afterwards his successor in the see) both express their own personal sense of loss and disappointment in the strongest terms. Nine years later, when the churchmen of New Brunswick had so increased in numbers and importance as to make them feel their need of a resident Bishop, some leading persons at Fredericton entered into communication with their former pastor, in the hope of effecting an arrangement by which he might be restored to them in that capacity. He was not unwilling to entertain the proposal, for he always cherished a strong affection for his first flock, and he had already been thought worthy of advancement to the highest order of the ministry, by those whom he knew to be well qualified to form a judgment; but the encouragement which had been held out respecting the provision to be made for the maintenance of the office was subsequently withdrawn, and the plan was necessarily abandoned for a time. A leading member of the society of Fredericton says on this occasion, "I shall not quite relinquish the hope of seeing you placed where not I alone, but all your friends here, are persuaded you would be eminently useful." Again, some eleven years afterwards, when the project of a Bishopric in New Brunswick was revived, the Governor of that province wrote to him, while he was administering the diocese of Quebec under the title of Bishop of Montreal, to express the great satisfaction which his translation to New Brunswick would give to the Church there. He never met his old flock, however, until thirty years after he had left them, when he passed through Fredericton, on his way from the district of Gaspé to another part of his own diocese, and the eagerness with which he was welcomed by men and women of all classes, rich and poor, white and negroes, shewed how lovingly his memory had been cherished, and how fruitful his short ministry had been. It was a great happiness to him to witness the many advantages which they enjoyed through the exertions of their own Bishop; and when he renewed his visit in 1853, upon occasion of the consecration of the cathedral, he was as thankful as any who took part in that deeply interesting service.

His youngest brother, writing from Fredericton, where he was quartered with his regiment, in 1825, says, " Your memory is universally respected and cherished, and the people sometimes disturb me by their unqualified preference of you to all rectors past, present, and future, in presence of Mr. B——, who is, however, very well liked, and deserves to be so." *

Some very rough notes of part of the journey from Fredericton to Quebec have been preserved. It was begun by ascending the river St. John in two small canoes, and a long *portage* was traversed by the rector and his wife on foot, with two children, of whom the elder was very little more than two years old, and the younger was carried in his arms. The fifth night after leaving Fredericton was spent at the house of a settler, where, the master and mistress being absent, they were received by " a disagreeable, wise, talkative old grandfather, a most uncouth lad, and a barefoot little girl with a handkerchief tied over her head and ears under the chin, to keep away flies in milking. Their extreme ill manners, without intentional incivility, tell us we may take the things when we ask for them. The young lady pops herself into the best bed. The lad sometime afterwards whispers to the old man that ' those folks ' should have this ; but after rousing the young lady, and some consultation, they decide

---

* This brother, in a letter written to Fredericton in 1816, says, " Next to my father's, I shall always receive your advice most gratefully, and your opinions most submissively, as I have more confidence in your goodness, more reliance on your judgment, and more respect for your character, than for that of any man, with the sole exception I mentioned." And about ten years later, he wrote of his brother George, " I much question whether there be a being in this world more beloved and respected by all belonging to him."

otherwise. They turn down some bedding for us from the loft (where the youth sleeps) which the old man, with an excess of partiality, commends for its cleanliness. We spread some of our own rugs, &c., on it, and sleep in our clothes, the old man having turned in by the side of the girl."

CHAPTER III.

Entrance on parochial work at Quebec—Appointment as Official—Journeyings in that capacity, and with his father on visitation.

THE change from **Fredericton to Quebec** had been made with the prospect of **a diminution of income,** but his father succeeded, during his visit to England, in procuring from· the **Imperial Government the appointment of two** Officials, for Upper and **Lower Canada** respectively, with **salaries of** £150 each. **His son was made** Official of the Lower province. The Bishop also **procured** an allowance in lieu of house-rent for the minister of Quebec. He failed in the main **object of** his visit to England, for he had hoped to be enabled to resign his charge into the hands of some younger man, and was detained so long before obtaining a decision upon the subject, that it was not till **1818** that he returned to Quebec. In the meantime Mr. Mountain had entered thoroughly into **his work.** He was impressed with the importance of extending religious knowledge and education **as the** foundation of that work: and at Quebec, as at Fredericton, one of his first acts was to take measures for the establishment of a Diocesan Committee of the S. P. C. K., as well as of National Schools for boys and girls; and both of these objects, in which he was well and cordially supported by the leading members of his flock, received a peculiar degree of his attention and regard as long as **he** lived. He lived to see the schools which he founded still flourishing some forty-five years afterwards, notwithstanding the springing up, with the increase of the population, of numerous others **of a similar class,** and to know men filling high positions **in different** learned professions who had there received their early education. Dr. Inglis, Commissary and afterwards Bishop of Nova Scotia, writes, in acknowledgment of a letter of the 18th March, 1818: "It is **matter of joy to me that you have founded a Diocesan** Committee **at Quebec, which, I doubt not, will be very** respectable. We do not look for marvellous and **instantaneous fruits** from our humble **labours, but may hope the blessing of God may** render them useful. **From our little effort here (and surely** you may entertain the fullest **hope of similar advantage) we** have good reason to **believe that Christian knowledge has been** promoted and extended, **and we can already perceive that our mode of effecting** this has served as a bond of interesting union among members of the Church. It has also saved many **of our members from turning their zeal and influence** and assistance to objects of **a more equivocal character. * * *** Rely upon it, your school will **succeed in Quebec."** At this time he was the only clergyman **in Quebec or its** neighbourhood, besides the chaplain of **the garrison who also held the** office of evening lecturer at **the cathedral. But while thus** actively engaged in his parochial **duties, he did not regard his** post of Official as a sinecure. **Early in January, 1818, he set** out, driving his own horse, **on a tour through the new settlements on the river St. Francis, first visiting Drummondville, where he spent** a **Sunday and held service, and from thence** proceeding **to Shipton, then inhabited almost exclusively by** Americans, **of whom he says that the men were, many of them,** absolutely **destitute of religion, and the women disciples of wild** fanaticism, **and brings forward some sad proofs** of the truth of this **remark. At Shipton he officiated in a** schoolroom, which **was the garret of a large wooden** building, of which the lower part was **unfinished and quite open.** "There was not a single prayer-book **to be found among the people;** I was obliged, therefore, **to read responses and all.** There was no chiming

in of *groans** during the sermon, with which they had saluted
Mr. Mills, agreeably to their previous habit. I found, however, that they approved of my 'discourse,' and some of them
regretted the want of a settled and authorized pastor. The
Methodist teachers have laboured hard to set them against the
Church." The next Sunday was given to Chambly, which
was reached viâ Sorel, the settlements beyond Shipton on
the St. Francis being in charge of the Hon. and Rev. C.
Stewart. At Chambly, service was held in a " guardroom
which was fitted up (if fitting up it can be called) as a temporary place of worship. At one end was a raised sleeping-
place on which the men sleep, and in the middle of this a kind
of tub has been built for the clergyman. I was much pleased
with the behaviour of the congregation ; the responses were
very well made, and the singing was excellent. After service I begged the resident members of the congregation to
remain, and told them the object of my visit," namely, the
establishment of a clergyman among them, for which matters
were put in a satisfactory train.

In September, 1818, he made a journey up the river Chaudière, some sixty miles from Quebec, to visit a German colony
which had been planted there by a merchant of Quebec, a
German himself, who had purchased seigneuries on that river.
This settlement was afterwards dispersed, chiefly in consequence of a disastrous fire.

In February, 1819, the visit to the St. Francis was repeated ;
and this time he reached Hatley, where he was most cordially
welcomed by Dr. Stewart, who, however, dissuaded him from
his purpose of proceeding farther. He speaks of travelling
in a stage in a driving snow-storm, on " a day after my own
heart, and only regretting that I was not facing it in an open
cariole." At one place he says, " I am all the better for a
good night's rest in a room where I stopped up the broken

---

* Marks, not of disapprobation, but of the contrary.

pane with my stockings, and put my beaver coat over the bedclothes in lack of any fire. The walls of the sitting-room are rough clay, furrowed however in diamonds, as an indication that they mean to put something else upon them. I assure you they have some ideas of elegance here, for not being possessed of a snuffer-tray, they brought in the broken-nosed snuffers upon a plate." His last letter written on this journey concludes thus; " I should have more spirit in the work, if there were anything to be done by a flying visit like this, but except at Drummondville it is scarcely worth while. There the people are anxious for the baptism of their children, &c., but in other places they will come with great readiness to hear you preach, as they will any body else, and will say you are ' a fine speaker ' if you have a loud voice, and there it ends." This somewhat desponding tone may, perhaps, have been occasioned by an illness which was then coming on, and which detained him at Hatley for many weeks. Dr. Stewart acted the part of a brother, giving up his own room to him, and doing all in his power to promote the comfort of Mrs. Mountain, who went up from Quebec (an arduous journey, in those days, for a lady) for the purpose of nursing him. By God's blessing on their care and kindness, he regained his strength, and was enabled to return to Quebec.

In December, 1819, he received the degree of D.D., on his father's recommendation, from the Archbishop of Canterbury, and was appointed by Government a member of the Royal Institution for the advancement of learning in Canada, in which capacity he visited and inspected schools. The operations of this body were afterwards confined to the control of schools of a higher order, and he always took a leading part in them while he continued to be a member of it.

In July of the following year he accompanied the Bishop on what proved to be his last visitation of Upper Canada. The facilities for travelling had much increased, though they had still to depend on the bateau for carrying the baggage

from Montreal, and themselves for part of the distance
between Prescott and Kingston. Steamers were available
between Quebec and Montreal, and Kingston and York
(Toronto), as well as, farther on in the journey, between
Fort Erie and Amherstburgh. The rest of the journey was
performed in waggons. From Amherstburgh they went by
land to Sandwich, (the farthest point reached) where a confirmation was held " in the new church," and Dr. Mountain
preached, as he seems to have done almost everywhere. A
confirmation (the first on this tour) had also been held at
Amherstburgh in a brick church lately built, " neat, but not
well-proportioned." From Sandwich they crossed to Detroit,
to take the steamer on their downward course, on board of
which a Sunday was spent, when divine service was held in
the morning, and Dr. Mountain preached to a congregation
consisting chiefly of Americans, who made a request for a
second service in the evening. From Fort Erie they proceeded to Queenston, where the Bishop met the Rev. B. B.
Stevens and other gentlemen, with whom he "went to see
the new church, and promised an assistance of £40, if they
placed the altar and pulpit properly." The next day a confirmation was held at Fort George, where a church was in
progress to replace one that had been burnt by the Americans
during the war. Confirmation was administered to about
seventy persons in the Indian Council House, and the Bishop
preached " with his usual energy and effect." At Grimsby
thirty persons were confirmed on the following day in a
school-room, " a remarkably pretty church" being not quite
finished, and in the evening they proceeded to Mr Leeming's
in the village of Hamilton, in Barton, " and drove thence
about three miles to Barton Church,"* where fifteen were

---

* This church is described in Dr Mountain's letter as " the property of the
public, and accessible to teachers of all persuasions ; an unpainted wooden
building of two stories with square windows ; a steeple, however, at one
end, and a chancel with arched windows at the other, have just been added

confirmed, the congregation being very small. Mr. Leeming,
(it is noted in the journal) " goes occasionally to the Mohawk
settlement upon the Grand River (about fifteen miles), and
preaches to them, and the Indian schoolmaster reads his
sermon to the natives. They have a church: they purchased
a bell: there are about twenty-one communicants : the school-
master reads prayers to them regularly in their own tongue,
and exhorts, or expounds some text of Scripture."

The Bishop held a visitation of the clergy of Upper
Canada (fifteen being present) at York, on St. James' Day.
" Dr. Strachan read prayers, Official Stuart preached. A
proper arrangement was made for delivering the charge,*
and the behaviour of the clergy and congregation was
conspicuously grave and attentive." The Bishop and clergy
all dined afterwards at Government House with Sir P. and
Lady Sarah Maitland. About eighty persons had been
confirmed on the previous Sunday, and on the next day the
Bishop presided at a meeting of the Clergy Reserve Corporation,† " which went off well. By-laws were passed similar
to those in Lower Canada." There are some remarks in the
letters of Dr. Mountain, written in the course of this journey,
which it is curious now to read. He had entered into conversation with some American fellow-passengers in a steamer,

---

to it." It may possibly be, sometimes, in comparison with buildings of this
description, that the architecture of some others is commended in the Bishop's
notes, from which the account of this journey, so far, is principally taken.

* Dr. M. says, " Certainly I never heard anything more impressive, and I
hope none of us heard it in vain."

† This body consisted of the Bishop and clergy of the province, though
the Bishop had, at its original constitution, recommended that laymen should
be associated with them, on account of his own residence at Quebec, and
the distances at which the clergy were removed from one another. The
functions of both corporations ceased after the settlement of the Reserves
question in 1840, when other bodies had become entitled to share the proceeds with the Church of England, and the management of the property
was assumed by the Colonial Government.

one of whom, a " colonel, spoke without any disguise as to
their views upon the Canadas, and without any doubt as to
their becoming an appendage to the Union. I forgave these
people a great deal for the sentiments which they expressed
upon the slave-question, which causes such a schism between
the Northern and Southern States. They all, except one young
man, who argued feebly and seemed conscious of a bad cause,
reprobated in the warmest terms the existing system of their
country in this point, and treated it as a disgrace to a nation
challenging to itself to be the very home and hearth of liberty.
But nothing short of a separation can give effect to the views
of the Northern States, since the Slave-States have already a
preponderance in the councils of the nation." " There is a
remarkable and not very gratifying contrast between the
American state of preparation for a future rupture, and our
own. Along this whole frontier they are building or repairing forts, and opening roads from the interior, by which they
could pour in invading myriads with ease ; while on our side
the few defences which exist are going rapidly to decay, and
exhibit every symptom of neglect. It is impossible not to
contemplate the alienation of the province from the British
Empire at no very remote period, and the contemplation casts
a damp upon all the interest which one feels for the advancement of the colony, and even of the Church within it. I
trust, however, that we shall have laid a good foundation for
the establishment of an episcopal clergy, as we did before in
the States." Near " the little village of Cleveland " they fell
in with an English traveller who had been to Michilimack-
inac and told them that the endeavours of an American
clergyman to convert the Indians at that place had proved
abortive. " They said that a person very like him came to
persuade them to the same belief about seventy years ago,
and that the Great Spirit sent the small-pox among them,
which they interpreted as a chastisement for having listened
to him. It is a remarkable coincidence that this clergyman

had hardly left them before the small-pox appeared again among them." Referring to this incident in a letter written some years after this, he writes, " Another instance of their rejecting the Gospel was also singular enough, accompanied by strictures in which there were but too much reason and truth. They appointed Redjacket, one of their chiefs, to reply to a recommendation of the Christian religion. ' But, said he, ' my people have charged me to speak their sentiments, and I must be plain. Your forefathers came to this country few in number, and after a while obtained from ours a little space of ground to carry on trade with them. They invited others over, and by little and little grew too strong for us. They then claimed to be our lords, and drove us into the back parts of the woods. You have hurt us in many ways, and made us dwindle to nothing, and taught us to drink firewater, and do other bad things, and now you tell us that we must be of your way to make us good and to improve our condition. We cannot believe you. But if you wish to convince us, there are some very bad white people at Buffalo, and they have often cheated us : go first and try your experiment upon them ; if you can make them good, we will believe that your religion will be for our benefit also.' "

One or two extracts of another kind from the letters written at this time may serve to exhibit the manner in which, through life, he reconciled himself to a lot very different from that which he would have chosen for himself, as well as the nature of his occupations, and the tenderness of his domestic affections. He often used to say that the height of his ambition, and his ideal of happiness, had been the charge of an English country parish. Writing from Grimsby, after the confirmation, he says, " Certainly it is in a complete *country* church and congregation that a clergyman must enjoy the most unmixed satisfaction in administering and guiding the offices of religious worship. Yet this is a gratification rather of taste than of principle, since the farther removed is the congregation from the simplicity and purity of the Gospel, the greater is the need of spiritual improvement, and the greater the field of usefulness and exertion. Even our more amiable feelings, therefore, and more chastened views of life are not always **safely to be indulged** : and thus on **all sides** we are discouraged from bounding our ideas of happiness **below, and** attaching ourselves to this world as to our ultimate destination." From York he writes, " We shall be at Montreal on the 20th, and leave it probably on the 23rd, August, to come straight *home*. *Home* is a monosyllable *qui renferme beaucoup*. My father is waiting for my finishing this letter, that he may close up the packet before he goes to bed : and I have to write, before I go to bed, **to every** clergyman in Lower Canada. We go off to-morrow morning early ; good night, therefore, and God bless you. Give my kindest love to all friends, and tell C—— that we drank her health yesterday.* Sir P. M. did the same, although he deviated from his usual practice in drinking wine."

Writing on the night of the 1st August, at Kingston, he **says,** " you may judge of my anxiety not to 'stint' you, when I tell you, that having **brought some** ink into my bedroom, and finding myself without a pen (all the household having retired to rest), I bethought myself all at once of a toothpick, and having fashioned it at the point, stuck a pencil into the top for a handle. And I flatter myself that you have found it a very good-spelling, easy-describing quill. I shall tax its powers no farther at this sitting than to wish you good night, it being now about that ambiguous hour which causes the Hibernian to ask ' whether it be to-night or to-morrow morning.'—2nd August. As it is now, out of all controversy, ' to-morrow morning,' and the anniversary of our union, I must begin by wishing you joy of your good fortune in the event which took place six years ago, and to which, **as**

---

* His sister's birthday, referred to in "Songs of the Wilderness," p. 81.

it has greatly promoted your happiness, I am generous enough
to be perfectly reconciled myself. I could indeed, my beloved
Mary, say a great deal, and in a much more serious tone, upon
this occasion, but I am content to leave you to interpret my
feelings by your own. May God continue to bless our union,
and spare us, if it be good for us, the strokes which we have
already suffered." Reference is made in these last words to
the loss of two infant children, his first two sons, in two successive years, 1818 and 1819. It was God's will to try them
again, for in May, 1821, they lost another infant, a daughter.

The following extract shews how some of his tastes and feelings had been displayed in boyhood :—" Your surprise at my
particular fondness for the Bride of Lammermoor, when I
' do *not like tragedies,*' is founded upon a little mistake. I
never had any objection to the feelings excited by tragedy,
but (though I was thoughtless and careless enough) I had
a certain degree of constitutional infirmity, which made me
afraid of exposing myself, and I used to think of those lines,—

> ' How sometimes Nature will betray its folly—
> Its tenderness—and make itself a pastime
> To harder bosoms.'

I remember when I was a boy, that in reading the story of
the Judge, in the Théatre d'Education, I cried so bitterly,
that I was obliged to stop, and walk up and down the room.
It sounds excessively ridiculous for a man to say these things
of himself, but I do it with the less reserve, because I am not
speaking of my *present* self. My nature is harder now. I
have seen so much real misery in the course of my profession, I have witnessed so many scenes of deep and complicated
distress, full of everything that is disgusting to a refined
sensibility and repulsive to a fastidious taste, that I have
learned to disjoin these qualities, in some measure, from the
exercise of compassion, to think less than I used to do of the
more delicate afflictions of my equals and superiors, and to
rate *that* as the best order of humanity, not in which you

indulge your feelings, but in which you have much occasion to *do them violence*, of which the repetition wears them harder than they were wont to be ; else would they be perpetually sore.   But what is lost in mere feeling in such a case, is supplied by principle, and the love of our neighbour is more fruitful when the freshness and the fragrance of its bloom have passed away. Still, I would not have you think me dead to the softer—but quite enough of myself, and of general reflections drawn from my own case ; and, besides, I suppose your opinion of me is not to be formed from this letter, but from the experience of those years which we have spent together."

There are many parts of these letters which contain descriptions of the country and other details which it is interesting, at this date, to read. But I must be sparing of these, and content myself mainly with extracting from them an account of the remainder of the journey, with reference to its special object.   Having to visit different places between York and Kingston, the Bishop could not avail himself of the steamer, which appears to have gone direct from one port to the other.   The journey was performed, therefore, partly by land, partly in a bateau, and partly on foot.   The first confirmation, after leaving York, was held at Hamilton, the head-quarters of the mission of the Rev. W. Macaulay, and as it was on a Sunday, it was settled that the Rev. Mr. Thomson should bring his candidates to that place, (five miles distant,) from Smith's Creek, " now called Port Hope, where there is a rising village."   The Bishop and his chaplain " slept at Mr. Macaulay's house, who, for a bachelor, is really in very snug quarters, and has a very good library for a young clergyman. Hamilton is the county town, and it was in a wooden building which is both court-house and jail that the service was performed. My father preached extempore on the gospel of the day ; and certainly, if I could do it as well, I should never address a country congregation

in any other way. About thirty were confirmed. Mr. M.'s
church is building about a mile from his present residence
and place of worship, in a village called Cobourg. There is
a wooden church in forwardness at the Carrying Place, at the
head of the Bay of Quinté, and some of the leading inhabitants expressed to my father their desire to have a clergyman
sent among them. One of these is an old man, who talks
always in a rattling style, and just as if all the world wanted
to be put to rights, and he was the person to do it. The
clergy at home, according to his account, were strangely deficient in overlooking Canada as a channel by which to draw
off some of their exuberant wealth, in the way of assistance
in building churches. He would not give any of them more
than a dollar a day ; it was quite enough for preaching. * *
* * At Belleville there is a brick church upon an eminence,
building, or, at least, half built ; it is at a stand ; and one
principal cause of this presents itself to your eye when you
go in ; for under the beams of the yet unlaid floor, there is
the grave of a Mr. Taylor, who was the great promoter of the
undertaking, and had taken the contract himself." Thirteen
persons were confirmed at Bath, in the township of Ernest-
town, on the 1st August. "The church is an unpainted
wooden edifice, and is one of the oldest in the province ; for
Ernest-town was the residence of Mr. Langhorne, and the
centre of his exertions, which were not small nor lightly
appreciated. He built two log churches in adjacent townships, at which he occasionally officiated. Kingston is much
increased since I saw it in 1813. It is the largest town in
Upper Canada, and the place of greatest trade. The confirmation was held here on the 3rd August, and my father preached
his sermon on the blind man restored to sight, which doubtless you remember, and which I think is one of his very best.
The church is a long, low, blue, wooden building, with square
windows, and a little cupola, or steeple, for the bell, like the
thing on a brewery, placed at the wrong end of the building.

They are taking measures, however, to build a new one. On the following Sunday a confirmation was held in the court-house at Brockville, a high brick building, which seems to stand as a representation of mortified ambition, for it is upon an eminence, and, for such a place as Brockville, built in an aspiring style, but has never been finished; and half the windows are stopped up with old boards. There is no church, which is a great shame, considering the advancement of the place. The Presbyterians have got the start of us, having built a very decent stone kirk. The court-room was very full, and there was a pretty large confirmation, as the people from Augusta, where Mr. Leeds serves the church, also came over. My father preached. After an early dinner, we went a stage on the Perth road, for the days being all fixed for confirmations below, we had no time to lose, and we found that we could not get through to Perth in one day. All the roads which I have described before were turnpike and bowling-green to this. Roots, rocks, sticks, stumps, holes and bogs,—these were the component materials of the road. The journey of Monday was divided into three equal stages of about seven miles, and each of them, exclusive of baiting, took us three hours. The holes, however, and the sloughs are of course much worse in the wet season, and travellers have sometimes been obliged to leave waggon and horses sticking fast till they could procure a yoke of oxen to pull them out. An Irishman in the service of Major Powell of Perth, being asked by his master how he had got along upon the road (with a waggon), replied, that he had got along pretty well, for he had found bottom in every place but one. The settlement of Perth, so laboriously reached, affords one of the most encouraging examples of the kind that I have seen. It appears hardly credible that, less than four years ago, it was a portion of the wilderness, unex-plored except by the wandering Indian hunter. Streets laid out, and the building lots occupied, in some instances, by very good and neat houses; two places of worship erected; gardens and farms under cultivation, and yielding abundant returns; a very tolerable society, enjoying the intercourse of civilized life; and everything wearing the aspect of cheerfulness and competence;—such is the scene which the skill and industry of man have carved for him so quickly out of the depths of the trackless forest. The churches are Roman Catholic and Presbyterian. Mr. Harris officiates in the school-house, but will have a church in progress soon. Mr. H., owing to accidents on the American Lake Ontario steamboat,* had not reached Perth, but this we were quite prepared for, as we had been unable to hear of his arrival åt Brockville, and my father thought it best, at all hazards, to go on and see the place, and shew the people his determination to visit them." There was, therefore, no confirmation. At a house where they slept on their return from Perth to Brockville, "in the course of the evening, the hostess apprized us of the arrival of ' a lady,' who having heard of my baptizing Mrs. T.'s children on the way up, had brought her's to the house for the same purpose. The ' lady ' was an Irish blacksmith's wife. In an hour or so more, ' another lady ' came with the same request, bringing two children, the youngest of whom was a most lovely little creature. I felt a great satisfaction in entering these little innocents into the family of their Lord, which very likely never would have been done for them otherwise." Proceeding down the St. Lawrence, the Bishop " went ashore at Fort Wellington, (now Prescott), to speak to some of the persons engaged in the erection of a church, of which the frame was up. When the churches are completed which are now building in this province, I suppose that the number will be treble what it was when I last went through it in 1813. The new churches also along the American frontier appear to be principally

---

* Apparently on his return from the visitation at York.

episcopal. There is one built of stone at the little town of Waddington, which we passed. There are now in the States four hundred episcopal clergymen." The Bishop stopped also " in the township of Matilda, at the house of a Colonel Fraser, to encourage him to put the church in repair, and get things in forwardness for the reception of a clergyman. This is a church built by the Lutherans, which, in conformity with the example given by their neighbours in Williamsburg, they have made over to us. We reached, by a late dinner hour, the parsonage house of Williamsburgh, that *is* so red, close by the church that *was* so blue. The blushing honours of the former are unimpaired ; the honours of the latter remain only in name ; it is still called by the boat-people the blue church, though no stranger could now discover that it had ever been painted." About fifty persons were confirmed in it on the 11th August, and Dr. Mountain preached. A curious custom prevailed there. When there were collections in the church, " the money is received in a little bag, at the end of a long stick, and within the bag is a bell, which is intended, as we were gravely told, to wake any person who may happen to be nodding when the collector makes his circuit." The next place visited was Cornwall, where "the church appears to have increased since Mr. Salter Mountain's arrival, for there were only seventeen confirmed on the previous occasion, and to-day there were sixty-five. I cannot forbear from telling you a story about a bell. My father had found it troublesome to *call* for his own servants or those of the house, and he asked the girl, ' Pray is there any bell here ?' ' Yes, sir.' ' Well, and where is it, pray?' ' Sir,' said the girl, with all the simplicity in the world, ' it is in the church.' A house-bell was a thing which she had no conception of." This was the last confirmation held in Upper Canada. The parishes or missions of fourteen clergymen had been visited, and as the number mentioned as attending the visitation included the minister of Quebec, this was, probably, the whole number in the province. In 1862, there were three Bishops, and two hundred and forty-three clergy within the same limits.

Mr. S. Mountain accompanied the Bishop from Cornwall to Quebec, as well as to St. Andrews on the Ottawa, where his lordship confirmed, and his son preached, on the 18th. " The confirmation was held in the school-house, which is roughly fitted up as a place of worship. There was a very respectable attendance, but a small number only were confirmed."

The visitation of the clergy of Lower Canada was held at Montreal on the 22nd August, when fourteen were present, and the Official of the Lower Province was called upon to preach, as the Official of the Upper had been at York, and was requested by the clergy to publish his sermon. The Bishop had preached and confirmed about one hundred and fifty on the preceding Sunday. The church is described as being "very large and handsome, but not in so good taste as the church at Quebec. The ornaments are like those of some large public room. In some points, however, they excel us, Mr. Shuter having made them a present of a clock, which cost three hundred and fifty guineas. They also intend to have a peal of bells very soon, and to build a vestry-room, the want of which is a strange deficiency in so handsome a church. This church will have cost about £20,000 when it is completed. The organ cost £1,700. Montreal is very much improved and increased since 1813, and many very handsome private houses are now building."

Quebec was reached after an absence of nearly two months.

During this time, the Rev. Dr. Mills, chaplain to the forces, had taken charge of the parish, and the letters of the rector are full of proofs of his thoughtfulness for its wants and interests, especially those of the poor. Systematic relief was afforded to such as were in need by means of the voluntary offerings of the congregation, which were expended under the direction of the minister. One of his letters speaks of the expected arrival of an assistant in his parochial duties, who was to leave England in May. For early in this year, the Bishop, in writing to the S. P. G., had stated that the congregation at Quebec was "greatly enlarged, and the duty of the rector so much increased as to be greater than any one man could hope to sustain for any long period. Within three months, the funerals alone had exceeded one hundred; and other duties, particularly visiting the sick and poor, received from the rector a more than ordinary degree of attention. His employments were so multiplied, as not only to leave no space for reasonable relaxation, but not even for reading, nor such leisure for composition as it must be painful to every serious clergyman to be debarred from." In the year 1819, an Emigrant Society, (of which the plan had been sketched out by the Duke of Richmond,* then Governor of Canada,) for the relief of destitute emigrants, was established at Quebec, and the rector had, for about fifteen years, the greater part of the labour, and that by no means slight, which it entailed. An emigrant hospital was fitted up at the same time, in some barrack-rooms lent for the purpose, where, besides visiting the sick, Dr. Mountain regularly held stated services, with sermons. In fact, until his consecration to the episcopate, a very large portion of his time was necessarily given to the poor immigrants, who used, in summer, to throng his doors, before the establishment of a public department for their relief.

In 1821, the parish of Quebec was erected by letters patent, and Dr. Mountain appointed rector. Mr. S. Mountain had used the title of "rector of the English Church at Quebec." He afterwards styled himself "officiating clergyman," and this title was adopted by his successor till 1821.

---

* The first sermon which Dr. Mountain published at Quebec, at the request of all the leading parishioners, was upon occasion of the death of the Duke in 1819.

CHAPTER IV.

Visitations as Archdeacon—McGill College—First visit to Gaspé.

In 1821, two Archdeaconries were established in the diocese,
one including the whole of the Upper, and the other the whole
of the Lower province, the respective Officials of which were
promoted to the dignity of Archdeacon.   Archdeacon Mountain's first journey in this capacity was made in the autumn of
1822, when he visited the Eastern townships again.   He had
intended to spend the first Sunday of his absence at Eaton, but
was obliged to remain at Sherbrooke for lack of the means
of conveyance.   He "could hear of nothing like a horse in
the village," in which a church was in course of erection.
The Sunday was spent at Lennoxville, "better known by the
name of the Upper Forks," (Sherbrooke going by the name
of "the Lower Forks,") which was reached "by a horse-path
through the woods" from Belvedere, where he had been hospitably received.   Mr. Le Fevre, at this time, had charge of Lennoxville and Sherbrooke, and found "it necessary to have
double service at each place on alternate Sundays, instead of
one service at each every Sunday, because the roads are so
bad through which a part of the congregation have to come,
that they expect two services after such an exertion."   The
Archdeacon preached twice in the school-house, the church,
("a two-story wooden edifice, with sash-windows below, and
arched ones above,") being unfinished.   From Lennoxville
he went on to Eaton, Hatley, Shefford, Dunham, Frelighsburgh, Philipsburgh, Clarenceville, Isle aux Noix, Sorel, St.

Andrews on the Ottawa, and Rawdon, visiting the churches and schools, and preaching at most places. The journey from Three Rivers to Frelighsburg was performed on horseback.

Towards the close of the year 1822, the Bishop was desirous of sending a person to England, to represent the injustice done to the Church in some attacks which had been made upon her, and to endeavour to counteract their injurious effects, particularly with reference to the benefits to be derived from the Clergy Reserves. These lands had been appropriated by an Act of the Imperial Parliament to the maintenance of a "Protestant Clergy," and a share in those benefits began now to be claimed by other parties. The Archdeacon was at first designated to this mission, but he was very unwilling to leave his flock, and it was finally arranged that the Honourable and Rev. Dr. Stewart should be requested to undertake it. Dr. Stewart was at this time Visiting Missionary of the diocese, an office corresponding, to some extent, with the more modern one of Travelling Missionary, it being part of his duty to visit and report upon new fields of labour. With this, however, was combined inspection of the missions of the S. P. G., and the experience which he thus gained, and his intimate local knowledge of the wants of both provinces, as well as the love and reverence which his guilelessness and single-hearted devotion to the work of Christ everywhere won for him,* were no mean qualifications

---

* A remarkable proof of this is found in a letter addressed, at the time of his first arrival in Canada, by the sister of his predecessor in the see, to him who was destined to be his successor. "We have had a most wonderful young man here, who has charmed us all, and, indeed, even those who were prejudiced against him.—I mean Mr. Stewart—who, you doubtless know, came out here as a missionary, and so unusual an undertaking in a man of family and independence could not by the world in general be attributed to any but an enthusiast and a methodist. The papers mentioned his coming to convert the Indians, and I saw many a contemptuous smile when his name was mentioned. Yet see the effect of such conduct as his. With no

for the higher office to which he was afterwards called. The Archdeacon was sent from Quebec in March 1823, to communicate to him the desire of the Bishop that he should proceed at once to England, and to furnish him with the necessary instructions. He was uncertain where to find him, but fortunately, after leaving Quebec, obtained information which proved to be correct, that he was at the scene of his earlier labours, in Hatley. The Archdeacon " left Sherbrooke on Saturday morning at five o'clock, and proceeded to Hatley to breakfast, after which, (he writes on the following Monday,) I spent the day with Dr. S. at his lodging, and arranged everything with him relating to the business of his mission to England. He undertook it cheerfully, and went off to Boston either yesterday afternoon or to-day. Few persons could have been found who would have required such short notice. Had it not been Sunday, he would have even gone off yesterday morning. Yesterday I left Hatley at five o'clock, went back to Sherbrooke, (eighteen miles,) to breakfast with Mr. Le Fevre, assisted him in the service and in the sacrament, and preached for him; proceeded immediately afterwards (twenty-four miles) to Shipton, stopped at the school-house door where the congregation were assembling; went in and robed myself, and performed service, (according to an arrangement made on my upward journey,) and preached to a very attentive congregation, who, to the credit of Mr. Wood's * diligence, make the responses far better than many others who have regular service

---

advantages of person or address, with real disadvantages of voice and manner in the pulpit, before he left Quebec he gained general respect, and certainly did make converts of those who were disposed at first to call the real goodness of his design in question. He met with every discouragement here, except from a very few persons, yet he continued steadfast in his perseverance."

* Then rector of Drummondville, from whence he paid occasional visits to neighbouring townships.

very Sunday. Visited the family of the man who had driven me, and baptized six of his children; received a visit at the inn from the schoolmaster at Melbourne, who came to state to me the prospects of establishing the Church in the two townships; got some tea and toast and a beefsteak; and after reading a chapter to the family and praying with them, retired to my bedroom, where, a little after twelve, I got to bed, having to start again at five in the morning, and having had just about four hours' sleep the night before. So that you see I have not run away from you and my parish to be idle on the road. The man who was to drive me this morning called me at twenty minutes past four, instead of five, at which time I accordingly rose. About eight we baited at the hut of an old soldier whose family were at a plentiful breakfast, but the apparatus was not very inviting, and I did not signify any desire to partake. My driver offered me a sort of home-made cake, or biscuit, of which he had several with him, and this, with a glass of spring water, formed my breakfast. I contemplated, indeed, breakfasting with Mr. Wood at Drummondville, where I arrived at half-past ten, but he took it for granted, I fancy, that this ceremony had been performed, and as I did not want to lose time, I thought it just as well to forbear from giving him any hint. My biscuit and glass of water, therefore, held me out till seven o'clock this evening, at which time I sat down to a very good travellers' dinner." Speaking, in a letter written on his way to Hatley, of the possible difficulty of ascertaining where he should find Dr. Stewart, he says, " If I appeared dull and low the evening before I left Quebec, these uncertainties, coupled with the more important uncertainties yet remaining, which regarded Dr. S's concurrence in the business and its ultimate success, must have contributed to shed some gloom over my mind. I had been *wound up* to do my part, and had got through the share which I was to discharge at Quebec, and then, as it often happens, *I ran down and stopped,* and began to think that it was all in vain. I am unalterably convinced, however, of the duty lying upon us to keep watch and ward in defence of our Zion, and to sally out, if the proceedings of the other party render it necessary. But it would seem to human weakness a happier lot for a clergyman to have, as Chillingworth says, ' no enemies but the devil and sin ' in the discharge of his duty, and mine seems so different a case, that I shall be ' fit for treasons, stratagems, and spoils,' if I continue to be exercised in the sort of struggles to which our Church is here exposed. .... At Labaie, I hired a habitant to take me to Drummondville, who flattered my French so far as to express his surprise at finding that I was not either a Frenchman* or a Canadian."

I have given these extracts, because they exhibit two points for which he was always conspicuous. His power of enduring the want of food† was very great, but he never would have made it a subject of remark except in letters addressed to his immediate relations. And in giving the account of his Sunday's labour, he was fully understood, by the person to whom he wrote, as doing so in no boastful strain, for it was well known that he always thankfully acknowledged his health and strength as special blessings received to fit him for his work, and that he possessed a keen relish for varieties and even adventures in travelling (a gift, mercifully, no doubt, bestowed in order to qualify him for what he had to encounter in his "journeymgs often,") which others might even have esteemed hardships. Some proof of this will appear a little farther on. He was in

---

* This used to happen frequently. A similar anecdote, with reference to German, is mentioned in the memoir of his brother, Col. Mountain.

† He was remarkably abstemious at all times. I remember the present Dean of Montreal, who had known all of the name who had laboured in Canada, saying to me, "The Mountains are remarkable for two things, charity to the poor, and abstinence from wine;" and these are very much akin to the two points to which I am here referring.

the habit of writing home (whenever he had leisure,) **as
full** an account as possible of **his journeys, knowing how
eagerly it was welcomed there, and the interest which the**
novelties, or sometimes the dangers, **of the way excited in**
himself he strove **to impart to others, to whom** he wrote
without reserve.   **In writing journals for the Church** Socie-
ties, he used to do violence to his own feelings when **he**
interspersed with his **narrative any** mention of personal
adventure or privation, for the sake of what seemed **to be**
characteristic of the state of the country, and likely, therefore, to interest his readers, and so tend **to advance the**
great object that he had always in view.   **He seldom did this
without a kind of apology.**

The second of these extracts **expresses what he felt more**
and more strongly **the longer he lived.   No man ever more
ardently longed for peace, or felt more deeply, in his own**
spirit, **the misery of strife.*** Again and again **has he** expressed sentiments **of a similar kind.   Yet he was** always
ready to put a force upon himself, and do effectual battle for
the Church **at the call of duty.** His experience, however,
never made him **"fit** for treasons, stratagems, and spoils."
He not only could not endure strife,—for it was pain and grief
to his tender nature, and too directly opposed to the meekness for which he was conspicuous,—but he was too guileless
to use their own weapons against **those** who descended to
such acts.   Even the necessary forms of business were distasteful to him.   He often said, with reference to the part
which he was obliged to take in introducing synodical **action**
into his diocese, and carrying it on, that it was not congenial **to** him, that he could not bear anything like "diplomacy"
or "parliamentary work," that he was not fit for it, and

---

* A drawer full of papers relating to painful occurrences in the diocese,
was marked "The drawer of thorns," and the words were added, "But of
what, O Lord of glory, was Thy earthly crown composed?" Another memorandum was, "Let it be remembered that *thorns* are to be *burnt*."

longed to be employed only in preaching the Gospel to the
poor, and carrying the ministrations of his office to destitute
settlements.

Some of the attacks which he felt himself called upon
to meet involved no small amount of theological study,
or which, in the midst of his duties as Archdeacon, and his
unremitting parochial labours, he contrived to find time. In
1822, he published "a letter to Mr. S. C. Blyth, occasioned
by the recent publication of the narrative of his conversion
to the Romish Faith, by a Catholic Christian." It is an
octavo volume of nearly three hundred closely printed pages.
He was also a frequent contributor to a magazine called the
Christian Sentinel, of which he was, indeed, one of the chief
supporters.

In September, 1821, on the arrival of the charter of McGill
College, Montreal, the Bishop submitted a plan for its establishment as a University to the then Governor in Chief,
which he had drawn up for the Duke of Richmond, by whom
it had been approved. It met with the same approbation from
Lord Dalhousie, who also, as well as the Lieut. Governor
of Upper Canada and others, expressed his hearty approval of
the Bishop's recommendation of the Archdeacon of Quebec
as Principal. The will, however, having been contested, the
establishment of the college was delayed. In order to comply
with its conditions it became necessary, towards the close of
1823, to make a *pro formâ* appointment of professors, whose
names the Bishop was requested to submit. "While the
Bishop felt it his duty to project the frame of the University
in a manner consistent with the English National Establishment (both from the consideration of the erection of the
Canadas into a diocese forming an integral part of the Province of Canterbury, and also for the sake of that uniformity
of system which it must be so obviously advantageous to
introduce,) he endeavoured, at the same time, to throw open
the advantages of instruction to all denominations of Chris-

tians, without interference with their religious principles, and proposed to make such of the Professorships as the above mentioned considerations would permit tenable by graduates of the Scotch Universities." The Archdeacon was accordingly nominated honorary Professor of Divinity and Principal of the College, and held these offices till 1835. He never, however, acted in his capacity of professor, for up to that date the Medical Faculty only had been organized, and there were no resident students. As a Governor of the College he had, however, for many years, a great deal of labour and correspondence. From the letters which passed on the occasion of his appointment, I cannot forbear from selecting one from Sir Francis Burton, the Lieutenant Governor of Lower Canada, with the Bishop's reply:

" MY DEAR LORD,

" On my return from the Council I found your Lordship's letter of this date, with its enclosures. How could you think it necessary to send the testimonials of a character so highly beloved, respected and esteemed as the Archdeacon Mountain? I have read them, because I love to see worth like his so duly appreciated, and that feeling alone induces me to forgive your Lordship's supposing me capable of requiring any inducement to exert myself, where your Lordship and the Archdeacon are personally interested. In the instance of McGill College, I owe so much to this province, that I must have at heart the interests of it, and particularly those of the rising generation ; and for that reason, although I did not feel myself so much alive to its establishment as, perhaps, I ought to have done, yet as there is now a prospect of the young men of this province being placed under the care, guidance, and instruction of such a person as the one your Lordship recommends, I shall do everything you desire to further so desirable an object."

" DEAR SIR,

" I beg leave to thank you, in my son's name and my own, for the very kind answer which you have given to my application. If, upon this occasion, I had been guided only by my own opinion of the fitness of my son for the situation in question, or of your Excellency's benevolent and friendly disposition towards us, I should not, perhaps, have thought it necessary to give you the trouble of reading testimonials ; but it was not to Sir Francis Burton in his private capacity that I was to address myself, but to a

Lieutenant Governor of this province, and a Governor of the college to be established ; and it, therefore, appeared to me proper to lay before him whatever, in the exercise of his kindness, might serve to justify him to himself, the Royal Institution and the country."

I find a letter addressed to the Bishop, in this same year, by Bishop Hobart of New York, thanking him for kindness received at Quebec, in which he expresses his concern at an accident which had happened to his "inestimable son, the Archdeacon." He had been thrown out of a carriage, and broken his leg. This accident confined him for a long time to the house, and he never entirely recovered from its effects.

The mention of the labours of his pen has drawn me away from any attempt to exhibit some of the peculiar features of his character. In the account of one of his journeys, in 1822, he writes, "I am going to say a foolish kind of thing for a person who has for some time ceased to be a boy, and one which may, perhaps, be thought inconsistent with the solemn soberness of the profession to which I am devoted, but it has often appeared to me, that a tinge, not only of poetry, but of romance, is an addition to our happiness, if it be moderated and subdued by purer and higher feelings and principles. Many an untoward adventure, many a bleak and dreary way, many a circumstance which, to an ordinary traveller, carries unmixed discomfort and difficulty, borrows a charm from the sources of which I speak, which totally alters its nature and aspect. A driving storm, a solitary ride at night over a bad road, and through a dark, forlorn-looking wood ; an accident, an aberration from the road, a retardation which bids you seek refuge at the hearth of some sturdy tenant of the woods and shift as you can for the night's accommodation, may not only be talked of afterwards with pleasure, but yield pleasure at the time ; and I almost think that I should find an unpleasant insipidity in that perfection of travelling which secures you against the possibility of adventures, and leaves nothing to be provided for by thought, or encountered by

determination.   Travelling on horseback is far more in
unison with this set of ideas than any other mode of conveyance, and I am almost ashamed to cónfess, even to you,
that I had rather wrap my cloak about me, in traversing
these wild woods and mountains, than button my great coat.
But there is no romance in dirt; and this, as you well know
from your experience of some nights we passed on the road
from Fredericton to Quebec, is not unfrequently one of the
characteristics of the ruder sort of travelling in these countries.   My repugnance to a bed of equivocal cleanliness is
what I can never surmount, and what sadly spoils all the
shadowy delights of imagination.   The character, also, of
the American population, although they are a hardy and
enterprising race, expert and perfectly at home in all that
belongs to the field and the forest, is far from harmonizing,
in other points, with the romantic and the picturesque.   Their
democratic familiarity of manner, their anti-rural costumes,
their trafficking and speculating habits, their keen and wary
way of dealing, the tout-ensemble of their outward, as well
as of their moral, intellectual and religious man, is the most
opposite possible to that of a peasantry, interesting in the
point of view which I am considering.   The same sort of
remark may be applied to the character of the buildings and
the villages in the Yankeefied parts of these provinces.   But
with respect to the people themselves, is it possible to conceive a state of things more at variance with rural ideas than
one in which forging bank-notes is among the prevailing vices
of the youth of the country?"   (Here his father has written,
in red ink, " To all this, though an old man and a Bishop, I
heartily subscribe.")

    " It was no great adventure which gave occasion for this
page of writing.   I had only a couple of miles to ride and
not above one through the wood, but as I dipped down under
the ample covert of the trees, and heard, in the stillness of
the night, the rivulets rushing through them which have been

swelled by the recent rains, the train of thought which I have here exposed to your observation was passing through my mind. But I must not let you think that I am occupied by no thoughts of a better kind, in performing a journey which has for its object the interests of our religious establishments, and I will tell you therefore (although the religious thoughts which more directly concern ourselves are sensitive, as it were, and seem to be hurt by any contact, to receive some taint and diminution of their purity if they are unveiled) I will tell you that I have often called to mind, when I have been subjected to inconvenience or fatigue or disgust upon a journey, and when the people of the house, perhaps, have beset me with their apologies, as if they thought that the city-bred gentleman could scarce accommodate himself to the ways of the woods, that I am the immediate servant of a Master Who, though the foxes have holes and the birds of the air have nests, had not where to lay His head." (Here the Bishop has remarked " And this, I need not say, I like still better.")

Such thoughts found expression, on one occasion, in the following lines :

ON RETIRING TO A HOMELY BED IN A HUMBLE DWELLING.

> My Heavenly Master had not where
>   To lay His Blessed head ;
> Too thankful, then, may I repair,
>   To this—to any bed.
>
> Shield us this night, Almighty God,
>   And when we sink at last
> To sleep beneath the kindred sod,
>   On Thee our charge be cast.
>
> O grant that when that dark repose
>   By millions shall be burst,
> Our lot be found in Christ with those
>   Ordained to rise the first.

These lines form a fitting introduction to the account of his first visit to the district of Gaspé, in 1824, for he had no natural liking for water-travelling, except in an open boat or canoe, and it was only the remembrance of Him Whom he served that could reconcile him to what he was often called upon to endure on board small fishing craft. I remember the word "impossible," escaping half-uttered from the lips of a clergyman who had proposed to accompany him on one of his later visitations, when he saw the accommodation of a schooner, which was quite luxurious in comparison with what he often submitted to. The following are extracts from his journal of 1824:

" Within the space allotted to me are two berths, which occupy its whole length, being something less than six feet, one on either side. They are partly boarded up so as to screen the head and feet, but the open intermediate space is so short that it was with extreme difficulty that I climbed in, the berth being very little deeper than a coffin, and its perpendicular dimensions yet farther contracted at this point by a transverse beam of the cabin. But having once got in, although I found nothing within to gorge myself withal, I was nearly in the predicament of the mouse (or weasel or whatever it was) in the fable, who having found access by a very small hole to some depository of grain, was unable after he had unthinkingly indulged in plenty to squeeze himself out again. Having, however, extricated myself at last, I directed that my bed should be made in the opposite berth, in which, though Procrustes would have curtailed me by some inches to match me with its length, I am upon the whole as comfortable as I can expect to be upon the water. The other berth I have assigned to William (a servant-lad), not choosing to let him sleep forward, in a hole with the sailors whose habits and characters I do not know. This you may tell his mother, if you please, and you may add that I make him read a chapter in the New Testament to me every forenoon, and in the Old every evening, upon which I afterwards question him or explain it as I see necessary. I see that he

reads his Bible at other times besides. As to myself, I have
with me, besides the Bible and Prayer-Book, the Pensées de
Pascal, Cicero de Oratore, and another little Latin book
which I pitched upon on account of its diminutive size. I
wish not to let my Latin get rusty, and having little portable
editions of these, I thought I might also obtain some hints
for correcting my faults in public speaking, and improving
myself in composition. It is by preaching the Word, after
all, that I must expect to do most good in the world, (though
this itself can do but little if the life of the preacher do not
correspond,) and to preach as well as we can, therefore,
should be an object of great importance with the clergy, in
the attainment of which the auxiliary resources of learned
discipline are not to be despised." * * * After describing some of the scenery of the St. Lawrence, as he drew
near the end of the voyage, he says: "If I had not other
work to do which makes it the better for me, the less I
am entangled ' with the affairs of this life,' I should like to
plant a great massive old-fashioned château, with a sheltered
antique garden, laid out in alleys and rich with the bloom of
roses and domestic flowers, in some choice spot among these
wild heights and ravines, and to form some rude yet comfortable hamlets in some of the buried recesses round about,
where I would plant my *censitaires*,*—all picked and chosen
folk, who should come to my own chapel when the sound of
the bell should swing through the wilds, and frequent my
open hall when the Christmas fires were blazing upon the
ample hearth. And then we would have a few select friends
on a staying visit, and a good library, and horses (for we
must make some roads), and boats: and now and then we
could warm and comfort a tempest-driven crew who might
seek shelter in some cranny of our coast. All this would

* The name given to the occupiers of land in the seigneuries of Lower
Canada.

be really very delightful ; yet it is better, unspeakably better, to fight against the vices and miseries, to stand, as it were, between the living and the dead and stay the plague of sin or suffering, amid the most repulsive population of the most uninteresting and vilest commercial town, and to carry the consolations and remedies of religion into hospitals and prisons, and the foul and crowded lodgings of the city poor. And yet, if I could consign more of the mere routine of parish work to others, and enjoy something like retirement and leisure, I feel as if I could turn it to some account in a way from which I have been precluded since I learned to value time." He had left both his wife and his father very unwell ; but he says, "I keep a good heart, and enjoy both those balms of hurt minds than which the unhappy Voltaire seems to have thought there were no better vouchsafed to man, 'l'un est le doux sommeil et l'autre l'espérance.'" Gaspé Bay was reached in five days. At St. George's Cove there were "two places of worship ; one a little Protestant chapel, in outward appearance like the houses, the other a still more diminutive edifice, of which the purpose is indicated by a rude wooden cross planted in the grave-yard which belongs to it,—a sufficient and in itself a proper and becoming distinction—for why should we abhor the emblem of our faith because it is perverted by superstition?" The people of this settlement, being from Guernsey or Jersey, could, in many instances, not understand English, and "finding that I spoke French, and said grace in that language, and that I was furnished with a French copy of the liturgy in preparation for the christenings which I was to perform, they conveyed a request through their preacher that I should hold service and preach to them in French. To preach extempore in French, or to preach at all in French was what I had never done, and as I had two houses to visit, each at some little distance, I saw that there would be but little time to digest and arrange my thoughts beforehand. But I had a stronger objection in my doubts of the propriety of preaching in their chapel. Yet when I considered, on the other hand, that, although they were Methodists, they would not, probably, have become so, had an authorized pastor resided among them ; that they did not, according to their own notions, regard themselves as separatists from the Church, to whose ministrations they always resort for the sacraments, marriages, and funerals, and whose ordinances respecting sponsors, churching, &c., they punctiliously observe ; that they attended upon the preaching of the clergyman whenever they had opportunity, either by his coming (which he can but rarely do) among them, or by their finding any convenience for going to hear him at the distance of a dozen miles ; that the clergyman himself, when he visited them, made use of this chapel, and that I should convey a reflection on that good man by declining to do so ; that the building was designed to receive the Church-minister when he should come, as well as to hold their own meetings in when they could do no better ; that I should, probably, prejudice the estimation of the Church among them, in a sensible degree, and set them more adrift from her communion if I refused, as, on the other hand, my compliance might help to pave the way for some future introduction of her stated ministrations ;* when I recollected also that at Montreal our congregation hired the use of the Presbyterian place of worship when the Church was building, and that my father had himself held a confirmation, in Upper Canada, in a church which, at that time, was held in co-partnership between the Presbyterians and our people, but has since been vested exclusively in the Church, I came to a decision, which, indeed, I had no time to revolve in my mind, but in which I hope I was right, to suffer them to spread the notice of a service in French. After visiting the two houses and per-

---

* This building was subsequently made over to the Church of England, and a church built in the neighbourhood also.

forming the baptisms, I occupied the remaining time in such
preparation as it would permit: and taking an appropriate
text from St. Paul (Rom. x. 10), I wrote a sort of introduction to a famiiir exposition of the creed which was to follow
extempore, and the outline of which I framed in my own mind.
This introduction I have preserved, rough as it is, because
having mentioned the day (which was St. Bartholomew's) I
took occasion to advert to the ordinances and constitution of
our apostolic Church, in a way (according to my endeavour)
to avoid hurting their feelings, and at the same time to counteract any impression that my proceeding was a sanction of
Methodism and lay-preaching. I have entered thus fully
into my reasons and mode of proceeding, because I wish
to preserve memoranda of the case for the opinion of my
father. The little chapel was well filled, and I succeeded,
not so much to my own satisfaction as to do me any harm in
the shape of particular self-gratification in this new experiment, yet sufficiently well to prevent my being confused or
guilty of hesitation." Two or three days were spent at Gaspé
Basin, which were occupied with business relating to the
progress of the Church. On one of them the Archdeacon
preached in the church, where he heard " what we cannot
boast of in the cathedral of Quebec, the bell inviting the
worshippers to the temple. The temple itself, however, was
a mere unpainted barn, yet it is a surprising building when it
is remembered that the materials grew in the woods on one
Sunday, and formed a Church, framed, roofed, and boarded,
in which service was held on the next." On the night of
the 27th August, the Archdeacon set off with the missionary
of Gaspé Bay (then one of the only two clergymen in the
district) in an open boat, to visit the settlements along the
coast. They both took their turns of steering and rowing.
Stopping at Malbaie, spending Sunday at Percé and L'Anse
à Beau-fils, they reached Paspébiac, where the Archdeacon
remained several days, holding services and preaching (as

he did everywhere) inspecting schools, and putting matters in train for the erection or completion of churches, and the establishment of new schools, and visiting sick and aged persons. The missionary of Gaspé Bay, in the meantime, took advantage of the opportunity of his visit to the Bay of Chaleurs, to carry his own ministrations across into the province of New Brunswick, where the people were quite destitute of religious ordinances and had requested him to pay them a visit. The Archdeacon assumed the responsibility of this intrusion into another diocese, with the authorities of which he communicated afterwards on the subject. A church was nearly finished at Paspébiac, and the frame of one was up at Carlisle. The Archdeacon was " rather surprised to hear the missionary, after giving out the psalms for the day, add the following hint to the people, ' very pleasant to hear the responses after the clerk,' and after giving out the singing psalms, he said, ' St. Paul says that we must sing with the spirit and sing with the understanding.' There were some other peculiarities in his manner of performing the service, but they had been partly introduced for the assistance of a congregation unaccustomed to frequent the worship of God, till the Bishop sent a clergyman among them." After a visit to Hopetown, the Archdeacon, in company with the missionary of Gaspé Bay, who had returned from his visit to the New Brunswick shore, proceeded in a boat up the Bay of Chaleurs, and held services at New Richmond and Ristigouche. From thence he took a bark canoe, with two Indians, and ascended the Ristigouche and Matapediac rivers for about seventy-five miles, walking about twenty-five more to the shores of the St. Lawrence, through the woods. He passed one house on the way inhabited by an English family, where he baptized some children ; but, with this exception, there was no occasion for the performance of official duties on this part of the journey. The Indians were Roman Catholics, and " they asked many questions about the Indian tribes in the higher parts of the country, some of whom they had heard were ' de bons gens *comme nous*,' and others reprobates ' qui ne croient pas au bon Dieu.' I asked them whether they would not desire the advantages of education, the most obvious of which I pointed out, and they heartily acquiesced ; but though I encouraged them, as far as occasion could be taken, in every moral and religious feeling of a correct nature, I did not think it my business to endeavour to wean them from any of the errors of the church of Rome. The only effect of such an endeavour would have been to alienate them still farther from a religion whose professors interfered with the soundness of their own. I made it my object to give the conversation such a turn as might tend in some degree to conciliate their good will to Protestantism, and thus at least I might be instrumental in improving their charity. I know there are some zealous Protestants who would think me wrong. And I should think *them* so. * * * We fell in with a small party of lumberers, and as I had a very short allowance of bread and biscuit, I asked them for some flour, and they give me about eight pounds, for which I gave them money, but they returned it, unobserved by me, to the Indians, who faithfully informed me afterwards of their having received it. These people were just going home, having spent the summer upon their task. I asked them how they distinguished the Sunday in the woods, and found that it was simply and solely by abstinence from work. I gave them a couple of tracts, which I had with me. I had the Bible in one pocket and Cicero in the other." They pushed on in their walk through the woods so as, if possible, to reach Metis, where there were a few Protestants, by Saturday night. The Archdeacon describes his appearance as being very little like that of a " dignitary." Lame, from a strain which he had met with on the march, " and tattered, a long staff made out of an old canoe-paddle in my hand, the scratches of my skin seen through the holes of my trowsers and stockings, without a neckcloth, my clothes soiled

by the march, my shoes tied with twine, and my trowsers confined at the ancle, to prevent their catching in the branches,
with pins and strips of cedar-bark. To this equipment was
afterwards added, at the instance of my friend François (one
of the Indians), who had the promise of inheriting my trowsers,
(as Jean Baptiste had already done my discarded waistcoat),
and who by no means contemned the expected prize, a coloured
handkerchief round one knee to prevent the enlargement of a
very serious solution of continuity, to which pins had repeatedly been applied with little effect." The journal continues,
" We met with so many delays in hunting for the path, and
made so many deviations, that night closed upon us in the
wood, and we accordingly made our camp within about four
miles of the waters of the St. Lawrence, where, finding
that our crackers would hardly eke out a slender supper for
William and myself, I divided them with so rigid an equality
as to split the odd one which remained into halves. The
Indians had no bread, and supped upon fish alone. In our
way through the wood to the beach the next morning, we met
with some partridges, two of which the Indians brought down
with sticks, and they proved afterwards a most valuable addition to our *sea-stock.* At eight o'clock we stood on the beach
of the St. Lawrence, which is here forty miles across, and
had a couple of miles more to walk before we could reach a
house. From this house we were pulled about a league, in a
boat gaping with leaks, to the Point of Little Métis, by a
Scotch settler and his son, a lad of eighteen whom I had put
to the national school at Quebec. Nothing could have fallen
out more happily, though it had not been in the least within
my original calculations, than my arrival in this place on Sunday morning, and I spent a most satisfactory day. I had, in
fact, been mortified by the failure of my intention to devote
this day to the Protestants of a settlement fifty miles below
Quebec, but it happened that the schoolmaster of that very
place had come down to look at some land at Métis, and I

learnt from him that I should not have collected a congregation of half-a-dozen persons, and that, at the moment, there
was not a single child to be baptized there.   I took means to
spread the notice of my arrival and to convene the congregation for the afternoon.   They had never had but one pastoral
visit, which was when the seigneur, a Scotchman, brought
down the Presbyterian minister from Quebec, four or five
years ago.   At the appointed hour, about forty persons
assembled, and ten children were presented for baptism.
Some of the persons who had been married upon the spot by
means of a written contract, a copy of which they had lodged
in the hands of the seigneur, spoke to me apart, and expressing some uneasiness of mind at the insufficiency of the form,
solicited me, if possible, to give effect to what they had done
by a regular solemnization.   It grieved me to refuse, but I
did not conceive that the law would permit my marrying
without either licence or publication of banns.   As, however,
they had acted in good faith, and their marriage was likely
to be comprehended in some of those Acts of the Provincial
Parliament which are passed, once in a while, to give validity
to irregular transactions of the kind, I was enabled to comfort
them, both as it regarded conscience, and the recognition of
the legitimacy of their offspring.   The public prayers, the
psalm-singing, the preaching of the Word had all the zest
to these people of a rare and unexpected occurrence, and
I never was more thankfully received.   One of them said to
me, in tendering the acknowledgments of the congregation,
' We can only thank you and love you.'   They profited by
a recommendation conveyed in my sermon, that they would
make arrangements among themselves for meeting together
on Sundays for public worship.   It would not, perhaps, be
presumptuous to say that my own plans were happily over-
ruled, and my steps directed so as to spend the Lord's day
in a place so rarely trod by the feet of them that bring glad
tidings of peace."   On the following day the Archdeacon,

after sundry difficulties and delays, embarked in an open boat
for Rimouski, where, being unable to obtain any land-convey-
ance, he took another boat to Trois Pistoles, in which he spent
two nights (the distance being about forty miles) and "never
suffered so much from cold." From thence the journey to
Point Levi was comparatively easy : but it is curious now to
read of difficulties within sight of home. " Being determined to proceed direct to Marchmont (where his father then
lived, and his own family were staying), I stopped, myself at
the little Indian encampment on the beach at Point Levi to
bargain for a canoe, and directed William to go across in the
steamboat* to Quebec. The only disposable canoe belonged
to a squaw, and they told me it was too small to venture in
with the degree of wind and swell which prevailed. I then
applied to some Canadians for a boat, but as they had the
conscience to ask me ten shillings,—the price, as William
observed, of a steerage passage in the steamboat to Montreal,
—I cut short all negociation with such extortioners at once.
While I was going in quest of another boat, the squaw came
up and offered her canoe, declaring now that it would do
extremely well. As the day was wearing fast away, I closed
with her offer and embarked. She steered the canoe herself,
and a male Indian paddled in the bow, but they were sadly
unlike my Ristigouche friends. The man, I found, was quite
drunk, and the woman, a bragging, brazen wretch, who cursed
him furiously, and talked to him like a slave, dealing her
offensive slang among the crews of the vessels which were
within hearing, and talking in the same breath of our being
in the hands of Providence, and of our looking to the mercy
of God if anything should happen. At length when we had
reached a place just below the middle of the race-course, she
declared she would go no farther, and put me ashore upon

---

* There was only one at this time plying between Quebec and Point
Levi, and that not at regular intervals.

the beach. I did not insist upon her proceeding, for I have seldom felt a more painful disgust than she caused me, and I was glad to be rid of such evil company. I ought not, perhaps, in strict prudence, to have come with them, but I was deceived by my recent experience into confidence in Indians: and after all, as far as safety is concerned, you never hear of any accident in their canoes. This woman, by the way, pronounced me to be a " Français de France," which was the third time on this journey that I was so mistaken. After waiting a little while on the beach, I found a Canadian lad whom I engaged to carry my portmanteau to Marchmont. He shewed me a precipitous path up to the plains, and I thence led the way across to the house. * * * * * If we are now upon the eve of a longer separation, on this 23rd of March (1825), to which time my scant enjoyment of leisure has protracted the conclusion of my journal, let us pray that it may please Him to grant us to meet in health and happiness."

CHAPTER V.

Visit to England—Death of his Father.

THE separation, to which reference is made in the concluding
words of the last chapter, was caused by his compliance with his
father's desire that he should go to England, partly as the
agent of the Clergy Reserve corporations, who commissioned
him to take fresh steps towards obtaining from the Imperial
Government the preservation of their interests, with particular reference to a proposed measure for the sale of a portion
of the lands to the Canada Company ; and partly to urge,
in the same quarter, the necessity for affording some relief
to the Bishop, whose infirmities now began to make him
unequal to the labours of the episcopal office, by the division
of the diocese. The Bishop hoped, indeed, that an arrangement might be made for his own retirement, and desired to
see the two provinces of Upper and Lower Canada each
constituted a diocese, with Dr. Stewart presiding over the
former, and the Archdeacon of Quebec over the latter.
But if this might not be, he was content to retain the charge
of Lower Canada, if Dr. Stewart, to whom he was prepared
to surrender £1000 a year from his own income, might be
consecrated to the charge of the Upper province, and afford
occasional help, if it should be necessary, in administering
confirmation in Lower Canada. Some communications with
reference to this subject had already passed between His
Majesty's Government and Dr. Stewart, when he had been in

England in the preceding year, and the Bishop was secure of His Majesty's approval of his nomination. Dr. Stewart enjoyed his Lordship's full confidence ; and a proof of that which he himself placed in the Archdeacon may be found in a letter in which he " readily " says that he " shall be satisfied with any arrangement you may make for me respecting my being a Bishop in Canada, my salary," &c., &c.; though with reference to this last point he states his opinion in another letter, with characteristic disinterestedness, that " if the two future Bishoprics are not equal, that of Quebec ought to be the largest. I am disposed to prefer Upper Canada."

The Archdeacon left Quebec on the 30th March for New York, which, with pretty hard travelling, was not reached till the 9th April. At New York he was detained till the 1st May, waiting for a commission* to act on behalf of the Clergy Reserve corporation of Upper Canada. He had undertaken this task with very great unwillingness, and only because

---

* The following is the commission :—

" Reverend Sir,—The Corporation for superintending and managing the Clergy Reserves in this province determined at their last meeting to petition the Imperial Parliament, praying that the Clergy Reserves may be withdrawn from the purchase contemplated by the Canada Land Company, and that no sales be made of such Reserves, except by the Corporation with the concurrence of the Government, and to be heard by counsel against the passing of any bill authorizing such purchase that may be under the consideration of the Imperial Parliament.

" As the Corporation have full confidence in your zeal and abilities, and your knowledge of the state and prospects of the Established Church in this province, you are hereby appointed their agent to urge the prayer of their petition, and to take such other measures, with the advice of counsel, as may be found expedient.

" John Strachan, D.D.,

" Rector of York, Upper Canada, and Chairman of the Corporation for superintending, conducting, and managing the Clergy Reserves in the said Province."

his father believed it to be necessary for the interests of the Church. He shrank very much from the responsibility which was imposed upon him, and was very apprehensive that he might fail in his object through want of proper management. His distrustfulness of himself seems to have caused more perplexity and uneasiness than there was any real occasion for ; and possibly the separation from his father and his wife, both of whom were far from strong at this time, may have tended sometimes to depress his spirits. His letters to them (which contain descriptions of New York which it is now interesting to read,) are full of tenderness and diffidence. To the latter he says—" Your letters are an inexpressible comfort and delight to me, and whatever anxieties or perplexities I may have to encounter abroad, or whatever chicane to deal with,—nay, whatever domestic afflictions it may please God to hold in store for me—*my home* will always be a resting-point to which my soul will turn itself as to nothing else which there is, or can be, here on earth. I bless God for all His undeserved mercies to me, and am determined not to let my mind sink in any vexations which may occur ; but for none which partakes of an earthly cast do I more bless His Name than for that which enables me to call myself *yours*, my own excellent and best beloved M——." Well was this confidence deserved and repaid ; for he had, indeed, an help meet for him. His letters are full, not only of directions as to parish matters, relief of the poor, &c., but also as to those in which his place might, to some extent, be supplied to his father ; and this while she had a more than ordinary share of maternal care, and had not been able, notwithstanding the meekest resignation, to overcome the physical effects of the repeated sorrows to which reference has already been made. His father, in a letter on which is written " the last which he addressed to me, and the last but one which he was able to dictate," expresses his regret that he had not been able to go into Quebec as often as he had proposed to do, but adds, " with

Mary's activity, and Mr. Archbold's* assiduity, I trust every thing is going on well." In a note to his father, written the day after leaving Quebec, the Archdeacon says: " I omitted, in a hurried note to M——, to convey my feelings of duty, of love, of thankfulness to Marchmont. I therefore seize a moment to do it now, although how shall I ever sufficiently acknowledge or requite all the kindnesses I have experienced from parents such as no other children are blessed with ?" †

The Archdeacon reached England on the 21st May, but the delay which he had met with at New York proved fatal to the success of his mission with regard to the Clergy Reserves, for the bill against which the corporation petitioned had already passed the Imperial Parliament. Its object was to empower certain commissioners to fix a uniform price at which Crown Lands should be sold to the Canada Company, the introduction of whose capital into the country was considered to be so great an advantage, that they were able to obtain very favourable terms, and the petitioners desired to exempt the Clergy Reserves from the operation of the bill,

---

* A missionary of the S. P. G., who assisted in the duties of the parish of Quebec, and of whom the Archdeacon wrote in 1832 : "I was happy in the opportunity of intercourse with this valued friend (then rector of Cornwall) and unaffectedly devoted servant of God and His Church, who is an example to us all. So zealous and devout, but so humble, so genuine, so single-hearted, so entirely given to the work to which he is called, it does one good to be in contact with him, and we may well desire to learn from him."

† The Bishop would probably have replied, that never parents had such children. In a letter written by his Lordship's sister to the future Archdeacon, in 1809, while he was at Cambridge, I find the following passage : " The accounts we hear of you and your dear brothers from every one afford the most heartfelt satisfaction, which is increased by the idea of the solace it must prove to your parents under every trial ; when they call to mind the goodness of their children, it must counterbalance every evil. May this comfort ever be theirs, and may you all be rewarded for the conduct which holds out so much gratification to us and them."

and to give the corporation some voice in their disposal. The highest authorities in the colony declared themselves in favour of the reasonableness of this claim, and the secretary of State for the colonies (Lord Bathurst) was warmly attached to the Church, but the bill passed notwithstanding, by which " the Company were to enjoy the full benefit of the valuation of three shillings and sixpence an acre, and that payable by instalments, without interest, in fifteen years." But a letter from the under secretary of State to the Archdeacon, declared " it to be the intention of Government to place the Church upon the same footing as before, restoring the one-third of the Reserves if the Company will accept other lands as an equivalent, or substituting these other lands for the support of the Clergy, if they will not." The Archdeacon derived much valuable assistance in the conduct of this business from Mr. Robinson, Attorney-General of Upper Canada, who had been his fellow-passenger across the Atlantic, and was a sincere friend of the Church, and thorough master of the subject. In his other object he was greatly aided by the counsel of his friend and connection, the Honourable A. W. Cochran, secretary to the Earl of Dalhousie, Governor-in-chief of Canada, who had accompanied His Excellency to England at that time. No two laymen have rendered more faithful and efficient services to the Canadian Church. In later years the one was the confidential friend and counsellor of the Bishop of the Lower Canadian diocese, the other the confidential friend and counsellor of the Bishop of Toronto. The college, societies, and other institutions of the Church, in each diocese, owe much to their legal knowledge and general experience, as well as to their hearty devotion to their interests.

The Society for the Propagation of the Gospel seconded the efforts of the Archdeacon, by making representations to the Colonial Office, with the view of securing to the Church the advantages just mentioned. The Bishop of Quebec had furnished him with written instructions,* and full information, as well as careful calculations made by the rector of York. He discharged his part with unintermitting diligence, but the whole business was exceedingly distasteful to him.   Writing to his father from England, he says, " I cannot express to you how much I should desire to have done for ever with public men and public offices, and to hold some charge in God's Church which might leave me independent of the favour or frowns of political power, and unconnected with any engines of government."   It was probably this feeling that withheld him from carrying out his father's wishes with regard to the other object of his mission as fully as he might have done ; for he proposed to the Government only the division of the diocese, with the transfer of Upper Canada to the hands of Dr. Stewart, the Bishop retaining Lower Canada, or the assumption by Dr. S. of the charge of the whole province, the Bishop in that case being allowed to retire.   The result of his negociations is contained in the following letter addressed to the Bishop, which was submitted to, and approved as "perfectly correct" by, the under-secretary of State :

" I am happy to be enabled, by the kindness of Earl Bathurst, to inform you that some conclusive arrangements respecting your affairs have received the approbation of the Archbishop of Canterbury, upon his Lordship's recommendation, and are in train to be executed, which I trust you will consider as entirely satisfactory.

" I am authorized to state, that these arrangements will be as follows :

" H. M. Government being unwilling, except in cases of strong necessity, to permit the resignation of a Bishop, and being also desirous, on the other hand, of embracing the present opportunity to divide the laborious and extensive diocese which constitutes your charge, have decided upon this latter expedient as the mode of providing for your relief. You will, therefore, continue Bishop of Quebec, but under a fresh patent, and with diminished labours ; the limits of your diocese being reduced to those of the province

---

* The last words of these are, "Be not at all disheartened ; you have nothing to fear. Keep up your spirits. May God bless and protect you, and prosper your undertakings. Amen."

of Lower Canada, and the Upper province being taken out of your jurisdiction and erected into a separate diocese, to the charge of which Dr.
Stewart will be consecrated.

"In order, however, to meet the wants of the case, in whatever shape they
may present themselves, Dr. Stewart will receive his appointment upon a
distinct understanding that he is to assist you, as far as may be necessary,
during your life, and that the charge of the whole of both dioceses shall,
for that period, devolve upon him, if your health should render you incapable of your duties, or require your return to England."

Having so far fulfilled the objects of his voyage to England,
the Archdeacon turned his thoughts again to his parish and
his home. They had never, indeed, been long absent from
them, and though he had originally promised himself the
pleasure of seeing some of his early friends, he devoted himself so unsparingly to business as to leave time for scarcely
more than forced and flying visits to his nearest relations
and one friend* who claimed the privilege of calling herself
his "second mother." He accomplished, besides, a brief
visit to a brother of Dr. Stewart, to whom he had given a
promise that he would do so. An account of the effort this
cost may serve as a specimen of the manner in which his
time was filled up. "I have had a life of constant, unceasing hurry since I first came to town, (immediately after
his landing at Liverpool,) and if it were not for the satisfaction of what little I am to see of my brothers and friends,
could heartily wish myself out of England every hour. Yesterday (Saturday) I left town at four o'clock, to go down to
Mr. James Stewart's, at Clapham Common, at whose house I
dined and slept. He has been very kind to me, and has

---

* Mrs. Harrold, of Horkesley Park, Essex, an early friend of his mother's,
whose husband, inheriting her property and her friendship, became afterwards the great benefactor of Bishop's College, Lennoxville. His munificence to the great Church Societies was unbounded, and generally anonymous. Mrs. Harrold's brother and sister gave as "a clergyman and his
sister" the funds for the erection of one of the Bethnal Green Churches.
Her delightful letters to her "dear son" would form a most interesting
addition to this memoir.

entered into all my business. With his family I went to church at Clapham. From the church door I got into a stage-coach ; from the stage-coach office in town, without going to my lodging, I went to afternoon service at Westminster Abbey ; thence I came home, and having dined off a little rye loaf which I bought two days ago and put in my pocket, and a glass of lukewarm London water, I addressed myself to writing, having previously to my luxurious repast read your letter and my mother's. And this is not the only day, I assure you, that I have gone without my regular dinner, or any use of those beverages which are given to make 'glad the heart of man.' The writing which I have to execute to-night, if I can get through it, is as follows: a letter to the Archbishop; ditto to the secretary S. P. G. ; ditto to Lord Bathurst, respecting the disposal of the petition ; two private letters ; then, on your side of the water, I must write to my father, to Major Hillier, to Dr. Strachan, and Dr. Stewart. If I should not have time for the last, will you make a copy of the letter to Lord B. about the Bishops, and send it to him, and tell him that his brothers have been very civil to me ; his brother James, who seems to be an excellent man, particularly kind." I cannot forbear from giving one or two more extracts from letters written at this time. " I have received your letter, containing a lock of our dear little boy's hair for G., the sight of which made me more foolish than I choose to tell you of. But how can I be thankful enough to have such delightful accounts of you and your occupations, abroad and at home ? The parish and the family seem to go on so well in my absence, that I think I had better stay away, and would do so on purpose, if I could put so much force upon certain strong and yearning inclinations which every day's absence serves to increase. What you and your coadjutors have done about the Red House* delights me. Tell the dear

---

* A building secured as a home for houseless poor.

little girls that it makes me very happy to hear of their behaving so well about reading prayers, etc., which I trust may be taken as a proof of their behaving well in all things. I write, as usual, in a hurry; it is the old story over again; trudging all day, or waiting upon official people, and writing half the night. The watchman has been singing out ' past one,' for some time, and as this is not my closing operation, I wish you and my children good night, and may the Almighty have you ever in His holy keeping." * * * * " I am to be in London again on the 18th (July) to meet one of the principal merchants concerned in the Canada Company, and work may be then cut out for me which will protract my stay. I left town on the afternoon of the 7th, and came that evening to Bourchier's. The next day, after breakfast, we came through Easton, where we visited our old school-boy haunts, and several of my old friends* among the cottagers, to Thaxted, where my aunt's gig met me and took me on to Bardfield, where I spent Saturday and Sunday; and on the latter day preached, as it were, among the shades of my maternal forefathers, and over their very bones, in Little Bardfield church. Nothing can exceed the kindness of all my friends, nor can I describe to you the longing that I feel to have you here among them; but, as to our taking up our abode here, I see no prospect of it whatever, and every year that I remain away removes farther the probability of my obtaining preferment at home. We must make ourselves happy, therefore, where Providence has cast our lot, and be thankful for all our blessings, remembering that here we have ' no continuing city,' and if we must not look to England as our land of promise on earth, there is a resting place for us all, to which the way is never long."

---

* One of his brothers, writing to him a description of his own visit to these scenes some years later, says, " Old Mrs. F. cried when she spoke of you."

Although the Archdeacon did not put forward his father's views with regard to himself, he was furnished with testimonials from different persons to whom they had been communicated, from one of which, from the Earl of Dalhousie, I make the following extract:

"It gives me great pleasure to seize this earliest opportunity of placing in your own hands, to be used as you please, my most earnest hope that your claims and pretensions to preferment over that diocese will be received by H. M. Ministers, and considered as they justly merit. To give my own personal recommendation on that point would be a poor expression in your favour, and I have no hesitation in going so far as to say, in the name of the whole protestant population of the Lower Province, that whenever you shall see fit to lay your claims before the proper quarter, you may rest assured of the cordial wishes of all who have already had the advantage of knowing and of appreciating your indefatigable labours in the performance of your duties among them. I shall be ready, at all times, to bear testimony in your favour, in preference to any other person, from the conscientious conviction that your knowledge of the people there, your experience, and your well-known abilities would have greater weight in promoting the great interests of the Church and of the people than any other person whatever."

Before the date of the letter which he addressed to his father, announcing the arrangements which he had been able to effect for him, that father had been taken to his rest. He died on the 18th June, 1825, having given scarcely any previous grounds for alarm. It was a heavy blow to his sons, none of whom were permitted to be with him, but especially to the Archdeacon, as he was the only one who could reasonably have expected to receive his parting blessing, and it may naturally have added to his grief, to reflect that so far as his father was personally concerned, his mission to England had proved of no advantage. The intelligence of his loss reached him on the 22nd July, as he was making his final arrangements for leaving England, but he was detained another week by business preparatory to the return of his mother to her native land. I must draw the history of this year to a close, or it would be a satisfaction to place on

record some of the testimonies which the death of the first
Bishop of Quebec drew forth from different quarters, public
and private. I confine myself to an extract from the letter
written by the Archdeacon on hearing of that event. It
bears strong marks of agitation, which rendered writing difficult, though the place from which it is dated (Colonial Office)
shews that he had braced himself up so as not to suffer any
interruption of his work. " I have received your letters, and
I have seen Mr. B. (from Quebec.) The will of God be
done! I trust He will support us all and teach us to submit,
and that He will grant me the comfort of speedily rejoining
you. You are, indeed, a comfort to me ; the thought of you,
and the account which you give of your own strength in this
trial, and the support that you will be able to administer to
those more immediately connected with him whom we mourn,
are mercies for which I fervently bless my God ; and how
many mercies have I received at His hand! But I cannot
trust myself farther upon this subject now. *   *   *   As
for you, my beloved children, I know that your young hearts
will grieve for the loss of your kind, your good grandpapa.
You love your own father, and can judge of his feelings ; but
your blessed grandfather is gone where, I trust, we shall all
meet him, and though our hearts are broken now, it will be
a comfort to us even in this world to think of his virtues and
his kindness to us all. You are old enough always, always,
always to remember how good he was to you. Do not think
that I shall give way. Writing to Quebec agitates me, but
with God's help I shall brace up again." His eldest brother,
writing at this time to his mother, says, " George's conduct
has been delicate, feeling, firm and judicious. His success
cannot but be a source of comfort to you, and of lasting
satisfaction to his own heart. My father's mantle has not
wholly fallen to the ground ; part of it has rested upon
George. God bless him." Another brother, writing a little
earlier to himself, had said, " I think I may congratulate

you upon the success of your negociations, which I hope will make you some amends for all the harass and hurrying about that you have had, and it ought to reconcile us, in some measure, to seeing so little, almost nothing, of you, but we must be allowed to feel vexed and disappointed on this account. This must not be reckoned a visit to England. You must come again and bring your family with you. God bless them and you. Your very truly affectionate brother,

"G. R. M."

From London the Archdeacon went down to Tunbridge Wells, to take a hasty farewell of his wife's family, between whom and himself there subsisted the strongest affection. He left them on the morning of the 30th July, (in days when there were no railways,) and dined the same day with his brothers at Hemel Hempsted in Hertfordshire. After a stay there of about an hour and a half, he was driven by one of them to meet the Liverpool mail, and reached that place between nine and ten the next evening. The following morning he sailed for New York, where he arrived early in September. Before leaving the ship, his fellow-passengers presented him with a letter, conveying their thanks for his " religious attention to themselves and the ship's company during the voyage," and the assurance of " their individual esteem and sincere wishes for his happiness and welfare."

As he lay in his berth, soon after leaving Liverpool, the thoughts which were uppermost in his mind found expression in the following lines:

Speed, speed, good ship! for home and friends
One heart is here that sorely yearns;
And they to whom the traveller wends,
How oft to thee their fancy turns!

O speed him well—tho' not that home
Will wear a look his heart to cheer;
Ah! wherefore was he bid to roam,
So dark a change then lurking near?

Yet speed him well,—a widow grey,
His mother now, will want her son ;
Alas! that in that mournful day
Of all her four she clasped not one!

O speed him fast,—his gentle wife,
Partner of all his joy and pain,
   .   .   .   .   .
   .   .   .   .   .

Ye children that he loves so well,
Sweet sister, too,—fair drooping flower !
Kind brother whom the tidings fell
Have brought before this weary hour ;

With you, with others near in love,
He longs to mix in mutual grief;
To draw, from streams which spring above,
In mutual use, a blest relief.

He longs to find the healing charms
Of home, albeit in sorrowing mien ;
And fold within a father's arms
Th' unconscious child he has not seen.

O sacred links! and fastened deep
Beyond the world's infectious reach,
How well, whom many mourners weep,
How well didst *thou* their value teach!

Yet not within the narrow walls
Of home his only wishes lie ;
He owns the power of other calls
Fulfilled beneath a father's eye.

Aye, so fulfilled—but that is done—
No earthly father now shall mark
The course of this inferior son,
Who yet emits a kindred spark.

O Father of the saints above
And men below, it is to Thee,
To Thee we must commend our love,
Altho' no human eye should see.
   .   .   .   .   .   .
   .   .   .   .   .   .

O Thou, upon th' eternal throne
Of heaven, Who rul'st the changeful waves,
Whose wonders in the deep are shewn,*
The avenging arm, and that which saves,

Thou in Whose hidden treasures lie .
The ready winds,† and in Whose hand
Is all which once, in earth or sky
Sprung and stood fast at Thy command,§

Deign Thou the wanderer's way to guide
Who thus his lone affliction sings ;
And o'er his kin, whom seas divide,
Stretch forth, O God, Thy guardian wings.

O truly guide them all to find
The haven where they hope to rest, ¶
—Left but a few brief days behind,
They join THE DEAD FOR EVER BLEST.

---

* Ps. cvii. 24.   † Ps. cxxxv. 7.   § Ps. xxxiii. 9.   ¶ Ps. cvii. 30.

.

CHAPTER VI.

Bishop Stewart—Labours in the parish of Quebec, for the diocese and
for different institutions.

Dr. Mountain had been nearly six months absent from
Quebec, though scarcely more than two had been spent in
England.   His labours were not lightened by his being relieved of those which properly belonged to the office of chaplain, for during the vacancy of the see additional responsibility was, of course, laid on the Archdeacon, and this, with
his parochial duties, left him little leisure. The new Bishop
was not consecrated till January, 1826, and was unable to
enter on the administration of the diocese for about a year
after the death of his predecessor. He had gone to England in
1825 for consecration, and the Government declining to carry
into effect the plan for the division of the diocese on the ground
that it had been rendered necessary only by the failing health
of the late Bishop, the charge of the whole of Canada devolved
upon him.   But it was more than any one man could bear,
and soon wore out the strength of Dr. Stewart, which had,
perhaps, been already impaired by twenty years of apostolic
labour.   It would have been a great comfort to him if he could
have persuaded His Majesty's Ministers to agree to the erection of a new diocese, and could have seen his friend the
Archdeacon of Quebec placed over it; and in this feeling,
the clergy of Lower Canada may be presumed to have shared,
for in the conclusion of an address of condolence in his bereavement which they presented to him upon his return from Eng-

land, they say, " That return is cause of rejoicing to your family, your friends, your flock, and the Church of God Whose ministers we are ; and, gratified as we are at the prospect of the elevation to the vacant see of that distinguished missionary of noble birth, whose exertions in the cause of religion, and whose sacrifices to promote it, none can know how to appreciate better than ourselves, we must yet be permitted to express the satisfaction we shall feel at any arrangement, whether near or remote, which may have for its object your own advancement to a situation of higher honour and more extensive usefulness in that Church of which you have shewn yourself, on all occasions, the able and vigilant champion, and which already owes so much to your services and your zeal."   Bishop Stewart, indeed, seems never to have lost sight of this object, for he made repeated efforts for its accomplishment before it was at length attained.   He was well able to judge of the qualifications of his Archdeacon, for never was Archdeacon more truly the " right hand " of his Bishop.   The Bishop leaned upon him for advice and assistance in all that he undertook, and the most perfect affection and confidence subsisted between them.   He became his lordship's examining chaplain, (an office which he had filled under his own father,) and his pen was more than once employed in writing pastoral addresses which were sent forth ·· *from the Bishop of Quebec.*"   The first ordination by the new Bishop was held in July, 1826,* when the Archdeacon preached the sermon, which was published.   It was nearly the same as that which he had preached at the visitation at Montreal in 1820, and which he had not then published, as it formed one of a series intended for his own flock, the whole of which he had designed to give them in print, but the necessary leisure for doing so having been denied him, this one was now published separately.   He constantly laid down exact

---

* Two hundred and five persons were, in this year, confirmed at Quebec.

rules for the distribution of his time, but he was so completely the servant of others, that it was scarcely ever possible to observe them. Besides discharging the duties of Archdeacon and chaplain, he undertook, in January 1827, and continued for several years, to superintend the studies of some candidates for Orders resident in Quebec, for which no other provision could be made, and they used to come to him for a certain number of hours every week.* All this while he was working a large and scattered parish, with charitable associations which depended on his activity for their welfare, and without the regular machinery which would have afforded him relief. The National Schools, Sunday-Schools, Hospitals, Jail, Jail Association, S. P. C. K. Committee, Clergy Reserve Corporation, Royal Institution, Emigrant Society, and several other public institutions,—all claimed a large share of constant labour and anxiety. There is a likeness of him, taken in 1826, on which he has written with reference to the premature grey hairs and other marks of age which it exhibits,

> Confiteor facere hæc annos; sed et altera causa est,
> Anxietas animi continuusque labor.

And besides all these, there was a ceaseless recourse to him, by all sorts and conditions of men, for every conceivable kind of assistance, spiritual and temporal. He sometimes longed for relief from some of "the drudgery of parish routine," which might have been equally well performed by inferior hands, leaving his own more free for higher things. He generally, indeed, had an assistant in the week-day work, but this clergyman used to devote the Sundays to destitute settlements in the neighbourhood of Quebec. There was not at this time more than one resident clergyman in the district

---

* He also drew up, by desire of the Bishop, a sketch of the heads of lectures, &c., for the guidance of others, which has been preserved.

of Quebec, beyond the limits of the parish itself, and the Archdeacon was constantly called upon to visit sick persons at a distance. His labours were also shared, particularly in the duties of some of the institutions above mentioned, by the Rev. Dr. Mills, chaplain to the forces, and evening lecturer at the cathedral, and the Rev. E. W. Sewell, incumbent of a proprietary chapel in Quebec, (which had been built in 1825, by the father of that gentleman, then Chief Justice of Lower Canada,) who had also relieved him of the pastoral charge of such members of his flock as became pew-holders in the chapel. His Sunday duty consisted of the greater part of two services in the cathedral, a service at the jail, superintendence of two Sunday schools, baptisms, churchings, and funerals nearly every Sunday, and an evening service in the suburbs. I find some rough memoranda of his employment on particular days, which are specimens of his general work. " Sunday, June 22nd, 1823, read altar-service, and preached in the cathedral in the forenoon; christening; visited the boys' and the girls' Sunday school at Hope Gate. Prayers and preached at the jail, and visited a prisoner in his cell. Prayers P. M. in the cathedral, two women churched, two christenings; went to the burying-ground at half-past seven, and performed a funeral. Evening service, and preached at the burying-ground. One woman churched, a private baptism at the sexton's house." On the 14th August, in the same year, (a week-day,) there is a list of visits paid, which, from their distances, and the variety of business arising from them, must have cost an astonishing effort to accomplish. And on All Saints' day, 1825, he has noted down, " Family prayers and chapter. After breakfast, walked out to emigrant hospital, (about a mile from his house) and administered Sacrament to a sick woman; returned by a quarter past ten; made some memoranda and preparations for other business; went to church, where delivered a lecture upon the day (as he did on all festi-

vals) ; returned home ; a young woman received instruction
for Sacrament first time ; drafted three letters in the diocese
letter-book, wrote fair, and sent them ; a note to S. respecting his allowance from society ; Mr. Archbold called to consult me respecting a baptism without sponsors ; called at
office of Civil Secretary to make arrangements respecting
transport of Government Bibles, etc. ; visited widow W.,
prayed with her ; went to Neptune Inn, Lower Town, to see
Mr. M., from Bay of Chaleurs ; woman of the house begged
me to see her mother, dangerously hurt,—conversed and
prayed with her ; called on M. A. ;* returned home to dine ;
played with the children ;† wrote some portion of blue-book ;
family prayers and chapter ; read some portion of " Conver-

---

* His cousin, Miss Mountain, who died in Quebec in 1845. She is the
person referred to in the note, at page 33, and her practice well illustrated
her precept. The following extract, from one of her letters, written to Fredericton, will shew the affection that existed between them. " None, I may
venture to say, feel your absence more than my aunt and myself. We
have not much to do with the business or pleasures of the world, and the
loss of the society of one endeared to us by the ties of near relationship, by
the fulfilment of the promise of early excellence, and still more by his
daily and uniform affectionate attention, forms a blank to us which your
letters only reconcile us to, as they tell us you are happy, and we strive to
silence all selfish regrets." On one of her notes relating to an act of kindness done to himself, he has written, " Blessed be she of the Lord, who
hath not left off her kindness to the living and to the dead."

† The pains which he took to promote even the innocent amusements
of his children ; his mindfulness, when in the midst of his most pressing
occupations, of their little wants and wishes; the manner in which he
entered into their feelings ; his constant desire for their improvement, and
his efforts to aid them in it, were eminently characteristic of him. And
this same tenderness of disposition shewed itself, in its degree, in his in-ter-
course with all children with whom he came in contact. When his children grew up, and left their home, he scarcely ever missed an occasion of
writing to them, even if he had only time to say that he was " glad of
every little opportunity of renewing a father's blessing;" and he still
entered into all their pleasures, as well as strengthened them by his judicious and affectionate counsels. An absent child was sure to be specially
mentioned in the family prayers.

sion of Struenzee." Another memorandum, which is scarcely
intelligible, shews the forenoon of 23rd January, 1826, filled
up in a similar way: " In the afternoon, drove Dr. to Stoneham, visited sick man and baptized a child, the state of the
weather and roads being such, that returned at three A.M.
on 24th." I will give only one other, which seems to have
been made as a matter of curiosity; the date is, probably,
early in 1826: "Things done before eleven o'clock, on
Monday morning, a Saints' day: 1. Orders and directions
written for the messenger of emigrant society; 2. A man
wanting a note to procure admission for a sick woman into
hospital; 3. A boy wanting relief for his mother; 4. A man
wanting a recommendatory note to be employed as a tide-
waiter; 5. A man wanting the time fixed for the interment
of a child; 6. A woman wanting a note to procure a place
at service for her son, and requiring my interposition with
Colonel B. for permission for a soldier to marry her daughter;
7.-8. A visit from two ladies, (mother and daughter,) the
former wanting arrangements made for placing her son with
some clergyman, to complete his education in preparation
for the Church; the latter bringing her certificate for her
pension, as an officer's widow, to be signed, and to have the
blanks filled up; 9. Another man about the funeral of a
child, requiring a note to Mr. Sewell, and an order to the
sexton; 10. A visit from a tailor, wanting the pattern of my
coat and cassock to make ditto for the Archdeacon of York;
11. A visit from Captain T. respecting business of emigrant
society; 12. Some alteration and adaptation of part of my
lecture for the day."

Wants like these were attended to at once, for he never
refused to see any one, to enter fully and patiently into
their business, and to do what was wanted, whenever possible,
at whatever cost of time and trouble to himself. Self, indeed,
never entered into his thoughts. The number of persons
who, in summer, when immigration was at its height, used

literally to besiege his house, was so great, that it was often very difficult to make one's way across the entrance from one room to another, or to get through the crowd who stood in the street waiting for room within, and it was sometimes necessary to use chloride of lime in the house after the crowd of visitors had dispersed. To the duties already mentioned he added, for several years, a week-day evening service, for which was afterward substituted one at eight o'clock on Sunday morning, chiefly for sailors, in a room at a cove about three miles from his house, and thus prepared the way for the erection of St. Paul's, or the Mariners' Chapel, which was consecrated, and had a district assigned to it, in 1833. In the same way, he had an evening service on a week day in a ship-yard on the river St. Charles, which formed the nucleus of the congregation of St. Peter's Chapel, which acquired a separate existence in 1834. He had also a monthly service on Sunday, in French, at the burying-ground, for the benefit of Jersey and Guernsey people. The Sunday evening services at that place were, however, his chief delight. He began in the end of 1822 with a large room in the sexton's house. This very soon became too small for the congregation, and the whole house was then thrown into one. In 1827-8 the windows were arched, a cupola was built, in which a bell* was placed, and the interior was fitted with open benches, and decently furnished, so that it had a sufficiently ecclesiastical appearance. His sermons here always consisted of plain and familiar expositions of Scripture, delivered without a book, and there was scarcely ever standing room in the chapel. About 1830, an addition was made, by a kind of transept, which added greatly to the accommodation. The service and singing were most hearty, and he so loved to preach the Gospel to the poor, that often on Sunday

---

* A peal of bells was procured for the cathedral in 1831, the only one, for many years, in Canada, or, I believe, with one exception, in America.

nights, when he came home nearly worn out in body, he would say his " soul had been refreshed." I shall never forget his sorrow when he saw the place he loved so well destroyed by fire, on the night of the memorable 28th June, 1845. His Sunday Schools were also his special care, and he took an active part in the " Sunday School Association" for promoting uniformity of system throughout the diocese, over the Quebec branch of which he presided with the most constant care. He had a large number of teachers, and a board hung on the door, with their names written on small blocks of wood, which they drew out, so as to make them project, as each entered the school, in order that, on his own entrance, he might see at a glance who were punctual in their arrival. He was extremely punctual himself, without which, indeed, he could never have accomplished what he did. He was always earnest in promoting habits of devotion among his flock, particularly in their families, and in urging the duty of attending to the spiritual interests of servants and dependants, of which he was eminently careful to set an example in his own house. The pains which he took, and the minuteness of his efforts, were truly wonderful. A sermon which he preached in February, 1822, in relation to these points, and partly as an appeal for the National Schools, was published, and contains evidence of his anxiety for the spiritual growth of his flock, and its promotion by the use of the ordinances of the Church, which he was firm in the conviction that Christ had appointed as the means to that end. One or two extracts from this sermon may be given to illustrate the principles on which his ministrations were based. " O, far be it from our views, and alien may it always be held to christian principles, to turn them loose upon the world, that they may choose, in matters of religion, for themselves! to send them into the thickening warfare of temptation, unprotected by the shield of faith, unfurnished with the helmet of salvation, and the sword of the Spirit, which is the Word of God. We make,

indeed, an exception, in this point, for those who are claimed
by their parents, as members of other regularly constituted
folds;* our local rules, in that respect, are public. We are
willing, we are glad, to give them education without meddling
with their tenets or religious discipline, but utterly do we
renounce the maxim which would forbid it to religion to have
her share in the public training of youth, or would divorce
her from the national establishments, from the education of
the different classes of the nation. The Madras system has
been called exclusive, but I know of no exclusion so injurious
as the exclusion of religion. And, unless we mean to subvert
the whole constitution of the country, both civil and ecclesiastical, in what shape shall it be introduced, (for it would be
a perfect Babel of confusion were we to open the door to all
at once,) in what shape but according to the received form
of the country itself ? Are we to be so afraid of training
children to be churchmen that we will not contribute to their
chance of being christians ? We are very wise, very enlightened ; we have undeniably made great strides in civilization, but there is a wisdom in which we have gone back from
our venerable forefathers, by full as many steps as those by
which we have outstripped them in another field.'' And in
a note appended, on the publication of the sermon, to the
words, " tracts inspected and approved before they pass, and
stamped, as it were, for sterling doctrine," he says:

" The Incorporated Society for the Propagation of the
Gospel has laid it down as a rule for the guidance of the
missionaries, that the tracts which they disperse shall be
taken from this catalogue. There are, probably, many per-

---

* One of the rules of the schools was as follows : " The children of Roman
Catholic parents, and of those who are members of the National Church of
Scotland, will be allowed to attend their respective places of worship on
Sundays, instead of going with the other children to the English cathedral,
and the former (and if the parents should desire it, the latter also,) will be
exempted from learning the catechism of the Church of England."

sons to whom such restrictive provisions may appear rather
in the light of an objection than of an advantage, but they
might be led, perhaps, to view the subject very differently,
if they saw it more in its details. Among the religious wares
which are circulated in these days with an unwearied zeal,
there are too many which are unsound, and the practised
hand can readily detect in what forge they have been fabricated, and what peculiar interests they have been calculated
to serve. And hardly is there a more imperative point of
duty in the work of promoting religion, than to guard against
the insinuation of adulterated materials. I had intended to
exhibit some specimens of this nature, and to have left it to
the judgment of the reader, to pronounce whether a clergyman, at least, may not be pardoned for some jealous anxiety
with respect to the quality of the food which is to be given to
his flock. But I should have swelled this note too far, and
upon this occasion I forbear. Volumes, indeed, might be written to point out the hurtful effects which arise from the manner in which particular doctrines (relating chiefly to conversion, regeneration, and what is called assurance,) are warped,
upon the danger of mixing in with things spiritual and unseen,
the gross alloy of physical causes, and the meretricious excitement of the imagination; upon the temerity, pregnant with
mischiefs to the cause of religion, which seats itself in the
chair of inspiration, and challenges to enjoy those favours
which were peculiar to the times of visible interposition and
direct revelation from on high. Volumes might be written
upon the shades and gradations of these mistakes in religion,
upon the effects of adopting a certain turn of phraseology,
and wearing the marks, as it were, of affinity to this school of
doctrine, upon the system of precisely identifying the success
of this school with the extension of the gospel. But let it be
well remembered, on the other hand, that there is a far more
usual and less excusable manner of promoting error or ex-

travagance in religion. It is by turning our own backs upon it, by coldness and indifference to the characteristic doctrines of the Gospel. The comforts of the Gospel *will* be sought, and if food be withheld in one quarter, it will be asked for in another. I am aware that such observations as the foregoing often bring upon the clergy the charge of broken charity. And I take the risk. I do more. I boldly plead not guilty. We are the special guardians of sound doctrine ; we are pledged in the most solemn manner to execute our trust in this point. Charity in religious matters is not indiscriminate approbation. Charity has no field where this exists, no subject of trial. It is the delicate part of true charity, while she earnestly contends for a sound faith, to go fearlessly on to her mark, and to keep clear, at the same time, from all animosity of feeling, from all harshness of thought or expression, from all spirit of misconstruction or ill-will. And, at least, it is no worse charity in us to uphold vigorously what we conceive to be a right system, than in others sedulously to undermine it."

For several years, beginning in 1823, he also took his turn, once a fortnight, at a weekly service which he established at a sort of a poorhouse, called the Quebec Asylum, or more familiarly the Red House, by which name it has been mentioned before, nearly two miles from his residence. At all these new openings, he seems to have begun by going back, in his teaching, to "the first principles of the doctrine of Christ," so as to insure a good foundation for future labours.

CHAPTER VII.

Second visit to Gaspé—Journey to York—Visitation of Eastern townships, and district of Quebec.

In the autumn of 1826, the Archdeacon made a second visitation of the district of Gaspé, in the whole of which, owing to some unfortunate occurrences, there was not at that time one resident clergyman. He obtained a passage in a small vessel belonging to the provincial Government, which was going to Halifax, and called for him, on her return from that place, to take him to Quebec. He visited all the places where congregations had been formed, and went as far as Nouvelle in the Bay of Chaleurs, administering the Sacraments and other ordinances, and enquiring into all that concerned the welfare of the Church. Speaking of the congregation at St. Georges Cove, to whom he again preached in French, he says: "The little chapel was very full, and the people were all glad to have the services of the Church performed among them again. The great body of them could be easily kept fast in their attachment to her, if she could afford them some regular care and attention. It is a defect in our system that we have no workmen of a humbler class whose services might be disposable for purposes like these, and that people living scattered in new and small settlements must go without religious ordinances, if they adhere to the Church. We ought to have deacons, as a *distinct order*, and persons ought to be admitted to it for particular objects, whose pretensions are not such as to allow of their looking higher. At any rate we might have catechists acting as lay-readers; and, if such a system had been organized and carried into effect in time, it might have gained us some members, and preserved to us a great many more. While we leave the people unprovided, how can we blame them for using the only means within their reach, and how can we expect that they can transmit to their children any attachment to a system, or veneration for a Church, in the ordinances of which they have few or no opportunities of partaking?'' Another little extract will shew the effect upon his mind of his admiration of striking scenery: " It is a romantic little spot, and put me in mind of some of the scenes of Salvator Rosa. Its general character is not unlike that in which he lays the preaching of the Baptist in the wilderness. It was ' to a desert place apart ' also that Christ retired to pray, and such solitudes assuredly fit the frame of the mind to devotion. *For the time, you do not belong to the world.*" * At one place on the coast, he

---

* In one of the letters of his brother, Colonel Mountain, a very similar expression occurs: "I quite agree with you as to the effect of scenery upon the mind. I always feel, when alone (or genially accompanied) with nature, whether in her grander or gentler moods, nearer to nature's God, soothed and raised in feeling and resolve. Strange and humiliating, that the being who stood, almost as an angel, upon yon hill, should become again a monster on transition to the tracasseries of life and the trammels of office. But so it is with human nature, save with the happy few who have overcome their nature." There was a wonderful similarity of taste and sympathy between these two brothers, and I am tempted to give an extract from another letter in a similar strain, dated Simla, May, 1849. " My dearest brother, This is a most lovely morning, and all nature rejoices, and I would fain give you greeting! Many a day must elapse before these lines meet your eye, but when they do, if ever they do, it may be, perchance, on as sweet a morn. Oh! it is a great privilege to retain freshness of mind, power of enjoyment, appreciation of the works of God. Nothing so lames the elasticity of spirit necessary for this accessibility to pleasurable feeling, as the being *usé* in the world, as the consciousness of sin; but weighty cares and anxieties in continued wearing course and weak health, are also lamers of the spirit, and you and our dear C. are as much perhaps, losers of many sources of pleasure around from

mentions a person who "officiated very respectably as clerk, but in the churching of *women*, being determined to avoid the singular, said, ' and let our *cries*,' etc."

Part of the voyage round the coast was performed, as before, in an open boat, but at Percé he was persuaded to take passage in a small decked vessel, where he suffered the greatest discomfort from " dirt, closeness, evil odours, sea-sickness, tedium, and utter loneliness as to all sympathies of taste and feeling," amid which he says, " my thoughts turned to my own dear and happy home, and all the blessings,—one there was very prominent in the picture,—which God has given me there. But you must not suppose that I allowed the contrast to produce any present impatience or dejection in my mind ; for though I know full well that there are many occasions when I do not behave as I ought to do, yet, when the discomforts and inconveniences of travelling begin to be serious, I make it a practice to think of the real and severe sufferings to which others are exposed, and it is a rule which can hardly fail to reconcile the mind to these lesser evils." One more extract will shew, like this, that he was not un-

---

the latter causes, as I from the first. But, thanks be to God and to my earthly father who took pains to cultivate in me a love of nature, I do yet feel, despite the writhing effect of my own sins and follies, the susceptibility of delight in the beauties of the creation, and particularly in the genial influences of morning and evening." In a letter dated in 1824, the younger brother thus expresses himself: " There are many points of resemblance between us ; the same things give us pain and pleasure ; the same tincture of romance, the same chivalrous feeling, the same respect for the olden time, the same enthusiastic love and early perception of the beautiful, the gentle, and the peculiar in nature, in art, or in human character, the same love of justice and indignation of injustice, live in both our breasts ; in yours, enriched by originality of humour, supported by talent, softened by patient temper, regulated by habitual piety, and always subservient to the great end of your existence, the good of others, and the care of your own soul. • • • I have often been moved, even to tears, by accidental circumstances, such as a fine sunset or sunrise, the sudden view of sublime scenery, or the magnificence of a storm."

mindful of his own failings. "**I laid** my hands upon a book, the only one in a room where I was waiting, and just turning the leaves **over to see** the **order** and distribution of the contents, I stumbled upon a passage at once, treating directly of a fault of which I had that very day pronounced myself **not guiltless; and** reading on, I found what was calculated **to benefit me, and I hope may have done so."**

Early in 1829, the Archdeacon was sent by the Bishop to settle a dispute respecting **the site of a** church at a settlement some distance above Bytown, and took occasion to visit **the other** settlements on the Ottawa River,—Hull, St. **Andrews, and Lachute,**—preaching everywhere, according to **his usual practice, as** well as inspecting schools and the affairs **of the Church generally. The only** clergyman resident on **the east side of the Ottawa was at St.** Andrews, Hull being **served from Bytown.** A similar dispute caused a journey **to Rawdon on his way home, to** which place he was driven **by the rector** of Montreal, from whom he derived much help **in** the object of his **visit.** Sorel and Three Rivers were also **visited.** He had gone to Bytown by way of Cornwall and **Hawkesbury, and the** journey **between these** two places was performed **on horseback.** He passed through Glengarry, **where he called on** the Roman Catholic Bishop McDonell, **who received him " in** his frank and friendly way, assisting himself **to unstrap my** valise, and giving directions, in Gaelic, **to his people, about a** little repair required **in one** of **the straps. He made me stay to** dine with him. The Bishop **said a short grace in English like our own, and after** dinner **proposed the health of our Bishop." ***

---

* When the first Bishop of Quebec arrived there in 1793, the Roman Catholic Bishop appeared unfeignedly rejoiced, and greeting him with a kiss on each cheek, declared that it was high time that he should come to keep his people in order. The following letter addressed soon afterwards to his lordship will exhibit a proof of the same spirit of friendliness:

"Monseigneur, j'ose me flatter, d'après les témoignages sensibles de vôtre estime dont nôtre communauté fut honoré lorsque vôtre seigneurie

A winter journey to the capital of Upper Canada, in January, 1829, is the next of which I have any account. It was difficult and fatiguing after entering Upper Canada, where recourse was had to wheels. The object of this journey was to confer, by the Bishop's desire, with the Lieutenant Governor of Upper Canada, whose guest he became, and the Archdeacon of York, on measures to be taken respecting the Clergy Reserves. On the way down, he had for a fellow-passenger " the Scotch minister of Kingston, whose movements were caused by the same competition on the part of the kirk which produced my own journey. We did not touch upon this topic, however, and got on very harmoniously together, our conversation being, in a great measure, religious, and our views, as far as they were mutually developed, very much the same. * * * When I was at ———, on my return to the inn from drinking tea with Mr. ———, I engaged the landlady, who is of our own Church, in conversation respecting her attention to her religious duties, and the religious care of the family and household. Speaking of Mr. ———, she said he was ' a fine man and a good man,' but she might go to hear him seven years without having the same insight into the truths of the Gospel, and the importance of attending to them, as in this short familiar conversation with me. Do not think that I mention this with any feeling of vanity, or that it inspired any feeling of the sort. I

---

nous fît la faveur d'entrer dans notre monastère, qu'elle voudra bien agréer l'honorable et gracieuse liberté que nous donne le renouvellement d'année pour nous procurer l'indicible satisfaction de lui présenter nos très humbles hommages et assurances des vœux que nous adresserons au ciel pour sa précieuse conservation et prospérité de son illustre famille. C'est avec ces vifs sentimens que nous avons l'honneur d'être, avec le plus profond respect, monseigneur, de votre seigneurie les très humbles et très obéissantes servantes, Sr. Thérèse de Jésus, Sup. aux Ursulines des Trois Rivières, le 30 Décembre 1794."

A very similar letter was addressed to his lordship, about two years later, by the successor of this lady.

assure you it only made me humble, and partly sad, to think how great a responsibility attaches to us, if so much may be done by opportunities so often neglected by us all, and partly thankful that I had turned the half hour to so good account. It also led me to reflect how very, very faulty many of our clergy are, in firing over the heads of our audiences. Do not shew this to any body. * * * I have often reflected since I left you upon your labour and persevering assiduity in making that transcription (of a series of lectures for Saints' Days) and upon many other testimonies of your goodness and your love. All the little difficulties which this winter journey has presented remind me of those far more serious ones which you encountered to visit me in my illness at Hatley. Let us always most dearly cherish a tender mutual affection, and unreserved mutual confidence; and do not think that I love my family the less because the duties to which I am called draw me away from their society much more than accords with my own desires. Domestic affections are the first earthly comfort that I have, and they are, indeed, so sanctified when cultivated under the guidance of religion, that they are not merely worldly; but no interfering claim of domestic tie or duty ought, according to the conviction of my conscience, to lessen the amount of service which I actually perform as a minister of Christ. 'He that loveth father or mother more than Me is not worthy of Me,' and in competition with that service, we must hate, in figurative language, all our nearest and dearest connections, and our own lives also, or we cannot be His disciples. But the domestic love of one who feels this conviction is more worth having than if he did not feel it. We will talk these things over when we meet."

Early in 1829, another visitation of the Eastern townships was undertaken. Passing through Three Rivers, the Archdeacon instituted the new rector of that place, the Rev. S. S. Wood, who accompanied him to Shipton. At Drummondville the same ceremony was performed for **Mr.** Wood's successor, the **Rev.** G. M. Ross. The number of resident clergy in the St. **Francis district had been increased, since** the Archdeacon's last visit, from three to four, by the appointment of the Rev. A. **H. Burwell** to Lennoxville. The provision for the maintenance **of schools** under the auspices of the Royal Institution seems **to have** been much larger than has since been the case, **though the** expenditure was not perhaps in every case **justified by the results. A great** deal of business arose out of their **inspection.** The Archdeacon visited all the stations of **the clergy, and preached in** all their churches (there were five in the district), and in several school-houses. But his chief care **seems to have** been bestowed **on destitute settlements.** In this way **he had spent a Sunday at Nicolet,** and officiated in Shipton, Melbourne, and Durham **(his labours in these three townships** being shared **by Mr. Wood). Writing of a visit to one of** these, **he says:** " It was a very humble cottage,* but there were plenty of hot cakes, and **a most cordial** welcome, which, with the opportunity of a kind of pastoral conversation with people who rarely see **a** clergyman, and gladly avail themselves of it, made me feel as happy as a king. I have indeed often felt that **if I** had not other duties marked out for me, **I** would gladly devote myself **to such** scattered sheep as these about the country ; **and I am well** persuaded that a clergyman who would give **himself to** the **work,** and engage, **at** once with kindness **and zeal, in** guiding and gathering them

---

* At a house where **they slept, having reached** it at two A.M., " **though** all else was comfortable enough, **we detected the signs** of preoccupancy in the sheets, which deterred us from going between them, and inspired W. with the following **parody, with which he greeted** me in the morning :

> No dirty sheet encircled my breast,
> With no quilt or blanket I wound me,
> But I lay like a clergyman taking my rest,
> **With my camlet cloak around me,"**

together, would decidedly fix them by degrees in regular
habits of religion and compliance with all the ordinances of
the Church. We settled what psalms should be sung, and
proceeded to the school-house, which was excessively full. *
* * On the way back I stopped to call on a family which
I had not had time to visit in going, and in which I had baptized the mother and several children at once, in 1823.
These persons, or the survivors of them,—for the mother was
dead,—I wished to remind of their baptismal covenant, and I
found other work besides in the house, for the step-mother
was seemingly in a hopeless consumption, and willingly received my ministrations, added to which there was a young
infant to be baptized." At Eaton, mention is made of a
Scotch widow* "whose zeal and perseverance in attending
the services of the Church are so great, that at certain seasons,
she makes light of wading a ford on foot above her knees,
having previously walked in an overflowed path for about a
mile, and this she does without ' undressing ' her legs or feet,
which the stony bottom would render very painful in its consequences. She told Mr. Taylor that she was once in her life
subject to rheumatism, and that she did not know what had
cured her, unless these aquatic walks had done it." At
Lennoxville the Archdeacon assembled the clergy of the district together for mutual conference, after divine service, and
he recommended it to them, " to appoint quarterly meetings
with each other, read over together their ordination vows,
confer on all points of pastoral interest or difficulty, and hold
a public service on a week day." The last services performed in the St. Francis district were at Hatley, where the

---

* I remember, many years after this, seeing an Irish widow at Lake Beauport who had brought two of her children, when a snow storm had blocked
up most of the roads, a long distance, which in winter could never be traversed but on foot. On my remarking that she must have left home early
in order to reach the church when she did (soon after ten o'clock) she said
' Well, we set off about six ' "

Archdeacon instituted Mr. Johnson to the rectory, and " was called upon, without previous notice, to preach two sermons at the dedication, as they term it, of the new church. They know little or nothing of our form of consecration by the Bishop, and the opening service with sermon is considered by them as the dedication." At this point he passed into the Montreal district, preaching in school-houses at Waterloo Village and Granby, and in a church at West Shefford. At Yamaska Mountain, (to which, at his suggestion, the name of Abbottsford was afterwards given, the Rev. J. Abbott being at that time the missionary of the place,) there was a church, of which it is remarked, "Many of our churches in this diocese are not placed according to rule, their steeples being at the east end, and the communion-tables at the west; but in this instance, it seems to have been resolved to be right in one of the two points, for both are placed together, the recess for the altar being in the lower part of the tower, which is at the farther end from the entrance." At Granby, having occasion to ask for a pen, in transacting some business respecting the Clergy Reserves, one was brought to him made out of an eagle's plume, which suggested the following lines :

> " How fleet is a glance of the mind !
> Compared with the speed of its flight,
>   The tempest itself lags behind,
> And the swift-winged arrows of light."—COWPER.

>   Trace my thoughts, thou eagle plume,
>   Far to those I love they fly ;
>   Ne'er shalt thou thy flights resume,
>   Traveller of the boundless sky.

>   Fleeter than thy flights of yore,
>   Speed our thoughts and farther range,
>   Traverse time remote, explore
>   Space, and ah! remember change.

Years, O years, for ever fled!
   Thought can all your track pursue;
Sleepers with the peaceful dead,
   Thought full well can picture you!

Homeward still the wanderer's care
   Flies athwart this waste of snow;
When, he knows not, knows not where
   Fate may deal some withering blow.

Wanderer, cast thy care on One
   Who to care for thee descends;
Think what He for man has done,
   Trust to Him thy home and friends.

Lift, O Lord, our thoughts on high,
   Teach our truant hearts to soar;
Thought can pierce beyond the sky,
   Pierce where change shall be no more.

Lord of lords, and King of kings,
   Bear us all our journey's length;
Bid us ride "on eagles' wings,"
   Sheath us in eternal strength.

At Abbottsford he preached on prayer, "and there was a woman in the congregation whom Mr. S. observed to have been repeatedly in tears, and on his enquiring who she was, we found she had been a careless person in religion. If those tears were like the tears which washed the feet of the Saviour, this was a day which I ought thankfully to note. How many days might ungrudgingly and gladly be given to be rendered instrumental in an event which causes 'joy in the presence of the angels of God!'"

From Abbottsford the Archdeacon proceeded to Dunham, where he preached, and afterwards addressed the people on the duty of contributing to the support of divine worship. Here again the rector was instituted, a measure for the legal erection of parishes according to the establishment of the Church of England, on an extended scale, having been recently adopted by the Government. The same ceremony was performed, farther on in the journey, at Clarenceville and Sorel. The rectory of St. Armand had been established at an earlier date. To this place the Archdeacon was driven by the Rev. James Reid (who had come over to Dunham to meet him) the successor of Bishop Stewart at Frelighsburgh, of which he still holds the charge.* Between him and the Archdeacon there always existed a strong mutual respect and regard. They "spent the evening with a family who really are patterns of what such families should be. All that they possess is the fruit of the father's own industry blessed from above, for he made his war originally upon the forest, with no resources but the weapon with which he waged it. All within the house was plain, substantial, plentiful, orderly and neat. The father of the family is a placid, benevolent, and humble-looking man, with his grizzled hair smoothed down upon his forehead, and falling behind in cleanly locks upon his collar. All the eleven children, several of whom are grown up, are exemplary young people. The girls are among Mr. Reid's church singers, and their father is one of his church-wardens. The farm is large, fruitful, and well-stocked, with appendages of orchards, etc. The whole family are steadfast church-people, and such as we should wish church-people to be; they are devout, but in a sober, settled, and enduring way, and the blessing of God seems, as it were, to rest visibly upon the house. Mr. Whitwell came up to meet me from Philipsburgh. Mr. Reid's infant was baptized, and I was one of the sponsors. We must bear our god-children in mind, for although we have not perhaps undertaken the office in any case where we are called upon to interfere, we ought not to lose sight of our obligations. There is one way in which we can always remember those with whom we have contracted

---

* Since these words were written, this venerable man has rested from his labours.

this voluntary relationship. I preached, and after church visited the school and some of the families in the village with Mr. Reid, who drove me to the house of his other church-warden, where I was to sleep on the road to Philipsburgh. He is a very substantial person, lately married to an American, a warm-hearted woman, who is an episcopalian. The Bishop is an especial favourite of hers, and nothing seems so much to delight her as to get a clergyman under her roof. The comfort and feeling of confidence which is engendered by church-fellowship and community of religious sentiment may furnish an idea of the happiness of Christian society at large, if it were more like one fold under one Shepherd, for which I firmly believe that episcopacy must be the common bond of external union, and that the correction of prevailing lax notions respecting irregular assumptions of the ministry must be an indispensable pre-requisite. God remove such faults among ourselves as help to obstruct a consummation so devoutly to be wished! I was pleased to see in this house the retention of old customs brought from the home of our fathers. The wall of the room was decorated with the word 'Christmas' in large letters, and some ornamental flourishes wrought with some evergreen plant or creeper. It had been put up at that season, and suffered to remain."

After the usual duties at Philipsburgh, the Archdeacon was driven by an American clergyman, who had come across the lines purposely to meet him, to Clarenceville, where this gentleman took part in the service, " having no sort of scruple about praying for King George." At the two churches in Mr. Townsend's mission, at St. John's, Chambly, (where some divinity students were under the charge of Mr. Braithwaite) and Sorel, similar duties were performed, and the Archdeacon had now visited all the parishes and missions south of the St. Lawrence. The number of clergy was fourteen in all, and these, with one on the Ottawa, and three on the north shore of the St. Lawrence, made up the whole number in Lower

Canada, with the exception of those resident at Quebec and Montreal. The last letter written on this journey is dated 25th of February: "I preached at Sorel yesterday, and instituted and inducted Mr. Jackson, at whose house I was quartered. It was, you remember, St. Matthias's Day. There was a very good congregation, and the singing, accompanied by instrumental music, was, for a country church, excellent. Part of the service was chanted, and an anthem was performed. This afternoon I preached in the diminutive stone church at Rivière du Loup, to a congregation of forty-two persons. Small as this church is, and without steeple or tower, I like it better than the township wooden churches. I cannot avoid attaching the idea of something trumpery, and as it were a make-shift, to a wooden building, however neatly finished. This little church has very thick stone walls, and looks as if it belonged to institutions on a permanent foundation. I am obliged to confess, however, that these walls were cracked, and the churchwardens, with the concurrence of the minister, made application to me for aid towards repairing them." This aid the Bishop afterwards granted, on the condition of local exertion being made for the object.

The account of this journey was embodied in a report to the Bishop, which was published* by the S. P. G., from the concluding portion of which I make the following extract :—

"That the Church, speaking generally, is in a positively prosperous and flourishing condition in the tract of country comprised in this visitation, is a belief of which severe and impartial truth will not permit us to lay the flattering unction to our souls :

"That her condition here, as in other parts of the diocese, would have been more flourishing and more firm, if she had not been unfairly attacked in the province and unfairly represented at home; if encouragement had not been afforded by circumstances to continue this system of aggression; if her rights as an establishment had not been suffered to be so long and

* See Annual Report for 1830, Appendix, pp. 110 and seq., where will also be found some regulations for catechists in the diocese of Quebec, drawn up by Archdeacon Mountain.

loudly questioned, and the various mischiefs arising from the unsettled state of the Reserves question, so unhappily, though no doubt unavoidably, protracted, is what we may pronounce, I think, as confidently as we can pronounce upon any thing which *would have* been, *but is not:*

" That the situation of her clergy is extremely difficult and trying, and such as calls for the most devoted zeal and watchful circumspection for themselves, but at the same time for much indulgence and allowance towards them on the part of others; and that sensible good is effecting by their means, both as it regards the salvation of souls, and the planting of that Church whose system and all its provisions are to be directly regarded as instruments for that grand object, and whose success is only to be desired in conjunction with it,—is what must, in common candour, be acknowledged."

In the course of this tour, the Archdeacon met with exceedingly heavy storms and drifts, which, on one occasion, suggested the following lines :—

THOUGHTS OF A TRAVELLER IN A VERY VIOLENT SNOW-DRIFT IN LOWER CANADA.

Blow, winds, and crack your cheeks, rage, blow,
　*　　　*　　　*　　　*
I tax not you, ye elements, with unkindness.—K. Lear.

Rage on, thou whistling tempest !
Sweep high the snow in air ;
Ye blinding gusts, relent not,
I can your fury dare.
O we might heed but little
The storms which blow above,
If man upon his fellow
Would breathe the breath of love !

I pass the homes of peasants,
Thick scattered through the land :
I mark each spire, a banner
For God which seems to stand :
I hear the bell which calls them
To bend the duteous knee ;
I see them troop responding,—
Alas ! it calls not me.

O who can speak the sadness
That chills the Christian heart,
To think that in Religion
We have not common part !

That as you hold us outlawed
From holy Church and hope,
We mourn your deep enchantment
Beneath a sorcerer Pope. (*a*)

'Tis not alone the children
Of old usurping Rome ;
They who her yoke have broken,
Are dissidents at home :
To thee, loved England's Zion,
On different sides alike
There stand whose will is evil,
Whose arm upraised to strike.

Each spokesman of the people
Insidious wrongs thee still ;
Each newsman's weekly trumpet
Remorseless blows thee ill :
Their teeth are spears and arrows,
Their tongue a sharpened sword : (*b*)
With mischief to thy children
Their ready lips are stored. (*c*)

O for the dove's free pinion,
That I might flee, and find
The rest (*d*) which you refuse me,
My brethren of mankind !
Ah me! the post of duty
Is not for soft repose :
Our term of toil and conflict
The grave alone can close.

O sure and peaceful shelter,
Which none but God can break,
When all who lie expectant
The general trump shall wake :
Then in their promised country
Thine Israel shall be blest,
O Captain of Salvation,— (*e*)
It is *the land of rest.*

---

a. Rev. xviii, 23 ; *b.* Ps. lvii., 4 ; *c.* Ps. cxl. 3, 9 and Prov. xxiv, 2 ; *d.* Ps.
lv, 6 ; *e.* Heb. ii, 10.

My God, before Thy greatness
No child of man may boast—
Yet look on us thy servants,
And go before our host : (a)
Beset by many a danger,
And soiled by many a sin,
O from without defend us,
And purify within !

We have not wronged this people—
We have not proudly dealt ;—
Thy Word we freely tender,
If this a wrong be felt : (b)
We draw, to do them service,
Our wages from afar,
And rob, for this, the Churches (c)
Beneath a different star. (d)

We count among our shepherds
True hearts the fold to tend ;
None to be spent more willing, (e)
None readier seen to spend :
Far through the gloom of forests
Their welcome steps are traced ;
Their hands the rose of Sharon
Plant in the howling waste. (f)

Turn, turn, good Lord, Thy children, (g)
That they may all be one,
E'en as, O Holy Father,
Thou and Thy Blessed Son :— (h)
When shall we see the leopard
Lie gently by the kid,
And with the bear to pasture,
The fearless kine be bid ? (i)

Full many a stone of stumbling
Must from our path be hurled ;
Full many a fault be weeded
From this misjudging world ;

---

a. Exod. xiii, 21., xiv., 19 ; b. 2 Cor. xii, 13 ; c. 2 Cor. xi, 7, 8 ; d.—alio sub sole jacentes ; e. 2 Cor. xii, 15 ; f. Caut. ii, 1 ; Is. xxxv, 1 ; Deut xxxii 10 ; g. Lam. v, 21 ; h. S. John xvii, 11 ; i. Is. xi, 67 ;

Full many a speck be purged
From things we love and prize ;
Full many a schism repented
Ere that blest Sun shall rise.

Far hence the hollow seeming
Of unity and love,
Which leaves to choice of fancy,
Truths given from God above ;
Far hence their pliant baseness,
Whom from their standard sways
Poor meed of fashion's favour,
Or breath of mortal praise.

The gems of truth to barter,
We purchase peace too dear ;
Pure faith and ancient order
Must still be guarded here ;
All, all, we love, we pray for,
All holy zeal commend : (a)
But for the rule delivered
Of old, we must contend. (b)

O come, O come, blest Kingdom,
O Saviour, bid it speed :—
One Spirit, one rite baptismal,
One hope be ours, one creed ! (c)
'Tis then the Cross, blest ensign,
One way we all shall wave ;
Nor more with dissonant trumpets,
Proclaim its power to save.

In seemly strength and order
Shall march our conquering band ;
And Christ shall win the Paynim,
With followers hand in hand :
Till God shed wide His glory,
Earth's utmost verge to sweep,
E'en as the rolling waters
O'erspread the boundless deep. (d)

---

a. Gal. iv, 18 ; b. Jude 3, 9 ; c. Eph. iv. 4, 5 ; d. Hab. ii, 14.

I

The Archdeacon returned to Quebec just in time to witness the opening of a new parochial institution, an asylum for female orphans belonging to the Church. This was undertaken by the zeal of several ladies, in whose labours Mrs. Mountain took the prominent part. Some rooms were fitted up over the National School, which had been removed from Hope gate to its present site near St. John's gate. He always took a special interest in these orphans, and the fifth of March was an anniversary which he never forgot, and which was observed, while he lived, by assembling the ladies and children, as well as the friends of the institution, to whom it was his practice to deliver an address whenever he was in Quebec. In 1842, when he was prevented from doing so by illness, he addressed a letter to the clergyman who was to take his place, in order to convey to the ladies the assurance of his regret that he was unable to be with them upon an occasion connected with many interesting and many sacred associations, adding, " I cannot unite, in bodily presence, in the prayers which it will devolve upon you to offer, but although absent in body, I shall be present in spirit. * * * I cannot conclude without requesting you to say one word from me to the children themselves. Although my occupations do not permit me to visit them often, and my illness has prevented me from seeing them for more than four months, let them know that the Bishop of the Church cares for them, and prays from his heart that they may please their Heavenly Father, Who cares for them too, and may be enabled by His grace, given for the sake of Christ, to make a good and dutiful return to the ladies who have been so kind to them. To Him I now commend both them and their benefactors." This institution was removed, in 1862, to a wing of the Church Home, which was formally opened on the 2nd August in that year, after the service held in the cathedral to mark the completion of the 50th year of the Bishop's ministry. That day was also the anniversary of his union with her to whom the asylum was chiefly indebted for its existence, but who was not permitted to see it upon earth.

In June, 1829, the Archdeacon accompanied the Bishop to York, for the purpose of assisting his lordship in the examination of the candidates who were to be admitted to Holy Orders at that place.* On this occasion they first became acquainted with Sir J. Colborne, the Lieutenant Governor of the province, whose guests they were, and who, like his predecessor, was sincerely attached to the Church, and anxious to do his utmost for the cause of religion. I make extracts from two letters written from York: " An Indian chief, called Yellow-head, with four or five of his train, was introduced to the Bishop by Sir J. C., and we had a good deal of conversation with them through the interpreter. They were very dark, and partook a good deal of the olive in their complexion. They have recently become Christians, and the adoption of Christianity is spreading most rapidly and with most blessed effects, producing a marked and total change of character and habits among the Indians in this province. The principal instruments of this blessing have been persons in connection with the Methodists; but whoever they are, and whatever mixture of error may be found in their opinions, we must rejoice and thank God for what has been effected, and is now proceeding. Our own mission among the Mohawks is prospering, and we have now sent another labourer there, who has been among them some time learning their language, and who brought testimonials to the Bishop in Mohawk as well as English, (the Rev. A. Nelles, ordained Deacon on this occasion.) * * * * We had some conversation with a person of the name of Jones, who, with his brother, was the chief

---

* In a letter to the S. P. G., the Bishop mentions having invited the Archdeacon to accompany him on this occasion, not only as his examining chaplain, but that he " generally might have the benefit of his counsel and assistance, well knowing how valuable they would be whenever he needed aid or advice which might be useful to himself or the Church."

engine, in the first instance, of the conversion of the Missis-
sagas, settled, or as it is called, villaged, by Sir P. Maitland
on the river Credit. He told me that the number who had
embraced Christianity since the late impulse was given was
from twelve to fourteen hundred, including the children of
believers. We had also a visit from Mr. M., a Hungarian,
and once a Romish priest, who applied to the Bishop some
time ago, and has undergone a kind of probation, the result
of which is that the Bishop has felt satisfied in deciding to
ask the Society for £50 a year for him, in addition to what
the people on the spot will do. He is to continue officiating,
with a German translation of our Prayer book, to a large body
of settlers from Alsace, who are established at the lower end
of Lake Erie. * * * On Sunday I woke with a bad headache,
having sat up rather late in preparing notes to preach for the
ordination (for I have had no possible time to write a sermon);
and preach I did, thank God, though not without some little
degree of inconvenience, yet without any which was apparent
to others, but I found myself obliged to leave the church
immediately after the sermon. * * The Bishop, with his usual
kindness, provided a doctor, who unexpectedly marched into
my room, and prescribed just what I should have done myself
without him; but I gained the advantage of having my malady
and symptoms, as well as the mode of cure, embellished with
sundry learned names." The other extract is from a letter
addressed to one of his children on her birthday, June 18,
1829: "There are many celebrations, my sweet ——, of
this day; and I am not insensible to the glories of the public
anniversary: for the battle of Waterloo turned the fate of
the world, and the British arms were the instrument of Providence to strike a decisive and final stroke which changed
the whole aspect of European affairs. But the day has a
domestic interest which touches me more nearly, and my
thoughts are not occupied with scenes of carnage, or the
political effects which follow them: they fix themselves rather

upon my dear child, who is now both of an age and disposition to have some serious thoughts of her duties to God and her fellow-creatures. You may well believe that I do not forget my child in my prayers ; never do I forget any of you : but I now specially pray for you that you may be happy here and for ever ; that you may still advance in serving God as He grants you year after year; that His blessing and grace may be with you through your time on earth, and that you may enjoy, through your Saviour, an eternity of blessedness in Heaven. * * * On Monday the 16th there was a confirmation at York. Fifty-one persons were confirmed ; the sermon was assigned to me, and the Bishop addressed an exhortation to the young people. The next day there was a confirmation at a church on the road called Yonge Street, seven miles from York, and the church was consecrated at the same time. Lady Colborne, her sister, and the children, went with us; and we filled two carriages ; the private tutor and one of the sons going on horseback. The horsemen, being a little before us, went to the house of a farmer, who is a most zealous churchman and a great promoter of schools and other good works, but a strange kind of man, where, the conversation turning upon religious subjects, Mr. —— (the private tutor) asked him if he had heard the Archdeacon's sermon on Sunday, (meaning mine.) ' Why,' said the farmer, 'I thought you were the Archdeacon.' Mr.—— explained to him that he had no pretensions to be so regarded.* ' Well, then,' said he, ' you are some piece of the Bishop's furniture.' We robed ourselves in a shed which stood in the church-yard, there being no vestry-room, and proceeded to the solemnity of consecration, a service in which I had never taken a part before. It is extremely impressive, and we had Archdeacon Strachan and two other clergymen with us, in their surplices. The sermon was again allotted to me, after which

---

* The gentleman referred to is now a Bishop.

twenty-six persons were confirmed. * * * Upon the whole, this is a residence in which I should delight to live and let my children run loose, and in the neighbourhood of which we might enjoy many agreeable walks and promenades ' en voiture ou à cheval.' But the calls of duty fix my residence in a town, and with all the manifold blessings and advantages of a country life, it must be admitted that many more opportunities of personally doing good present themselves at Quebec than at Stamford Cottage, not only to me, but to all of us. And at any rate, we have abundant cause to be thankful for the portion which we enjoy. We must cultivate our rural predilections by driving out when we can, and once in a while, on special occasions, making holiday in the country."

On their way back to Quebec, (where another ordination was held on St. Peter's day) the Bishop and Archdeacon took part in the " ceremony of taking possession of McGill College," when the Archdeacon, in his capacity of Principal, delivered an address, and conducted the devotions. "It was an interesting occasion, and it is a nice place: I should have no objection to live there, and fulfil my present nominal charge. * * * Altogether we are pressed to pieces with people and business." A confirmation was held at Montreal, when the Archdeacon again preached.

It has been already mentioned that the Bishop had been anxious all along for a division of the diocese. Having so far failed in the accomplishment of this desire, and feeling strongly the great need of a resident Bishop in Upper Canada, his lordship, after this visit to York, determined to procure a house there, and divide his time between that place and Quebec. In the summer of 1829, the Reverend Dr. Mills, being about to visit England, was intrusted with a commission to obtain the consent of the Imperial Government to the erection of a separate see ; and two years later the Bishop himself went home chiefly for the same purpose.* The difficulty of procuring the necessary funds seems to have been an insurmountable obstacle.

Early in 1830, the Archdeacon made a circuit of the townships in the district of Quebec, south of the St. Lawrence, where there was not one resident clergyman. They had, however, received stated visits from a missionary of the S. P. G., whose time was chiefly so employed, but in these they shared with the settlements on the north shore, so that the supply of the ministrations of the Church was but scanty. This being the first mention of these townships, I shall give some extracts from a continuous account of the visit.

The Archdeacon left Quebec in his own vehicle on the 6th March for West Frampton : baited on the road at St. Henry : then " I betook myself very thankfully to my canister, and doled out a cracker or two to the children of the house, as well as some biscuit for myself, after which I begged for a little milk, and this a pleasant-looking good-natured lass, as there was none in the house, procured at once from the fountain-head ;—' je m'en vais tirer la vache.' We baited again at the toll-bridge on the River Etchemin at the house of Woodhouse, respecting whose family Mr. Archbold is interested. I made the little girl whom he particularly mentioned say her prayers, the belief, &c., to me in English, but it was in miserably broken English. She seems to be almost losing her own language. The people would take no payment. They promised to come up to service the next day at West Frampton, and I was much disappointed at not seeing them." On Sunday, the 7th, he held service and preached at the house of Mr. Ross at West Frampton, where sixty-five persons were assembled, and " after service addressed the people in a more familiar way respecting family prayer, service on Sundays, teaching their children the catechism, preparing for the com-

---

* It was on the occasion of his lordship's return from this visit, that the bells of the cathedral of Quebec rang out their first peal.

munion, &c. There was a second service at which about fifty persons were present, with sermon and catechising." An appointment had been made for service at East Frampton, the next day, but the Archdeacon was so unwell that he was detained till the following day. The weather was such that, when he got up in the morning, water freshly brought into the room became crusted over in a few moments, and "I really suffered in dressing, but it would be a shame indeed to complain of suffering no worse than this, and a strange forgetfulness of the charge of St. Paul to the Christian minister, 'thou, therefore, endure hardness, as a good soldier of Jesus Christ.' On arriving at East Frampton, I was mortified to learn that the people had assembled the day before in a strong muster to meet me, and that there was also a full attendance at the school in expectation of my visit. To-day I fear that I shall have hardly any congregation; the people waited so long yesterday, and so much snow has since fallen, that I can hardly expect the settlers to come again. I have been to the school." He had, however, a congregation of thirty-five, children included, and then returned to West Frampton, and on his way "passed the house of a settler who had built his house not upon but against a rock, a huge mass of stone forming one end of his dwelling, against which he makes his fire, which, when the whole face of the mass is heated, protects him against the most intense cold." The whole of the 10th, from nine a.m. to half-past ten p.m., was occupied by the journey to Aubert Galleon on the river Chaudière, where, on the 11th, service was held, as well as at a neighbouring settlement, with sermon and baptisms, followed by the examination of the school. The next note is dated Broughton, 13th March: "I have only the time which will be occupied by stowing away the things in the cariole (the horse being at the door) to say that I am well, and I hope not proceeding without, at least for the moment, doing some good. God bless the seed which I scatter, and bring it to effect! I have had service this morning in the loft of a mill, where I also baptized a child. I have thirty-five miles to go before night, through desperately heavy wood-roads the greatest part, I fear, of the way : snow-storms, as usual, have escorted me on my route. Leeds, 14th.—I may as well see the whole line of country through which the Protestant population is scattered, and add my report to that of others as a ground for endeavouring to establish a mission here. Three Sundays are not much to be away on such a circuit, when it begins on a Saturday and ends on a Monday. It is, indeed, very insufficient for all that is required. The heavy rain, however, of last night and to-day is discouraging. The people in New Ireland are all running into the wildest enthusiasm : they have fourteen preachers, as I understand, among them. I arrived here at about twelve o'clock last night. I have been preaching here this morning, and am going on four miles to preach at five this evening : to-morrow I expect to preach twice, once at the end of my journey, at the house of Mr. Lord in New Ireland, and once at Sergeant Lee's on the way. As to my doing any of my writing, I see no chance of it whatever, and pray tell the Bishop so. I wonder what fresh disagreeable work awaits me, at which you hint in your note. God grant me wisdom, perseverance, patience and charity! they are all wanted enough." One letter of the series is unfortunately wanting, but the whole portion of the county of Megantic (in which there was not a single church) where there are now missionary stations seems to have been visited. The last letter is dated St. Giles, 20th March, and speaks of service at that place, in its neighbourhood, and at Plomer Range in Inverness. A rough memorandum of a report to the Bishop shews ten places in the county of Megantic, besides Frampton, the Chaudière settlements, and St. Giles, at which service had been held. At each place the congregation averaged from forty to one hundred persons, and twenty-two children were baptized, although the Rev. R. Burrage had baptized about the same number on a similar circuit, about two months before. The Archdeacon appeals earnestly " for the establishment of at least one resident missionary in this district, whose head-quarters should be at Leeds. The charge is indeed much too extensive, but an active and zealous missionary would, under the divine blessing, prove a great comfort to the people and effect much good, and there are many circumstances which indicate that no time should be lost." He also adverts to the spiritual destitution of the townships of Melbourne and Shipton, mentioned in his former journal. Both these points were soon afterwards gained.

CHAPTER VIII.

Archidiaconal duties and journals, 1830.

THE visits of the Archdeacon to the parishes and missions within his archdeaconry were continually called for by the necessity for taking measures for the establishment of new stations, and sometimes by local difficulties which required his presence in order to their removal. They were necessarily every way different from the visitations of an Archdeacon in England, and he never followed the English practice of assembling the clergy of any one district to receive a charge. In this respect the visitations of colonial Archdeacons are, perhaps with scarcely an exception, alike. But he always had a note of certain points of enquiry or recommendation on which he took occasion to enlarge in private conversation with them. These are mentioned in one of his journals as being, "first, catechizing; second, Sunday-school; third, pastoral visits from house to house; fourth, preaching at out-posts; fifth, observance of certain holydays; sixth, conformity of the people to certain ordinances, such as the institution of sponsors, churching of women, etc., and manner of obviating prejudices and difficulties, or of exercising discretion in making out a case of necessity to dispense with rules; seventh, font for baptism; eighth, ecclesiastical dress, wearing of canonicals recommended in preaching at out-posts and performing the occasional offices of the Church in private houses; ninth, family devotion, and attention, in travelling, to the performance of family prayer and the read-

ing of Scripture by the clergy in the houses where they pass
the night ;* tenth, correspondence with the S. P. G."

He always kept notes, more or less full, of his journeys,
which took the shape of letters to his family, and from these
the foregoing extracts have been taken. About this time,
however, he began to endeavour, as he had leisure, to draw
up a more formal and official report of his journeys, addressed
to his Diocesan, and generally intended also for the information of the S. P. G. In June, 1830, he says, " I keep a
journal of my proceedings, but it is very different from any
that I have kept before, and I feel a difficulty in keeping it,
which makes it stiff and constrained. It may possibly be
sent home to the Society, and as the object of sending it is
that they may have something favourable or interesting to
tell the public about the Canadian Church, I ought to make
a good, or at least, decent figure, as the hero of my own tale ;
* * * the interest which we feel about religious objects, the
pains which we take to promote them, the manner in which
we endeavour to let our light shine before men and to recommend the Church when we have to give an account of them
with our own pens, and when this account itself is to be calculated to recommend the Church at home, produce a divided
feeling between a natural backwardness, on the one hand, to
all semblance of puffing, and a desire, on the other, to do
justice to the cause which we support, and to meet the expectations of the Society. A simple narrative of facts without a
single touch of description or a single glow of feeling would
be found cold and dry ; yet how far to indulge in description,
what subjects for description to select, how to carry the reader
into the interest of the scene and to sustain his attention without making more of one's own part in it than it deserves, or

---

* I have seen a note to a clergyman who, from being a comparative
stranger to the state of things in a new country, might, it was feared, omit
attention to this point, in which it is suggested with great kindness and
delicacy.

more than one likes,—in short, without thinking one's self egotistical,—are points which it passes my skill to manage to my satisfaction." With this preface, I give some extracts from the journal of 1830, which is the only one of this kind, except that of the preceding year, which has come into my hands. Leaving Quebec on the afternoon of St. John Baptist's day, he spent one day at Three Rivers, where two divinity students were under the charge of the rector. "It is an arduous but a blessed task for which these young men are training themselves, and all who pray for the peace and welfare of our Jerusalem should remember those who are preparing to stand as watchmen upon her walls * * * At Nicolet I had the satisfaction of finding the family engaged in prayer, upon which even the Roman Catholic servants of the house attend. I promised, if possible, to spend a Sunday here on my return, and perform service in the church, which depends upon such occasional visits. Much pains are taken by the family of the seigneur to keep up a spirit of religion among the scattered Protestant settlers, by the distribution of the Scriptures, the liturgy, and tracts of the S. P. C. K., by instructing the children in the catechism, and by reading the prayers of the Church and a printed sermon, coupled with the performance of psalmody, at the house on Sundays. Among the most constant attendants at this service are the members of a family who occupy a solitary clearing back in the woods, at a distance of from twelve to fourteen miles from the spot, and who have no means of coming but on foot. The man and his wife attend alternately, each accompanied by some of the children. Upon some occasions they pass the night on their way back at a house on the road, and whenever the woman proceeds the whole way home, she is provided with a candle, without which she will not venture through the darkness and depth of the wood. * * * Nothing can be more ugly or dreary than the swampy parts of the road to Drummondville, yet along its edge,—as there is always something beautiful to be seen in creation,—besides some other little flowering shrubs, the lovely and blushing calmia, now in the height of its flower, grows in the richest profusion. I have often reflected with thankfulness on the circumstance that whatever trifling privations and occasional little rough-nesses of travelling, just enough to do us good, we may en-counter in our circuits of official duty, yet go where we will, we have the best which the country affords, our visit is regarded as a special favour, our accommodation is zealously studied. We often meet with discouragements, and some-times with opposition, in the discharge of our duty ; but how different is our lot from that of the early planters of the faith who were ' made as the offscouring of all things,' and from that of many missionaries of modern times ? How careful ought we to be to cultivate a spirit which could accommodate itself to humbling circumstances and contemptuous treatment in the world, and would ' know how to be abased ' as well as ' how to abound !' How watchful against the indulgence of any habits or feelings which would unfit us for such humiliations, and cause us, in the event of reverses in the Church, to shew ourselves unprepared, unmeet to be the servants of a Master Who ' came not to be ministered unto but to minister,' and ' had not where to lay His head !' Yet as long as we do our duty, I am persuaded that we shall always meet with kind treatment.　＊　＊　＊

" Sunday, June 27th. The Bishop in his instructions to me had marked out this day to be spent at Drummondville, on account of the absence of Mr. Ross. He has desisted from attempting two services in the day, from the difficulty of collecting a sufficient congregation in the afternoon, most of the people living at a considerable distance, and having bad roads to pass. As the occasion, however, was peculiar, and the days were at the longest, and as Mr. Ross's absence might leave them some whole Sundays without service, I told them, after the morning service, that if twenty of them would attend in the afternoon, I would have a second. (There were about sixty present in the morning.) One of the settlers answered, that ' he lived as far off as any other, and that he, for one, would attend,' and trusting to this example, I decided at once upon having service at three o'clock. I was not disappointed, for there were about as many present as in the morning. I visited the Sunday-school, and questioned and instructed the children. As some of them ' came from far ' and remained for the evening service, I was apprehensive of their feeling the want of food, which a very few shillings would have provided for them, and I gave directions accordingly; but only one could be prevailed upon to take advantage of the offer, and the person who supplied him refused to be paid. Mr. Ross has other preaching stations, which he regularly attends. Every second Sunday he officiates at two different places, the nearest of which is fifteen miles from Drummondville. The persons who conducted the Sunday-school particularly expressed their want of a prescribed system, an example, among many others, which confirms the useful character of the endeavours set on foot by Mr. Archbold.* There are three brothers here, Canadians, whose father was from France, all of whom are Protestants. One of them is a churchwarden. The father, upon his first arrival in the country, experienced some difficulty from the priesthood respecting his marriage with a Protestant, and (as the son told me) upon his applying to the Governor himself, General Haldimand, for a license, and stating his case, received a French Bible from his Excellency, who told him ' that it was the Word of God, and he ought to consult it.' He appears to have profited by the advice, for all his children were baptized and brought up in the Church of England.

" June 28th. For the first ten miles of the way to Melbourne, (to which a resident missionary had been recently

---

* The S. S. Association mentioned in p. 101.

appointed,) the road lies through the woods. There are, however, habitations lying some miles off the road, accessible now by horse-paths, but not even thus in the first stage of the settlement, when the inhabitants could not get backwards and forwards except on foot, and in the wet season were in many places up to their hips in water in doing so. Their provisions and other necessaries they carried on their backs. Such are the hardships which men will submit to with the prospect before them of an independent provision to be transmitted to their children, and such is the sustaining power of hope, applicable to the highest purposes and objects to which the mind of man can be directed. I stopped at the house of a man who is a Roman Catholic, and whose daughter had just been driven from his house, because he would have forced her into a conformity to his religion. He had always expressed this determination, and she had, in the perplexity of her trials, more than once resorted to the expedient of feigning herself sick, in order to avoid receiving her *première communion*. It would have been right, no doubt, that instead of this she should have at all hazards declared the truth : but much allowance must be made for her, and she has, at least, evinced a resolute adherence to the dictates of her conscience. His wife, a Norfolk woman, told me that his zeal was most noisy and troublesome when he was in his cups. At other times he was often very quiet in his family upon the subject, but when he was in liquor, she said, then " Religion was all the crack.' She said, however, that he had a great respect for Mr. Wood, who is well known in all this part of the country, who, she hoped, might come and see them and have an opportunity of talking to him, for he had often declared that Mr. Wood was ' the best man in the country, let who will be the other.' *   *   * After preaching in a school-house twenty-two miles from Drummondville, I proceeded to Melbourne ; *   *   * crossed the ferry in a little ticklish canoe, in which it is the practice for the passengers to stand upright, to see the new church at Richmond village.

"June 29th. The church-building committee came to meet me, according to appointment, and I trust that things were put in train for the advancement of the work. * * * After a good deal of conversation with Mr. F., chiefly with reference to his approaching admission to Priest's Orders, I set out for Sherbrooke. * * *

"July 1st. Divine service was appointed at six p.m., and after my sermon I requested, acting in accordance with the wishes of the Rev. E. Parkin, that the heads of families would remain to consider some means for putting in better train the temporal affairs of the Church, all whose affairs, indeed, upon this spot (as cannot be wondered at after the defection to Universalism of the pastor who was lately in charge) wear an aspect disheartening to those who love her. Heresy running like wildfire through the neighbourhood; many tossed to and fro and 'carried about with every wind of doctrine'; many 'after their own lusts' heaping 'to themselves teachers, having itching ears'; two Universalist newspapers circulating in the village itself; among the adherents of the Church 'the love of' not a few waxing 'cold'; the languishing condition of religion intimated by the external face of things; the building out of repair and becoming unfit for service in severe weather; no collections established, nor any revenue raised whatever for the support of the Church; no churchwardens appointed; the last register of the mission carried off and not returned; the singing in the congregation faint or none; the burying-ground exposed without fence to protect the graves of believers from being trodden by cattle or upheaved by swine. * * * But God, if it be His pleasure, can retrieve His Church from the worst circumstances, and lift her up when she lieth in the dust. * * * Nothing can be imagined more delightful than many of the landscapes on the road from Sherbrooke to Hatley, if the fields were intersected by green hedges and scattered over with rural-looking farm houses, and here and there an ancient seat, or a grey

K

church-tower mantled with ivy.   *   *   *   But to conclude
this digression by bringing the whole question to its only sure
test, ' the fashion of this world passeth away,' and they who
' think that their dwelling-places shall endure from one generation to another, and call the lands after their own names,'
leave only a monument of the vanity of human projects.   It
is not, therefore, for the perpetuation of anything dear to our
particular associations, tastes, or prejudices, that our solicitude ought to be felt, but rather for the extended knowledge
of the Word of the Lord which shall endure for ever, and
the advancement of that kingdom in unity and strength in
which ' there is neither Greek nor Jew, Barbarian, Scythian,
bond nor free, but Christ is all and in all.' "   *   *   *   *   *

" July 4th, Sunday.   I performed the whole service at
Charleston, in the forenoon, to a congregation of upwards
of two hundred persons, whom I afterwards took the liberty
of addressing before they dispersed, to press upon them,
with some earnestness, the renewed cultivation of church-
singing.   I was impelled to do so by the mortifying occurrence of a psalm having been given out, which, after a
distressing pause, was followed by my resumption of my own
part of the service, not a single voice having been raised.   *
*   *   There are certainly some truly pious church-people
in this village.   Immediately after service I drove to the
new church in Compton, which is quite in an unfinished
state, and had never been used, but a temporary arrangement was made for the accommodation of minister and people.
The number present was probably something more than one
hundred.   It would have been greater, but a preacher of the
sect who call themselves Christians preached twice in the
township this day, because some mistaken information had
got abroad that our service was to be at four instead of three.
He would otherwise have dispensed with his second performance, for all or the greater part of his hearers would have
come to hear me, as it is a prevailing principle to go to hear

everybody; and he intended to have left them time to do so after twice hearing himself. Several of them came dropping in very late, and the preacher himself just as I was uttering the last sentence of my sermon. A psalm was sung, and a few persons had prayer-books, of whom three or four made the responses. A clergyman established as the pastor of these people must first win them to attend diligently upon his ministrations by his acceptableness in his public performances and the personal respect which he acquires among them, and may then succeed in teaching them a right knowledge and a just value of the Church and her ordinances. It is a great point if he is an able preacher, or, as some of them express it, a smart speaker, but it is of more importance still that he should be discreet, circumspect, spiritual, zealous and laborious. The Americans expect a great deal in a clergyman, and it is useless for a man to go among them in that capacity who will not seem to be truly a man of God. A hypocrite may sometimes succeed with them. A careless worldly clergyman never can. A sincerely devout and exemplary pastor will seldom fail to build up the Church among them, and to gain the respect and goodwill of those who conform but partially or not at all. Upon the whole, however, it must be plainly confessed that the difficulties of the ministry are great in the missions of this diocese. * * * On my way back I drove round a few miles to see a poor afflicted man crippled with rheumatism, whom I had once known in Quebec. We found his wife at a house on the way, where my friend who drove me from Charleston went in, and waited for my return while I drove the woman on in the waggon. The poor man and his wife most thankfully received my ministrations, and I baptized their two youngest children. They occupy a quiet and secluded spot, beyond which the road does not pass, and their farm would be a productive one if they had a hand to till it. But it is the suffering and want endured by one portion of God's creatures which afford exercise to the benevolence of another, and this poor family have found some neighbours who have shewn them great and continued kindness.

`" July 5th. I met this morning the committee for building the academy at Hatley, the frame of which, surmounted by a cupola, is already erected. The whole affair seems to be in proper train, and it is provided that the head-master shall be a clergyman of the Church of England, although, in the first instance, it has been considered that the inadequate state of the funds may warrant an exception to this rule. After taking leave of the Rev. T. Johnson, I got away about the middle of the day, a single-horse waggon having been engaged for me, which was driven by the church-clerk. His house being on our road, I went in and sat with his wife while he got his dinner. She has been in a declining state for many months, but she bears her burthen with a willing spirit and is constantly occupied in reading her Bible. I had much satisfaction in conversing and praying with her, and was interested by her relation of an occurrence which took place upon her first settling in this neighbourhood, then a howling wilderness of forest, about thirty years ago. It is well known that trees which grow thickly together depend partly upon each other for support, and many of them have no depth of root to resist the action of a tempestuous wind, when they are exposed to it by clearing. Thus, when a road has been opened through the woods, a tall hemlock is often seen uptorn and prostrate ; his roots, with the spaces between them filled up by earth, presenting a flat surface, like a table turned over, perhaps ten or twelve feet in height. The little tenement which this woman occupied was, of course, in the settler's first establishment, upon the edge of the forest. One night, when the wind blew violently, and, as it is sometimes expressed, the bones of the trees began to crack, the woman, who was alone with her children, became terrified, expecting to be crushed by their falling upon the house, and

she took her children without their reach, into a little clearing in front. But here it soon began to rain heavily. She
then considered that she was exposing the children to a
certain evil and to almost certain danger of illness by suffering them to remain all night in the wet, and took them at
once back to the house, confiding the issue to the Providence
of God. The storm raged on with unabated fury, and the
threatening sounds continued among the trees; but she assured
me, with evident marks of feeling, δακρυοεν γελασασα, that she
never in her life felt more strongly the presence of God, or
reposed more securely in His protection. * * * I had
been pleased during this day by an anecdote (new to myself)
of Sir H. Wotton, which I saw in a printed sheet, posted up
in the house where we baited. Being asked to pronounce
whether a papist could be saved, he replied, ' You can be
saved without knowing that.' We may, indeed, go farther,
for surely there are papists of whose salvation we have reason
to enjoy a comfortable hope, however deeply we may lament
their errors; but still the answer is excellent. I gather
something from all sorts of sources as I go along. * * *

" There is no encouragement at present in Stanstead for
planting the Church, there being no more than three or four
even nominal adherents to her communion. The British
Methodists and Close-communion Baptists are the sects who
occupy the ground. There are however many persons, no
doubt, who (as they would express it) have never joined
any society; and are pretty equally accessible by all except
Roman Catholics. The Church has been planted with success where there was no better promise at the beginning.
But there is no need to obtrude her unsought, where there
are so many demands for her aid which cannot be answered.

" July 6th. After crossing Lake Memphramagog we entered Potton. * * * The road passed through a kind of
defile, magnificently wooded on one side, but shut in on the
other by prodigious bristling crags, rocky, rugged and pre-

cipitous, which rise at a short distance, running parallel with
the road and the opposite ridge. Over the highest point of
this vast and rude elevation, we saw, 'sailing with supreme
dominion,' a bird which we could discover to be a white-tailed
eagle. We saw afterwards partridges and wood-pigeons,
perhaps destined to be his prey. Wonderful and warning
extent of the curse which came from sin, pervading all
creation and causing it to groan and travail together in pain!
We met several waggon-teams, and one (which I never saw
before in this country) drawn by six horses, drawing flour
and cases of merchandize from Montreal. The struggles of
the poor loaded animals in these dreadful roads, and up the
hills which constantly occur, did not tend to do away the
reflections suggested by the eagle and his prey. At present
the road is such that, with a light load and an excellent horse,
we could not effect more than fifteen miles in the first six
hours. *　*　* At Frelighsburgh there is a tombstone on
which the death was recorded by saying that at such a time
'her ethereal part became seraphic.' *　*　*　* It is
gratifying to see the number of schools established throughout the townships, and increased by the late grants of the
provincial parliament. Few or none of them, I believe, are
inefficient. The teachers are generally Americans, and the
books used are chiefly procured from the States. But no
republican kind of objection to render obeisance seems to be
inculcated among them, for the little barefooted boys and
girls rarely fail to make their bow and curtsey to the traveller as he passes. The former is frequently accompanied by
taking off the hat, and is performed by a jerk both forward
and downward of the head, very zealously respectful, but
almost ludicrous in its effect. But if they are trained to
'honour all men' and 'love the brotherhood,' the eccentricity
of their salutation should not be sufficient to provoke a laugh.

"July 12th. I had called a meeting the day before in church
to deliberate on some matters connected with the removal of

Mr. Abbott, who had already left the place, and the preparations to be made for receiving Mr. Johnson. The difficulties
related to a parsonage-house, for which no final and satisfactory arrangement had been made, and it is impossible for
any person unaccustomed to such modes of doing business to
conceive the intricacy and involution almost ad infinitum of
which agreements and proceedings of this nature are made
up, when the circulating medium is comparatively no part of
the various equivalents to be calculated. Payments in labour,
provisions, grain, goods, cattle, or transferred debts ;—whatever the Americans understand by the term trading ;—
demands conditionally relinquished, exchanges and private
arrangements passing from hand to hand, and comprehending
perhaps many of the foregoing items in the bargain ;—all these
are to be unravelled and disposed of before a clear result can
be obtained. * * * There was a thunder-storm towards
evening, and I never saw anything more exquisitely beautiful than the setting of the sun behind the Belœil mountain
which followed. The glories of creation may give us some
faint idea of what must be the grandeur of those things which
'eye hath not seen,' when we reflect that these visible works
of God are to be destroyed when they have had their day,
are as a nothing which will leave no void among the wonders
of His hands. Too happy if we can be made instruments to
forward, each within his sphere, the work of creating ' all
things new in Christ Jesus,' to be fully developed when ' the
restitution of all things' and ' the times of refreshing shall
come.' I had now completed all that constituted the special
objects of my circuit, and might have returned at once by
the most direct route to Quebec, had it not been that I had
promised to allot Sunday the 18th to the little unprovided
flock at Nicolet. It became my duty therefore, of course,
to consider in what way I could most profitably dispose of
the intervening time, and I decided to visit some settlements
at no great distance from Abbottsford, where there are sheep

of our own fold without a shepherd, although visited occasionally by some of our clergy. * * * I found a table provided for myself, and planks arranged for the hearers, in a school-house at Rougemont, where I preached to about forty persons. The people all knelt during prayer. I also baptized two children. * * * I gave a caution to the sponsors before I allowed them to make their engagements, endeavouring to explain the office in such a way as that the bystanders might benefit by the removal of objections against this custom of the Church, or by the communication of new impressions to their minds as to the seriousness with which the duty should be undertaken. * * * I got a comfortable dinner at the tavern, but the table was set out in the kitchen, which appeared also to be a place of rendezvous for persons whom business or gossip brought together; and if it had been consistent with my occupations and the purposes before me to catch and delineate the humours of the scene, there were strokes which might have been not unworthy of appearing in the pictures of Erasmus or Sir Walter Scott. American and Irish peculiarities were intermingled with the broken English of an old French Canadian notary from a neighbouring village. The people of the house, who had shewn me every attention and provided me with their very best, absolutely refused to receive any payment. * * * The family spoke in the warmest terms of the zeal, attention, affability, and cheerful submission to difficulties and privations, exhibited by our clergy and some of the divinity students who have come over from Chambly as lay-readers, from the time when the Rev. E. Parkin first began to visit them : snow-storms, severe cold, roads which broke their vehicles, and coarse entertainment after their fatigues, have been no obstacles to their coming to hold service and to extend their visits to more distant sick who needed those consolations which make the desert rejoice. As the necessity for my going off early the next morning precluded any inspection of the R. I. School in this settlement, I sent for the school-master, and spent some time in questioning and advising him ; and while I was setting before him the responsiblity of his charge, at the same time with its interesting nature, if rightly considered, and the extent to which the good effects of his assiduity in the day and Sunday-schools might reach, I saw the poor fellow's eyes more than once become moist.

" The line between the French Canadian and his British or American neighbour is still strongly and conspicuously marked, and the *bonnet-rouge*, the grey homespun dresses, the beef-skin moccasins, and the party-coloured *ceinture*, the close cap, the striped petticoat, and the skirted body, are not more decided distinctions of the people themselves, than their buildings and whole system of agriculture are of the tracts which they inhabit. In travelling through these tracts, these rural characteristics of a simple people, the uniform aspect of their institutions, their brotherhood in religion, the full and regular provision made everywhere for religious worship and instruc tion, their substantial churches, with the *presbytère* always immediately adjoining, and the glimpse, perhaps, of the *curé* himself in the distinctive habit of the priesthood, produce a favourable impression upon the mind, and convey ideas, at least much beyond the truth, of peacefulness, comparative innocence, good order, and well-timed discipline. * * * It cannot, I think, fairly be disputed that standing institutions and observances interwoven with the feelings and habits of the whole population,—order, unity and discipline existing in vigour in the administration of religious affairs,—although they may be found in bad company, yet produce in themselves a good effect upon the manners of a people. And when,—for whatever wild and visionary notions may be entertained upon the subject of the millennium, we are surely taught to look forward to a fuller and more blessed establishment of the kingdom of grace than has yet been seen in the world,—when that happier time arrives which is anticipated in the christian world, the evils of schism as well as of superstition and Church tyranny must be swept at least from the prevailing aspect of the scene. Roman catholic unity and order must be combined with Protestant doctrine and worship, and with Protestant enjoyment of liberty and light. * * * Close to the church at Sorel, upon an unenclosed level space of smooth turf, is an open *bocage* of pines, into which I was tempted to stroll. The breeze blew rather freshly through them, and I never heard to more advantage the sound which gave pleasure to one of the oldest of moral poets, a sound which is soothing in itself,

> 'Round an holy calm diffusing,
> Love of peace and lonely musing,'

and which often carries with it a kind of mysterious charm, wafting back a thousand fleeting associations and remembrances of a tender and pleasing nature, although they fix themselves upon no tangible object, and present no distinct picture to the mind."

I close this chapter with two short extracts from private letters written on this journey : " I cannot help being a little anxious, now and then, about private and public objects at Quebec : the singing in church, the mariners' chapel, the national school under its new master, are all objects of particular solicitude. I commit all to God above and to His blessing, but I must return prepared for some disappointments and vexations. * * * I stand prepared for changes, as I have often told you, and as far as I am personally and individually concerned, I think I could soon accommodate myself even to poverty : but God has blessed us with means far beyond what we could have once looked for ; and while we have them, we must do justice to our children, and cheerfully contribute our share to the promotion of good objects and the relief of distress. But I know you feel with me on all these points. Let us enjoy our present blessings, and endeavour to consecrate them by the manner in which they are used. 'The morrow shall take thought for the things of itself.' Although we must exercise a fair prudence, the future is in the hands of God, and there we must leave it, in confidence that all things needful will be done for them that love Him.'' *

---

* He made it a rule never to save any thing out of the income which he derived from his profession, although for many years he had no private means. And when he became possessed of these to a small amount, he employed them upon the education and setting out in life of his sons, rather than diminish his expenditure for other objects. It was not till these objects were accomplished that, for only a few years before his death, he allowed his private income to accumulate, and latterly, as he never wished "to be what is called rich," he devoted a large portion of it to objects of charity. When he succeeded to the administration of the diocese, at the death of Bishop Stewart, he had no salary as Bishop, the vote of the Imperial Parliament by which it had been supplied having been then discontinued, but chiefly through the representations of Mr. Pakington (now Sir J. Pakington) £1000 per annum were granted for his life. This was about the same amount as he had received as Archdeacon and rector of Quebec, and one-third of the salary of his predecessors in the episcopal office. It would have been very difficult for him, therefore, to meet his increased expenditure as a Bishop, with the expectations which his own habits of liberality, as well as those of Bishop Stewart, who was a single man, had formed, without retaining some portion of the income attached to the subordinate offices. His salaries as Archdeacon and rector were limited to his incumbency of those offices, and he always thought it desirable to retain these, rather than that the Church should lose this pecuniary advantage. He made repeated attempts to effect an arrangement for resigning them without loss to the Church, but without success. On his first assumption of the episcopal office he surrendered to the curate of Quebec one-half of his emoluments as rector, discharging, himself, to the last, a large share of the duties of that office, and he was then certainly a poorer man than when he had been only Archdeacon and rector. For many years before his death, when his private expenses had been diminished, he gave up the whole of the rector's salary to other clergy in the parish, and for several years devoted that of the Archdeacon also to Church purposes within the diocese. He was always eminently self-denying in personal expenditure.

CHAPTER IX.

Journeys as Archdeacon continued—1832.

I HAVE no record of any journeys in the year 1831, though I remember accompanying him, for the first time in my life, in a short one which he undertook in the summer of that year to the township of Frampton, which was still without a resident clergyman. At this time he had an assistant in the parish of Quebec, who lived in his house, and devoted part of his time to the instruction of his sons. In February, 1832, he set out on a journey to the Ottawa river, on which a new mission had been established at Grenville, and a congregation formed at Vaudrueuil which was served once a fortnight from Côteau du Lac. The description of the rectory at Three Rivers is worth preserving, now that the house has been modernized. It was originally a convent, the chapel of which is now the parish church. " I delight in the character of this strange rambling building, especially in this country, where there is so little that approaches to the venerable in the works of man. The walls are of a most massive thickness, but what I like most is a heavy arch under which you pass to gain the stairs, and the staircase itself, which is very wide, with an antique and cumbrous banister, or balustrade. In the lower part of the building, which is rude and strangely divided, owing to the different uses to which it has successively been put, and in which, although I cannot say that the hands of the builders have been employed ' to raise the ceiling's fretted height,' nor in 'each panel with achievements clothing,' nor in making

' rich windows that exclude the light,' yet there are plenty of
' passages which lead to nothing.' * * * The journey was
extended to Bytown,* respecting which he writes, ' I think I
never spent a Sunday with less comfort to my feelings than
that at Bytown and Hull. I began the day by officiating for
Mr. —— to the troops at the former place,† where, in the
unfinished Methodist chapel which we borrow for the purpose,
I read prayers and preached to a sergeant and eight men,
with just about an equal number of other individuals, including a christening party of country people who came from a
distance, and were no part of the Bytown congregation. Mr.
——then went across to the tavern where he puts up (he lives
about three miles off in Hull), and performed the christening
in a back-room : the apartment in front, divided from this by
a thin wooden partition, was occupied by loungers reading
newspapers, to whom every word of the ceremony was distinctly audible. I left them and passed into the other room,
where I found Mr. —— administering this solemn ordinance,
altogether in a manner and under circumstances not at all
tending to clothe it with reverence. He then drove me across
the river to Hull, (where I preached) which is in Lower
Canada, but the church of which, the largest and most showy
country church that we have in the diocese, is supposed to
accommodate such of the Bytown episcopalians as do not
attend the military service. My visit was expected, and it
must be presumed to have added something to the congregation, which nevertheless consisted of about thirty persons.
There was no singing, nor did anybody but myself make the
responses. The church was intolerably cold, though the day
was not severe, and several people left their pews to get over

* Mention is made of meeting sleighs carrying barrels of pork, flour, &c ,
from Montreal to Bytown, the owners of which performed the whole journey, both ways, for five dollars.

† Bytown, being in Upper Canada, was not within the archdeaconry of
Quebec.

to the stoves. Coldness, neglect, and unprosperous management seemed to hang about every thing. In the afternoon I
had an invitation to the military mess, none of the members
of which (with perhaps one exception) had been at either
of the services, which I declined. * * * The people of the
house were quite pleased at my performing the usual evening
devotions with them while I staid there, and said they had not
had such a thing in the house since Bishop Stewart was
there. On Monday I transacted business with the Rev.
R. Leeming, who came by appointment to meet me : at six I
went to dine with Colonel B——— : at eight a cariole called for
me by appointment to take me to visit a poor dying man in
the village : between nine and ten I returned to meet the
Rev. R. Short at the inn, who had also been summoned
from his station to meet me : afterwards I had prayers, and a
visit from a half-pay naval officer, settled far up the river, who
wants to get things in train for a church where he lives ; and
by the time I had packed and got ready for the stage which
was to be at the door by six o'clock in the morning, it was
half-past one A.M. The next day, in the township of Lochaber,
two lovely children were brought to me at the stage-house
for baptism, by persons who had heard of my passing through
the country. I had expected to proceed to St. Andrews,
although the stage puts up for the night at Grenville, but
the Rev. J. Abbott had made an arrangement, in consequence of a proposal of my own in going up, which at the
time he had thought hardly practicable, that the congregation
should meet for a week-day evening service in the school-
house. The place was crowded to excess, and the singing
was by far the best that I ever heard in a country place.
After preaching I detained the heads of families to arrange
some points respecting a church which is immediately about
to be built, in reference to which I had conferred with Mr.
Abbott, the churchwardens and others, on my way up. I
left Grenville by the stage, at five o'clock on the morning of

the twenty-second, which day was allotted to a visit to the Gore settlement, after we should reach St. Andrews, to which place we came to breakfast. Never was seen any thing in the shape of human habitations more wretched than the huts occupied by a number of Irish Roman catholics, who have established themselves along the line of the Grenville canal, having been drawn there originally by the labour offered in the works. They are constructed, in the rudest conceivable manner, of mud, sod, bark and other materials immediately accessible, and some of them are so excessively low and drifted over by the snow that they are hardly observable, except from some projecting corner, or the wreath of smoke which perhaps issues from an old flour barrel converted into a chimney. The Gore settlement lies among woods, rocks, lakes, and mountains (although of small elevation,) and is composed entirely of Protestants, all, but a very few, Irish and of our own Church. These poor people have no Church-service, except on a week-day once a month. The congregation was assembled in the largest house which the settlement afforded, and it was so insufficient that some persons at first had got into the loft, intending to catch what they could of the service through the floor. They all, however, squeezed into two rooms, but most of them were kept standing. They sang, and were led by an experienced parish-clerk. * * * I had written to the Rev. J. Leeds to meet me from the Côteau du Lac at Vaudreuil on the twenty-third, and had suggested that he should assemble the congregation. No Mr. Leeds, however, appeared, and no congregation met. From all that I heard, I was so convinced of the importance of my meeting these people, and endeavouring to put things in train for more effectual provision for their spiritual wants, that I came to the determination to return to them on Saturday from Montreal, and spend Sunday with them. While I was at Vaudreuil, old Mr. —— was brought in to see me. Till last autumn he was a worldly and irreligious man. At that time he met with

a fall which produced consequences rather of a serious nature,
and led him to think of death. For this he found himself
wholly unprepared. His sins rose up before him in the form
of dreadful accusers, and he began to despair of mercy. But
he has been graciously brought to find the way of pardon and
peace, and is in a most humble, penitent, and devout frame of
mind, self-abased and comforted at the same time. I talked
and prayed with him, and he wept like a child.   *   *   *
Proceeding with my little rat of a horse through heavy and
drifted roads (for there was a determined snow-storm all day),
I was so annoyed by the ceaseless curses and unmerciful
blows which the driver bestowed upon it, and there was so
little prospect of our getting to Montreal at night, that I
dismissed the man, and engaged another conveyance in the
parish of Pointe Claire. Here, in the village, is a large old-
fashioned Canadian house, which is one of what may be called
the branch convents scattered about the country for the
education of girls, and conducted by a couple of ' les sœurs.'
There are fifty children at present in this establishment. No
person can wish to see such things as these swept away in
any religious revolution which might shake the empire of
Romanism. I dined this day for two-pence. It was about
four o'clock, and I foresaw that I must be quite late in Montreal. I asked, therefore, for some refreshment ; and without
cooking, there was nothing to be had but dark-coloured bread
and butter. The woman declined to take any thing for it, but
three half-pence being paid for what my driver drank, I prof-
fered four, happening to have the vile coin about me, for what
I myself ate, and they were received as a favour. It is a
sort of maxim with me, and I find it useful, to accommodate
myself to any little privations or rough occurrences on a
journey, so that I do not in the least regard it as necessary
in travelling to have any regular dinner, nor sometimes,
indeed, any dinner at all, and it does not affect me in any
unpleasant way, if this happens for days together. The

ignorance of the Canadian *habitants* may be judged of from the circumstance that the man who drove me did not at all relish the idea of coming into Montreal after dark, because he had been told that there were persons going about the streets who clap an adhesive plaster upon your face, and then carry you off to murder you, in order to procure subjects for dissection, there being a contract with Government to send bodies home to England for this purpose. The origin of this story is evidently the account of the Burkism carried on in London, but it is curious to see how the poor Government is coupled with everything which carries odium on its face. The next day was a busy day, and indeed I am always busy, except when actually on the road. After breakfasting with Mr. Stevens, where Mr. Bethune came to meet me to digest and prepare all our arrangements for a meeting (to be mentioned afterwards), I returned to the hotel to see divinity students, catechists, &c., by appointment, and to write letters till the hour of the meeting. Its object was the establishment of a central committee for the district of Montreal of our new Sunday-school society, and of a parish Sunday-school in Montreal itself. It devolved upon me to preside. I had the evening to myself till ten o'clock, at which hour the secretary of the medical faculty of McGill college came to me, by appointment, on business. I had to write afterwards, and did not get to bed till between one and two. On the twenty-fifth I had appointments with Mr. Bethune and others, and Mr. B. assisted me in examining a catechist and lay-reader whom I then licensed for Terrebonne and parts adjacent. The day was fine in the forenoon, but my star pursued me: the heavens gradually became overcast and a snow-storm soon followed. I left Montreal at one o'clock, and stopped to bait at Pointe Claire, where I again dined, in spite of your* injunction, upon crackers and milk-and-water. As to your

* These extracts are from letters addressed to his children.

recommendation of roast-beef, although *rosbif* has become a standing dish in France where English travellers are concerned, this is not quite the case in Canada : the beef is not thawed, much less cooked for you, if there is any, but it is a hundred to one that there is none in such houses as those of which I am speaking. When I was passing through a room filled with Canadians, who were in company upon the road, and whose *traineaux* were at the door, I heard one of them say that I was obliged to stoop under the beam. As I had done this unconsciously, I turned round and told the man I thought he was mistaken, upon which some of them begged me to try, when, thinking it best to be complying when no harm is intended, I found by the experiment that he was right, upon which a kind of shout broke forth from the party which was not perfectly polite, and certainly not con istent with respect for the dignity which, whatever they thought at the time, they afterwards ascribed to me: for I heard, after I got upstairs, that I was '*l'archévêque* de Québec Anglais.' I walked into the church here for a moment, and I cannot help liking the Roman catholic custom of leaving their churches always open, the sanctuary at all times accessible. I also think their arrangement of the interior in one respect infinitely better than ours (according to our received custom rather than our rule), namely, that the chancel is very large, and the whole service is performed within the rails, instead of boxing up the clergyman in a tub-like enclosure, down among the congregation, and obstructing their view of the solemn offices performed at the communion-table. The pulpit is always, and properly, among the people. It is mere prejudice, and hurtful prejudice, to think that because the Roman catholic religion is decidedly corrupt and superstitious in doctrine and worship, therefore there can be no usage among them which is preferable to the corresponding usage among ourselves. I wish, indeed, that the observations could not be extended to points of more importance, but with respect to discipline in the

Church for the preservation of purity and order, they are better off than we are. Their discipline is imperfect and mixed with many things that are objectionable; our discipline at present can hardly be said to exist. I saw one thing, however, in this church which (I do not speak of the evidences of a superstitious and erring worship, which are matters of course) was very offensive, a row of spitting-boxes on each side within the chancel, for the use of the priest and his associates in the service. I thought it bad enough to see this in the Legislative Hall at Albany, but I never expected to see it in the House of God * * *. At Vaudrueuil I began the Sunday by a visit to the bedside of my hostess, who is in ill health. She was born of English parents, but brought up from the age of six years in the house where she now lives, and has reached sixty-five without any ministrations of Protestant clergy nearer than Montreal, till within the last year or two. She seems, however, to have read her Bible with regularity, and the Bible and prayer do a great deal to establish and preserve our intercourse with Heaven. I heard, in the course of this journey, of an old German settler, who lived in the woods ten miles from any other human habitation, and without any other inmate of his dwelling. A person happening to be at his house expressed some wonder at his choosing to live in so forlorn and unprotected a state. ' I have plenty of company,' he replied, ' and am taken very good care of,' and he then pulled out a German Bible, saying, ' there is my company, and there I find the promise of protection.' The school-house where I officiated was crowded, and is very insufficient for the congregation, who were chiefly Englishmen and church-people, and who sang three times, not without an appearance of devotion. I took occasion in preaching to advert to their own situation, and to recommend their making exertions for the erection of a church, and afterwards addressed the heads of families in a more familiar way on the same subject. I was obliged to stand at one side in the desk on account of a beam in the centre with which my head interfered. The epistle of the day (Sexagesima) is strikingly calculated to put us to the blush, if ever, for a moment, we are disposed to murmur or become impatient at the fatigues and inconveniences to which we may be subjected in the discharge of our itinerant labours. I could not get off again from Vaudrueuil before three o'clock. It was necessary that I should leave it on the Sunday, in order to effect the objects which I had in view in the time remaining at my disposal. I intended, indeed, to reach Chateauguay in the evening. But the drift, which still continued though the day was clear and bright, had so choked up the roads, that when we came to the Isle Perrault, the driver said it was hopeless to attempt crossing Lake St. Louis, and we drove to the Cascades, and put up at the stage-house, kept by a Highlander, and, apparently, a stiff sort of presbyterian. I introduced, however, a proposal, to which he acceded, for turning the Sunday evening to some improving account; and as there is no Protestant worship within reach, and there were eight or nine persons assembled, I rather lengthened the offices which I performed, reading and then expounding, and concluding with prayer. I thought the man of the house seemed to relax sensibly after this from a kind of repulsive manner which characterized him before. I had ordered my driver to be at the door at half-past five on Monday morning, but he was nearly an hour after his time, and the sun rose upon the earth in her mantle of snow, as we descended upon the ice to cross the mouth of the Ottawa to Isle Perrault, and lit up a golden blaze in the windows on the island's edge. * * * My business at Chateauguay was to meet Mr. Forest, a licensed catechist and lay-reader, and his report was such that I never more forcibly felt (what indeed I have had abundant reason to feel on this journey) that our case is, in this diocese, that the harvest 'is plenteous and the labourers are few,' and that we ought to pray earnestly to ' the Lord of the harvest that He will send forth labourers into His harvest.' He gave me a regular return of children requiring baptism, and candidates for confirmation and the Lord's Supper. There are forty-five unbaptized children of the Church of England in Ormstown alone. I regretted excessively that it was wholly out of my power to attend personally to these crying wants: it was indeed by a mere chance, if I may so express it, that I was able to take a visit to Chateauguay, which formed no part of my original plan nor of my instructions from the Bishop, into my circuit at all. I baptized three children there, and have since made arrangements with Mr. Bethune for devoting the time between two Sundays, next week or the week after, to this tract of country. * * * Mr. —— is very ill, and could not meet me at Montreal, so I have come to see him. I fear his sorrow is preying upon his constitution, and it will be a great consolation to me if I can pour oil into his wounds. He does not want to be guided by me, but ' as ointment and perfume rejoice the heart, so doth the sweetness of a man's friend,' and ' a word spoken in season, how good is it!' A little encouragement and a few soothing words from a brother in the ministry may possibly serve to cheer him. * * * On Wednesday morning I purpose to take the stage, which, if all go well, will bring me home on Thursday. Pray tell Mr. Brown* that I shall be glad to be with him again, and to ease his shoulder from part of the burden."

---

* Assistant minister at Quebec.

CHAPTER X.

New scenes of trial were before the Archdeacon in the memorable year which we have now reached. I have already given
an extract from one of his letters* in which he spoke.of its
being better than following even the highest bent of natural
inclination and taste " to stand, as it were, between the living
and the dead, and stay the plague of sin or suffering, and to
carry the consolations of religion into hospitals and the foul
and crowded lodgings of the poor." In this year he literally
stood between the dead and the living while carrying his
ministrations to his plague-stricken flock, augmented by a
large and continuous stream of immigration. Full well he
gave proof that those words had been no empty sound, but
expressed the full and deep conviction of his heart, for never
did his devotion to God and his fellow-creatures shine more
conspicuously than in the times of pestilence. With the
exception of the congregation of Trinity chapel, the whole
parish was still in the hands of the rector and his assistant
who lived in his house. The cholera broke out at Quebec
early in the summer of 1832.† and by the end of July it was

---

* See page 71.

† Its approach had been looked for, in consequence of the ravages it had
committed in other parts of the world. In a circular drawn up for the
Bishop by the Archdeacon on the 10th April, 1832, to accompany a proclamation of the Governor for the appointment of a fast, it is carefully pointed

estimated that one-tenth of the population, which at this time numbered twenty-eight thousand, had been carried off. The number of deaths, however, included those of immigrants and sailors. The number of interments by the clergy of the Church of England in 1831 had been three hundred and eighty-two. In 1832 it was not far short of that number in the month of June alone; and in the whole year it amounted to nine hundred and seventy-five, the number of resident church-people being rather under five thousand. The proportion of deaths, therefore, among them was as two to one in that among the whole population; and when it is remembered that many persons who demanded the services of the clergy recovered, it will be seen that their duties were sufficiently arduous. On two consecutive days in June upwards of seventy persons were buried by the rector, but he noted it as probable that in the distracting confusion which then prevailed, the bodies of persons who did not belong to the Church of England may have been sent from the hospital to be buried by him. I take these particulars and those which follow from the appendix* to a sermon preached on the last Sunday in 1832. He does not mention, however, what I well remember, that a horse was kept saddled day and night in his stable to enable him or his assistant to meet calls from a distance; their rule was to take night calls alternately, but on many nights they were both out, and for whole days together unable to return home. " Never can the scene be forgotten by those who witnessed it which was exhibited in the dusk of one evening at the emigrant hospital, before the forced exertions of some members and agents of the board of health

___

out that this observance should not be regarded as a matter of form, but that while " private discretion might be exercised as to the manner and degree of abstinence, it certainly ought to be understood as forming a subsidiary part of the humiliation enjoined."

* "Id quoque quod vivam munus habere Dei," is prefixed as a motto to this appendix.

had provided another building in the Lower Town, exclusively
for the reception of cholera patients. A house opposite the
hospital had been engaged to afford additional accommodation, but the unfortunate subjects for admission came pouring
in before any arrangements at all sufficient could be completed; and the desertion, in one afternoon, of part of the
servants who had been hired, rendered the attendance, before
most inadequate, so miserably inefficient, that the passages
and floors were strewed with dying persons, writhing under
wants to which it was impossible to minister, some of whom,
I believe, actually died before they could be got to a bed.
The health commissioners, the head of the medical staff, and
the first medical practitioners of the city were upon the spot
together, and doing all they could; but how could their skill
or judgment meet all the exigencies of such a moment?
Women were met at the doors bewailing their affliction, who
had come too late to take a last look at their husbands while
alive; parents or children were surrounding the death-beds
of those most dear to them; patients were, some clamouring
in vain for assistance, some moaning in the extremity of languor, some shrieking or shouting under the sharp action of
the cramps; friends of the sufferers were contending angrily
with the bewildered assistants; a voice of authority was
occasionally heard enforcing needful directions, but quickly
required in some other quarter of the establishment; a voice
of prayer was also heard, and the words interchanged between
the dying and their pastors were mingled with the confused
tumult of the hour. The clergy, in passing through some
quarters of the town, were assailed sometimes by importunate
competitors for their services; persons rushing out of the
doors or calling to them from windows, to implore their
attendance upon their respective friends, and each insisting
upon the more imperative urgency of the case which he
pleaded. I have no reserve whatever in mentioning my own
share in these occurrences, because to suppose that the

clergy are entitled to any extraordinary credit for not flinching from their plain and proper duty in such cases seems to involve a supposition, that men whose whole employment relates to the business of preparation for eternity, and who preach Christ as ' the Resurrection and the Life,' are less expected to be armed against the fear of death than all the other persons who are engaged in visiting and tending the sick, and performing the various offices successively required after death. There is, indeed, a canon which directs the clergy to visit their parishioners in sickness, if it be not known or probably suspected to be infectious; but the rubric of the prayer-book was framed in better days, which provides for the case where none of the parish or neighbours can be gotten to communicate with the sick in their houses for fear of the infection, and assumes it as a matter of course that their minister will visit them under such circumstances."

The appendix concludes with the following characteristic passage: " It was a remark that I often made during the continuance of the cholera, how little the face of nature betrayed the sadness of the time, or shewed any symptoms of that principle of death which was in such fearful activity among the delegated lords of the creation. I was particularly impressed with this kind of feeling upon some of the lovely summer evenings on which I officiated at the new burial-ground, then still unenclosed. The open green, skirted by the remains of a tall avenue of trees, and contiguous to the serpentine windings of the River St. Charles, beyond which you looked across meadows, woods, and fields dotted with rural habitations, to the mountains which bound the prospect, the whole gleaming in the exquisite and varied lights of a Canadian sunset, formed altogether a beautiful and peaceful landscape, and seemed ' a fit haunt of gods.' How melancholy and striking the contrast with all that had been deposited, and which it remained to deposit in the spot on which I stood! How full of deep reflection upon the ravages of sin! How coupled

with deep thankfulness to Him Who came to repair those
ravages in the end, and to ' make all things new.' "

These scenes of suffering were ordained to give occasion for
the exercise of true christian charity. Besides that which
was exhibited in attendance on the dying and the dead, the
case of the widow and the orphan called for sympathy and
exertion. A society was formed in Quebec to provide for
their wants, and the sum of £2750 raised. Many orphans
were adopted, and among the French Canadians in the suburb
of St. Roch, where the disease raged with great violence,
every individual orphan belonging to Roman Catholics was
thus disposed of. The number of inmates of the Church of
England Orphan Asylum was doubled, and the same head
and heart* which had conceived the idea of its establishment
now set on foot a similar institution for boys.

In an address to the members of the cathedral congregation, issued in November 1832, at the request of the wardens
and members of the select vestry, (a body of twelve persons
whom, about this time, at the rector's suggestion, it had
become customary to elect at Easter to assist the wardens in
the discharge of their duties) which is headed with the first
two verses of i. Corinthians xvi, it was announced that
weekly instead of fortnightly collections, beginning on the
approaching Advent Sunday, would be made for the poor, in
consequence of the increased demands created by the visita-

---

* In a letter written at this time from Montreal, it is mentioned that one
of the cathedral churchwardens, a man of extraordinary energy and un-
sparing self-sacrifice in times of emergency, in driving him down to the
steamer from the Bishop's house at Quebec, had said of the person here
referred to, that she was " a wonderful woman, and that he was more
convinced of it every day ; and if she took the male orphan asylum in
hand, it would go right, for she always saw things in a right point of
view." When the cholera revisited Quebec in 1834, it broke out in the
absence of the Archdeacon, and Mrs. Mountain, though there was illness
among her own children, left them at a distance of four or five miles, to
attend upon orphans in the asylum who were seized with it.

tion of cholera. The following extracts may be interesting as exhibiting some details of parochial history of which it may be desirable to preserve the record. " The collections in this church were originally made once a month upon each occasion of administering the sacrament. It is now exactly ten years since, in consequence of the increase in the numbers of the poor, an additional collection in the month was established,* one half of which was applied to the relief of their temporal wants, and the other towards the supply of their spiritual necessities, by providing for the expenses of lighting and warming a temporary kind of chapel for an evening service. Upon the alteration of this building in the beginning of 1828, to convert it into the regular chapel now known as St. Matthews, or the free chapel, a weekly collection was established in the chapel itself, to provide for its own current expenses ; and from that time the whole of the two half-monthly collections in the cathedral was made available for the temporal relief of the poor and some other parish expenses. Thus the necessities of the parish have, in two former instances, prompted measures for the augmentation of this fund. It must be unnecessary to point out that the immense yearly influx of emigrants, while, in one point of view, it advances the improvement and prosperity of the country, causes at the same time a constantly progressing accumulation of pauperism in this city. The Emigrants' Society, to which the community is much indebted in different ways, can of course relieve only the fresh emigrants of each year in succession. And when the Beneficent Society, instituted for the relief of sufferers by the late awful visitation, shall close its operations in the spring, the Church of England list of persons who are subjects of its bounty, comprising between thirty and forty widows, and upwards of sixty young children, will be trans-

---

* The annual circuit of the churchwardens from house to house was, however, previously discontinued.

ferred to the parish. * * * The management of the expenditure, which embraces all these six objects, is becoming more and more an extensive and complicated concern, and it is anxiously desired that the congregation should be aware of the pains which are taken to conduct it. * * * The labour having been too great for the unaided efforts of the clergy and churchwarden in charge of the poor-fund, the members of the select vestry have undertaken to hold sittings in rotation, accompanied always by one of the clergy or the churchwarden, every Tuesday and Friday, from nine to ten o'clock, to conduct and control this whole expenditure, and to receive and dispose of all fresh applications for relief."

The disease had so far abated by the middle of August, that the Bishop held a visitation of the clergy at Montreal, which had been fixed for an earlier day. The Archdeacon preached the sermon on this occasion, which was published. The few days spent there afforded no relaxation, though they occasioned some variety in his labours ; those, indeed, of the offices of Archdeacon and chaplain must have unavoidably fallen into arrear. He speaks of having scarcely left the hotel except to go to church. "The memorial from the Clergy Reserve corporation, the task of putting matters in train for getting the Sunday School Society in the diocese under weigh ; the business to be done with the professors, etc., of McGill College ; various matters to be attended to with various clergymen, and others to be disposed of with the Bishop before our long separation, altogether fill my hands completely." Before leaving Quebec, he had drawn up a short and very hurried memorandum of his wishes respecting his family and flock, respectfully representing to the Bishop what he conceived to be the best arrangements for the parish, in the event of his own removal. In the beginning of this paper are these words : " Commending my soul to Him in humble hope of forgiveness and acceptance through Christ, I commend to Him also the best and most exemplary of wives and mothers, my incomparable help-mate in private affairs, training of my children, and the works of my calling in which she could aid me. Words cannot speak her value;" and it concludes thus: " And, indeed, every clergyman who has anything to do with the parish ought to be content to deny himself hourly and take up his cross. ' None of us liveth to himself' ought to be unceasingly before his eyes. And none of us dieth to himself. If I die, I trust I die to the Lord. I am a poor sinner,—more in number are my sins than the hairs of my head, but I believe in Him Who is able to save."

The year 1833 was not remarkable for any occurrences of unusual interest, and I have no record of any journeys then undertaken. The extraordinary labours of the preceding year may have caused some addition, by way of arrears, to ordinary parochial duties, his devotion to which, during the summer of 1833,* was such that he was scarcely ever able to go to see his children, whom he had sent for that season into the country about four miles from town.

In 1834 he was engaged in a circuit among the destitute church-people on the Chateauguay river, (mentioned at pages 156-7) when the cholera reappeared at Quebec, though its ravages were mercifully confined within comparatively small limits. In the course of this journey he preached at the opening of a new church at Ormstown, which was crowded to excess. On another Sunday he preached and administered both Sacraments in the threshing-floor of a large empty barn, three miles from Huntingdon. The whole interior of the barn was filled, and a large number of persons stood abroad in front of the open doors. In the afternoon of the same day he preached and administered baptism in a small school-house at Hunting-

* In a letter from the Bishop, dated York, 29th April, 1833, his lordship says, "I think you are apt, in your zeal, to propose for the clergy, especially at Quebec, and for yourself, too much work."

don, where the people were jammed together in an oppressive
degree, and there were also auditors on the outside of the
windows.

The time was now approaching when the office of Archdeacon was to be held in conjunction with that of a Bishop
in the Church of God.   This part of the memoir may be fitly
closed with an extract from a letter, on a copy of which,
made by his desire, Bishop Stewart has written " Archdeacon's warning and exhortation to an unprofitable clergyman,"
and another from a correspondence in which he engaged
in 1833 and 1834 with a member of his flock, who, having
imbibed some predilection for Methodism, thought it his duty
to endeavour to correct the teaching of his pastor.   I give
these extracts, as illustrating the manner and spirit in which
his duties as Archdeacon and rector were discharged.   The
correspondence just mentioned is very long, and affords an
example of the patience with which he endeavoured to remove
the offences of even unreasonable men.*

"The charge of the flock of Christ is at all times a serious, an awful
charge, and if ever there were circumstances which could heighten the
responsibility attached to it, and call for a more than ordinary devotedness
and circumspection, the circumstances of the Church of England, at this
juncture, in the Canadas are such.   If there are ministers among us of
whom it cannot be said that they have fed the flock ' with a faithful
and true heart and ruled them prudently with all' their power, such
ministers are not simply unprofitable, they are injuring the cause, and sadly
exemplify the maxim that ' he that gathereth not with Me scattereth.'   I
fear, my dear sir, I greatly fear, that this description will apply too closely
to you.   I shall be sorry if I offend you, and I am too sensible of my own
deficiencies to desire to use any harshness which is uncalled for; but there
is so much at stake that I must waive apologies for the freedom with which
I write, and must only hope that I may be an instrument to open your eyes

---

* The names of the clergyman and objector do not appear.   In another
instance the signature has been torn from a letter of humble acknowledgment of sympathy and direction in difficulties, apparently because it referred to family occurrences of which it would not be desirable to preserve
the record.

to the condition of the charge committed to your hands, and to rouse you, ere it be too late, to effectual exertion, in which case you will acknowledge me to be your truest friend. The neglected state of your parish, and the seeming unconcern with which you leave your hearers to be seduced into the Romish Communion form the theme of conversation far and wide. • • • • The great subject of complaint is a general remissness and indifference; a total absence of that zeal and lively concern for the eternal interests of the souls committed to you, which characterize the faithful minister of Christ; an omission of that pastoral care and attention, that personal intercourse of the spiritual guide with his flock, that solicitude for their happiness and their improvement, which constitute some of the essentials of an effective discharge of the ministerial duties. • • • Awake, then, as out of a dream, and address yourself to your high and holy task. Read over, I do beseech you, the charge given you in the service of the ordination of priests, and the promises which you then made before the God to Whom we must render account of our stewardship. Cast yourself before Him in humble prayer, and seek 'a new heart and a new spirit' in the performance of the work committed to you. O what happiness will you experience if He shall graciously enable you to recover the ground that has been lost! What blessedness will be yours if you once seriously and vigorously devote yourself to the promotion of His glory upon earth, and the task of 'turning the hearts of the disobedient to the wisdom of the just'! if you make it your business and delight to 'preach the word,' 'in season and out of season,' and to warn your flock 'from house to house' of the truths which concern their salvation; if you promote in families religious and devout habits, and bring individuals to the knowledge of God and Christ; if you become an instrument of bringing the careless sinner to that repentance of which one single instance causes 'joy in the presence of the angels of God.'"

The extracts which I shall make from the letters to his parishioner are chiefly such as exhibit his own views and feelings and the character of his teaching and labours. I omit what is designed directly to meet the errors of his correspondent:

• • • "Those religious opinions upon which I build my own hope of salvation, and teach my congregation to build theirs, have rather too deep and solid a foundation to be shaken by a letter. Years of thought and examination, of prayer to be rightly guided, and search in the Word of God; of study, snatched, indeed, at scanty moments of leisure, but mixed, for the very same reason, with extensive and diversified professional experience; years in which I have had very advantageous opportunities of obser-

vation as it respects both ministers and laity, have brought me to conclusions in which I do not rest as if my having formed them exalted me above
believers who may differ from me; but they are conclusions not lightly
embraced — conclusions in which I am more and more confirmed. I wish
that I had more leisure to enter at large with you upon the subject, that
I might entertain a hope of convincing you. But it is with extreme difficulty that I can command time to throw together a few observations which
must be infinitely short, in their effect, of what I feel that I could say upon
the subject. My archdeaconry and my parish, combined with some half-
dozen or more appointments in different institutions or public commissions,
which peculiar local reasons have made me think it my duty not to decline,
besides the leading part which it devolves upon me to take in several
voluntary associations of a religious or charitable kind, so press upon
me that I have to lament the insufficiency of my attention to some important objects; and yet I do not see how I can well withdraw from any
department of my occupations. I am glad to have the opportunity of
making this observation, because it may account not only for my executing
the task now before me in an imperfect manner, but for a seeming deficiency
which I have often deplored in my desire to cultivate a familiar intercourse
with my flock. I have, indeed, more anxieties and more harassing occupation to contend against than most people perhaps imagine; and although
I bless God that He has not suffered me to sink under them, I am prompted
at times to adopt the language of the apostle, where he declares that he
has 'great heaviness and continual sorrow in' his heart. Being at the
head of a parish comprising five thousand souls professedly of the Church
of England, to whom I should give, or cause to be given, 'their meat in
due season,' I find in one quarter 'things ready to die' which must be
strengthened; in another, Roman Catholics plying their engines of proselytism among my people; in another still, infidels and even atheists indus-
triously circulating their poison; in a fourth, sectarians insinuating the
seeds of division and of error; and to crown all, my own hearers charging
their pastor with want of fidelity or want of spiritual knowledge. Without are fightings, within are fears. But I am sustained by the comfort that
man is not my judge.

"If you have ever supposed that when I have lamented, as I apprehend
that every faithful minister of every flock will feelingly do, the comparatively poor return of those labours which are expended in seeking to 'turn
many to righteousness,'—if you have supposed, upon such occasions, that
I have wished to produce such fruits as are produced by Methodist preachers,
rather than such as it has pleased God to make me instrumental in effecting,
you have entirely misconceived me. I have not the slightest desire to
render my ministry remarkable by such incidents among my flock as often
figure well in newspapers and magazines. I do not mean to discredit the
pious exertions of men whom I may think in some points mistaken. But I

do mean that there never was a time yet in the Christian Church in which that remarkable prophecy 'the time will come when they will not endure sound doctrine, but after their own lusts shall heap to themselves teachers, having itching ears,' was so strikingly fulfilled as in the present day. I do mean that, with all the undeniable advantages and improvements of the age, it is characterized by a restless love of excitement in religion, a rage for publicity and display, a pruriency of appetite, a morbid fondness for stimulants, and a disrelish for sober and wholesome food, which have opened a wide door to religious empiricism, and through fear of man's censure or love of his praise, or the mere contagion of feelings and opinions, have borne with some vitiating influence upon the minds of many—both preachers and hearers,—who are not drawn to the extravagant lengths of others.

"Whatever failures I may have had to lament in my ministry, it has not, thank God, been without its encouragements. When I came to the parish the cathedral was our only place of worship. We have now three others, with growing congregations, and shall shortly, I trust, establish a fourth. An improved spirit of religion has certainly, I think, been engendered, and is advancing. Our communicants have greatly increased, while, at the same time, a careless participation has become less common. We have four Sunday-schools, all prospering. My congregation in the little chapel where I expound the Scriptures to the poor has been a source of much comfort to me. The place is crowded to excess, and the voice of the worshippers is raised devoutly in the praise of God. Several valuable charitable institutions have been established among us, in which a persevering spirit of love has been called into exercise. In many individual instances, I have had consolatory testimonies that my labours have not been wholly in vain. Among others, several young persons who have attended my Lent lectures, and who have by this and other means been prepared for confirmation, have, I have reason to believe, imbibed impressions beneficial to their souls. One in particular, on her death-bed, made acknowledgments to this effect. The Rev. ———, whose preaching you admire, declares that he was first brought to a concern for his salvation through my means.* Many

---

* I have a letter from a gentleman who many years ago held a responsible office under the Crown in Canada, dated in 1854, in which, referring to the Songs of the Wilderness, the following passage occurs: "Independently of all partiality of affection, it would have been impossible for me not to be deeply interested in your tour, and delighted by your poems. The truthfulness and evidently heartfelt piety which pervade the whole production are of themselves sufficient to awaken corresponding feelings in all who read them. And it would have been strange if I, who owe my first awakening to a sense of religion to your friendly suggestions, were blind or indifferent to works sent forth to the world with the same object towards the benighted.'

M

persons have privately consulted me or unburthened their grief to me in a
way which has convinced me that numbers of those who are never talked
of as religious persons, but quietly and unobtrusively discharge their blame-
less part in life, have a deeper feeling of religion, and a more influential
faith in Christ than their fellow-creatures have ever given them credit for.
• • • There are thousands who never experienced certain precise symptoms,—perhaps never heard of them,—who have been truly born again, and
perfectly know the reality of the thing,—perfectly understand from the
history of their own hearts the significancy of the expression. They have
discerned their lost estate, repented of their sins, believed to the saving of
the soul, received the seed of the Word into ' an honest and good heart,' and
brought forth ' fruit with patience.' They ' perceive within themselves the
workings of the Spirit of God,' because they find that that grace for which
they have prayed has made them altered beings,—beings different from what
they would have been by nature ; and although humbly conscious of infirmity, they go on their way rejoicing, as they find their faith still gaining
strength, their steadfastness confirmed, their love to God and man increased,
their conformity to the will of God in inward affection and outward action
growing closer and closer, their discernment of spiritual things clearer and
clearer, their hope of heaven more bright, their application of the saving
power of the Cross more home-felt and consoling, and their attachment to
the world and the things of sense proportionably more faint.   •   •   •
For myself, I feel that, like my fellow-sinners whom I am appointed to
teach, I am as ' a brand plucked out of the burning.' I am sensible that my
sins ' are more in number than the hairs of my head '; yet, little cause as I
have to exalt myself, let those who tell me that I am not faithful and full
in delivering the message of my Master judge as they please,—I stand or
fall to Him. And when I look to Him I am most confirmed in the views
which I entertain. The fear of man's censure, the love of his praise, the
torrent of the accidentally prevailing fashion in religion, the noise of popular proceedings, might sway me in another way. But I can truly say that
I never felt more attachment to the principles which I have embraced, or
saw more cause to confide in them, than when they were brought to the
test of the late awful and appalling visitation; when I was morning, noon,
and night among the dying, and with so many ghastly pictures of death
before my eyes, could not fail to have the consideration of my own brought
home to my breast, and to feel myself standing, as it were, upon the very
verge of the world unseen.   •   •   •   The necessity of the renewal of the
heart, of the change to be produced in the natural man, of the conviction
of sin to be wrought by the influence of the Spirit, of the operation of the
same power to enlighten the understanding in divine truth, and to strengthen
the feebleness of nature against temptation,—the necessity of all this, and
of faith in Jesus Christ, in order to pardon and peace with God and comfortable sense of His favour,—these have been the constant subjects of my

preaching. * * * 'With me it is a very small thing that I should be
judged of you or of man's judgment,' so far as concerns my own self-love.
As it regards the effect of my ministry and the retention of those in the
unbroken communion of the Church whom I am set over in the Lord, I feel
very differently. * * * It has happened within the sphere of my own
experience that the most thoroughly devoted ministers, and most amiable
as well as steadfast private christians whom I have known, have entertained the views which I regard as orthodox.   I do not mean by this that
I profess to belong to any party, or implicitly to adhere to any set of men
and their particular opinions.   It would be the joy of my heart that no
distinctions should exist, and never do I bring them needlessly into view.
* * * I shall go down to my grave without having the stamp of approbation affixed to my proceedings by any set of men who can be called a
party in religion.   But oh! how little does it matter, if I am counted faithful in mine office, with all my sins and infirmities, by Him Who seeth in
secret, and can be instrumental, as I have the consolation of believing, in
saving souls by winning them to Christ! * * * I have, indeed, so
strong a dislike to anything controversial, and it costs me so much pain to
advert to religious differences, that nothing but a sense of my duty as a
guardian of the truth of God would ever cause me to utter a polemical
expression; and I was very near leaving out the very passage in question
simply from my love of peace.   But this feeling was overborne by a conviction that the passage was calculated to do good."

The following is the passage (appended to the first letter)
to which exception was taken in the sermon :

"But the servants of God, let their crosses and trials be what they will,
enjoy a better portion.   They 'dwell in the secret place of the Most High.'
'The love of God is shed abroad in' their hearts, and 'the stranger intermed-
dleth not' with their joy.   The profligate and the worldling are alike aliens
from the peace with which they are blessed.   We do not here speak of
those direct assurances, those communications from God to the breast of
man made sensible at the very moment, which some believers are too fond
of representing as the evidences of a state of grace; things which may, in
some extraordinary cases, occur, but in which it is notorious that men may
dangerously delude themselves, and to make which the test of our spiritual
safety is inconsistent with the state of trial and probation in which we are
here placed.   They resemble what, in the departments of human sciences
are familiarly termed 'royal roads' of attainment; for the business of salvation lies in a very small compass, if God once for all speaks pardon to our
souls, and we are then secure.   Let us remember that, although we may
entertain a deeply-seated trust that 'He Who has begun a good work in' us
'will perform it until the day of Jesus Christ,' and treasure a blessed con-

fidence that nothing shall 'separate us from the love of God,' our posture should be always a posture of watchfulness, distrust of ourselves, and dependence upon divine grace; that we are to work out our 'own salvation with fear and trembling'; that our course is that of 'patient continuance in well-doing,' and 'patient waiting for Christ'; that he 'that thinketh he standeth' must 'take heed lest he fall,' and that 'happy is he,' in this sense, 'that feareth always.' But at the same time, without any enthusiastic views, and without incurring the same liability to self-deception, we claim for the faithful followers of Christ, in a safer and surer shape, all the genuine and unpretending benefit of that sacred declaration, that 'the Spirit of God beareth witness with our spirit, that we are the children of God.' 'He that believeth on the Son of God hath the witness in himself.' The humble and thankful self-appropriation of the promises of the Gospel; the comfort of casting our care upon God Who careth for us, and the burthen of sin upon Him Who has promised to give us rest; the sense of the healing power of the Gospel in our hearts; our perception of the hand of God in His providence over us, of the inspiration of His Word, of the happy effects of His heavenly influence upon ourselves; the growing conviction of 'the excellency of the knowledge of Christ Jesus'; the consciousness of cherishing a hope that 'maketh not ashamed'; the exercise of that temper which the Gospel inculcates and which the grace of God imparts; the clear anticipation of a state reserved for the faithful after the struggles of this weary life; a state in which all the clouds of sin and sorrow and ignorance shall be forever chased away,—these constitute an irresistible testimony that their source is from on high, and that we are the sons of God, adopted heirs of immortality through the reconciliation of 'the first-begotten from the dead.'"

In the year 1833 the Archdeacon established a Wednesday evening service, with sermon, in the cathedral. This was some years later transferred to Trinity chapel, where he still continued for a long time to take his share of the duty.

CHAPTER XI.

Voyage to England in 1835—Consecration as Bishop of Montreal—Death of his mother.

THE efforts of the Bishop of Quebec to obtain assistance in the duties of his office had been unrelaxed; and in 1834 a letter was addressed to his lordship by the Governor in Chief (Lord Aylmer) on this subject, in which the following passage occurs; " I can have no hesitation whatever in stating my conviction that should such an appointment (of a suffragan Bishop) receive the sanction of H. M. Government, the selection of the Archdeacon of Quebec would be hailed with satisfaction by the whole of the protestant inhabitants of Lower Canada; and it affords me much gratification to be furnished with this opportunity of expressing the very high sense entertained by myself of the Archdeacon's eminent qualities." Finding it impossible to bring the matter to a satisfactory termination by correspondence, the Bishop in the following year prevailed upon the Archdeacon to visit England for this and other purposes. The maintenance of the clergy had become a matter of serious anxiety, in consequence of the withdrawal of the parliamentary grant from the S. P. G., whose resources were so much crippled that it became necessary to reduce the salaries of their missionaries, and to shut out any hope of increasing their number, though that of the members of the Church, particularly in Upper Canada, was receiving enormous accessions, year by year, from emigration. In order, as far as possible, to provide for their wants, a society had been organized at Quebec and Toronto for the propagation of the Gospel among destitute settlers and Indians, a branch of which was afterwards established at Montreal. Each branch maintained a travelling missionary, in whose duties in the Quebec district the charge of the quarantine station in summer was included.

The Archdeacon was furnished with a letter of general introduction from the Bishop to persons in public authority in England, in which his lordship said ; " The present state of my health and the pressure of business upon my hands, which in such a state I find excessive, rendering me desirous of avoiding any unnecessary writing, * * * I wish it to be known that he has my confidence, and that I commit it to him, in concert with the friends of the Church at home, to pursue all such measures as shall be judged advisable either with reference to H. M. Government, to religious societies, or to the British public. I commend him, therefore, and his endeavours to the blessing of God above, and to the prayers and co-operation of Christian friends." In a letter written about this time, the Bishop speaks thus ; " Your great kindness and partiality to me, and usefulness to the Church bind me in ties of obligation and affection for you more strong than for any other person almost. My prayers for you are very sincere and constant. God bless you ! Believe me always yours faithfully and affectionately, C. J. QUEBEC."

The Archdeacon left Quebec with his family on the 10th August, 1835. His parishioners presented him with an address on this occasion, which was no empty form, for I well remember the eagerness with which the congregation of St. Matthew's chapel affixed their names to it one Sunday evening. With reference to the chief object of his mission, the success of which he conceived to lie at the foundation of all the rest, he entertained, to the last, the hope that some English clergyman of experience and ability might be found willing to accept the office of suffragan. A difficulty, however, which proved to be insuperable, presented itself in the uncertainty of the pecuniary provision to be made, for the Bishop's offer of one-third of his own salary was necessarily limited to his life, and there was no hope of any renewal of the parliamentary vote. The Bishop, in the meantime, continued to urge his own acceptance of the appointment as the only arrangement which would be satisfactory to himself, unless, failing this, he could induce any one of three or four English clergymen whom he named, to take it. On the 14th November, 1835, his lordship wrote from Quebec, "I am sensible that it is my duty to spare no pains to accomplish the appointment of a suffragan to assist me in this see with as little delay as possible, and that I should urge, as far as I reasonably can, your soliciting the appointment for yourself. * * * I am disposed to refrain from positively recommending any one except yourself and Dr. D.;" and on the 12th December, to his own brother (who rendered essential service in the affair), "Your letter received to-day is very acceptable. As Mr. Stephen, Lord Glenelg, and Sir G. Grey are quite well-disposed with regard to a suffragan, I trust that Almighty God is about to will and to order the accomplishment of the work. * * * Is it not a good time for making an arrangement for providing a Bishop in Upper Canada and one also in Lower Canada?* I heartily wish that Dr. Mountain may concur in this plan, that I may be appointed to Upper Canada, but God's will be done! * * * I think the Archdeacon is so well fitted to be Bishop of this Lower province, that I earnestly hope that, D. V., a permanent provision may be made for it." The result of the negociations with the Colonial Office (all the authorities of which gave their attention,

---

* This was found impracticable until, three or four years later, the present Bishop of Toronto consented to take the office without salary.

with very marked kindness, to the subject) appears in a correspondence between them and Dr. Mountain, which was printed for the information of the clergy of Lower Canada. The Archdeacon was induced, by the advice of the Archbishop of Canterbury, the Bishop of London, and different friends, no longer to withhold his consent, which was urged upon him by Lord Glenelg in the following terms : " I can hold out no secular inducement to any one to assume the labour and responsibility necessarily attached to such an office. I am aware that when it was proposed to me that a suffragan Bishop should be appointed with a permanent salary, you expressed an unwillingness to accept the appointment, although the Bishop of Quebec was most desirous that you should be selected for this station. Sensible, however, as I am of the disinterested anxiety which you have evinced to promote the welfare of the Church in Canada, I am encouraged to hope that, under the circumstances which I have stated, you will not refuse your personal assistance towards carrying into effect the arrangement in question. If upon consideration you should feel yourself able to accede to this proposal, I shall have much pleasure, with the concurrence of the Archbishop of Canterbury, in sanctioning the appointment, and in submitting your name to His Majesty as suffragan Bishop of Quebec. I cannot doubt that much benefit will accrue to the interests of the Church in North America from the zealous and efficient discharge of the duties which will devolve upon you in that character." On the 30th December, the Archdeacon wrote to inform the Bishop that he had yielded to his wishes, adding, " It is just possible, however, that a person may yet be found, who, having an independent fortune, and being in all respects eligible, may be substituted for myself. * * * I am sure I shall have your special prayers, if I am to be called to a more arduous post in your diocese." In the next letter, four days later, he says, " I am thankful to have executed the arrangements respecting the suffragan in a way accordant with the wishes which you express, although it is not a very encouraging prospect. * * * Still I feel satisfied that, unworthy though I am, the path of duty is marked out for me. * * * I esteem it a matter of great thankfulness (this is on the 3rd February, 1836,) that I shall be associated with such a person as your lordship, whom as a Christian Bishop I unfeignedly and deeply revere, and to whom as a friend uniformly kind I am strongly attached. God grant me increased wisdom, humility, devotedness, and love to Himself and to my fellow-creatures in the more elevated and arduous post to which I am called! When the clergy hold their next meeting, request them all to remember me in their private prayers, with a special reference to the task which now opens before me. I sometimes feel discouraged and depressed, especially when I first wake in the morning; but I trust God will strengthen me, since it appears to be the will of His Providence that I should hold the office, for circumstances have conspired in a manner scarcely to leave me the option. I rejoice to think of the unity of sentiment which prevails between us, and although infinitely behind you in the race of godliness, I trust that I shall be found pursuing the same track, upholding in a consistent manner the interests of the episcopal Church of England, but always identifying them with the advancement of the kingdom of Christ, and regarding all maintenance of the claims of the Church as in subordination to her efficiency in promoting the genuine influence of the Gospel. When I look back upon the way that I have measured, I cannot but deplore my own unworthiness; but the greater it is, so much greater is the mercy which has called me to the office of pastor, and finally to that of Bishop in the Church of God; and I hope that my sense of this mercy will be an additional incentive to my devoting myself to the work assigned to me."

The Bishop replied, " I am inexpressibly obliged to you for your kindness in consenting to accept the appointment."

The consecration took place in the chapel of Lambeth Palace, on Sunday, 14th February, 1836, at the same time with that of Dr. Broughton, the first Bishop of Australia. The Archbishop was assisted by the Bishops of London, Winchester, and Gloucester. The preacher, the Rev. Dr. Molesworth, referred to the persons to be consecrated in the following terms:

"I have ample grounds of assurance that they are not persons who would lightly or unprepared encounter such a fearful responsibility. In the individual who is to be consecrated to the diocese of Montreal, we have one who has been long tried in all the duties of the ministry, and whose usefulness is placed on honourable record in the proceedings of our Church societies. He has had also to prove his devotion to the cause of his Master, as St. Paul did, 'in journeyings often, in perils of waters, in hunger and thirst, in cold,' and in those privations and hardships which the climate and the difficulties of the country have compelled him to encounter, and which he has encountered as one conscious of the service in which they were required."

The day after his consecration, his friend and former tutor, the Rev. J. K. Miller,* wrote to his elder brother:

"Your letter arrived yesterday evening, the day, it seems, appointed for George's consecration with his brother Archdeacon, now Bishop of Australasia. May all blessings from above attend him and both of them! As for the preferment or prelacy, I regard it much in the same light that you do. Congratulations would be—I was going to say—quite out of place; but at least they must have been steeped in pensive lookings-out, and certainly cleared of all worldly and carnal views, before one would think of offering them. Having undergone that process, they may, perhaps, be suitably presented; and if you write to your brother before I do, perhaps you will be so kind as to express our feelings to him accordingly. After all the rest of our household had retired to rest, S. and I knelt down to repeat the prayers contained in the office of consecration in behalf of the two new Bishops, with such alterations and additions as the case required. We begged that our voice might be added to that of the congregation, and our prayer not cast out, though we were distant, and 'small, and of no reputation,' and unworthy. And this petition, as made sincerely, I now repeat. And now congratulate me, if you please, on having a pupil a Bishop. Of

---

* See page 18.

such a Bishop I may indeed justly be proud. But how strange it seems! I dare say you participate in a great many of the indescribable feelings which crowd upon my mind at this development of time and Providence."

I cannot withhold an extract from a touching note addressed to him on the day of the consecration by his youngest brother, accompanied with a ring on which was a mitre and his crest :

"MY DEAR LORD AND DEAREST BROTHER :

"This ring was thy father's, and is now thine by thy mother's command.

"Thou wilt not value it the less because it has been nearly eleven years in my keeping, during the last four of which I have constantly worn it. * * * May the Lord God of our fathers bless thee ; may He fill full the measure of thy earthly prosperity ; may He reserve for thee that crown of happiness unspeakable which I, save through a miracle of His mercy for the sake of Christ Jesus our Saviour, may never hope to wear with thee."

There is a letter from his mother, dated 18th February, in which she says :

"My prayers were for you; my mind much with you. I am thankful to the Giver of all good Who has raised you to this responsible station, and assisted by His grace and Spirit I have no doubt but that you will endeavour to do your duty as you have in all situations. God will bless you, my own dear son, and reward you hereafter. May we all so conduct ourselves here as to hope to meet him who is gone before us in a blessed eternity! * * * The Archbishop told R—— he never laid hands on any one with more entire satisfaction, or looked with more confidence to the good such men would do. That you, my son, deserve such commendation fills my heart with thankfulness to Almighty God."

On this letter is written, " The last from thy hand, dear, honoured, sainted mother! God be praised Who gave me thee for a mother, and still bless the remembrance of thee to all thy children !"

It was on the 13th April that the mother whom all her children so deeply and so justly revered was taken from them. She had spent part of the winter at Southampton, to be near her son, the Archdeacon, who had a house there during his stay in England, and there her four sons (one from Canada

and another from India) met together for the first time for
upwards of five and twenty years. They met again at
Havant Rectory, to partake with her and one of their sisters,
for the last time, in the Holy Communion administered by the
Bishop, and to receive her parting blessing. On the 13th the
Bishop wrote to his own family :

"It is all over,—but, thank God, in a most blessed, blessed way. I
have lost the mother that bore me, that nursed me out of her bosom, that
tended me in helpless infancy and in many a weary hour of sickness by
night and by day, and that watched and prayed for all her children to the
last. • • • What suffering she has had in the last few days has served
only to leave an increased impression of her humble resignation. Yesterday she gathered us all round the bed, and, with joined hands and uplifted
eyes, prayed for us and blessed us,—a sweet prayer and memorable blessing,—and as we were leaving the room, she said, 'I have blessed you and
you shall be blessed.'"

Her children erected a monument to her in Havant church,
for which the Bishop wrote the following lines :

"Yes, thou art gone; thy children will not raise
The common notes of monumental praise:
What they have lost in thee, asks not for speech;
What thou hast found in Christ, words cannot reach."

I shall conclude this chapter with extracts from two letters
written with reference to this occasion. The first is from the
Bishop of Quebec. After mentioning that on hearing of Mrs.
Mountain's death he had called upon the only person then
bearing her name in Quebec, and prayed with her, he adds,
" I reflect with pleasure on the comfort and happiness I
derived from my acquaintance and intercourse with your
mother during many years." The letter ends with the words
" Pray for us frequently." The other is from the aged Dean
of Winchester, Dr. Rennell :

"Deeply as I lament the event of your excellent mother's decease, I cannot but feel some gratification in your lordship's thinking me worthy of a
communication of the sad tidings. Indeed you do me but justice in supposing that in every circumstance materially concerning your family I take

a sincere interest. Besides the veneration in which I, in common with all those to whom christianity is dear, hold your father's labours and exertions, the obligations I owe to him and his memory for the great kindness he shewed the orphan of the B—— family, and which has been so kindly continued by yourself, must leave a great debt of gratitude to you. Allow me to express my most sincere congratulations on your advancement to the episcopate, for which every requisite seems to meet in your character. Notwithstanding the boisterous storms and waves which seem to surround you in the quarter where your labours are to commence, yet the very dangers and conflicts are the high privileges of your calling, and you serve a Master Who will 'never leave or forsake you.' But I feel that I am guilty of much presumption in suggesting to so superior a mind thoughts that must have long occupied it."

CHAPTER XII.

ARCHDEACON MOUNTAIN was appointed to assist the Bishop
of Quebec, under the title of Bishop of Montreal. He had,
however, no separate jurisdiction, nor was any see erected
at Montreal, and he acted under a commission from Bishop
Stewart. The understanding between the Bishop of Quebec
and himself was that he should relieve him entirely of the
charge of Lower Canada, and render such assistance in that
of the Upper province as might become necessary. It was
also understood that on the occurrence of a vacancy he was
to assume the charge of the whole diocese.

During his stay in England, which lasted till the end of July
1836, he was constantly engaged in efforts for the advancement of the interests of the Church. He addressed the Colonial Office on the subject of the Clergy Reserves, with which
he had been specially charged ; but having been informed that
it had been comprehended in the instructions given to the
three Royal Commissioners who had then been recently sent
out to enquire into Canadian affairs, he thought it better to
leave it in the hands of the Bishop, to be brought before the
Commissioners at Quebec. With the societies for the Propagation of the Gospel and Promoting Christian knowledge he
was naturally in continual correspondence and intercourse.
But he was also much occupied with a new society which the
wants of Upper Canada had called into existence, and of

which the Earl of Galloway, nephew of the Bishop of Quebec, was the chief promoter.* In writing to the Bishop soon after his consecration, he says, "I have had the satisfaction, by attending the meetings at Lord Galloway's, and by correspondence with the secretary of the Upper Canada society, to get that vessel fairly launched, which before was only upon the stocks." He drafted its rules, and procured the adhesion to it of the Bishop of London. He also endeavoured to persuade the Rev. W. J. D. Waddilove, who had devoted himself with extraordinary energy to the cause of the Canadian Church, to take the same step. Mr. Waddilove had raised, by his own private exertions, a fund which was called, after the Bishop, (to whom he was related by marriage) the Stewart Mission Fund, and was the means of maintaining travelling missionaries in Upper Canada, as well as of affording some aid to Lower Canada, for many years. The Bishop of Montreal had a great objection to the unnecessary multiplication of societies and agencies, and ultimately succeeded in procuring the incorporation of the U. C. C. S. with the S. P. G. This venerable society had lately, notwithstanding its difficulties, increased its grant to the diocese of Quebec by £500 a year, by means of the sale of some of its capital; and the Bishop of Montreal, in consideration of the aid given to Upper Canada by the new society and Mr. Waddilove, put in a plea for Lower Canada in the distribution of this bounty, specially instancing the wants of the Chateauguay country, the Gore on the Ottawa, the county of Megantic, Kilkenny and Frampton. He addressed an appeal to the S. P. G. on behalf of the Canadian Church, which was published by that body, and in which all these places are particularly mentioned as affording striking examples of spiritual destitution. I extract what is said of Kilkenny:

* In a letter dated 2nd March, 1836, Lord Galloway expresses " the assurance how much gratification your consecration had given to myself and my friends * * * as a means of spiritual advantage to Canada."

"I have been assured that there are one hundred and twenty families in the township, and that they all belong to our own Church. I do not think that any of our clergy have ever penetrated to this settlement; and I have no reason to doubt the melancholy truth of an account given to me, that the people, hearing of a protestant minister whom some circumstance had brought into the adjoining seigneurie, came trooping through the woods with their infants in their arms, to present them for baptism in the name of the Father, the Son, and the Holy Ghost, to one who was a preacher of the Unitarian persuasion."

The Bishop landed at Quebec on Sunday, the 11th September, 1836.* On the following Sunday, the letters patent appointing him Bishop of Montreal, and his commission from the Bishop of Quebec were read in the cathedral after the Nicene Creed. The health of Bishop Stewart had become so impaired that he was obliged to make arrangements for proceeding immediately to England, instead of spending the winter at Toronto, and thus the charge of the whole diocese devolved at once upon the Bishop of Montreal. Bishop Stewart never returned to Canada. Becoming more and more enfeebled, he at last sank in July, 1837. He was able to write once only, on the 6th December, to his coadjutor after his arrival in England, and on the back of the letter, the person to whom it was addressed wrote :—" The last which I ever expect from the hands of that worn-out servant of Christ. God grant me a measure of the same spirit which was given to him." In his correspondence with the S. P. G. he thus refers to the death of Bishop Stewart :—" His decease deprives the Church in Canada of one who was her boast and her blessing, and the clergy of a father and a friend. I have myself lost a personal friend who had long honoured me with the most intimate confidence, and I succeed for the present to his charge with much fear and trembling, having no hope of ever doing what he has done, and being destitute of many

---

* By a curious coincidence the present Metropolitan of Canada, then recently consecrated under the same title of Bishop of Montreal, reached that city on exactly the same day fourteen years afterwards.

advantages which he enjoyed; but at the same time, with the determination, by the help of God, to follow up whatever he had put in train to the utmost of my power. I may well be content to be one day worn out like him, if I am worn out in the same service."

The Bishop of Montreal had secured in England the assistance of the Rev. George Mackie, B.A., of Pembroke College, Cambridge, who accompanied him to Canada to relieve him of the greater part of his duties in the parish of Quebec, as well as to act as examining chaplain. He still took, however, his regular turn in preaching both in the cathedral and St. Matthew's chapel, and continued to do so at the former place as long as he lived, and at St. Matthew's till 1858,* besides bearing an active part in the management of parochial institutions and constantly visiting his parishioners, especially the sick and the afflicted. For many years he preached on every Saint's day, as well as catechized the children of the schools and the congregation on Wednesdays and Fridays in Lent. And he took a large share of all these duties as long as he lived. He made repeated efforts to procure the appointment of Mr. Mackie to the rectory, but the consent of the Government could not be obtained to this arrangement, except at the sacrifice of the grant for the

---

* In May 1838, the Bishop removed from the town of Quebec to Marchmont, where his father had spent the latter days of his life, about a mile and a half distant. He fitted up a building in the grounds as a temporary chapel, where he regularly performed service and preached on Sunday afternoons, besides superintending a Sunday-school which he formed there, without any interruption of his regular turns at the cathedral or St. Matthew's. These labours were continued during the three years of his residence at Marchmont, and the recollection of them still lives in the memory of many poor who benefited by them. The Sunday-school was kept up for some time afterwards through the exertions of the ladies of a family who succeeded him in the occupation of the house. On his return to Quebec, after leaving Marchmont, in 1841, he had a Bible-class of young men chiefly candidates for confirmation, in his own house, and on every occasion of confirmation in Quebec he prepared some candidates himself.

rector's salary, which it was not thought desirable, in the existing circumstances of the Church, to lose. Soon after his return to Quebec, the Bishop established a parochial lending library of religious and useful reading, and organized a district-visiting society, in behalf of which he issued an address. A few extracts from this address may serve to shew the principles on which he worked himself, and invited the co-operation of others. A Church of England clothing society was established at the same time.

"We all profess to be disciples of the Lord Jesus Christ; and professing this, we must acknowledge the authority which tells us that, 'if any man have not the spirit of Christ, he is none of His'; that in kind acts of lowly condescension He has given us an example that we should do to our brethren as He did to them whose feet He washed; that even in suffering, if necessary, for others, He left 'us an example that ye should follow His steps,' and has charged us Himself that, as He loved us, so ought we 'to love one another.' These are very plain declarations, and there is no escape from their force. We must confess that they indicate our positive duty, or we must renounce the Gospel.

"But is it so that any of us can wish to escape from their force? Is it so that we desire to avoid being followers of the Lamb of God? Do we really believe that He died upon the Cross to save our sinful souls, and shall we refuse to recognize for the rule of our own practice the maxim of scripture that 'the love of Christ constraineth us; because we thus judge, that if One died for all, then were all dead; and that He died for all that they which live should not henceforth live unto themselves, but unto Him Which died for them and rose again'? If we are truly touched with any sense of what that love was which Christ shewed for us, we shall surely be prompted to evidence our sense of it, and impelled by our own feelings to do whatever little we can for His sake. We can render no benefit to Him, and, when we have done all, are unprofitable servants, but He graciously says that what we do for the love of Him to one of the least of our brethren, we do it unto Himself. And we have just seen how His own example is proposed to us. What then was the general character of that example? What was the business of His life while upon the earth? He 'went about doing good and healing all that were oppressed of the devil.'

"A little time, therefore, a little trouble, a little self-denial, a little effort to surmount obstacles, a little perseverance in spite of disappointed labour, will not be thought too great a sacrifice when we can hope to promote His cause on earth. And if you are willing to make this sacrifice, you have good grounds for such a hope in bearing your part in the work of **this** society. In so doing you will go 'about doing good,' promoting the temporal and spiritual good of your fellow-sinners. The rules of the society are before you; the instructions for the visitors are in your hands. You have only faithfully to follow them, and you may be instrumental to the welfare of old and young around you. If you can make one poor family or one member of it more orderly, contented and comfortable, it is some reward of your labour. If you can suggest thoughts to one erring soul which may lead to repentance unto life, you will cause 'JOY IN THE PRESENCE OF THE ANGELS OF GOD.'

" And this exalted privilege you may humbly hope to enjoy. You cannot tell, you cannot calculate, the extent of good which you may be employed in the hands of God to effect. An affectionate interest manifested for the poor by those above them may of itself open their hearts to new views and hopes. A plain remonstrance may draw the negligent to the house of God to hear that Word which may prove to them the savour of life. A judicious and impressive tract left in their houses may awaken in them a concern for their own salvation. An enquiry respecting the catechism and the habit of prayer, or an invitation to the Sunday-school may produce benefits to their children which will cause them to be numbered among the children of God and to transmit to their children's children the inheritance of faith. A simple recommendation of the Bible may lead them to open it, and, opening it, to apply its saving truths. A very few words of friendly and christian advice or comfort may prove to be seed dropped in a happy moment and destined to spring up into everlasting life. 'A word spoken in due season how good is it. "

The Bishop's **first** ordination was held on the 28th October, 1836. The number of clergy in the diocese at the date of his **assumption of the charge** was eighty-five. Of these thirty-four were in Lower Canada, equally divided between the present dioceses of Quebec and Montreal.* The number

---

* At this date it may be interesting to **give the names of the** stations of the Lower Canada clergy. Besides five resident at Quebec, three at **Montreal,** and one travelling missionary, there were, in the district of Quebec, only one, at Leeds; in the district of Three Rivers, only two, the rectors of Three Rivers **and** Drummondville; in the district of St. Francis, four, at Melbourne, Lennoxville, Eaton and Hatley; in Gaspé, **two, at** Gaspé Basin and Carlisle; in the present diocese of Montreal, fifteen parishes and missions (of which one was served from the Upper Canada side of the Ottawa,) at Sorel, Abbottsford, Chambly, St.

of churches in Lower Canada was forty-two, and this also was equally divided between the present dioceses. The increase in the number of clergy in the whole of Canada during the ten years of Bishop Stewart's administration had been twenty-four.

As soon as the Bishop was fairly settled at Quebec, he began to make arrangements for visiting the parishes and missions of Lower Canada, and in November issued a circular to the clergy, appointing confirmations. He left Quebec on his first visitation-tour, immediately after morning service on the feast of the Epiphany, 1837, "after one of the most remarkable snow-storms which had occurred within the memory of man." On this account the journey began with disappointment. His first mark was Rivière du Loup en haut (the Bishop of Quebec having recently held a confirmation at Three Rivers) which he reached, by the most forced efforts, at noon on Sunday the 8th January. The missionary at Sorel, within whose charge this place was comprehended, had been prevented by the snow-storm from coming down to conclude the preparation of the candidates for confirmation during the previous week, and abstained from doing so on Sunday, thinking the Bishop's progress impossible. From Lake Maskinongé, where there were other candidates, prepared by a catechist, who were to have come to Rivière du Loup, there was no egress for fifteen days afterwards. "It was some consolation, however, (in the words of the journal addressed to the S. P. G., from which the following passages are taken) that I had it in my power to officiate to the few Protestants

Johns, Clarenceville, Frelighsburgh, Philipsburgh, Stanbridge, Dunham, Shefford, Rawdon, St. Andrews, Grenville, Hull, and Côteau du Lac. To these Chateauguay, Nicolet, Percé, and Frampton were added very shortly afterwards. In November 1836, having learned that the sum of £600 per annum was available from the Clergy Reserve Fund, the Bishop applied, but without success, to the Royal Commissioners for the establishment of new missions.

who were sufficiently near to be collected for afternoon ser
vice, and I preached to about twenty persons in the little stone
church, which had never been opened since the visit of the
Bishop of Quebec, about a year before. On the 10th January
I held my first confirmation. Twenty-two young persons were
confirmed at Sorel ; eight were prevented from attending. I
addressed a charge to them and afterwards preached, which
practice, having no chaplain with me, I followed as a matter
of course in all the remainder of my visitation * * *. The
church at Rawdon has been built by the exertions of the Rev.
C. P. Reid, who, by the Divine blessing, has overcome great
disadvantages under which he entered on his charge. It is
a very homely, though at the same time a decent, structure,
being built of squared logs, and not having arched windows,
but it has a steeple surmounted by a large cross.* * * Twenty-
seven were confirmed, and among them two whose faces were
very familiar to me, they having been educated at the Quebec
National School. * * * On Sunday the 15th, I admitted
to Priest's Orders at Montreal, a deacon who had come from
Upper Canada for the purpose. He was in sole charge, owing
to the absence of the missionary of the Mohawks on the Grand
River. * * * There is a great deficiency of church accommodation at Montreal, the parish church, although very large,
being alone quite insufficient. Mr. Bethune and Mr. Robertson
do their utmost to supply this deficiency, by a service which
they have established, by candle-light, in the national school-
house. It is well attended ; but two clergymen, with all their
exertions, cannot do all the duty which the Church would
require at Montreal, especially as one of them serves the
church at Lachine.* Mr. Bethune is endeavouring to put
matters in train for the erection of another place of worship
and the introduction of another minister, to be supported by
the pew-rents. * * * In bearing my part in the solemn

---

* The rector at this time was acting also as chaplain to the forces.

ceremony of **confirmation, I have** been more and more struck
as well with **its impressiveness as its** importance, and with the
obligation which lies **upon** the rulers and pastors of the Church,
to turn to all the happy account of which they are capable,
means which may at once be believed to afford an actual con-
veyance of grace to the recipients, and, by the blessing of
Heaven upon the ordinary train of causes and effects, to
guard the lambs of the flock against a fatal estrangement from
the great Shepherd of their souls, and retain them also within
the regular bounds of the fold. * * * **The Bishop of Quebec**
had established a rule that no person should be admitted to
confirmation under the age of fifteen ; but I was requested by
the clergyman at St. Andrew's to dispense with the rule in
favour of a female, who, although she had not attained that
age, had been for some time married. * * * **If the Board**
should find that there is no prospect of obtaining from Govern-
ment what I have pressed upon the attention of the Royal
Commissioners, I must only hope that, in their own solicitude
to relieve the spiritual destitution of Canada, they will feel
warranted in applying for the same object a portion of the
funds of the society, and look to an increase by the Divine
blessing in proportion to the compassion which they extend.
On my way down the Ottawa I saw, between nine and ten
o'clock at night, so glorious a spectacle that I regard it as a
privilege to have been permitted to behold it in my day upon
the earth.   It was a display of the Aurora Borealis which
was **seen all over the colony and in the adjoining States, and**
was so brilliant that the reddening reflection upon the snow
was everywhere supposed, upon the first aspect, to be caused
by some neighbouring building in a blaze.*   In the centre of
the arch of heaven there appeared a kind of radiating crown,

---

* At New York it was said that the fire-engines were got out. At Quebec,
where it was seen a few hours earlier than is here mentioned, the appearance was not unlike that which is described in " Life with the Esquimaux,
the narrative of **Captain Charles Francis Hall.**"

diverging from which were **broad dependent streamers of** which the skirts **reached nearly to the horizon, and which,** when I first saw **them, looked almost like an assemblage of** united rainbows **covering the whole face of the sky; but the** only colours which remained **after a time were a beautiful red,** and a **brilliant silvery kind of white, the latter forming, as it** were, a broad edging to each **streamer of the former hue.** Nothing to be compared **to this display of glory has been wit**nessed before in the **Canadas, within the memory of man.* * *** From some want of **precision in the notice respecting the con**firmation at Vaudrueuil, **a mistake arose, and on my arrival** there on the evening **of the 25th, I found that Mr. Leeds** had appointed a meeting **with the candidates at twelve** o'clock the **next day, which I had fixed for the confirmation.** Having made my arrangements **to proceed to Côteau du Lac in** the afternoon, **I sent round messages to desire their attendance at ten instead of twelve, and I occupied the two hours before** his arrival in examining **and instructing them myself. Punc**tually **at twelve he came into the school-house, and** after he had read prayers, I confirmed **twenty-five** persons, with the evidences of whose preparation I had been satisfied. **I took** up **my** quarters at the Côteau at the house **of an** American of **the** congregationalist persuasion, **but with no prejudice** against the Church, and **always desirous of the** assistance of her ministers who may happen **to be under the roof in** family devotion. In describing the footing occupied **by** the ministers of his own communion among their flocks, he told me that having engaged a preacher, they kept him as long as they pleased and quarrelled with him when they pleased.* * * In emerging from a wood, on the road to Huntingdon, into a clearing full of stumps, we were at a loss to pursue the right track, **and** drove up to a log hut, where, **by a** light through the window, I saw a mother reading the Bible to her children closing round her knees. She was rejoiced to see me, and, bringing out a lantern, walked in front of us for some distance through the snow, and set us in our right course. * * * At Ormstown I confirmed seventy-two persons, and the number would have been much larger had it not been for the inability of some of the candidates to meet me at this point: and I baptized ten children. I preached at Huntingdon, in a small edifice of squared logs, 'contrived a double debt to pay,' being constructed for holding the sessions of the magistrates, and adapted also for use as a school-room. I had thirty-nine communicants, baptized eleven children, and churched the mothers. The next day at a settlement called the Gore, in a school-house of squared logs, I preached, administered the Lord's Supper to thirty-two communicants, baptized eleven children, and churched the mothers. At Chateauguay I confirmed twenty-six persons (making in all ninety-eight on the Chateauguay river), baptized two children, and churched the mothers. Part of the service was chanted, and I fully believe that a spirit of devotion pervaded the assembly. * * * Dr. A—— having had a stove put up in the church at Laprairie, which had been long closed, I officiated to between fifty and sixty persons, and encouraged them to hope for the renewal of regular services in the spring. I afterwards baptized two children. * * * The smallness of the number confirmed at —— was partly, I believe, to be accounted for by the strict standard of the requisites for preparation established by Mr. ——; and even if it was too strict (which I am far from meaning to affirm that it was), the error was on the right side. The people themselves, however, in places where, as here, the American population predominates, are so far from being disposed to laxity upon this point, that, in my judgment, their notions are often hurtfully overstrained. Instead of regarding the ordinance as an aid to those who are in an early stage of the Christian life, and whose voluntary engagement the Church may in good hope receive, if they manifest a serious impression of its nature, can give a distinct account of their own faith in Christ as the Saviour of sinners, and the leading points of scriptural truth, and are known to be religiously correct in their deportment, the persons in question are apt to exact as a pre-requisite a degree of spiritual attainment to which I conceive that confirmation, rightly understood, is one of the commencing steps. The communications of Divine grace to the soul are supposed to be wholly independent of any such means ; and confirmation is rather admitted as a public declaration of having experienced religion, with a peculiar sense attached to those words, than recognized as a solemnity in which the preparation of the candidate, sealed by his own promise and crowned by the prayers and benediction of the Church, which draw down the blessing from on high, confirms him in seeking the way of life. Some may, in this way, be prompted to come forward who have mistaken a transient excitement for a true conversion: others are deterred from doing so by the very humility which is the best qualification for approaching God. Nothing surely can be more contrary than all this to the evident spirit of the Church in framing her ordinances. Yet after all, as I said before, the error of strictness is the better of the two. * * * A few miles brought us to Mr. Reid's parish. The house was pointed out to me from a distance, on the road, in which the Bishop of Quebec first lodged, and we passed the site of the school-house, now demolished, in which he began his preaching. These are among the cherished traditions of the neighbourhood, which has none beyond the memory of living man. * * * We stopped to bait at a log farm-house close to the church. The mistress of it was a daughter of ——, who gave the Bishop of Quebec 800 acres of land towards the church-building fund which his lordship was forming for the diocese. Her husband was lying on his back in a rude and homely bed, having, at the age of more than sixty years, suffered a severe fracture of the leg. The son who lives with them had, a year before, broken his arm, which remains awkwardly bent. The woman herself had been for a great number of years afflicted with incurable lameness, proceeding from some disorder and causing continual pain. As I sat and warmed myself over their fire upon a hearth of ill-assorted stones (for they had no stove, and scarcely any comforts about them) I got into conversation with her; and I might rather say, perhaps, that I had an opportunity of learning than of teaching, for, as far as I could form a judgment from her words, I found her, under the circumstances which I have described, not only resigned and contented, but thankful and, in a manner perfectly plain and unaffected, able to express her sense of that goodness which weans us by affliction from the world, and conforms us to the example of a suffering Lord. * * * Divine service was held in the school-house in the evening, and I preached to a good congregation. They brought their own candles, and as they walked home through the snow with lighted candles in their hands, they had very much the appearance of some procession. At Abbottsford the impressive and affecting ceremony of adult baptism was administered to four persons by Mr. Johnson, who was well satisfied with their state of preparation. Twenty-one were confirmed. The state of the roads was very unfavourable. Four young persons, however, belonging to the family of an Englishman, came the distance of sixteen miles. Mr. Johnson received them all into his own house, and kept them for the night.* I had proposed to preach in the evening at the school-house in Granby, an offer which was very gladly accepted; but upon its being afterwards recollected that a congregational minister had previously sent to make an appointment for the same purpose, I withdrew my proposal at once, to avoid the appearance of opposition. I found, however, what may appear sufficiently characteristic of the state of

---

* A similar instance of hospitality on the part of a clergyman is recorded elsewhere in this year, where upwards of twenty candidates for confirmation were received for the night into the parsonage.

things among newly-established settlements, that the people, by communication with this minister, had made arrangements for my officiating as soon as he should have closed, and he was so accommodating as to limit himself in point of time. I thought it best to acquiesce in this arrangement, and the minister himself remained with the other hearers. * * * The Rev. L. Doolittle has opened a school at Lennoxville, and such has been the accession of respectable families of late to his neighbourhood, that I think I have nowhere seen in America such a collection of right English-looking youths of a gentlemanly stamp. * * * Mr. Slack, a half-pay officer of the navy, drove me to Eaton, and from thence to Bury, where we put up for the night in a solitary public-house by the roadside. The whole accommodation disposable for our benefit was one tiny room, in which was one bed. We set off early in the morning, and as I came out of the house, I was struck by the characteristic nature of the scene. Long icicles were hanging from the roof of the log-built house ; the snow freshly fallen was lodged in masses upon the branches of the trees ; and the only view was up and down the track passing in front of the house, which was broken through the narrow vista of tall wintry woods. It took us three hours to accomplish the eleven miles which we had to go to the Victoria settlement, which is a kind of focus of the operations of the Canada Land Company in this tract of country, and promises to become hereafter an important place. It had been arranged that I should take advantage of the day on which the settlers attend to receive their rations; and the issuing-house, a log-building having a counter within, was appointed as the place for service. The number present was at least seventy, and the house would scarcely have held more. I baptized one child and churched the mother. A great many of the Company's settlers are from Norfolk, my own native county, and I hope that it was pardonable, after the affectionate manner in which an apostle speaks of his ' kinsmen after the flesh,' to feel some

increased interest in them on this account. We returned the
same evening to the public-house before described. Among
the habitations which we passed on the way was one constructed of bark, without either door or chimney, but with
an aperture in the roof for the escape of the smoke. It was
almost buried in snow, which formed indeed the best protection of the miserable inmates. I stopped at two houses on
the road for the purposes of baptism and churching. The
settlers, dispersed about at different distances in the woods,
came flocking to meet me the next day at Bury Village, and
service was held at the appointed hour in a house belonging to
the Company, two rooms of which were occupied for the purpose. The people were jammed together, and there were
some who, after all, could not gain admittance. It was
calculated that three hundred were present. If, in the very
infancy of the settlement, at such extremely short notice, and
upon a week-day, so many people could be collected, and
those manifesting such eagerness to attend, it will be evident
how imperative is the claim of this place, combined with Victoria, for spiritual assistance ; and the Society will, I am sure,
approve of my having allotted to this station a portion of the
grant made in November, 1835, for additional missionaries.
As a provision, ad interim, for this object, I directed the Rev.
J. Taylor of Eaton to give one Sunday in the month to these
two settlements ; and the people appeared very grateful when
I announced my intention of making this arrangement, and
my hope of providing them, at no very distant period, with a
resident minister. Although there could be no confirmation
in these settlements, because there was nobody to prepare the
candidates, I am thankful that I was enabled to visit them.* *
The village of Sherbrooke, in which the district court is
established, and which the Land Company have made their
central point, is likely to become a place of consideration ;
and an impulse has been given to all the surrounding townships, which opens the prospect of rapid improvement and

accumulating population. Even the tracts of continuous forest may, before many years have passed, exhibit scenes of industry, cultivation, and social intercourse ; and the voice of the bridegroom, the sound of the millstone, and the light of the candle may be things familiar in what is now a vast howling wilderness. It is melancholy to think how meagre and precarious is the provision for the first interests of those to whose enterprise the stores of nature are thus laid open ; how utterly inadequate are the means at command, and, according to all earthly calculation, the means in prospect for furnishing to these successive aggregations of the human family what they want as immortal beings, and gathering them into the fold of the Church ' that they may be saved through Christ for ever.' The patrimony of the Church stands adjudged, in the purpose of Government, to other objects which are conceived to be more important ; and the Company, although they are obliged to make a certain expenditure in works of public utility, among which the erection of churches is especially mentioned, appear to have decided that this shall be the only work which they will omit. The plea for declining assistance in the case of the settlements at Bury and Victoria was the inexpediency of opening a door to applications of the same kind from different sects. But, even if it were admissible, in a reasonable or a religious view of the case, to place the claims of the national Church of England, preserving its hierarchy from the first ages of Christianity, upon a level with those of modern and irregular sects, it might have been considered that the great bulk of the population in these settlements are confessedly adherents of the Church. I am greatly mortified at this decision on the part of a body whose operations in other respects must be regarded as highly beneficial to the colony : and it may, perhaps, be judged proper by the Board to open some communication with the heads of the Company at home, in order to impress upon them the responsibility which it surely cannot be questioned that they contract, to provide for the religious interests of the thousands whom they remove from the home of their fathers, and in them of the millions of whom they must be believed to be the progenitors. * * * I had written on the 10th February to the Rev. W. Anderson, and to the catechist at Lake Maskinongé, in the hope of being able to repair the disappointment at the Rivière du Loup, where, as before mentioned, I had expected to perform, for the first time in my life, the office of confirmation, for which I now fixed Sunday 5th March. Upon my arrival there, I found that it had pleased Providence again to defeat my wishes in behalf of the little flock. Mr. Anderson had been suddenly called to Quebec, on account of the dying state of a near connection. My letter to the catechist did not reach him in time. No confirmation, therefore, could be held. The consolation remained, however, of spending one more Sunday with a congregation who had seen no clergyman but myself on my former visit for more than a year. I received a letter afterwards from the catechist expressing the most bitter disappointment. On the 7th March, I was within fifteen miles of Quebec, but had to set my face the next morning another way. A famine prevailed partially at this time in this province, and in some places dogs and horses are said to have been eaten: in the neighbourhood of Leeds, among the French Canadians, I was assured that there were families who had been living upon such food as bran and hay broth. After service, at Leeds, I was waited upon by a deputation with an address of congratulation on my appointment to the episcopal office,* which took me entirely by surprise. The authors of it stated themselves to be, in part, persons who had been members of my flock in Quebec. * * * At West Frampton, the Rev. R. Knight received me into his house, which I cannot forbear

---

* A similar address had previously been presented by the clergy of Lower Canada.

from describing. The walls of the principal room were formed of upright trunks of trees, smoothed off in front, but with the bark left adhering to them at the edge. The floor was composed of rough boards laid loosely together, and the ceiling was in the same unfinished condition. This may be truly called, even after its completion, 'the village preacher's modest mansion,' but close by the side of it is a hovel in the form of a shed, of which the elevation at the highest side of it is seven feet and a half, built of round logs with the bark on, with the rough ends projecting where they cross each other at the corners. Here the pastor dwelt before the erection of his present house. I confirmed forty-one persons in the little church, which was well filled, and fourteen in a private house in another part of the township in the afternoon, some of whom had come sixteen miles. I had much ground for being satisfied, according to all the evidence by which I could judge, with the pains taken to convey correct impressions to the minds of the young persons who came forward in this mission, as well in ascertaining their knowledge of the leading principles and objects of Faith, and requiring, in order to their admission, consistency of practice, as in founding their recourse to the means of grace upon a distinct recognition of their own natural helplessness and sinfulness; and thus exhibiting the only just view of those doctrines of repentance and faith which the Church insists upon as the two great branches of the promise made in baptism and confirmation. And, indeed, I think that very generally, on the whole visitation, the clergy were faithful in setting before the candidates for the latter rite, the nature of the covenant to which they were to declare their adherence, and warning them of their obligation to regard themselves as not their own, but ' bought with a price.'"

The confirmation at Frampton concluded the visitation, and the Bishop returned to Quebec on the 15th March, having been absent since the 6th January. The whole number of persons confirmed on this tour was six hundred and sixty-seven, of whom five hundred and forty, including one hundred and fifty-one at Montreal, were in what is now the diocese of Montreal, and only one hundred and twenty-seven in what is now the diocese of Quebec. The Bishop of Quebec had, however, very recently confirmed at Quebec and Three Rivers, to which place the candidates from Nicolet had been brought ; and other circumstances prevented a confirmation being now held at Leeds and Rivière du Loup, as well as at Hull in the district of Montreal. The number of candidates was also greatly diminished by the state of the roads, which, in repeated instances, prevented those who had been prepared from meeting the Bishop. " No one in the country remembered such a winter, as it respects the succession of snow-storms and the quantity of snow." All the missions had been visited, and services held at four places where there was no provision either by clerical ministrations or those of a catechist. Seventeen confirmations were held in the district of Montreal, including two where there was no resident clergyman, and only six in the remainder of the diocese. In what is now the diocese of Quebec, these six sufficed for all the fixed missions, except Leeds, Nicolet, and the two in the district of Gaspé. There were at this time six clergymen resident in the city of Quebec, and these, with one travelling missionary, made up the whole number of seventeen. The change which God had wrought before the Bishop rested from his labours, exactly twenty-six years from the day on which he began his first visitation tour, may surely teach us not to despise " the day of small things."

CHAPTER XIII.

THE visitation of the district of Gaspé was yet to be performed, in order to complete that of Lower Canada. There were at this time but two clergymen within its limits, holding charge, respectively, of the counties of Bonaventure and Gaspé. The Bishop left Quebec for this purpose on the 6th June, having been so fortunate as to secure a passage in a small vessel chartered by the Government for the use of the naval officers engaged in the survey of the St. Lawrence. On board this vessel he performed a short service daily, with exposition of Scripture (in which, as the officer in command expressed it several years afterwards, " he was peculiarly happy,") and the weather was so fine as to cause no single instance of its interruption. It did not, however, favour the progress of the vessel, for it was seventeen days before the voyage was concluded, though nearly one-third of it was performed in twelve hours by the aid of a fair breeze which sprang up towards its termination. " So remarkably like some pilgrims in their mortal course were they favoured at the close of a voyage which had been distinguished by circumstances perseveringly adverse to their progress." From Gaspé Basin to Carlisle the voyage was continued in an open boat. The churches of Gaspé Basin, Malbaie, Percé, Paspébiac and Carlisle, all of which, except the last mentioned, were unpainted, and most of them in a more or less incomplete

O

state, were visited : and confirmations were held in them all
as well as at St. George's Cove, L'Anse à Beau-fils (in a
fisherman's house) and Hopetown. The whole number confirmed in the mission of the Rev. W. Arnold was one hundred
and nineteen, of whom eighty came forward at the Basin
church alone. The Rev. A. Balfour had sixty-four on his
list, of whom fifty-two were confirmed. A large number in
every part of the district were, on this and every subsequent
occasion, deprived of the ordinance by their absence from
home, being engaged in the whale-fishery. On the last occasion of the Bishop's visit to the district (in 1862), he left
Quebec on the very first opportunity which presented itself
after the opening of the navigation, on purpose to provide for
the case of the whalers. It was so early in the season, that
the steamer which conveyed him was detained several hours
in the ice, before he could reach the Magdalen Islands.

One or two extracts from the journal of 1837 may here
suffice. Leaving the Gaspé Bay mission, the Bishop embarked
in a four-oared boat, with Mr. Arnold as steersman. " I was
anxious," he says, " if possible, to reach Carlisle before Sunday.
Like the disciples, we 'had forgotten to take bread,' and after
embarking returned to the house for a supply, which afforded
another, though a small, opportunity to the friendly people,
of manifesting the eager pleasure with which they rendered
us any service in their power. Our wind, which had been
favourable, having soon died away, we took to the oars, but,
with the object in view which I have stated, we persevered,
and at midnight reached a settlement where we knocked up
one of the Jersey traders, or rather, as he was himself confined to his bed by sickness, the two fishing lads by whom his
ménage was conducted. They got up half-naked, struck a
light, and kindled a fire on the rude hearth, over which we
were glad to crouch while the kettle was boiling. My travel-
ling-bed was spread upon the floor ; Mr. Arnold found some
place to throw himself down ; and we allowed ourselves and

the men, who remained abroad, two hours and a half for sleep.
* * * In every place where public worship is held in this
district, the congregation, according to the charge of the
Psalmist, sing praises lustily and with a good courage."

On the 7th July, the Bishop embarked at Carlisle to return
to Quebec, in a " schooner of forty tons, very roughly fitted
up, and the whole ship's company consisted of two men and
a boy. Having reached Percé on the evening of Saturday the
8th, and having encountered a foul wind, I sent word on shore
early on Sunday morning, to make arrangements for divine
service. I have recorded two occasions for thankfulness,
upon which a fair breeze had enabled me to dispose of my
two Sundays in the district to the best advantage : it now
occurred that the adverse elements caused my passing a third
at the very point where, if a choice had been given me in
the case of my detention, I should have wished to spend it,
Percé being an important point, and one for which there is
but slender spiritual provision.* Without presumptuously
claiming a special interposition, I could not but be grateful
that, in the course of events, these opportunities were so
happily afforded. I preached twice to good congregations.
On Monday the wind continued foul, but it happened very
well ; for a funeral came from L'Anse à Beau-fils with a
large train of followers, and, although the resident catechist
was in attendance, the people, who are so much strangers to
clerical ministrations, were rejoiced to find a clergyman to
officiate. Under these circumstances, I added a sermon to
the usual service. Towards sunset, the wind having shifted,
I returned to my vessel, which lay out at a short distance,
near the entrance of Malbaie : and, as the sun was now sinking,
and after it sank, a peculiar tint was shed over the landscape by
a very wild and yet bright evening sky which most beautifully

---

* One result of this visitation was the appointment of a third missionary,
who had charge of Percé, Cape Cove, and Malbaie.

heightened its effect. I do not remember to have been ever more impressed with the grandeur and the glories of creation. In going on board in the boat, I passed close under the enormous and frowning mass of the pierced rock (from which Percé takes its name,) and scarcely emerging from the very midst of that striking assemblage of objects which I have before described,—the rock itself, the site of the village, the mountain behind, the island opposite, the overhanging cliffs of the shore,—I saw before me on one side the broad expanse of ocean, and on the other, Malbaie, like a sheltered recess, with its mountains and its hills still retiring, range behind range, and swell behind swell. After beating about all the next day, without being able to weather Cape Gaspé, we came to anchor towards evening at Malbaie Cove. I went ashore and called to see one of the churchwardens. His children were brought to me to be examined, and I was reminded that I had christened the eldest of them, upon my first visit, thirteen years before. I believe it will generally be found that the children of our people in this quarter are at least taught the elementary truths of the Gospel, and the habit of prayer to God through Christ, a benefit which may often lead, it may be hoped, to happy results, and which they owe, under Providence, in a very great measure to the S. P. G. Since I have known the county of Gaspé, there have been among its protestant inhabitants no ministers or religious instructors of any kind (with the single exception of the methodist local preacher at St. George's Cove) but those supplied by the Society. Bibles and prayer books have been largely supplied by the S. P. C. K. * * * On the voyage up to Quebec, I made it a practice to collect my shipmates together (there were four steerage passengers) every day, and after a few prayers from the liturgy, to lecture familiarly upon one of the portions of the 119th psalm. How far any seed may have been blessed which was thus dropped, I had no very decided means of judging, but in such cases we have always

the comfort of being permitted to hope that good may have
been done, although mixed (at least in my own case) with a
feeling that the opportunity of communicating the benefit
might have been more zealously improved. * * * On
Saturday 22nd July, I went ashore at Berthier, and found a
Canadian on the beach, who engaged to give me breakfast
and drive me up to Pointe Levi. The change was indeed
refreshing from the schooner to the shore. The beach was
profusely ornamented with hare-bells; the meadows looked
fresh and rural through which we passed up to the house; the
road-side, as we travelled, was fringed with the wild rose, the
convolvulus, the spiræa frutex, all in blossom, with other shrubs
and flowers; the day was bright and beautiful, and the breeze
seemed to give fresh life to nature; the greater part of the
drive, through the villages on the bank of the St. Lawrence
with the Island of Orleans opposite for twenty miles, and the
mountains of the north shore beyond, presents scenery and
views of an enchanting character. My driver was a simple
but substantial *habitant*, dressed in the grey home-spun of
the country, and every thing in his house and establishment possessed that rural character, not absolutely rude, but
appropriate to a frugal and simple race very moderately
advanced in the arts of life, which few travellers, whatever
their deliberate judgment may pronounce upon it with
reference to the improvement of human society, can avoid
contemplating with emotions of pleasure. There was a huge
ancient and mutilated folio in the room where I breakfasted,
which I found to be the *Vie des Saints.* In the mood which
is inspired by such scenes and objects as I have described, we
are disposed to more indulgence than the truth will warrant
towards the errors of an adulterated Christianity, and there
is something soothing to our own minds in the large exercise
of what seems to be an amiable charity of judgment upon the
subject. But although there is danger here and deception too,
and although it is the part of genuine charity to be intent, if

God seem to open the way, **upon** the communication of better
light to souls possessed by hurtful superstition, and to promote
this object by all judicious and temperate endeavours ; yet,
after all, in the exercise of that grace, hoping all things,
believing all things, and seeing that certainly in some points
a salutary effect is produced by the discipline and instruction
of the Church of Rome, we may be glad that, till their ' times
of refreshing shall come,' the truth reaches them in part, and
may believe that, through the very intercession of Him Who
is obscured to their view, a measure of grace is not denied to
them, and the sins of their system are not always visited upon
their individual heads. At present I do not think that we can
gather it to be the will of Providence that any effectual impression should be made upon the Roman catholic population of
Lower Canada ; and all the resources which we can command
are inadequate for the spiritual instruction of our own people.
I am disposed to believe that, under existing circumstances,
we best prepare the way for recovering this branch of the
Romish Church to the primitive system of faith and worship,
by exhibiting before the eyes of the people the proper fruits
of spiritual religion ; letting our light so shine before them, that
they may see our good works.   The great obstacle to their
conversion is our disunion.   Their only strength lies in our
being divided (speaking of protestants collectively) into
sects, and our fatal admission of the principle that men may
set up new standards, and create new ministries at will
within the Church.   The greatest friends to the prosperity of
Romanism, although often the most eager assailants of the
Romish system, are those persons who have low and loose
views of the Church.   But, although it is not for us ' to know
the times or the seasons,' it is impossible not to feel a longing that the French Canadians should be enlightened, when
the effects of their ignorance are seen.   *Fortunati nimiùm
sua si bona nôrint,* they enjoy a condition, in temporal matters, as happy as any people upon earth ; and are so well off

and so entirely exempt from any painful or irritating pressure received in any single point from the Government, that, unless they were very ignorant, it would seem impossible that they should be engaged to enter into rebellious plots for obtaining changes by which they must infallibly be losers; to which it may be added that, unless the received principles which mould and actuate them were defective, they could not seek to compass their object in the spirit which they have manifested. This people, who have so much reason to be happy, and who present a picture to the eye of a peaceful simple peasantry, with much that is courteous in their manners and amiable in their attachments, have shewn, in too many instances, when acted upon by designing and unprincipled demagogues, the latent and unsuspected wickedness which is in the heart of man; and with whatever just horror we may regard the leaders who would plunge such a peasantry, so situated, into causeless revolt, we are compelled to admit, at the same time, that among the people themselves a disposition both sanguinary and treacherous seems only to have been dormant within many bosoms, by the sudden fierceness with which it has broken out. In this point of view, our own religion, as it exists in this province, is a precious deposit which ought zealously to be fostered and protected as the leaven which may yet be destined to leaven the whole lump: and this consideration may be an additional incentive to the venerable Society to continue its pious endeavours for the support and extension of the Church of England in Lower Canada."

Some idea of the incessant character of the Bishop's labours may be formed when it is stated that it was not till February, 1838, that he was able to write the journal of this visitation, which had been concluded more than six months previously. He had been absent from Quebec about four months in 1837, during which he had travelled 2208 miles. This first visitation of the diocese was concluded by a visit in February, 1838, to the county of Megantic, when seventeen persons were confirmed at New Ireland, and thirty-five at Leeds. The church at Leeds was consecrated at the same time. This journey added 140 miles to the number just mentioned, and brought the whole number of confirmations in Lower Canada up to thirty-three, and of persons confirmed to eight hundred and seventy-seven.

The charge of the whole of Canada had passed into his hands on the death of Bishop Stewart in July, 1837, and the correspondence which it involved both within the diocese and with societies and other benefactors of the Church at home, all of which was conducted without any assistance, was enough to fill the hands of one man, besides that which came upon him daily, ' the care of all the Churches' and especially of his own parish of Quebec.

On the 1st August, 1838, the Bishop delivered his primary charge in the cathedral to the clergy of the city and district of Quebec, whose number had then increased to fourteen. On the 7th of the same month twenty-three clergymen were assembled for the same purpose at Montreal, where, on the following Sunday, an ordination was held. From Montreal the Bishop proceeded to Upper Canada. There being no immediate prospect of the erection of that province into a separate see, he thought it right not to leave it any longer without the ministrations of the episcopal office. The Earl of Durham, who had been sent out a few months before as Governor General and High Commissioner to enquire into the condition of the Canadas, provided the Bishop with the means of taking a clergyman with him on his tour through Upper Canada, for the purpose of assisting him in procuring information on the state of the Church. The visitation occupied upwards of three months, and was extended to all the missions. Confirmation was administered to 1995 persons at fifty-nine places, the largest number of candidates being at Perth, where 156 were presented. Nine churches were consecrated, and ordinations held at Toronto, Woodhouse, and Bytown, besides that already mentioned, and another held on the way down, at Montreal. The episcopal charge was delivered at Toronto, where upwards of fifty clergy were present. The number of miles travelled from Quebec and back again was 2500. From a report which the Bishop rendered to Lord Durham, it appears that at this time the number of persons professing adherence to the Church in Upper Canada was roughly stated at 150,000, the number of clergy exercising their ministry was seventy-three, and the number of churches built or in progress about ninety. Between London and Goderich, in a tract of country sixty miles in length, there was not one clergyman or minister of any denomination. Between Woodhouse and St. Thomas, a distance of upwards of fifty miles, which could be travelled by two roads, there was not one clergyman on either, though a great body of Church-people was scattered over that part of the country. In the district of Wellington, which was everywhere spread over with a Church population, there was one clergyman ; in the district of Newcastle there were six. In the words of the Bishop,

"The importunate solicitations which I constantly receive for the supply of clerical services—the overflowing warmth of feeling with which the travelling missionaries are greeted in their visits to the destitute settlements—the marks of affection and respect towards my own office which I experienced throughout the province—the exertions made by the people, in a great number of instances, to erect churches even without any definite prospect of a minister, and the examples in which this has been done by individuals at their own private expense, are unequivocal and striking evidences of the attachment to Church principles which pervades a great body of the population. I would here beg leave to draw the attention of your Excellency to the bearing of these facts upon the question of supporting the clergy by the voluntary contributions of the people. Here is a deep sense of the value of religious services, and a strong manifestation of attachment to the Church. The moving principle, therefore, is not wanting ; and if with this advantage the system cannot work successfully in Canada, it may be inferred that it cannot succeed there at all. And I am more deeply convinced than ever that such is the fact. In the few examples in which the experiment has been tried, it has rarely been otherwise than a failure, and in most cases it would be hopeless to attempt it. Even if the country were far more advanced and the people had some command of money, I am persuaded that a faithful, respectable, and independent body of clergy, sufficient for the wants even of that part of the population who already appreciate their labours, much more for that whom it is their duty to win to a care for religion, can never be provided by the operation of the voluntary system. * * * The observations which I have submitted are, in great part, of common application to both provinces. * * *

There has been no census of the population of Lower Canada since 1831, at which time the Church of England population was estimated at 34,620 souls. The clergy are now forty-four in number, with thirty-two or thirty-three churches or chapels built or in progress. From fifteen to twenty additional clergymen would, I think, provide for the present wants of this portion of the diocese. In Upper Canada I believe that employment would be found for one hundred beyond the existing establishment.

Nothing can be less uniform and systematic than the manner in which a meagre supply of clergy is at present eked out and distributed over the diocese. One portion is paid from the imperial treasury (the salaries to be discontinued, one by one, as vacancies occur) another from local resources at the disposal of Government; another is composed of missionaries from home, and there are four different religious bodies (besides an individual of singular zeal in the cause) to whom the diocese is in this way indebted; and another still, though an exceedingly small portion, is dependent, in whole or in part, upon the people. Thus the establishment of clergy, imperfect and insufficient as it is, is made up by means of shifts and expedients, and to a great extent is without any permanent character; and the task of the diocesan in procuring supplies, and maintaining communication with the different parties who afford them, is complicated in a distressing degree. I am thus led to a subject which I have reserved as the last to be brought under the notice of your Excellency. The care of this diocese is altogether too much for one man. Certainly one man cannot do justice to it, situated as I am. Your Excellency is, I believe, aware that negociations have been for some time on foot for the erection of a separate see in Upper Canada. It is indeed high time that this measure should be carried into effect. In executing the duties of the visitation in the two provinces, I have travelled nearly five thousand miles; the extreme points which I visited in the length of the diocese being Sandwich at the head of Lake Erie, and the Bay of Chaleurs in the gulf of St. Lawrence. Of the state of the communications in the interior parts of the country and among the new settlements, your Excellency is not without information. No provision exists for enabling me to employ a single functionary in conducting correspondence with the Government, the clergy, and the societies at home, keeping in proper order and arrangement the accumulating records of the see, or **transacting those ordinary forms of ecclesiastical** business which are proper to the episcopal office; and in those departments of labour where the Bishop can receive assistance from the Archdeacon, **I am deprived of the benefit, as far as Lower Canada is concerned,** because, under the existing arrangements, I am compelled to hold the office of Archdeacon myself."

The object which the Bishop here sets forth as of so great importance was accomplished, by the divine blessing, in the following **year,** when he was relieved of the charge of Upper Canada **by the consecration of the present venerable Bishop of** Toronto, **who had been Archdeacon of York since 1825.** In order to **expedite this object, the Rev. R. D.** Cartwright had been sent on **a mission to England early in** 1838.

In **writing to the S. P. G. the Bishop describes the result** of this **visitation as "very highly satisfactory indeed, and** abounding **with matter of thankfulness to** God, as it respects **the character and** labours of the clergy as a body, the attachment **of our people to sound Church** principles, and the tone of **morals and religion which** pervades our congregations."

The clergy **of the Midland, Eastern, Johnstown,** and Bathurst districts in Upper Canada presented addresses to the Bishop of Montreal on their withdrawal from his jurisdiction, expressive of their respect and affection, and, in one instance, their "admiration of persevering exertions in the discharge of duties peculiarly **arduous,** of the faithfulness and devotedness with which he entered on the work of his Divine Master, and acknowledging, at the same time, the kindness of the christian so exemplified in intercourse with the clergy." In another "brief and simple testimony of filial affection," it is said;

"Your lordship **presided over us with firmness united to urbanity,** and dignity mingled with condescension. During a period of great danger to the Church, while the enemies of Zion, endlessly divided among themselves, have yet united in **the** cry, 'Down with her, down with her, even unto the ground,' your lordship has pursued **a noble** and elevated course, superior to vain ambition and restless policy.

"Your lordship, apparently without designing it, has succeeded in gaining the respect of enemies, the devotion of friends, and the admiration of **the** Church."

CHAPTER XIV.

THE second triennial visitation was begun by the confirmation of one hundred and seventy-two persons, among whom was the first of his own children on whom he laid hands, in the cathedral at Quebec, on the 13th October 1839. Early in the following January, the Bishop set out on a journey through the districts of Montreal, Three Rivers, and St. Francis, an account of which was afterwards published by the S. P. G. I shall make, therefore, only a few extracts, chiefly of passages which serve to shew the manner in which the services of the Church were appreciated, besides giving the general results of the visitation, and some particulars which may help to exhibit the progress of the Church during the three preceding years.

At St. Andrews several young persons, who had been prepared for confirmation, but had not received their tickets, having called for them early on an intensely cold day, on which the confirmation was to be held, were all frost-bitten in some part or other of the face. Some candidates who had been disappointed at Huntingdon followed the Bishop to Ormstown, and " not being sufficiently protected against the weather, had suffered greatly from cold in their tedious progress," the roads being nearly blocked up from the effects of a snow-storm, and they had to measure their way back after dark ; " but in commending them," says the Bishop, " for their exertions, I exhorted them cheerfully to endure this and greater things, if called upon, for their religion, and reminded them of the distant journeys which men were prompted to make, under an inferior dispensation, to keep the ordinances of the Lord's House at Jerusalem." Three others who had been disappointed in the same neighbourhood afterwards went fifteen miles for confirmation, and the clergyman who brought them " travelled about forty miles to bring them, and went immediately back with them. Two young Irish girls, sisters, came from Milton to Abbottsförd ; but having, in consequence of misinformation, gone a vast way round, they arrived after the confirmation was over, and I learned nothing about them till after they had gone home again. Mr. Johnson, however, had told them to meet me at Cutler's school-house the next day. Considering their long journey, their disappointment after all their efforts, the continued rain throughout the day, and the very bad state of the 'roads, as well as the distance between Milton and the school-house, I expected that they would give it up. They came, however, and as I spoke a few simple words of exhortation to them after they had been confirmed, the two standing together (for no confirmation had been appointed at the place), the tears rolled down their cheeks. These little incidents serve to shew what feeling there is to work upon in the bosoms of poor settlers in the woods, and ' who hath despised the day of small things ?' "

At Shefford a young man and woman, who had been prevented by circumstances from being examined, came into the vestry room before service " soliciting, with tears, the blessing of confirmation." At Drummondville, it is mentioned that " a young lad, who was working in a *shanty* thirty miles off and earning high wages, not only came down on foot to be confirmed, but came to his own family a week beforehand,

sacrificing the profits of that week, to spend it in study and
preparation, and this in opposition to the strong remonstrances
of his companions.   At Rawdon the church was so thronged
that one man described himself as having been for a quarter
of an hour with his person half in and half out of the door
without being able to move an inch.   Ninety-one persons
were confirmed, six of whom, on account of the crowd and
some confusion in the lower end of the church, did not get
forward at the proper time, nor make known their disappointment till after my robes were packed up again, and I was
leaving the church.   The little trouble, however, of again
putting on my vestments to administer a separate confirmation
to them was well repaid by their thankfulness, and better
still by the very deep marks of feeling which they evinced
as recipients of the rite."   In several other instances the
candidates are spoken of as " deeply and sensibly affected,"
and speaking generally, the Bishop remarks ; " I am indeed
thankful to say that a deep reverence and deliberate self-
dedication to Christ did seem to characterize the candidates
in the different places which I visited ; and I cannot but
hope that, in many instances, their future walk will evince
their sincerity in this important act of their lives."

The Bishop was accompanied through the district of Montreal by the Rev. M. Willoughby, agent of the Newfoundland
School Society, whose object was to ascertain the wants of
the district with respect to education, which in many instances
he was enabled to supply.   In accepting the office of Vice-
President of this society, a few months before, the Bishop
said :

" The want of good common schools in which a scriptural education is
afforded is grievously felt by a great portion of the protestant inhabitants
of this province, and I do trust in God that the society will have the happiness of being instrumental in the prevention of much moral and religious
and, I may add political, evil, as well as in the production of much positive good in the field newly opened.   I shall regard the society as aiding
instead of interfering with the ancient protectress of the colonial Churches,

the venerable society for the Propagation of the Gospel, the department of labour which the former has assumed being evidently subservient to the objects of the latter, and still not being identical with them."

In the course of the visitation an ordination was held at Sherbrooke, when Mr. Willoughby was admitted to Priest's Orders, together with the Rev. W. Dawes. The names of both these good men are connected with the increase of the Church at this period, " and in their deaths they were not divided," for both were taken away by fever which they contracted in their attendance on Irish emigrants in 1847. To Mr. Willoughby, too, belongs the honour of initiating the operations of the society just mentioned; while Mr. Dawes filled the office of secretary of the diocesan Church society, with remarkable fidelity and earnestness (qualities which indeed pervaded his character in everything which he under-took), from its formation till the time of his death. Mr. Willoughby was the first incumbent of the first chapel which was built in Montreal, where, till the date which we have now reached, there was no place of worship, besides the parish church,* belonging to the Church of England. Trinity Chapel, built at the sole expense of Major W. P. Christie, was consecrated in May 1840. Mr. Dawes, as travelling missionary of a local association already mentioned at Mont-real, was the pioneer of the district lying to the south-west of that city, now for the first time visited by a Bishop. His labours had been carried on for about fifteen months. He had established eighteen stations at which he preached twenty-five times in every four weeks. Four churches were either in progress or in immediate contemplation, and forty-one persons were presented for confirmation at Russeltown, sixty-five at Hemmingford, and forty-one again at Napier-ville. Fifteen more at Hemmingford and several at Russel-

---

* An evening service had been established in the parish church, at which all the pews were thrown open.

town were prevented from coming forward owing to the roads being completely blocked up.

Besides in this tract of country, confirmations were held now for the first time at the Gore on the Ottawa, Kingsey, Bury, Compton, and Lake Maskinongé. Most of these places had been previously visited by the Bishop in his capacity of Archdeacon, and since his former visitation he had been enabled to fix missionaries at the three first mentioned, as well as at Stanbridge. Before the conclusion of this journey, Compton was erected into a separate charge, and measures were taken for conferring a similar benefit on Granby, as well as on Portneuf, and for dividing the labours of Mr. Dawes by assigning a portion of them to a second missionary within their range. The association which maintained Mr. Dawes maintained another missionary in the settlements north of Montreal, whose head-quarters were at Mascouche, where the church was consecrated during this visitation. Another had been consecrated at Upper Durham on the St. Francis. All the places visited in 1837 were revisited this year with the exception of Hull, for which a confirmation had been held at Bytown in 1838. In the district of Montreal twenty-seven confirmations were held, and eight hundred and ninety-five persons confirmed, including one hundred and twenty-five at Montreal. In the districts of St. Francis and Three Rivers two hundred and sixty persons were confirmed at twelve places. The Bishop was absent from Quebec two months. The number of clergy in Lower Canada had been increased by ten, and about the same number of churches had been built, or were in progress, or in immediate contemplation. The Bishop says, " Churches (God be praised for it) are springing up so fast, that I must beg for more help as soon as I shall have forwarded the account of money already paid or promised from the Society's grant of £500. * * *

At Laprairie I received the refreshing intelligence, (together with the announcement of aid granted towards the erection of churches,) more than I had dared to hope for, that the Society had undertaken to maintain the eighteen new missions which I had stated to be required. God only raise up for us faithful men to fill them up, and to preach among them the unsearchable riches of Christ."

The visitation of the district of Gaspé was performed in the autumn of 1840, in connection with which the first mention is found in the records of the diocese of the destitute settlements on that part of the coast of Labrador which lies within the limits of Canada. The Rev. E. Cusack, missionary at Gaspé Basin, having learnt the wants of the inhabitants from whalers belonging to his own flock who frequented the coast, had gone across, just before the Bishop's visit to Gaspé, to pay them a visit. Their number was very inconsiderable, and for many years the attention which the missionary resident within the limits of Newfoundland (appointed in 1849) was able to bestow upon them was considered, in the existing condition of the diocese, to suffice. Yet so early as 1841 the Bishop of Montreal brought their wants, for the second time, before the S. P. G., and said, "That mission will demand great activity and great devotedness in the person who will undertake it; but God does not deny to His Church, among the servants of the society, men who are willing to take up their own cross, and to glory in the Cross of their Master."

There is mention of only one new station in Gaspé,—Port Daniel. No confirmation, owing to a recent change of missionaries, could be held in the Bay of Chaleurs. At the unfinished church of Cape Cove, twenty-one were confirmed, making twenty-five in that mission. In the mission of Gaspé Bay, there were twenty-nine, a much smaller number than in 1837; but the interval between the visit of that year and the last which had been paid by the Bishop of Quebec had probably been greater than usual.

The visitation was completed during the following winter by a tour in the district of Quebec. On the south of the St.

Lawrence seven confirmations were held, where three had sufficed in 1837, and one hundred and sixty-nine persons were confirmed. One woman came on foot nineteen miles for the purpose. A missionary had been established at St. Sylvester, whose labours were carried over a large tract of country, including the settlements on the Chaudière river.

So far, twenty-four confirmations had been held in what is now the diocese of Quebec, at which six hundred and sixty-five persons were confirmed, out of one thousand five hundred and sixty in Lower Canada. Four others appear to have been afterwards held in the district of Quebec, but I have not the means of stating at what particular places. The total number of confirmations in the diocese had been fifty-two, of which twenty were at places where the ordinance had not been administered before.

The journeyings of the Bishop were not confined to those which came in the course of his regular visitations, for occasions constantly arose demanding his personal intervention for the supply of local wants or the adjustment of particular difficulties. He was always specially anxious for the spiritual welfare of the city of Montreal, which he used very frequently to visit, and where he was accustomed often to hold ordinations both in summer and winter. He never lost sight of the object which he had greatly at heart, of erecting it into a separate see; and it was chiefly on this account that, though actually administering the diocese of Quebec, he retained the title of Bishop of Montreal, instead of being formally appointed to the see of Quebec. He wished, as he often said, to keep before the public the necessity of making this title a reality. But his travelling was the least arduous part of his labours, except perhaps on the occasions of visiting Montreal, where he would be incessantly occupied for days together in the same way as at Quebec. The increasing wants of the diocese, and the measures necessary to be taken for their supply, involved a vast deal of correspondence with public and private persons, in addition to that which grew out of the ordinary business of its administration, and which in the case of colonial Bishops is much greater than it would otherwise be in proportion to the number of clergy, from the comparatively unformed and unsettled state of the Church, and the necessity of the direct reference to the Bishop of subjects which may be disposed of by inferior authority where it exists. His journeys, in fact, though sometimes attended by more or less of what some men count hardship, were a relief, and afforded a break in the ceaseless course of sedentary and anxious employments which filled his time at home, and which otherwise must have worn down his strength. He never suffered his own convenience to interfere with the claims of business. Rising up early, and late taking rest, he was ready at all hours to attend to the wants of his flock. In a letter written from Montreal, in June 1841, (where he had held an ordination in the preceding February,) he apologizes for " firing a shot with a nerveless arm," being, as he was obliged to confess, " rather what is called, ' done up.' I came last night, in the middle of the night, or rather before it was light this morning, from Port St. Francis in the steamer. I was busy about the town till four P.M.; then I took a luncheon with F., and immediately afterwards a hot ride with him of twelve miles to St. Martin, where I had business to transact with persons engaged in the erection of a church; then a cooler one, in the dark, back to Montreal, where, at ten o'clock, Mr. W—— met me by appointment with a candidate for Orders, after which I wrote to ——, and now I am writing to yourself."

He was at this time engaged, and continued for three or four years to be so, in correspondence with the Hudson's Bay Company, the clergy resident in their territory, the Archbishop of Canterbury, the Bishop of London, and the Church Missionary Society, respecting the missions in Prince Rupert's Land, to which he anxiously desired to carry the ministrations of his office, with the object of paving the way for a resident Bishop in the territory. He always felt deeply that the Canadian Church was debtor to the original proprietors of the soil.

There were two other objects, nearer home, which were now occupying much of his time and thoughts,—the foundation of the Church Society and that of Bishop's College. He had mentioned, in his primary charge, his hope that a church society might be organized similar to that which had already been established in Nova Scotia. In July, 1839, he informed the S. P. G. that it was projected, and soon after the division of the diocese in the same year, he engaged in correspondence with the Bishop of Toronto on the subject of the establishment of a joint association for the two dioceses. He drew up an outline of his plan with proposed constitution and by-laws, and also made, in September, 1841, at the request of his brother Bishop, the draft of an episcopal address, to proceed from both, to the churchmen of Canada, with reference to the undertaking. Both Bishops desired opportunities of full consultation with their clergy before finally bringing their plan before the public, and the Bishop of Toronto finding a feeling to exist in his own diocese in favour of two separate organizations, it was agreed that each should pursue the plan for himself. The efforts of the Bishop of Montreal were interrupted by a severe illness with which it pleased God to visit him during the winter of 1841–2, and which for several months caused deep anxiety to his friends ; and it was not till the clergy of the diocese were assembled at a visitation held at Montreal in July 1842, that the Church Society of the diocese of Quebec was finally formed.

At this visitation fifty-one of the sixty clergy of the diocese were present. The Bishop, in his charge, especially commended the two institutions just mentioned to the prayers and support of the clergy, and stated that since they had last assembled in visitation, he had ordained twenty-one clergymen to new stations in Lower Canada, and admitted six others, already in Orders, to new cures, making in all twenty-seven new missions opened in less than four years, adding:

"Let none suppose that we have grasped indiscriminately at all opportunities of procuring additional hands; for the overtures are not few, whether for ordination or for the employment of ordained ministers, which I have declined to entertain. * * * The number of additional churches has fully kept pace with the advancing list of our clergy; and it is with feelings of overflowing thankfulness that we must acknowledge our accumulating obligations under God to the Society for the Propagation of the Gospel, nobly seconded by the sister Society for Promoting Christian Knowledge * * * I pass over all the subordinate supplies afforded for the greater solemnity and decency of worship, for the better facilities of religious instruction, for the more enlarged acquaintance with the Word of Life,—but what shall we say of that provident as well as pious munificence which has undertaken the perpetuation of all these blessings, by gradually creating endowments for the Church?"

Reference is here made to the purchase of glebes in Lower Canada by the S. P. G., which that body was enabled to accomplish, owing to the increasing demands upon its funds, in only a few instances; but this object was specially kept in view in the formation of the Church Society.

So large a proportion of the clergy came from a great distance, with very imperfect means of communication, that they could not be detained long from their cures; and a great deal of business was therefore necessarily crowded into a few days. The Bishop himself spent ten days at Montreal, and, writing from thence, says;

"I have never, I think, in my life been more incessantly occupied, morning, noon and night, than since I came to this place. The ordination, visitation, formation of the Church Society, and laying the first stone of the new chapel (St. George's), all carried with them, except indeed the last, a vast deal of business, compared with which each formal occasion was very little. The work of preparation for the Church Society was immense; the whole of my charge to the clergy was written here; the examination of the candidates for Orders was conducted by myself; and the forms to execute, business to transact, conference to hold, and counsel to give among fifty-one clergymen, most of whom I see only once in three years, amounted to no trifle. Many other persons have wanted me for other things, and I have preached six times besides delivering my charge."

One of these sermons was preached at St. Thomas' Chapel, then recently built.

At this visitation a large number of the clergy addressed the Bishop in favour of the adoption of a more distinctive clerical dress, which he was known strongly to approve. He referred the matter to the Archbishop of Canterbury; and his grace, though entirely concurring in their feeling on the subject, did not feel prepared to recommend the practice in the case of a single diocese, while the general custom remained unchanged.

In a letter written in the following November, the Bishop says, referring to the Church Society:

"We began well, but it has not pleased God that we should, as yet, proceed with a very prosperous course. The extreme commercial depression of Quebec and Montreal is against us very much, and we have had other difficulties too. There are also other objects which I have deeply at heart for the benefit of the Church, in which I have encountered great discouragement; but we must regard these occurrences as trials of faith, checks to presumption, and incitements to redoubled prayer and diligence. If it has pleased God to suffer me, in some departments of my charge, to be an instrument of good, I have been and am sufficiently schooled, on the other hand, to humility and watchfulness by mortifications and disappointments, in my career of labour, of no common kind."

One of the objects here referred to was, doubtless, the foundation of Bishop's College, already mentioned. So long before as in 1839 he had said to the S. P. G. that it "had long been his ardent wish and prayer to establish a college," and in December of that year the Society voted £200 per annum towards the maintenance of divinity students. In the following autumn he decided on placing all the recipients of this bounty at Three Rivers, under the charge of the Rev. S. S. Wood, M.A., of Corpus College, Cambridge, rector of that place, whose theological and classical attainments eminently qualified him for the task. In April, 1841, he informed the society of the completion of this arrangement, adding; "I have thus paved the way, I hope, for the establishment of that institution,—I shall be thankful if I can say that college,—the rough project of which I communicated to you in November last."

The rectory-house at Three Rivers, which was originally a monastery, seemed to offer some peculiar facilities for this purpose, both from the general character of the building, and particularly from its connection with the parish church, which had been the chapel of the monastery. But before these arrangements were finally completed, the Rev. L. Doolittle came forward, on behalf of himself and several residents of Sherbrooke and Lennoxville, with the offer of large contributions in money and land if the site of the college were fixed in the neighbourhood of those places. The situation of Three Rivers had been considered sufficiently suitable for a theological institution, but it was proposed now to give the college a more general character, with the special object of affording the advantages of a superior education to the English families who were daily flocking in to the Eastern townships, and of retaining within the province, and so moulding in English tastes and principles, the young men of American origin who were in the habit of seeking those advantages in the United States. The Eastern townships being the head-quarters of the English-speaking population of Lower Canada, and every day increasing in importance, the Bishop saw at once the benefit which the successful planting of such an institution among them would confer, not only upon the Church, but upon the country at large. There was no difficulty in his mind with regard to McGill College, already established at Montreal, partly because he foresaw that the day could not be far distant when the wants of the population would equal the resources of both institutions, and partly because McGill College had been deprived of the religious character which was a necessary feature of an establishment designed as a place of theological learning. The consent of Mr. Wood having been obtained to his removal to Lennox-ville as principal of the institution, measures were at once put in train for the erection of the necessary buildings on the site which had been secured; and while the theological stu-dents, awaiting their completion, remained at Three Rivers, a preparatory school was opened at Lennoxville, under the charge of Mr. Edward Chapman, B.A., of Caius College, Cambridge. In February, 1842, the Bishop furnished the society with a detailed account of the proposed college at Lennoxville, of which he said he considered a chapel as a most essential part, in connection with the formation of the habits of the students, and he shortly afterwards published similar statements in Canada.

The year 1842 was also marked by an event of some importance to the parish of Quebec, the completion of the rectory house, under an arrangement with the vestry of the cathedral by which the Bishop engaged to pay rent during his incumbency of the parish. A wing of the building was fitted up as a chapel, which was consecrated on All Saints' Day, 1842, under the name of All Saints, when the Bishop of Vermont preached the sermon. This chapel was designed to be used for week-day services or minor festivals, as well as the performance of acts of occasional duty. Immediately after its consecration, the Bishop assembled in it regularly a class of candidates for confirmation, whom he was himself preparing, and the first person confirmed in it was his own son, who, being unexpectedly called to join his regiment on receiving a commission in the army, and being therefore unable to wait for the general confirmation, was not allowed to depart without the blessing of the Church conveyed in the laying on of his father's hands.*

---

* The Bishop always looked back on this occasion with feelings of pecu-liar thankfulness. A person who was present described the scene as

The Bishop also established in **All Saints' Chapel**, a monthly service, with a lecture which he delivered himself, on the Fridays before the communion. The foundation-stone of St. Peter's chapel in Quebec, removed to its present site from a building which had been for some years used partly as a chapel, and partly as the Male Orphan Asylum, was laid in July of this same year. The orphans were then transferred to the National School building, which had been enlarged to receive them.

---

unusually striking, from her knowledge of the pains that had been taken to prepare the candidate, and his appreciation of them, when the Bishop armed the young soldier for the fight against sin, the world, and the devil. The son himself, writing to his father very soon afterwards from England, says: "I hope I shall not forget the day. I have felt much happiness ever since. I do not say this by way of boasting, but I know that it will be a comfort to you to know that I do not forget my vows." The Bishop furnished him with a most valuable manual of hints, drawn up originally for his elder son when leaving home to prepare for Oxford. *See Appendix.*

CHAPTER XV.

Third triennial circuit.

THE year 1843 opened with the first act in the Bishop's third visitation. On the festival of the Circumcision he confirmed two hundred and seventeen persons in the cathedral of Quebec, and the next day set off on a tour which occupied him till the 15th March. An account of this tour, together with that of some subsequent journeys to complete the triennial visitation of the diocese, was published by the S. P. G.* But it contains such striking proofs of the progress of the Church during the three preceding years, that this narrative would not be complete without longer extracts from it than it might otherwise be necessary to give. The first that I make describes a peculiarity of Canadian winter travelling; the others refer mainly to places where new ground had been broken for the Church, or her ministrations multiplied.

"In the tract of country in which we were now travelling, which is more or less rude and unfrequented, and in which the winter track (as is often the case in Canada East) was in many places carried through the fields, away from the summer road, we encountered brooks and ditches which had broken their confinement, and were so swollen with continued augmentations from the melting snow as to offer some obstructions to our passage across them. The driver of the sleigh which followed us would here go forward with a pole, to sound the depth; but when it was ascertained that we could pass, (which we did in every instance but one, when a circuit of some miles became necessary,) it was a matter of very nice man-

---

* Church in the Colonies, No. ix.

agement to prevent upsetting, the bottom being very unequal and broken
up. In some places the driver only could go, it being necessary that he
should stand up and balance the vehicle in its passage. Then the rest of
the party crossed on foot upon rails which the country people had laid
together for the purpose, taken from the fences; or we had recourse to the
fences themselves as a foot-bridge, holding on by the upper rail, and moving our feet along a lower one. In one place the little low-runnered
cariole was floating. These scenes brought forcibly to mind that passage
in the 147th psalm, where, after describing the intensity of frost, the
psalmist says, 'He sendeth out His word and melteth them; He causeth
His wind to blow, and the waters flow.' The roughnesses which I encountered here or elsewhere in the journey are such as are constantly familiar
to the missionaries, and I could by no means call them severe; but I had
deep cause for thankfulness to God for being able to go through them,
such as they were, without any sort of injury or improper fatigue, when
I remembered that at the same time last year I was in a condition
which caused my friends to augur that, if spared, I should be disabled for
life." *

---

* I cannot forbear from giving an extract from a letter written on the
21st February, 1842, and exhibiting not only the thankfulness here expressed, but cheerfulness. The illness had been very severe, and the sufferings
most acute. "Through the goodness of God I am a great deal better and
stronger, but it does not yet suit me to sit up regularly to write, and I am
now doing so in a lazy, recumbent posture, with a couple of pillows on my
lap for a desk. I have not been downstairs since the 2nd January, and I have
not used my legs since the 24th; but on Valentine's day, the anniversary
of my consecration, I ascertained that I could stand alone; and if my good
doctor had permitted me, I should, I think, have performed much greater
exploits by this time. The mercies by which I am surrounded, and the
alleviations which I have had at command in this illness, while thousands
of my fellow-creatures are suffering tenfold what I have done, with the
aggravations of want, hardship, neglect, and unkindness, are what I never
can acknowledge with sufficient thankfulness. The tender and anxious
watchfulness of your dear mother, the affectionate and assiduous attentions
of your sisters and brother, and the kind sympathy manifested in a variety
of ways, by many friends, have been such as I can never forget; nor have
the inferior members of my household been deficient. Those who have
immediately attended upon me have always seemed to do so with interest
and attachment, and, among other little instances, John, the other night,
in lifting me into bed with the aid of Robert, (a service which I hope very
soon to dispense with) said to me with a sort of pleasurable laugh, 'your
lordship is getting heavier.'"

Mascouche, which was mentioned in 1840 as the head-quarters of a travelling missionary, had since been formed into a fixed mission, the range of which was, however, still sufficiently extensive. It included Kilkenny, (mentioned at page 183,) and on this visitation the first episcopal visit was paid to that place as well as to New Glasgow. From Mascouche, " we drove to the church at Kilkenny, passing on our way what is jocosely called the ' cathedral of Kilkenny,' being a little log school-house, roofed with bark, and lighted by four panes, in which the missionaries formerly officiated. The church is a small, wooden, unpainted building, with square-topped windows. But it harmonizes with the present state of things in the township, and I verily believe it to be attended by worshippers who worship the Father in spirit and in truth. I consecrated this humble edifice, which is regularly fitted up for public service in the interior, and confirmed twenty-four persons. They asked me to give the church a name, as I had objected to their proposal of calling it the ' Mountain Church' which was partly intended as a compliment to myself, and I called it after St. John the Baptist, as being built for preaching in the wilderness, with which they were highly pleased. God grant that the preachers, calling upon men to repent, and at the same time indicating the Lamb of God Which taketh away the sins of the world, may prepare the way of Christ among the people." Nearly a week was spent at Montreal, where two hundred and ninety-one persons were confirmed and two adults baptized in the parish church by the Bishop. By this time there were three chapels in Montreal, making, with the parish church and a temporary chapel in Griffintown and a small chapel at the Cross, below the city, six places of worship in all, and others were in contemplation. A new mission had been formed under promising auspices at Huntingdon, in the Chateauguay district; but if this step could have been taken earlier, it might have been attended with more effect, for the village of Huntingdon, the Bishop says,

"May be taken as one among many examples of the deplorable effects of schism in a new country. Here, in a spot scarcely reclaimed from the woods, is a little collection of houses, a good mill, a tavern* or two, some few tradesmen, and some commencing indications of business. One good spacious church might contain all the worshippers ; one faithful pastor might tend them all ; and their resources for the support of religion, if combined, might provide for all the decencies of worship in a reverent manner, and for the comfort of the minister and his family. They might, in laying their foundations for the future, exhibit in the article of religion,—which should be their all in all,—the picture of a little christian brotherhood, and the village not drawing, or drawing comparatively little, upon the bounty of colonial cities or societies at home, the aid derivable from these sources might the more largely supply the unprovided tracts of country in the wilderness. But here are four protestant places of worship,—altar against altar,—all ill-appointed, all ill-supported, and while discordant preaching is going on, or unholy leagues are made of two or three irregular sects against the Church, and violent excitements are resorted to, like the getting up of the steam, to force on a particular interest at a particular conjuncture, many a ruder and more remote settlement is supplied only at wide intervals by the extraordinary efforts of this or that minister, and these again marked often by a mutual jealousy, heightened, where the Church is the object of it, to acrimonious and unscrupulous hostility. In these instances, the forbearance and dignity of the Church have, I think I may say without prejudice, stood in most advantageous contrast with the proceedings of other parties. But what cause have we to imitate the prayer of the Lord Himself ' that they all may be one', even as He and His Father are one !, to pray and long for a nearer approach to that happy consummation described by the apostle, ' that there be no divisions among' them ; and that they may ' be all perfectly joined together in the same mind and in the same spirit !' The Church, whatever opposition she may encounter, can be the only possible instrument of bringing on these blessed results ; and the conviction of this truth will surely be a stimulus to all the friends and supporters of the venerable society to add to its means of planting her standard in the rising settlements of the American colonies."

Notwithstanding difficulties like these, the Church was everywhere making way and taking root. The field which had been occupied by the labours of Mr. Dawes had been divided into two, one of which, though nominally the station of a fixed missionary, was still so extensive and important,

---

* The word tavern is commonly applied in Canada to what are properly inns.

that the Bishop decided on a sub-division of it, and immediately after visiting it placed a second clergyman within its limits. The Rev. R. G. Plees had succeeded Mr. Dawes in the post of travelling missionary, and "his charge, although lying within fixed limits, was still wholly of an itinerant character. At St. Rémi, which is his home, (so far as he has one) he officiates upon one Sunday and one week-day in the month. Both these are evening services, to which he returns after labouring elsewhere. He has four other Sunday stations in his mission ; eleven regular stations for appointed services in all. He officiates twenty-three or twenty-four times every month, and his monthly circuit is one of two hundred and thirty-five miles, besides all extra calls." Laprairie also now enjoyed the advantage of having a resident minister, and a new church was consecrated at L'Acadie. At Christieville a church and parsonage had been built, and an endowment provided by the founder of Trinity Chapel at Montreal, and a new church was in progress at Henryville.* Passing from the seigneuries into the townships, the Bishop visited a new mission at Brome, and took measures for the immediate settlement of a missionary at Granby and Milton. At Compton, the first confirmation ever held was on this visitation, and the Bishop baptized thirteen adults.

"In the conflict of religious teachers and talkers, the confusion of surrounding sects, and the array of prejudices drawn up against the Church in this neighbourhood, it was not without many struggles, and much earnest and devout search for truth, that a good many of the parties here brought forward to baptism and to confirmation had arrived at last at the comfortable conviction of mind with which they sealed and ratified the covenant of their God in Christ."

At Lennoxville, the Bishop presided at a meeting of the local committee for the affairs of the college, who were

---

* New churches followed, as a matter of course, on the establishment of new missions. This one was within the limits of an old settled charge.

encouraged by the bounty of the S. P. G. to resume their suspended labours, and it was resolved to take immediate steps for opening the institution in temporary buildings. At Danville, another new mission, which the Bishop had never before visited, nineteen persons were confirmed.

The last confirmations on this tour were at the three stations in the mission of Portneuf, (in two of them for the first time) which had been erected into a fixed charge shortly after the last triennial visit. The whole number on this circuit was forty-three; the number of persons confirmed, one thousand seven hundred and seventy-three; and four churches were consecrated. In 1840, the confirmations on the winter circuit had been thirty-eight, but this number included four on the Ottawa, which had not now been visited.

In the conclusion of his journal, the Bishop makes the following general observations:

"Reviewing this whole journey, and all the evidences which it affords respecting the existing order of things in the country, it is impossible not to be affected by many heavy solicitudes and heart-rending reflections. It cannot be without feelings of sorrow and shame and fear that we see that a mighty government like that of Great Britain, which has spent *millions* in this country upon fortifications and military works, and which can allow a sum probably not short of £100,000 to be spent in a few months, (in a particular instance,) for little more than matters of parade, should suffer its own people,—in broad and reproachful contrast, in every single particular, to the institutions founded for the old colonists by the crown of France,—should suffer its own people, members of the Church of the Empire, to starve and languish with reference to the supply of their spiritual wants; establishing no institutions for educating and forming the youth of the country; making no provision whatever for planting houses of God over the land, or for creating, training, and supporting an order of 'teaching priests' for the people; interfering with and abridging the means which do exist for the maintenance and perpetuation of religion in the country; declining to follow up in any efficient manner the plans laid down when the see of Quebec was established; limiting to the lives of the present incumbents the salaries which, in half a dozen instances, are enjoyed by ecclesiastics of the Church establishment; parcelling out among different religious bodies the very clergy reserves which had belonged to the Church alone, and keeping the management of them in its own hands, under a system which impedes

their profitableness, and threatens the most alarming sacrifices in the shape
of sales ; leaving its emigrant children to scatter themselves at random here
and there over the country upon their arrival, without any digested plans for
the formation of settlements, or any guide (had it not been for the society
which I am addressing) to lead them rightly in their new trials, tempta-
tions and responsibilities. The value of the missions and other boons
received from the society may be well estimated from this melancholy
survey of the subject. The influence which has presided over the proceedings of government in relation to the Church in these colonies appears, in
the mysterious counsel of Divine Providence, to have resembled some
enchantment which abuses the mind. I do not believe that there is any
example in history of any public measures based more decidedly upon false
data or distorted facts than those which have affected the interests of the
Canadian Church ; and here I allude specially to the information upon
which the report of the committee of the House of Commons was framed
in 1828, and to the materials of which the late Earl of Durham made up
his far-famed report to Her Majesty ten years after that period.

   " Yet, on the other hand, when we look at the advances which, through
all these difficulties, and despite all these discouragements, the Church has
been permitted to make, we have cause to lift up our hands in thankfulness,
and our hearts in hope. The Church in Canada has two Bishops and more
than one hundred and sixty clergymen; and in this diocese alone, which,
in point of Church population, is of secondary magnitude, I have just shewn
that there will be not less than sixty-seven confirmations on the visitation
now in part accomplished. Now, there are persons living,—and yet far
from any indications of decrepitude,—three of them are among my own
acquaintance,—who were confirmed at Quebec by the first Bishop of Nova
Scotia, the first, and then the only Colonial Bishop of the established
Church in the whole empire, towards the close of the last century, at which
time there were, I believe, half a dozen Church clergy in all Canada·
When I contemplate the case of our missionaries, and think of the effects
of their labours, I look upon them as marked examples of men whose
reward is not in this world. Men leading lives of toil, and more or less of
hardship and privation—often with their families in unpainted rooms, and
with uncarpeted floors,—the very consideration which attaches to them as
clergymen of the English Church establishment exposing them to worldly
mortification, from their inability to maintain appearances consistent with
any such pretension,—they are yet, under the hand of God, the dispensers
of present, and the founders of future, blessing in the land. There are many
points of view in which they may be so regarded ; for wherever a Church
clergyman is established, there is, to a certain extent, a focus for improvement found. But nothing is more striking than the barrier which the
Church, without any adventitious sources of influence, opposes to the
impetuous flood of fanaticism, rushing at intervals through the newer

parts of the country, and those especially which lie along the frontier. Nothing else can stand against it. The irregular sects are frequently seen either to yield through policy, and mix themselves with a stream which they cannot turn, or to be forcibly carried along where it leads them, and finally to lose the stand which they had held."

The journeyings for the accomplishment of the visitation were resumed in May, 1843, the first confirmation being held at St. Martin, near Montreal. The Bishop had made his arrangements for leaving Quebec on the 8th of that month, but the ice on the St. Lawrence held so firm till within four days of that date, that he had begun to fear that he should not be able to adhere to them. From Montreal he went up the Ottawa, but his progress was a matter of considerable difficulty, though he reached a higher point than he had ever before visited. The description of the state of the country at the time is so characteristic, that a long extract from his journal (also published as a number in the series of the " Church in the Colonies ") will not be uninteresting.

"Early on the morning of the 15th, a day of determined rain, I embarked in a small and ill-appointed steamer, having to ascend the Ottawa upwards of seventy miles before reaching the next missionary station at Hull. The waters at this season are extraordinarily high, and the river, like Jordan in the time of harvest, having for long spaces a margin of no elevation, over-floweth all its banks, so that the woods both on the shore and also on the islands (which are level) appear to be continuous masses of forest, or, in the latter case, detached clumps of trees growing in the water. They consist, in these tracts, chiefly, if not wholly, of a deciduous growth. The current in this fulness of the waters was of great power, and there was also a vehement head-wind, so that on the morning of the 16th I found that our unhappy little steamer, upon whose disordered machinery the captain and all his people had been expending labour to no purpose during the whole night, was absolutely incapable of being urged forward at all; and to make the case complete, there was no boat on board for getting ashore. The shore, fortunately, was not distant, and the water was shallow ; one of the men, therefore, fastened a couple of boards together, and standing upon them, poled himself in with a long stick. A canoe was thus obtained for my landing, and I managed to procure as rough-looking and roughly-accoutred a horse as can readily be imagined, to proceed on my way, leaving my servant and baggage to toil up, with such hands as could be mustered, in the canoe, against wind and stream; but this they soon found impossible, and actually carried the baggage on their backs. My way for a great part of the eight miles which I had to go, before reaching the mouth of the river Gatineau, lay along a low ridge of land next the river, upon which I followed the footpath, the road in the rear being under water. The whole scene was eminently characteristic of a newly opened country; here and there was a tolerable frame-house; but I passed many cabins, not five feet high in the sides, nor six under the highest part of the roof, made of trees put together with the bark upon them, the rough ends sticking out at the intersections in each corner, the roof plastered over with mud, and perhaps formed of bark, or else consisting of what are called 'scoops,' i. e., hollow halves of trees, generally lime-trees, the convex and concave scoop being laid alternately all along, from the ridge of the roof to the eaves, and so keeping each other together by their mere position, and, without any joinings, keeping out the wet. Out of this roof you might see a rusty stove-pipe to issue, or if there be a chimney, it is of clay and sticks.* The fields adjacent were full of stumps; and the woods beyond, in all the desolation of recent clearing, edged with dead or half-burnt trees. The bridges were made of trees unshaped by tool, and presented a surface wholly uneven, from the manner in which they were put together. Yet in such scenes as these there is already independence and a full sufficiency of the common necessaries of this life, and there is that impulse given to improvement of which the effects proceed in an accelerating ratio; there is the commencement made perhaps of a highly prosperous settlement, and still advancing civilization. The resources which lie in the bosom of the Canadian wilderness, prepared by the hand of God and offered to the enterprise of man, afford subject for deep and thankful reflection; but it is saddening to think of the spiritual destitution of many settlements and of the wretched provision which exists for the education of the children. We are not earnest enough in our prayers that the Lord of the harvest would send forth labourers and all requisite helps into such a harvest as this. The particular field here described will fall within the range of labour to be assigned to the travelling missionary in the district of Montreal, for the maintenance of whom, so soon as I find the person, the Church society of the diocese has provided, as well as of another in the district of Quebec; but his visits will necessarily be few and far between. God put it into the heart of those who are able to help the venerable society at home, to keep up her means and strengthen her hands, that she may do as she would desire for the many souls in the colonies, left, after all that she has already done and is doing, to hunger for the bread of life!

---

* In some parts of Canada it is not unusual to see an old flour barrel made available for this object.

"May 17th. My detention from the accident already described, and the prospect of farther detention from the want of conveyance upward by steam, the boats not having commenced running for the season, were very vexatious and disheartening, because I foresaw that it would be impossible to keep my appointment at Clarendon; and a delay there, sufficient to collect again all the scattered population who were to meet me, would oblige me to break the whole chain of my appointments downward, with much doubt of having the means at command for sending fresh notifications in time. But these contretemps will occur; and even when they seem to hinder the work of the Gospel, we must be patient, and remember that worse hindrances have been permitted in greater labours performed by holier hands. I crossed over with Mr. Strong to Aylmer village, in Hull, the residence of the Rev. J. Johnston, the society's missionary at that station, and made arrangements with the agent of one of the principal mercantile houses in Quebec, engaged in carrying on operations in the lumber trade upon the Ottawa, who was to proceed up the lake the next day in a canoe, and obligingly undertook to give me a passage. Mr. Johnston and the building committee submitted to me a plan of the stone church immediately about to be erected in Aylmer, for which Mr. Charles Symmes, a merchant of the place, has liberally given a very desirable site.

"May 18th. I rose at half-past four, and drove down to the landing. The canoe which was in waiting was one of birch bark, with ten paddles. Mr. Strong accompanied me, so that, with the agent, there were four passengers on board. There is an indescribable charm attaching to this species of vectitation upon the water, harmonizing so well in its character with the scenes through which you pass. The rush of the ten paddles, of which the short, strong, rapid stroke was kept in perfect accordance, was soon united with the bell-toned voices of the men, who struck up one of the peculiar old Norman airs (not much resembling, it must be confessed, either in the words or the music, the voyageur song composed by the poet Moore, of which the scene is laid in this very river) imported by their forefathers from France. They are all French Canadians, and there is a stamp about that race of people, even of the lowest classes, in their manners and deportment, all unenlightened as they are, which gains a feeling of good-will, attributable in a good measure, no doubt, to an inherited national courtesy, but also, as a long residence in Canada has led me to believe, to one real and high advantage, which, together with many deep and sore evils, attaches to the system of the Roman catholic Church. Order, unity, discipline, habitual and unquestioning conformity to rule, common and fraternal feeling of identity with the religious institutions of the whole race,—these, although in connexion with superstitions, abuses and corruptions, do of themselves produce a favourable effect upon the character and demeanour of men. I do not know whether it is worth while to trouble the society with such passing observations as these, which incorporate themselves in a manner spontaneously **with my** journal; but I think that the contemplation of the **effects just** mentioned carries with it a great lesson to the **protestant world, who might enjoy** all the blessings which I **have enumerated, in conjunction with a** pure **and** scriptural religion, and **with all those blessings of a higher** order which follow in its train.

"The Lac de Chênes which we ascended, is about thirty miles long; and after reaching the Chats, corruptly called the Shaws, at its upper termination, we made two portages, (the men carrying the inverted canoe and the baggage,) the former of which was above a quarter of a mile in length, the latter perhaps a mile and a half. The Chats are a series of low waterfalls, nine in number, stretching across the top of the lake, divided from one another by rocky and wooded islets, between which the foaming and tumbling waters issue as from so many portals. The effect is singular and striking. The whole length of the range of falls and islets appears to be about a mile. Above is a complete labyrinth of wood-clad islets, estimated by the voyageurs at the number of two hundred, a wilderness of wood and water, without visible bound or seeming choice of course. Mr. Noel, **the** agent, obligingly carried me beyond his own destination, to a house of entertainment about twelve miles up the second lake, where I was to sleep. We entered a room in which a group of canoemen and labourers, a dozen strange-looking and unkempt figures, were crouching over a fire in a rude chimney made of rough stones, and looking like a natural cave; they all most respectfully made way, and we were glad to get over the same fire ourselves. They afterwards disposed of themselves on the floor for the night, wrapped in the sails of their rafts or canoes, or whatever other integument came to hand, and lying close packed, side by side, like bodies in some crowded cemetery. We passed into an inner room, where we each got some kind of bed.

"May 19th. I rose again at half-past four, and crossed the lake to Clarendon in my own diocese, a distance of perhaps half a dozen miles, **in a** small row-boat, which they call here a 'bun.' Mr. Strong was obliged to remain behind, fearful of not getting back for his Sunday duty at home. Upon landing in Clarendon, at a spot where there were several scattered settlers along the low margin of the lake, or more or less withdrawn from it, I walked a mile and a half into the interior, to the house of a Mr. H——, a respectable young Englishman to whom Mr. Strong had recommended that I should address myself. (Neither I nor any other Bishop had **ever** been in Clarendon before, the mission having been first established since my last visitation.) It may be mentioned as a specimen of the state of things in the new parts of a colony, that Mr. H—— went three times to Bytown, a distance of fifty odd miles, to be married, and was only successful on the third, the clergymen, on the two former occasions, having been absent upon other calls. I found him exceedingly obliging and attentive; **and the first matter to** be arranged was to get information **circulated**

along the lake shore, up and down, appointing a time for the people to
meet me at the church in the afternoon, since I was a day after my original
appointment, and to procure the means of conveyance for proceeding to
the church myself, which was six miles farther in the interior. Messengers
were soon found for the first object. The other was not quite so easy of
accomplishment. No part of the neighbourhood afforded a single vehicle
of any kind upon wheels; the people using ox-sleds for drawing any articles requiring to be moved from place to place, even in summer. Men and
boys were despatched in different directions, to seek for horses to ride.
The first which was brought was taken from the plough, and it was no
small sacrifice for his owner to make, although I believe that it was cheerfully done, for the season was precious for his labour. He had on the
head-stall of a cart-harness, with its winkers, and a halter underneath.
The bridle-rein was a piece of rope. The saddle was in a condition just
to hold together, and no more. I mounted him at once, feeling it important to push on to the church, that notice might be given in good time at
some straggling habitations on the way, and that I might arrive also
sufficiently early to have all persons within any practicable reach collected by notices sent after I should get to my point. Mr. H—— accompanied me upon a mare far gone in foal, whom he was doubtful about
taking; but he had only the choice between this animal or none. My
servant was left to follow, if a horse should be brought for him, and was,
in that case, to bring my portmanteau, containing my lawn sleeves. I
had put up in a carpet bag, which Mr. H—— was good enough to carry,
what might serve to officiate with in case of absolute necessity. Our way
to the church was by a narrow wood-road, between high ragged pines;
there were many bad places, and there was much corduroy; but the chief
difficulty arose from the necessity of going round the prostrate giants of
the forest, thrown down by the storm of Monday and Tuesday, and lying
directly across the road, probably in not less than twenty places in the
course of the six miles. This is a sufficiently common occurrence in newly
opened roads in the woods; the trees in the dense forest, depending upon
each other for support, have no tap-roots, and when the passage of the air
is freely let in to act upon them, they are apt to blow over. In these
places we had nothing for it but to fight through the younger growth and
the bushes, making a circuit, and so regaining the road; but when I found
the nature of these obstructions, I gave up the idea of their being successfully combated by my servant with the portmanteau strapped at his back.
The Rev. Daniel Falloon lodges in the neighbourhood of the church,
which stands upon a road where there is something like a continued line
of settlement; and the expedient resorted to for circulating notice was to
send off the school-children as messengers, who fortunately were at their
lessons in the school-house. The appointment now made for service was
at three in the afternoon, before which time my servant, to my great sur-

prise, arrived. It was very saddening to think of the unavoidable disappointment of those persons who were beyond all reach of notice, in the townships of Lichfield and Bristol, and who had come great distances through bad roads* to meet me the day before, according to my original appointment. But there was much compensation in the alacrity manifested by all who were accessible to the information now sent in travelling over the same ground again, especially when the state of the roads and the poverty of conveyances are considered. Eighty-six had received tickets from Mr. Falloon; fifty-one were confirmed: about forty other persons were present. Two of the subjects for confirmation arrived after the conclusion of the service, and were then separately confirmed. One of these, a lad barely of sufficient age to be passed, had been employed in the morning running in quest of horses for me, and had travelled on foot twenty-two miles that day. Many of the males were in their shirt-sleeves. I have detailed all these particulars because they set before the society, in their aggregate, perhaps as lively a picture of the characteristic features of new settlements as any of my travels will afford; and they are interspersed, as cannot fail to be observed, with many evidences of good feeling, which one is willing to trace to an appreciation in the minds of the people of those spiritual privileges which they enjoy through the care of the society and the Church. The labours of Mr. Falloon have been exemplary, and not, I trust, without a blessing, nor without an intelligent participation among his people in the ordinances of the Church, as well as a discernment and practical application of saving truths. It was in part, I doubt not, with such feelings and such principles, that a knot of people gathered round me, (after I had mounted my horse to return for the night to Mr. H.'s,) and poured forth the most earnest remonstrances with the unrestrained vehemence of their country (they were Irishmen) against the removal of Mr. Falloon, who had become engaged to take charge of a chapelry in Montreal.† I took a longer but rather better road home, and reached Mr. H.'s house at nine o'clock, full of thankfulness that the exertions which I had been enabled to make to repair the effects of my detention below, and to get through the duties lying upon me in this quarter within the necessary time, had been so amply repaid.

"After this statement, the society may judge what the need was of Church ministrations before the opening of this mission only a year and a half ago, at which time the nearest clergyman to it in the diocese was distant fifty miles or upwards; and the blessings, present and future, may be estimated,

---

* Some of them had come from the two extremities of the mission, each fourteen miles off, on foot.

† I am happy to state that Mr. Neve, who succeeded to the charge, has fully kept up the credit and influence of the Church. Sept. 1844.

which are procured by the expenditure of the missionary allowance of £100 a year. There is in Clarendon alone a population of one thousand and seventeen souls, of whom between eight and nine hundred belong to the Church of England.

"May 20th. I rose at a quarter past four, and took an early breakfast with Mr. and Mrs. H——. In surveying the premises and the whole scene round the house, I was struck with the perfect specimen which they exhibited of the battle with the wilderness in the early stages of settlement. A gentleman told me the other day that a friend of his who has settled in the woods of Canada declared himself never to have understood the full force of the text, 'replenish the earth, and subdue it,' till he had to create his establishment and his farm in the heart of the forest, applying to this labour the latter of the two verbs. Here was to be seen a decent two-story framehouse, occupied for some time, but by no means finished, nor likely soon to be so,—out-buildings and appendages, being added by degrees, were partly wanting, partly standing incomplete. Nothing could be rougher, more dreary, more disfigured than the homestead and the scenery in view. Ragged wooden fences, fields full of stumps, like a grave-yard full of monuments; the whole space irregularly shut in by burnt, half-burnt, or singed trees, many of them simply enormous poles, with a few blackened branches near their tops; all idea of order, neatness, comfort, or finish in any of the accessories of the picture, all approach to these advantages, utterly out of the question, for a long, long time to come. Yet Mr. H—— is an enterprising, and, I hope I may say a prosperous, young man, who, besides his farm, has other undertakings in hand upon the spot, and has the prospect before him of living in plenty, improving his condition from year to year, and passing a handsome property to his children; advantages which, amidst the smooth and smiling scenes of Old England, might probably have been shut against him for ever. So it is that the gracious hand of Divine Providence balances and tempers the lot of men in this lower world; and—

> * * * * 'if countries we compare,
> And estimate the blessings which they share,
> Though patriots flatter, still shall wisdom find
> An equal portion dealt to all mankind;
> As different good, by art or nature given
> To different nations, makes their blessings even.'

"After breakfast I went down to the Lake, leaving my horse, with many thanks to the owner, at his house on the way. Close to the water side there is a half-pay officer of the army settled on a farm, and living in a low log dwelling, whose wife and daughter, a slight delicate-looking girl of fourteen or fifteen, have lately joined him from the immediate neighbourhood of London. He apologized to me for her not having been up at

the church, saying that he was obliged to keep her at home carrying water
to put out the fires which had been kindled in the new clearings, but which
might have spread in a dangerous manner if they had not been checked.
Here was an example not recommendatory of a new country. Where the
means of labour are not at command within the family, or the means of
hiring it at the high prices which prevail are found wanting, it is not wise
to embark in the task of the settler.

"The 'bun' had come over to meet me by appointment, and I crossed
the lake to Sand Point, after which I descended to the Portage. The wind
being fair, the boatmen stuck up one of the oars for a mast, and affixed to
it a bedquilt which they had on board, for a sail. At the head of the lower
Portage I found Mr. Strong, who would have accompanied me to Clarendon
had he foreseen that I could have returned so quickly. I was now pushing
my way to pass the Sunday at Aylmer; and when I reached the village
of Fitzroy Harbour at the termination of the Portage, close to the Chats,
I found that the steamer from Aylmer had been sent up expressly for me
before her intended time, and that several of the proprietors had made the
opening trip of the season in her. One of the principal among them, Mr
Charles Symmes, already mentioned as having given the church-site at
Aylmer, had despatched a messenger on horseback to Clarendon (fifty odd
miles and back) to apprize me of this arrangement. I had left Clarendon
before he arrived, but my own movements had brought me within benefit
of the thoughtful kindness exerted for me.

"Among the remarkable features of Canadian travelling, the transitions
encountered in the means of accommodation and modes of conveyance are
not the least. Steam navigation, with all the internal economy of steamers,
appears to be associated with the most advanced state of improvement,
the most artificial condition of society, and the most diffusive application
of resources productive of general convenience; yet, in visiting the newer
parts of this country, you pass at once from steam travelling to such rude
scenes and adventures as I have described. The inventions of a refined
age, and the results of long accumulated experience, are transported at a
stroke from the ancient seat of empire, where they develop themselves, to
remote dependencies, of which many portions are in the very infancy of
their progress. How happy would it be, and what abundant blessings
might it be expected to draw down, if the rulers of affairs at home, and the
country at large, were alive to the duty of communicating, as the foremost
boon to those dependencies, the means of religious light, and the necessary
provisions for the establishment of the Church of God in the land."

The last confirmation on the Ottawa was held, on the
downward journey, at Vaudreuil, where another new mission
had been opened, and forty-nine persons were presented.

At Sorel a new church was consecrated to replace the first that had been built in Canada, and there was what the Bishop calls " a double consecration ; besides that of the material building, a self-dedication to God, with the Church's benediction, of those who, in the solemn rite established by the apostles, presented their bodies a living sacrifice, holy and acceptable to God ; lively stones, built up a spiritual house, growing unto a holy temple to the Lord. Happy auguries ! never perhaps to be realized without exception, in surveying the participants in any religious ordinance, but fairly to be indulged in behalf of every group of youthful believers who present themselves for confirmation after having been faithfully prepared and trained by their pastor."

In the following October, the Bishop paid his third episcopal visit to Gaspé, where he reached a point upwards of eight hundred miles from the farthest to which he had penetrated on the Ottawa. The peculiar circumstances of this district not admitting of much immigration or agricultural settlement, it affords less room for change or progress, and therefore less occasion for remark, than other parts of the diocese. One new church (at Sandy Beach) is mentioned. At St. George's Cove the Bishop preached, at the same service, both in English and in French, for the benefit of a mixed congregation. Six confirmations were held, and eighty-six confirmed.

In the May journey, at eight confirmations, two hundred and forty persons had received the rite. The Bishop preached on a great many occasions where there was no confirmation.

Six missions yet remained to complete the circuit of the diocese, which were visited early in 1844, and in which twelve confirmations were held, two hundred and nineteen persons confirmed, and two churches consecrated. Valcartier, New Ireland, and Rivierè du Loup had become the seats of fixed missions, and the two former had each three churches.

The whole number of confirmations in the diocese had been sixty-four, and two thousand two hundred and eighteen persons were confirmed. The proportion of these belonging to the present diocese of Quebec was thirty-seven confirmations, and nine hundred and twenty-five persons. The contrast between it and the district of Montreal had already begun to appear, for there thirty-three confirmations had sufficed for nearly thirteen hundred persons.

The whole number of miles travelled in accomplishing the circuit of the diocese was three thousand seven hundred and fifty-two, exclusive of about four hundred on separate journeys for the consecration of churches in the year 1843.

CHAPTER XVI.

Visit to the Red River—Surplice question—Views on some other points—
Manner of dealing with opposition—Corner-stone of Bishop's College
laid—Visitation of the clergy—Fires at Quebec—Opening of Bishop's
College—Pastoral letter.

THE desire which the Bishop had long cherished of visiting
the missions in the Hudson's Bay territory has been already
mentioned, and as soon as this visitation of his own diocese
had been accomplished, he undertook a voyage to Red River.
All necessary arrangements had been made with the Church
Missionary Society, by which the entire expense of the
voyage was cheerfully borne, as well as that of providing the
services of an additional clergyman in the parish of Quebec
during the Bishop's absence, and some remuneration to a
clergyman who discharged, in addition to his own, the duties
of one who accompanied the Bishop as acting chaplain. The
Governor of the territory, Sir George Simpson, afforded
every facility in his power, and though the degree of exposure and privation to which he would necessarily be subjected
in a long canoe-voyage had raised some apprehensions on the
part of some of his friends* (which he had effectually quieted

---

* It was not often that those nearest to him grudged his yielding to
higher claims than their own. One of my sisters writing to me from
Quebec in 1847 (the year of ship fever) said, "My dearest father talks of
going to Grosse Isle again. I cannot think he is called upon to do so,
though, were the danger and labour greater, and it were his duty plainly
to go, I am sure none of us would hesitate a moment."

by saying with St. Paul, "What mean ye to weep and to break mine heart?") the whole undertaking was regarded, in reality, more as a relaxation than anything else. Although he could not, of course, forget the cares and anxieties of the charge which he had left behind, yet the forced leisure, the constant familiarity with nature, the novelty of many of the scenes through which he passed, and, above all, the deep and lasting comfort which the exercise of his ministrations afforded him, formed a break in his life of continued toil, and presented opportunities of actual enjoyment which could not fail to produce a beneficial effect upon himself. He beguiled the time which he spent in the canoe by the composition of some small poems, which he afterwards published under the title of " Songs of the Wilderness," and which sufficiently serve to shew the spirit by which he was animated in undertaking the journey. An account of his visit, in letters addressed to the Church Missionary Society, was also published by that body.* He acted under a commission from the Bishop of London, who had a nominal jurisdiction over these extra-diocesan regions. On the 12th May the Bishop held an ordination in the cathedral of Quebec, and preached a sermon, which was published by desire, from 2 Cor. x. 15, 16.

---

* The first Bishop of Rupert's Land, writing to him soon after his arrival in his diocese, said, with reference to this journal, " It was from its simple and forcible statements that I felt so interested in the condition and prospects of the Indian that I at last determined to accept the call" to the bishopric. "The diocese owes so deep a debt of gratitude to your lordship for its formation, and for the interest with which it is regarded by the Church at large, that one of my first desires, on my arrival, has been to write to tender my thanks for all that you were enabled to do in 1844, and for that account of the condition of the people which drew the attention of the Christian world to the necessity of a resident Bishop." It appears, also, that it was the Bishop of Quebec who first drew (in 1850) the attention of the S. P. G. to the wants of British Columbia (see summary account of S. P. G., 1860, p. 13,) so that he lived to see six new dioceses to the westward of his own, which had either formed part of that of Quebec, or in the erection of which he had been himself concerned.

The next day he set out for Montreal, and on the 16th embarked in his canoe at Lachine, on his voyage of 1800 miles. The season during which it was safe to travel in bark canoes being very short, he was enabled to spend only eighteen days in the territory after the completion of his voyage. In these (which included three Sundays) he held two ordinations after examining the candidates, confirmed 846 persons, preached thirteen sermons, delivered five lectures to the candidates for confirmation in the different congregations, addressed the Sunday School children, and visited all the principal inhabitants of the settlement. The "Indian Settlement" on the Red River was reached by great exertions on the morning of Sunday 23rd June, and the Bishop preached twice to the Indians through an interpreter. One of the missionaries says :

"The Indians were quite delighted with the sermon, and said it was not the first time their Chief Praying Father had preached to Indians, for he appeared to know so well what suited them. The next day his lordship drew out a plan for the services during his stay. I am sure we ought to feel that we owe him a debt of gratitude which we can never discharge. After the hardships of a thirty-nine days' voyage, his lordship's plan looks little like one drawn up by a lover of ease. It reminds us very forcibly of the primitive ages of the Church."

Another writes of the effect of a sermon, into which the subject of confirmation was introduced, that " many persons who before had treated the rite with indifference, became interested in it, and his addresses to the candidates, male and female, married and unmarried separately, were in a similar strain." The episcopal visit greatly cheered the hearts and strengthened the hands of the missionaries, and expressions of gratitude abound in their communications. Thus Mr. Cockran writes :

"We feel ourselves under lasting obligations to the Bishop for visiting us, and for the great effort which he has made, during his short stay, to make his visit useful to us. His amiable simplicity and fervent piety will be long remembered by us. Should it please God to raise up such a Bishop for Rupert's Land, we should then expect, under the Divine blessing, to establish a permanent Church here."

And in the same strain Mr. Cowley observes:

"His lordship was most gratefully received everywhere. He seems to have captivated the hearts, and called forth on his behalf all the best feelings and wishes, of our people. The good he has done is, I think, altogether incalculable. It may, indeed, be said of the Red River settlement, as it was of Samaria, when Philip went and preached Christ unto them, that* there was great joy in that place."

Mr. Smithurst:

"His parting address drew tears from many eyes. He will long have a place in the affectionate remembrances of both clergy and people, and many, I trust, will be the prayers offered up at Red River on his behalf."

It was impossible that such feelings, to which a more formal expression was given in addresses from the clergy, the heads of British families, and the Indians, could fail to be mutual; and when to these was added the thankfulness with which he had witnessed the effect of the Divine blessing on the work of Christ, particularly as it was contrasted with the condition of the stray savages whom he had encountered on the route, the Bishop ever afterwards looked back to this visit with inexpressible gratification and interest. In a letter written on his return from Red River, he thus describes his feelings on first approaching it:

"To come upon such a settlement, and to see the Indian children all decently clothed, with their books in their hands, and in their deportment in school or church incomparably more quiet and reverent than I ever saw in an equal number of whites, after having come freshly from the naked or ridiculously tricked-out, and often dirty, heathens—the men sitting all day basking motionless in the sun, with pipes in their mouths—and after having seen some of their places for sorcery, &c., does indeed fill the mind with the most thankful emotions of delight and the most earnest longing for the extension, by God's good hand upon the laborers engaged in it, of so blessed a work."

The Bishop reached Lachine, on his return, in safety on the 14th August. He closed his letters to the Church Missionary Society with a strong and earnest appeal for the immediate establishment of a Bishopric in Rupert's Land:

---

*This was the text of the last sermon ever preached by the Bishop.

" A move should be made at once—an earnest, a determined move—with
the eye of faith turned up to God, the heart lifted in the fervency of prayer,
and the hand put to the work without looking back."

The Archbishops and Bishops who constituted the Colonial
Bishoprics' Committee appointed a sub-committee for the purpose of promoting this object, who issued a statement in the
following year, consisting mainly of an extract from the
Bishop's letter, than which they said they could not " make
a more forcible appeal." He continued to use every exertion
within his power until the bishopric was finally established in
1849. In the meanwhile he did what he could for the oversight of the territory by means of correspondence with the
clergy, who seem to have found comfort in seeking his advice,
and reporting their progress and their difficulties as to their
own diocesan. He often said that, but for certain considerations, he would willingly resign his see for the charge of Rupert's Land.

The Bishop found some trouble awaiting him on his
return, from the indiscreet proceeding of a clergyman who had
undertaken to write anonymously in the newspapers on the
question, then agitated elsewhere, of preaching in the surplice.
Some diversity of practice had begun to prevail on this point,
and the Bishop, early in 1845, addressed a letter to his clergy
on the subject, in which he declared himself, after considerable
research and the citation of various authorities, in favour of
the gown as a general rule, but adopting the recommendation
of the Archbishop of Canterbury, that no change should be
made in places where either practice had been fairly established. The Bishop had addressed a circular to the clergy
of his diocese before leaving them for the Red River, commending himself and the work to be performed there, as well
as the cause of the Church society, to be cared for in his
absence, to their special prayers, and had taken occasion in
it to refer briefly to this question, reserving his judgment upon
it till his return. He was therefore the more pained that
any " Presbyter " should have undertaken to anticipate his

judgment, and to animadvert on its expected character.   He
had a good deal of correspondence on the subject with the
present Archdeacon of Maidstone, and Canon Jebb, and his
letter was re-published by some of his friends in England.
A brother bishop on the English bench said of it :

"It will set the disputants an example of the tone and temper in which
controversy ought to be carried on."

Some farther notice of the question was taken in the notes to
his charge in 1848.

It is not to be supposed that this was the only opposition
or discouragement that the Bishop was called upon to encounter in the discharge of his episcopal functions.   He had
to deal, of course, with men of like passions with the rest of
mankind, and offences must needs have come.   I prefer to
leave in the oblivion to which he was always thankful to
consign them all personal or local difficulties ; and I allude to
this, as I shall be obliged hereafter to do to some others, only
because they relate to questions of public and general interest,
and form part of the history of the diocese, for which this
imperfect memoir is designed to furnish some materials.   The
sensitive tenderness of his nature caused trials of this kind
to sink deeply into his heart, where other good men might
have been able to regard them with comparative unconcern,
or to find relief to their own minds in administering official
censure.   The saying of St. Paul was constantly on his lips,
" Who is weak, and I am not weak ? who is offended, and I
burn not ?"   And though in the judgment of man a more
prompt and decided exercise of authority might, in some
instances, have seemed at the time to afford a readier escape
from present trouble, yet the meekness and gentleness which
he had learnt from his Divine Master prevailed in the end
over all opposition, and contributed to leave the diocese,
when he was called from his labours, in a much more united
and hopeful state (as has been often publicly acknowledged)
than a different system of administration might have been ex-

pected to produce. Innumerable are the instances in which, by heaping coals of fire on the head of those who had opposed themselves, he melted their hearts, and it is but right to say here that the "Presbyter" to whose indiscretion allusion has been made, came forward afterwards with an entirely voluntary and unexpected acknowledgment of the authorship of the letter, and of sorrow for his offence. Often have I seen occasion to apply to my father's case the words of the Psalmist, " When a man's ways please the Lord, He maketh even his enemies to be at peace with him." There is but one human being now on earth who has witnessed the struggles and sufferings, for which private prayer (unintentionally overheard), with many tears, was alone able to strengthen him, when persistent opposition carried wounds to his very soul. But while he was tender towards those who took what he conceived to be a wrong view of their duty, and even to those whose sins were open beforehand, he never compromised his own principles, or shunned to declare them. His charity was able to distinguish between the judgment to be passed on opinions and the feeling to be entertained towards those who held them ; and he enjoyed, particularly in the later years of his life, the unspeakable comfort of being dealt with himself by the same rule. Throughout his life, indeed, he lived on terms of close friendship with persons from whom, in many points, he differed ; but none were more forward in acts of personal attention and respect, accompanied by tokens of sincere affection, or in doing honor to his memory after his death, than some who, as he was always willing to believe, from conscientious motives had taken a leading part in opposition to his public acts.*

* " In delivering and in publishing, with the notes which have been appended to it, the foregoing charge to my clergy, I have made a great effort, 'in weakness and in fear and in much trembling,' to face a variety of questions more or less difficult, and to dispose, as I am best able, of some points of a thorny and contentious aspect. Let me hope in God that I

R

Having been led to these remarks by the mention of the surplice question, I am prompted to insert here one or two extracts from his private letters on other points agitated at this time, though his charges and published sermons, as well as the whole history of his ministry, sufficiently exhibit his principles and opinions. In a letter dated in April, 1842, he says:

"How lamentable it is to think that a set of men like the Tractarians. who 'did run well,' who, up to a certain point, rendered admirable service to the Church, corrected many loose and low notions which widely prevailed, and kept in check many irregular tendencies, should have pushed their principles so far beyond the line of truth as not only to propagate mischief, but to undo to a great extent the good which they had themselves done; for the avowed dissenters from the Church, and the half-dissenting party within her, have now the unhappy advantage put into their hands of being able plausibly to represent all maintenance of ancient order and discipline, reverence in the solemnities of worship. and adherence to primitive views of the Christian ministry, as tending towards popery. In itself, there can be no greater mistake in the world; for the relaxation which is seen among protestants of some of these points, and their abandonment of others, constitute the very strength of the cause of Rome. I trust, however, that there is a large body of our clergy who are neither Tractarians nor low Churchmen, and who are equally prepared to make their stand against the insinuating advances of popery, and the disorganizing proceedings of schismatics and their abettors."

Later in the same year, he wrote:

"I regret that you lost the opportunity of seeing the consecration of the five Bishops in Westminster Abbey. I am truly rejoiced that, among other improvements in the Church, the unhappy practice has at last been broken through, of doing in a corner the things which are calculated to excite the

have—in this department of my duty, at least—exhausted the task; and that if I am permitted to meet my brethren again in the same way, I may have the comfort of confining myself to topics of simple edification in the plain and unquestioned duties of our holy calling. My earnest prayer to God, with reference to the *last* as well as to the *daily* close of my labours, may be expressed in the familiar words of good Bishop Ken,—

'That with the world, myself, and Thee,
I, ere I sleep, at peace may be!'"

(*Concluding note of Appendix to Charge of 1848.*)

interest of our Church-people and strengthen the cause by their publicity.* It is curious to see that many points which, years and years ago, I made the subject of thought, and not only so, but committed roughly to paper, with a vague expectation of expanding those rough hints, and preparing them at some day of leisure (should it ever come) for publication, have latterly been brought forward by this and that person or party, and their recommendations are beginning to be acted upon in the Church. If I could enter into the spirit of the old saying, 'pereant qui ante nos nostra dixerunt,' I should have abundant ground for uttering the malediction. But I rejoice that, without my mighty help, the world is opening its eyes to the importance of recovering discipline in the Church, preserving the reverence of public worship in matters of exterior, distinguishing the clergy as men of God by their proper ecclesiastical habit, throwing open to the members of the Church at large the high and solemn occasions which are connected with the investiture of her ministers in their sacred office, &c., &c."

One or two of the rough memoranda here mentioned have been preserved, the date of which is apparently about fifteen or twenty years earlier than that of this letter. They are as follows :—" 1. Disused, or made to deviate from their original intention, which ought to be restored. Deacons. Church clerk. Fasting. Saints' days. Clerical habit (Canon). Religious office for circuit of parish bounds (Homily). Sidesmen and questmen. Excommunication, &c. Daily service. Separate offices for different hours, containing repetition if blended together, and lengthening forenoon service too much (Collect, ' beginning of this day'). Rubric before communion-service. Manner of women's attendance for churching, making it necessary to prefix a sentence for which there is no rubric. Marriage and baptism not performed in the congregation. Inconsistencies and bad effects of this deviation. 2. Corrigenda. Enclosed desks. Desks in body of church. Pews. Manner of kneeling and making

responses. *Private* not *public* worship. Should face the
minister (*i.e.*, the east end of the church), and visibly and
audibly send up one voice. Anthems should be reserved for
particular and rare occasions, except in particular congregations. A non-sequitur in the second prayer ror the king at
the altar. 3. Works wanted. History of religious delusion.
Familiar ecclesiastical history. Series of psalms and hymns
adapted to the Sundays and Holy days. Series of sermons
on Church government, ordinances, doctrines, lectures on the
festivals, to be *read* (out of the book,) brief and plain; style
more familiar than in MS. Lectures or homilies to be *read*
on Wednesdays and Fridays in Lent, or on Sunday evening by
the deacon, &c., &c., taken in part from the old homilies.
The constitution and ordinances of the Church to be distinctly
explained in the course of these. The Creed and Commandments also may be used after catechising, and taken in part
from MS."

Soon after his return from the Red River, the Bishop had
the satisfaction of laying the corner-stone of Bishop's College
at Lennoxville. This ceremony took place on the 18th September, 1844. Mr. Wood had, before this time, seen reason,
to the Bishop's great disappointment, to relinquish the idea of
taking the charge of the institution, and another clergyman in
the diocese, a graduate of Oxford, having declined the offer of it,
the Bishop entered into communication with his friends in England in the hope of procuring the services of a competent person
from home. The funds at his command were, however, at this
time so small that he could offer no higher salary than £100
a year, and the matter was, therefore, one of great difficulty.
A connection of the Bishop's, being a Michel fellow of
Queen's College, Oxford, was found willing to accept the
post on these terms; but before the arrangement with him
was finally completed, the liberality of the Bishop's aged
friend, who, upon his attention being particularly drawn
to the wants of the diocese of Quebec, sent him £6,000 stg.

to be applied at his discretion to their relief (a sum which he thought should be appropriated unbroken to some one permanent object), enabled him to raise his offer for the services of a principal and professor of divinity to £300 currency. He applied this donation to the endowment of the college, reserving, however, £400 towards the chapel, which he considered " an essential feature of the institution."

The Bishop closed his third triennial visitation by assembling the clergy of the diocese in the cathedral of Quebec to receive the episcopal charge, on the 2nd July, 1845. An ordination had been held on the preceding Sunday, while the flames of the second great fire of that year (in which St. Matthew's chapel had been burnt, as St. Peter's had been in the first, exactly a month before) were still unextinguished. The Rev. J. Reid, one of the senior clergymen of the diocese, was to have preached at the ordination, but the Bishop dismissed the congregation with a few words from the altar instead of a sermon, that they might go to aid in the work of providing shelter for those who had been rendered homeless. In his charge delivered on the following Wednesday, the Bishop referred to the fact of his still bearing the title of Bishop of Montreal, as furnishing " a standing testimony to those wants and claims on the part of the Church which ought never to be lost sight of." He had, a few months previously, declined a proposal for the annexation of the district of Gaspé to the new diocese of Fredericton, chiefly on the ground of looking to the erection of a see at Montreal.

Towards the autumn of this year, Bishop's College was opened, though the building itself was not completed. The new principal, with the students who had been removed from Three Rivers, occupied part of a building at Lennoxville, another part of which served as a store, though not without being called upon to submit to some inconvenience and privation, which they were taught to regard as part of their training for missionary work. There the Bishop paid them a visit in October. In the beginning of the winter he had occasion to address a pastoral letter to the clergy and laity of the diocese in explanation of a direction given for withdrawing the offer which had been made, in a particular parish, of the use of a chapel belonging to the Church of England to the Wesleyans, that body having been deprived of their own building by fire. This letter contains a clear and powerful exhibition of the principles which, with all charity to those who differ from the Church, render such proceedings inadmissible, and this was freely acknowledged by the clergyman whose kind feeling had prompted the act without, perhaps, sufficient consideration. It often happened, in the course of his visitations, that meeting-houses were placed at the Bishop's disposal for holding confirmations or other services, and he was always fully ready to acknowledge the kindness which prompted such offers. Yet he was never able to accept them without difficulty, from the fear of producing an unpleasant feeling when it was known that such accommodation could not be reciprocated.

CHAPTER XVII.

Fourth circuit of the diocese—Ship fever—Visitation of clergy.

THE next circuit of visitation was begun early in 1846, in which year 325 persons were confirmed at Montreal on the 22nd January, and 218 exactly a month later at Quebec. The settlements on the north shore of the St. Lawrence, between the two cities, were visited on this journey, or soon afterwards, the number of miles travelled being just 500. On the 23rd June, the Bishop again left Quebec on a tour through the districts of Montreal and St. Francis, which occupied him till the 1st September. His journal of this tour, with a preface containing some interesting statistical information, was published by the S. P. G. as No. xviii of the " Church in the Colonies." On Sunday, 5th July, which was one of the hottest days he ever remembered to have felt in his life, the Bishop held an ordination at nine a.m. at Montreal, when his own son was admitted to the diaconate, for which he had not been of age on Trinity Sunday, and his services were immediately required at the quarantine station, where the Bishop always regarded it as " very important, independently of concern for the sick, dying, and bereaved, that the Church should greet settlers belonging to her on their first arrival, and connect their first impressions with religious faith and duty." On the same day, the Bishop afterwards attended four other services, preaching four times, and administering the Lord's Supper once (besides at the ordination), " leaving off at very nearly the distance of twelve hours from the time at which he had begun, and with hardly more interruption than was necessary for passing from church to church,"* and he says, " I had great cause to be thankful at the close of the day for an additional proof of the physical fitness for the labours devolving upon me, with which it has pleased God to bless one of His servants, very sincerely and keenly conscious of much less aptitude for them in other and higher points of view. I felt no fatigue in the least degree hurtful or distressing."

While engaged in this visitation, the Bishop received the intelligence of the death of a brother, whom he describes as " younger than myself, but far before me in the Christian race." On a letter which he had received from him some time previously, he has written : " The last ! O might I hope to be ready like thee when I am called!"

The visitation of the district of Quebec was completed in the spring and summer of 1847, and that of the whole diocese by a voyage to Gaspé late in the autumn of the same year. It is a year much to be remembered in the history of the Canadian Church, as having tested the energy and devotedness of her clergy, and their willingness to expose themselves to danger and death for the sake of their brethren for whom Christ died. The fever which had been produced in Ireland by famine was imported to Canada, and though it did not spread to any great extent through the country, its ravages among the immigrants in the hospitals and sheds at Quebec and Montreal, and other points where they were collected in any considerable numbers. but, above all, at the quarantine station, were fearful. The Church Society of the diocese had always provided for the spiritual wants of the quarantine station by the services of a travelling missionary, who made his head-quarters there in summer; but this was an excep-

---

* In his memoranda of sermons, I find that in Christmas week, 1844, he preached eight times.

tional year, and even if the strength of the missionary
appointed for the season had not given way early, it would have
been necessary to make some provision for duties which
far overtasked the continuous labours of any one man. The
hospitals at Grosse Isle contained accommodation for about 120
or 150 patients, but the season had scarcely opened before ten
times that number were landed on its shores. All the sheds
designed for the accommodation of healthy emigrants were
converted into hospitals; the churches and every available
building were soon turned to the same use; tents were procured, and every possible means used to provide for the sick,
who came pouring in by hundreds, and still there was not
room enough. The Bishop suggested it to such of the clergy
of the diocese as seemed to be most able for the work, to
offer themselves for the service, each taking a week. He
took the first in the turn himself,* and though everything had
been done that the most strained efforts and unwearied energy
of the chief authority at the island could possibly effect, there
were still hundreds of sick whom it was impossible to remove
from the ships. There were about 800 sick afloat, and upwards of twice that number on shore. From early morning
till late at night he devoted himself to the ships and hospitals,
leaving those in the tents to the care of the chaplain who had
not yet retired from the scene, and passing from ship to ship
without allowing himself time for refreshment or repose. He
often said that he found refreshment enough in the comfort
which the faith and patience, in repeated instances, of the

---

* The same spirit of self-sacrifice prompted him, some years later, when
he heard that the delay in the appointment of a Bishop of Sierra Leone arose
from the difficulty of finding any one willing to run the risk of labouring
in a climate which had already proved fatal to more than one occupant of
the see, to write to the secretary of the S. P. G. to enquire whether that
difficulty had been surmounted. If this had proved not to have been the
case, he told me (what no one else ever knew during his life) that he
intended to offer himself for the post, that he might "wipe away that
reproach from the Church of England."

poor sufferers afforded him, though the scenes in which he
passed his days were such as, perhaps, no human being would
naturally have recoiled from more. In a letter written from
Grosse Isle at this time, he says; "If it were not for the
sense of one's utter inability to do all that is wanted, I would
cheerfully give myself up to this kind of work."

The wretched condition of the sick in the crowded holds
of the vessels, without care or attendance of any kind, may
be more easily imagined than described. The state of some
of the ships was such that no one else could endure to go below,
much less to remain there, and the Bishop was obliged to destroy the clothes which he wore while engaged among them.
He made some very rough notes of the work in which he was
engaged, in which he records the—

"General thankfulness in receiving ministrations, occasional examples
of faith, resignation, patience, and humble devotion, most pleasing. No
murmur, no bewailing of condition, but tears in listening to prayers and
exhortation. . . . Sunday—System now begun of landing passengers
in health. Mr. S— and police collected seventy-five a little before noon.
Chose spot in corner of field, under birch trees, affording shade to all.
Having put on surplice, began regular service of day; whole body of
worshippers knelt upon green grass. First time of officiating in open air:
mill, barn, school-house, prison, private house, borrowed meeting-house,
deck of ships of war, packets, merchant vessels, steamers, schooners,
(officiated in before.) Extreme beauty of day, preached on former part of
Ps. cvii., its peculiar appropriateness. . . . 14th. Administered H. C.
to Mrs. C. before breakfast; three other communicants in ward partook.
She died shortly afterwards. Usual rounds. Sailor visiting shipmates in
church informed me of sick on board Lady Gordon. Went on board with
him. Found eighteen protestant sick, all presbyterians, thankful to receive
my services. Returned and completed rounds, except one or two unimportant visits. Mr. Torrance's arrival. My joy thereat."

Besides the churches, and eighty-nine tents, there were
seventeen large wards in the hospital proper and sheds, and
three large buildings in course of construction, one of which,
capable of holding about 125 patients, was just ready when
the Bishop left the island on the 15th June. By this time the
arrangements had begun to improve, and the number of immi-

grants to diminish. Yet there was work enough to be done, and misery enough to be witnessed, and the clergy of the diocese were not backward in responding to the call, and following the example, of their Bishop. The majority of those who took their turn caught the fever, but by God's mercy they all recovered except two, who, at the very close of the season, when all expectation of extraordinary danger had passed, voluntarily outstaid their time, neither being willing to leave the other to serve alone. The whole number of clergy who served at Grosse Isle in 1847, including the Bishop, was seventeen, of whom nine took the fever. Of these last, the Rev. J. Torrance, who succeeded the Bishop in June, was one. He was relieved by the Rev. Official Mackie, from one of whose letters, dated 29th June, I make the following extracts :

"All the sick had been received on the island, and had been accommodated, after a fashion, on Saturday evening last. Since then several ships have arrived, but for the most part, in far different trim from that which your lordship was called upon to witness. It was a perfect treat to inspect the Solway. There are upwards of 300 protestants* in the hospitals, tents, sheds, &c. I visited 185 yesterday, administering to each such consolation as I was enabled to offer. . . . I have been pleased, on the whole, with the hospitals, but the sheds, how shall I describe them ? Conceive the *improvement* which the intense heat of the last few days was likely to effect in these buildings, such as you recollect them to have been, and you may form some idea of what they are. . . . Some of the nurses, especially the protestant nurses, appear to behave in an exemplary manner, but some of them have become patients themselves within the last few days. The nurse—the *only* nurse—in one of the new buildings, containing ninety-three sick, seems desirous to leave her post. I induced her to remain a little longer, on the ground of Christian duty. One nurse and two orderlies for a hospital of ninety-three patients does seem to be small allowance, and yet these hospitals, by contrast, appear to be well kept. I was agreeably disappointed on visiting them for the first time, and am still of opinion that wonders have been done by Dr. Douglas. . . . The

---

* The Roman catholic and protestant patients were all intermixed, which greatly increased the labours of the clergy of the Church of England.

cry for wine and milk is very general—painfully so; and yet yesterday's supply of milk was 158 gallons, and the steward informs me that a pint of milk and half a pound of meat a day is the average allowance for each adult, and that about twelve dozen of wine are consumed in a week. . . . I am thankful to say that I am in good health. I do not very well see how I can remain longer than the time which your lordship fixed in your last letter, but, of course, should God spare me in life, I will again share in the duty of the mission."

One clergyman died of fever at Quebec, another at Montreal, and a third at St. John's. The whole summer was a most anxious one for the Bishop, and in a letter written on a short tour for confirmations, undertaken in July, he says :

" It is most painful to me to be away from Quebec when there is such a time of trial for the clergy, and such an extraordinary demand for clerical service; and I cannot help feeling very anxious still about Mr. Torrance, though I cling to the hope that God will spare him to us, lest we 'should have sorrow upon sorrow.' I feel uneasy, too, lest anything should have kept Mr. Rollit from coming down, but as I believe that I am doing my duty in coming into this part of the country, I must endeavour to be reconciled."

The Bishop took a second week at Grosse Isle in August, and though the state of things had greatly improved, there was enough still to move his pity, as may be gathered from the following " specimens of familiar scenes " then witnessed, and roughly noted down :

" We have neither father nor mother, and none to take care of us (two little orphans sitting on ground). People brought ashore opposite church cry for water. Old man crawling, in his filthy shirt, out of bed on hands and knees, with his pot to get water out of a dirty ditch. Bedless persons in tents; saw two lying on wet ground in rain, one a woman very ill, with head covered up in her cloak, on a bed of rank wet weeds. Bundle of rags lying on floor of tent; orphan covered up within, dying, and covered with vermin from head to foot, unowned, and no connection to be traced (this the case with other orphans also); gave his name in sharper voice than could have been looked for from the little exhausted object, without uncovering himself; voice came out of the rags. Inmates of one tent, three widows and one widower, with remnants of their families, all bereft of their partners on the passage. Filth of person, accumulated in cases of diarrhœa. Three orphans in one little bed in corner of tent full of baggage and boxes, one of the three dead, lying by his sick sister. Dead boy under the tree, who passed on foot, in a division of sick, from east end, and sat down to die on his road. . . . Difference in state of religious knowledge among lower orders since time of my entering the ministry. General acquaintance with grand articles, &c., and often happy dependence, without presumption or fanaticism. Sailors. Visited three ships. Protestant sick, extremely few on board. Upwards of 2,000 sick, of whom perhaps, not much more than one-tenth are protestants." *

The triennial visitation, which was in some degree interrupted by these events, was closed, as already mentioned, by a voyage to Gaspé, a passage having been procured in a steamer belonging to the Trinity House. One hundred and thirty-eight persons were confirmed in the district, making a total of eighteen hundred and ninety-seven in the triennial circuit, of whom one thousand one hundred and sixty-two were confirmed at thirty-eight confirmations in the district of Montreal, and the remainder at forty confirmations in what is now the diocese of Quebec. Ten churches and five burial-grounds were consecrated. The number of places at which confirmations were held, was considerably greater than in the previous visitation, as the number of stations occupied by

---

* Since this was written, the following passage has been pointed out to me in an account of a speech delivered by the late Lord Elgin, in 1856, on behalf of the Memorial Church at Constantinople: " It was not intended, by erecting this building, to encroach on any other Church. There is one kind of proselytism which it may promote—the influence which is exercised over the mind of strangers by the spectacle of Christian worship in a pure and simple form, and by good examples of Christian practice. His Lordship concluded by paying a touching compliment to the Bishop of Quebec, and related an instance of the effect produced on eye-witnesses by the Bishop's unwearied and fearless attention to those patients who were sick with the plague in the quarantine station at Grosse Isle."—*Mission Field*, *June*, 1856. I may, perhaps, be pardoned for mentioning here the effect produced by the Bishop's character on another nobleman who also filled the office of Governor General of Canada, and who said that before he knew him, he had not thought it possible that so strong a feeling could be entertained for any one with whom his opportunities of intercourse had been so slight.

resident missionaries increased, though no new missions had been opened, with the exception of Granby and Sherrington. Confirmations were held at seven places for the first time, two of which had never before been visited by a Bishop. At two places visited in 1844, in the heart of the French population, no confirmation was now held. At the beginning of 1847, the number of clergy in the diocese was seventy-eight, of whom fifty-two were missionaries of the S. P. G. They served two hundred and twenty stations, exclusive of those visited by travelling missionaries.

It was on his return from Gaspé, in this year, viâ New Brunswick,—the season being so far advanced as to make it a matter of difficulty to reach Quebec by any other route,—that the Bishop paid his first visit, mentioned in an earlier chapter, to his old flock at Fredericton. On his way thence to Quebec, he also paid his first visit to Bishop's College, after the building had been completed and occupied, where he had the comfort, also for the first time, of being received under the roof of one of his own children. He reached home in time to hold an ordination on All Saints' Day, when one bearing his own name was admitted to the diaconate, and another advanced to the priesthood.

The fourth triennial visitation of the clergy was held at Montreal, in July, 1848, at which sixty-one clergymen were present, one of whom, having come from Gaspé by land, had travelled 700 miles for the purpose, nearly all the way on horseback. Their numbers had just been reinforced by the ordination, on Trinity Sunday, of seven deacons and three priests. Speaking of this visitation, the Bishop said, " I felt very strongly the arduousness and responsibility of my position, at the head of so widely scattered a body, with so many difficulties to contend with, but comforted and encouraged, at the same time, to see so goodly an assembly of my brethren around me, from many of whom I might learn lessons of duty, and to reflect that our number in Lower Canada has consider-

ably more than doubled since I delivered my primary charge
ten years ago."

The Bishop thus alluded, in his charge, to the events of
the preceding year :—

" My Reverend Brethren,

" The last occasion upon which we were permitted to meet in visitation,
was marked, as most among you will remember, by an exceedingly awful
public calamity, upon the spot where we were assembled. We stood in the
midst of yet smoking ruins,—the second conflagration, which within a
month after the first devastated the ancient metropolis of the province,
having just freshly occurred. Alas! there is a deeper gloom now thrown
over our meeting : we meet under the effects brought home to our own
body, of a far sadder scourge from the hand of our God. We look for the
familiar faces of some of our brethren in the ministry of the Church, who,
according to all human calculation, would have been among us to-day—
but gaps have been made in the circle :—they are gone, and their place is
nowhere found upon earth. A recent stroke has added one to the mournful
list of the victims of the past year—a stroke the more felt because unexpected ; for circumstances, which are of public notoriety, have diminished
the extent and altered the character of emigration from Ireland, and the
amount of sickness and the number of deaths at the quarantine station,
during the attendance of our lately deceased brother, so far from resembling the state of things which marked the summer of 1847, was, beyond
all precedent, small—(in fact, only one death among the protestant patients
had occurred at the station when he left it)—added to which, the ample
provisions which, in consequence of the severe lesson of a former season,
have been made by public authority to meet the demands of the case, and
the admirable regulations which have been established in the hospitals, have
sensibly lessened the danger of infection, which I believe to be less at this
moment than in any former year.* Yet, so it has been ordered by the wisdom of God that, although with the exception of the memorable afflictions
of last year, it had never happened that we lost a clergyman in this service,
the very first of our faithful volunteers who now undertook it, has already
fallen. ' Precious in the sight of the Lord is the death of his saints.' Honoured
be the names among men, and dear be the memories of those devoted servants of God who counted not their lives dear unto them, while ministering

---

* This opinion has been since justified by events. No other clergyman,
no medical gentleman, nor any of the subordinate functionaries and attendants at the island, have contracted fever up to this date (the middle of
September). The number of protestant interments during the whole summer has been eighteen.

to their humbler brethren in **scenes** of death and horror, **and** who, melancholy and grievous as has **been the loss to** their families **and** friends, have themselves finished **their course with joy** and gone **to their** reward in **Christ. To me, I hardly need point out that** as I was to a certain extent **concerned in causing this exposure to danger** of such among our martyr-clergymen **(in this sense) as contracted** the disease at the Quarantine **Island (being one-half of the whole number who** have died), there is here **an aggravation of poignancy in the sorrowful** sense of our loss. Yet suffer **me to mention some comfort which I have derived** from the thought not **only that our clergy, with no suggestion from their** Bishop, were found at **the post of danger in every other spot where the fever prevailed,** and that **the case, therefore, was not peculiar of those to whom I** proposed last year **(of course without enjoining it), a share of the quarantine duty ; but also **that even including those who served at that station, there was not one victim who fell simply in the execution of the duty which I had indicated. The **established term of duty was only for a week—the** two who were taken **from us last autumn, both voluntarily out-staid** their time,—one **of them by his own express and earnest desire had remained** six weeks **at the Island, —and, in human probability they might, but for** their spontaneous extension of their term of service, have been here among **us this** day. With **reference to the present season, you are aware,** my brethren, that I made no **suggestion whatever to individuals upon the** subject,—the occurrences to **which I am here adverting having caused me to** shrink **from assuming such a responsibility.

" Deeply as we must deplore the loss of so many valuable lives, and severely as it must tell upon the interests committed to us, there can, I think, be but one sentiment, when the case is fairly and fully considered, respecting the plain duty lying upon the Church to supply the service in question. It would have been monstrous, it would have been outrageous, to leave the protestant sufferers at Grosse Isle, after our chaplain became disabled, untended by the ministry of the Gospel ; and no means existed to supply this want, but in the succession of visits from clergymen at a distance. Upwards of five thousand four hundred bodies were buried in the Island during the single summer of 1847. In such a scene of death and human wretchedness, dreadful beyond conception in some of its details, and unsurpassed in the annals of history, it was not the part of the Church of England to leave her people to die like dogs, or to deny to the bereaved and desolate survivors, to the helpless orphans and the heartbroken widows, who multiplied from day to day upon the Island, the soothing ministrations and the seasonable care and counsel of her faithful pastors. Among the sick and dying themselves, there were, no doubt, many examples of a condition in which, from the operation of different causes, the ministrations of the Church can be of little avail—but even in these it was a satisfaction to be at hand and to do all of which the case might admit—while in a vast multitude of other instances, the clergy, I well know, and I may appeal to brethren who are here present—I might appeal to the testimony of those who are gone, and the assurances of the last of whom, to this very effect, are, as it were, still sounding in my ears,—the clergy, I well know, are prepared to say that they found their labours most affectionately appreciated, and, as they had reason to hope, profitably applied —that their presence was hailed and the return of their visits was longed for by the languishing sufferers among whom, from building to building and from tent to tent and from ship to ship, they made their unceasing rounds,—and that a gleam of joy,—yes, and not seldom of holy joy,—would light up the sunken or all but closing eye, at seeing, charged perhaps with the sacred memorials of the sacrifice upon the Cross, the messenger and representative of Him Who, in the days of His flesh, ‘Himself took our infirmities and bore our sicknesses’; ‘Who went about doing good and healing all that were oppressed of the devil’; and Who, in laying down His life for us all, bequeathed to us the lesson, as we are expressly taught, although our deaths cannot make the purchase of souls, that we ‘ought to lay down our lives for the brethren.’ The case here in our contemplation has been practically recognized by the clergy of this diocese as constituting such a call : they have not all taken a share in the task—it was not needed, it was not possible, that they should,—nor is any inference to be made on this account in the way of unfavourable comparison—but in every place where the call existed, clergymen of the Church have been found to respond to it—and may God give us all grace, more and more, to appropriate the language of the holy Apostle, in this or in any other case, should it ever arise, seeming to involve a risk of life in the cause of Christ, ‘Yea, and if I be offered upon the sacrifice and service of your faith, I joy and rejoice with you all.’

“I have been prompted to make these observations, because among the laity of the diocese, who lament the loss of their clergy, and who have not personally witnessed the exigencies which called them into scenes of danger, there have been questions raised, here and there, respecting the expediency or even justifiableness of their being so employed ; and reference, as I suspect, has in some instances been made to a Canon (the 67th) which exempts a clergyman from any compulsory attendance upon persons in his parish labouring under maladies which are known or probably suspected to be infectious. The rubrics, however, in the Office of the Visitation of the Sick, which I conceive to be decidedly the preferable authority of the two, plainly suppose the attendance of the clergy, even in the deadliest prevalence of plague. Would it not have been a reproach—a disgrace would be the more appropriate term—to the Church of England, to have left all the sick and dying protestants at the Quarantine Island to the care and instruction of priests of the Church of Rome, never slackening in their labours, never shrinking from their task, never abating in their zeal for proselytism, and, in the case which we are supposing, having all the advantage accruing from a discouraged or exasperated feeling of the protestant patients on account of the neglect with which they were treated by their own Church? Would it not have been a reproach, would it not have been a disgrace, would it not have been an indelible, an everlasting stain in the pages of our history in the colony, if, while physicians and magistrates and nurses and policemen and grave-diggers were found capable of braving the danger, and while mere secular motives prevailed to engage some of these parties in their respective service at the Island, or in other places within the province where fever-hospitals were established, the clergy of the Church of England had turned their backs upon the scene of death and sorrow, and had shut their ears against the cry of the sick for their ministry, and the wail of the widow, needing to hear the words of life and peace?

"The clergy who served at the Island had a sufficiently hard service to perform; and in the confusion of last summer, from the overwhelming flood poured in of misery and disease, and the imperfect provisions which were at command for meeting the emergency,—the sick dying at one time by wholesale from the mere want of attendance, and the entire establishment, notwithstanding an incessant watchfulness, and a wonderful degree of energy and administrative skill exhibited by the chief authority upon the spot itself, being carried on for a long time by strained expedients and inadequate shifts,—it was not easy to provide for the comfort and accommodation of the clergy, in such a manner as might have been desired. But if any idea has been suffered to go abroad that the illness of the clergy was liable to aggravation from any oversight in these points, the means are not wanting emphatically to contradict it. The diocesan Church Society and other authorities concerned did their utmost to provide all that was needful in this behalf. The society charged itself unhesitatingly with the expenses to be incurred for the object, as well as with all the expenses to which the clergy were subjected by their visits to the Island; including, in the case of those in whom the fever appeared after their return home, the charges of their medical advisers; but the Government ultimately took the whole upon itself, and the society was reimbursed.

"It may be proper for the clergy to know that, a public fast having been observed at home in consequence of the calamities of Ireland, and communication of the form adopted having been made to the Bishops of these colonies, (in some of which it was followed out in practice), I did not fail strongly to urge the issue of a proclamation for the same purpose, during the prevalence of the fever among ourselves; but objections were found to exist which I did not succeed in my endeavours to overrule.

"In parting with this subject, I cannot forbear to express the thankfulness which we all ought to feel in seeing now among us some of our brethren who were, in consequence of their share in these labours of love, 'sick nigh unto death,' but who have been spared to us, lest, in their cases, we 'should have sorrow upon sorrow,'—and spared, as we hope, for years of usefulness in the husbandry of God."

After the visitation at Montreal, the Bishop paid a visit to a rude and secluded settlement, in reaching which an hour and a quarter were occupied in making a distance of three miles. The clergyman lived in "two little unpainted rooms: his dinner consisted of a plate of fried salt pork, and another of potatoes, with bread and butter, both very good, a jug of milk, and another of water; such fare he was content to live upon."

In one of his letters to the S. P. G., at this date, the Bishop says, with reference to the general condition of the diocese, "There are some pleasing incidents and promising appearances, but it is not all a sunny or smiling landscape. There are difficulties, perplexities and discouragements enough, and something more than enough, for powers such as mine, but I still hold on by the hope that while it is the will of God to keep me at the post I shall not be wholly deserted or left to myself."

CHAPTER XVIII.

IN 1849, the cholera re-appeared at Quebec, and the Bishop
thought it a fitting time to establish a daily early morning
service, although the mortality did not at all approach the
number which it had reached even in 1834. The community
sustained some very severe losses. Among these the Bishop
had to deplore his faithful friend and counsellor, before mentioned, the Hon. A. W. Cochran. In all matters relating
to legal affairs, and in many other points, the Bishop found
another sincere friend and adviser after this loss, and this he
always regarded as a special cause for thankfulness. The
best legal advice that could be obtained in Lower and in
Upper Canada was always ready in the cause of the Church,
and afforded in the most disinterested manner. Towards the
close of 1849, the Bishop, who very rarely indeed took any
part in political affairs, felt it his duty to print, for private cir-
culation among members of the Church, some " Thoughts on
Annexation," which he had originally drawn up in the shape
of a pastoral letter. The necessity, however, for sending it
forth in this form had happily passed away before it could
be issued, but he was anxious, as far as possible, to exhibit
the duty of churchmen towards the Church and Realm of
England, to which he was himself thoroughly and devotedly

attached, and to dissuade them from being carried away by any passing excitement of discontent. The two great institutions, for the establishment of which he had laboured so long, were both now fairly established, and, by God's blessing, prospering. But they still demanded a large share of his time and thought, as well as frequent journeyings to Lennoxville and Montreal, the former not being, for several years after the date we have now reached, accessible by railroad. The college, indeed, was at this time in temporary difficulty of a financial kind, but this was met, partly by a subscription of £250 a year for three years, raised in a few days at Quebec, and partly by the voluntary sacrifice, by all the professors, of a portion of their salaries. In reference to this, the Bishop wrote to the S. P. G. : "The college has received a check, but it has been met by a spirit of faith and resolution on the part of those whose private interests are immediately affected : they are willing to do all they can to recover, by prudence and exertion, what the institution has temporarily lost, and are prepared, if they must suffer, to suffer cheerfully, and still to do their duty as heretofore." But there was another object, and one of wider interest, another need which had been long felt, to provide for which matters began now to be put in train. In his charge delivered in 1848, the Bishop referred to " the grievous detriment done in many ways to the Church, by the denial to her of her inherent privilege to meet, by her accredited representatives, in stated and solemn deliberation, whether in general or diocesan synods, upon her own affairs, and some peculiar consequences of this anomaly affecting the colonial branches of the Church," in which " a weight of labour and responsibility, often very oppressive and very disheartening, is thrown, as things now are, upon individual Bishops, of which they ought to be relieved, as well by opportunities of reference to the great council of the Church at home, as by the collective wisdom of both prelates and clerical deputies within the colonies, assembled in the same formal manner, and seeking, in united supplication, the guidance of the Spirit of truth and love." In the hope of maturing some plan for the accomplishment of this great object, he was engaged in correspondence with the other North American Bishops, now five in all, that a preliminary conference might be held on the subject. This took place two years later, as we shall presently see. Since the departure of Bishop Stewart, a few days after his own arrival at Quebec in 1836, he had not seen the face of a brother Bishop of the Anglican Church, until he visited Fredericton in 1847. It was in 1849 that he met the Bishop of Toronto, for the first time after his consecration ten years previously : they met when each was engaged in administering confirmation on the Ottawa, where it is spanned by a bridge. " Their opportunities of conversation were brief, but the mutual greeting was cordial, and no inconsiderable interest attached to their interview." It was in this year, too, that the efforts he had used for the establishment of a bishopric in Prince Rupert's Land, were brought to a happy issue,* and he began more earnestly than ever to labour for the farther division of his own diocese. The S.P.G. resolved, in April, " in compliance with his urgent and frequently-repeated recommendations" to do its part towards the establishment of a see at Montreal. The Clergy Reserves, of which the administration had been confided to the Crown Lands Department of the provincial Government (the Clergy Reserve Corporation having been dissolved), had become available, to a very small extent, in Lower Canada. An accumulated sum of about £9000, in addition to the annual revenue, had been placed at the disposal of the S. P. G.,

---

* In his letters to the S. P. G., on hearing of this, he says, " I bless God to learn that my prayers have been heard, (though better prayers than mine have been given for the attainment of the object) on behalf of Red River. * * * It is a measure of special interest to me, and I am full of thankfulness that it has been accomplished."

the legal trustee of the fund, and the Bishop proposed that this block sum should form the nucleus of an endowment fund for two bishoprics in Lower Canada. The urgency of the case seemed now, however, so great that it was proposed to provide at once for the new see. But the Secretary of State for the Colonies objected to its appropriation for this object, while no provision existed for the endowment of the see of Quebec itself, and it was accordingly arranged that it should be so applied instead, and allowed to accumulate during the continuance of the parliamentary grant. The Society, however, took immediate measures for raising, by private subscription, a sum for the endowment of the proposed new see, on behalf of which a special appeal was issued by the Council for colonial bishoprics, on the 12th March, 1850. This appeal was so successful, that on St. James' Day, in the same year, the present Metropolitan of Canada was consecrated at Westminster abbey, to the great joy* and relief of him who surrendered to him the title of Bishop of Montreal, receiving himself fresh letters patent appointing him to the see of Quebec, which he had administered for fourteen years. The new Bishop arrived in Canada on the 11th September, and was met, on first setting foot in his diocese, by the Bishop of Quebec and a large number of clergy at St. John's, where

---

* In a letter to the secretary S. P. G., dated 10th August, 1850, he says: "With deep and unfeigned thankfulness have I received this morning your letter of the 26th July, announcing the consecration of Bishop Fulford, and I am gratified to learn that the ceremony in the abbey was performed with so much solemn and impressive effect. My prayers are with him, and I shall gladly give him the hand of a brother, and pass to him a portion of my charge, in the firm hope that his supervision of it will be to the glory of God and the benefit of His church." And again, on the 26th October, 1850, "Nothing can be greater matter of thankfulness on behalf of the interests of the Church of England in Canada, than to witness the passing of the new diocese, with the important city of Montreal as the see, into hands such as those of Dr. Fulford, and to observe the general appreciation of his eminent qualifications for his charge, on which I pray and trust that the blessing of Almighty God will be seen to rest."

it 'had been arranged that, before proceeding farther, they should go together to the house of God, and administer together the Holy Communion. After this they went on to Montreal, where numerous addresses of welcome were presented to the new prelate, and of congratulation on the attainment of an object which all knew to be near his heart, mixed with affectionate regret at the necessity of separation from him, to his predecessor. The Bishop of Quebec was formally enthroned in his cathedral on St. Matthew's Day.

The last visitation made by Bishop Mountain of the undivided diocese had been completed a month before the arrival of Bishop Fulford, by a voyage to the settlements in the Gulf of St. Lawrence. It had been begun early in 1849, when the district of St. Francis was visited, and confirmation was held, for the first time, at Waterville, two other new churches and two burial-grounds being consecrated, and one other new church used for the first time for episcopal acts. In two instances, a Sunday was given to places where new ground had been broken for the Church, and where missions were afterwards established ; and in the same way, soon after his return to Quebec, a Sunday was spent at Cranbourne, which is still the *ultima thule* of settlement south of that city, a place almost inaccessible in summer, and inhabited by settlers of the very poorest kind. They are people, nevertheless, who have always shewn their appreciation of what has been done for them, both by their readiness to contribute, " to their power, yea and beyond their power," to the maintenance of their religious privileges, and the efforts of a different kind which they have made to secure the enjoyment of them. On a subsequent occasion, when confirmation was administered there, and the cold was indescribably severe, a poor paralytic girl was brought several miles, stretched upon straw in a sleigh with very insufficient protection, to be confirmed, and carried by her brothers into the church to receive the imposition of hands. Not expecting this, the Bishop had proposed to go to her house to confirm her.   The Bishop mentions a similar instance in his journal of 1849, which occurred in the district of St. Francis.   "I got into conversation with some women and children who were gathered round the stove, the weather being most intensely cold, and I observed one little girl barefooted. I asked the mother how she had protected the child's feet, in bringing her to the church. She told me that she had wrapped a quilt round them. I afterwards saw the father bringing up the vehicle to the church door in which his family were conveyed.   It was drawn by oxen, with a yoke only, and was a sleigh of that description which is called an ox-sled, consisting simply of the runners and a bottom, without sides, back, or front.   Upon this was spread a bundle of hay in which the wife and all the children nestled as best they might.   The family were from Suffolk."

Referring to Bishop's College, in writing to the S. P. G., the Bishop says, " I have so often mentioned the grounds of thankfulness to God, the Giver of all good, which exist in relation to this institution, that, although my soul overflows more and more with a sense of these blessings, I must put some restraint upon the repeated expression of it."

The visitation was continued through the districts of Quebec, Three Rivers, and Montreal, in June, July, September, and October. During part of it the Bishop was accompanied by the Rev. Ernest Hawkins, secretary of the S. P. G., who was then on a visit to Canada, and who took part in the services at the consecration of two churches on the Ottawa.   Three churches and four burial-grounds were consecrated, in addition to those already mentioned.   Early in 1850 another journey was undertaken, involving an absence from Quebec of a month, for the purpose of holding confirmations on the river Chaudière and in the county of Megantic, as well as an ordination of five deacons and a priest at Lennoxville, when an appointment was made to the new mission of Dudswell, in preparation for which the Bishop had again passed a Sunday at that place. Shortly after his return to Quebec, the churches immediately north of Quebec were visited, and in one of them (Lake Beauport) confirmation was held for the first time. In these journeys thirteen confirmations were required for 171 persons.

The most remarkable feature, however, of this triennial circuit was the Bishop's visit, in 1850, to the Magdalen Islands, lying about 600 miles from Quebec. These islands had originally been annexed to the colony of Newfoundland, and since their connection with Canada there had been so little direct communication with them, their trade being carried on almost exclusively with Nova Scotia and Prince Edward's Island, that scarcely anything had been known of them at Quebec. They lie nearer to Cape Breton, Prince Edward's Island, and Newfoundland,* than to any part of Canada. The Bishop had made enquiries at different times respecting them, but had never been able to learn that there were any other inhabitants than the Acadians, who are all Romanists. In the year 1847, however, Mr. Bowen, a resident judge in the district of Gaspé, having visited the islands on circuit, discovered a small number (125 in all, including children) of protestants, wholly destitute of the public means of grace, and though a very few belonged to the Church of England, he immediately reported the matter to the Bishop.

It is only in summer that the islands are accessible, and the next summer a clergyman was sent over with the judge from Gaspé, to ascertain the wants of the population. His visit, however, was unfortunately cut short by the illness of the judge, which necessitated his return to Gaspé. No other clergyman was disposable in 1849, and the Bishop himself was engaged in visiting other portions of his diocese. In 1850, however, he determined to see these few sheep in the wilder-

---

* One part of the Islands is a few miles nearer to a point in Anticosti than to Newfoundland, but Anticosti is uninhabited except by lighthouse-keepers.

ness with his own eyes, and after great difficulty in finding the means of conveyance, he at last embarked, on the 25th June, in a small brigantine bound for Halifax, the captain undertaking to land him at the islands, which lay in his course. Towards evening on the 3rd July, they approached the islands, but as the coast was unknown to the captain, he could not venture very near, except in daylight. The wind was favourable for the prosecution of his voyage to Halifax, and the Bishop, with his usual consideration and self-forgetfulness, proposed to the captain to transfer him and his baggage to a small fishing-schooner which happened to be in the neighbourhood. It was an unpainted, roughly-finished craft of thirty tons, "abundantly redolent of cod, and manned by six Acadian fishermen, as unkempt and as dirty a set of beings as could well be pictured to the fancy." In a letter describing this voyage, the Bishop says, "The wind was damp and chilly : but not relishing the idea of what was considered to be the cabin, I wrapped mine auld cloak about me, and sitting down upon the little hatchway, remained conversing with the man at the helm. I could not help thinking, as he sat bestriding the tiller, with gleams of light thrown partially upon his figure from the mouth of the hatchway to which he was opposite (there being a small fire, and a miserable, greasy, blackened lamp burning below), especially when Placide, a young lad belonging to the crew, brought him, at his command, a coal in the tongs to rekindle his pipe, which helped to discover his beard of about a week's growth ;—I could not help thinking what a subject I had before me for the pencil. I felt myself, altogether, in rather a strange situation. I had come upon this occasion without a single companion or attendant, and here I was, now a grey-headed Bishop of the Church of England, having tumbled, as it were, into this rude little French fishing-vessel which crossed my way by chance, driving along, in a dark night, upon the waters of the gulf, and seeking to effect a landing, where I knew not, but

anywhere upon the islands, which I had never visited before,
upon which I did not know a living soul, and after setting my
foot upon which I should be at a loss how to proceed or what
direction to take, in order to find the persons who could put
things in train for me to accomplish the objects of my visit.
I do not mean, and it must be needless to disclaim the idea,
that I was in an improper situation for a Bishop ; for I was
pushing my way to do part of a Bishop's proper work,
through some difficulties without encountering which I could
not, from particular circumstances, have accomplished my
object ; and if a thought of hardship or *læsæ dignitatis* had
come across me, it could not have failed to be instantly
repressed by the recollection of passages (and, as it happened,
I had been freshly perusing them) occurring in the iv.
chapter of the first, and iv. and v. chapters of the second,
epistle to the Corinthians, but more pointedly in the xi. of
the latter, verses 24-28. We must blush indeed, when
we remember our Master and the holy Apostles, if we shrink
from any of the passing *désagrémens* or exposure to the
roughnesses of travelling to which we may be occasionally
called ; and I go on in my narrative with a sort of undefined
apprehension that that which admits of what may be called
picturesque touches, with possibly even a shade of something
approaching to a romantic interest, in the description, may
seem, when so described, to jar against the train of thought
which is inspired by the high and sacred contemplation of the
labours and the sufferings recorded in the Gospel. * * *
When it approached eleven o'clock, I went below, and saw, to
my surprise, a rude stone chimney built into the vessel, and a
fire of faggots upon the hearth, which I was glad to approach.
I sat before it upon a chest occupying the little central space
between a couple of berths looking most utterly repulsive,
into which some of the crew managed to squeeze themselves,
who could be spared from above for their turn of sleep.
Others sat by me, ready for any call. I sat up the whole

night over the fire, which I took care to keep in activity.
At daybreak we ran into the shore and anchored, and the
men below were called up to assist in getting me ashore in
the little boat. Placide, however, was enjoying a slumber,
not only so placid, but so deep that he did not at all notice
the appeal. Another poor fellow had gone fast asleep at
his morning prayers, which were of some length, having
knelt down upon the cabin floor with his head in the berth.
It is a great reproach that men having inferior advantages,
and clinging to a system which is loaded with error, should
be far more exact and unfailing in their devotions than the
majority of those who profess our own faith. I thought, as
I have done upon many similar occasions, of a remark made
by Bishop Heber respecting the too great sensitiveness which
we often manifest in a principle right in itself, but one which
he thinks that we strain too far in the literal observance, at
all hazards, of the charge of Christ to seek privacy in our
prayers, so that our desire to shun observation produces,
under certain circumstances, an impression in the minds of
others, prejudicial in its effect upon them, that we do not
pray at all. It was nearly half-past four A.M. when I landed,
in the rain, at South-West Point. I had seen from the vessel
a couple of little log-huts or hovels, and the first living object
which I descried from the boat was a black pig, which led me
to hope that men were close at hand, but the huts were constructed only for objects connected with the preparation of
cod-fish, whose heads were strewed about the beach. * * *
The men went off to the nearest houses to seek the means of
conveyance for me to some quarter which might be considered
a point of reference in the islands; my baggage was stowed
away for shelter under an inverted *flat* or small boat, which
lay upon the beach. I took my post under my umbrella
against one of the boats, but presently espying, across a
diminutive brook, a little cavity which would just fit me,
sitting, in a low-browed cliff of red sand-stone, I proceeded to

occupy it, coming out in the intervals between the showers.
In an hour and a half the men returned, bringing with them
two or three people, and a low cart of the rudest possible construction, drawn by a wretched-looking little rat of a horse,
whose harness, home-made, was formed of strips of seal-skin
with the fur left upon it, the saddle, however, being worked
into a sort of parchment, and supported by a parcel of rags.
The head-stall was a piece of old rope, and the reins were of
the same material. Such a cart, it may be understood, had
no springs, but there was a board across the middle of it for
a seat. My baggage, however, quite filled it up. The cart
was driven by a French lad. Thus, then, I set out, having
fifteen or sixteen miles to go, in the first nine or ten of which
there is not a single house; an old Frenchman who had come
down with the cart prophesying, as we parted from him, that
the horse would not carry us through; and when I intimated
my intention of going on foot, he said that the horse would stick
fast in the fords, where both I and the driver must be in the
cart. This augury, however, was not verified. Our road
lay for the greater part of the way along one of those remarkable sand-beaches which so connect this cluster of islands,
that, with the exception of some more detached, not one of
the elevations is properly a separate island, although they all
appear so at no great distance. * * * On reaching
L'Etang du Nord, nine or ten miles from our starting point,
I went to the best-looking house to enquire for a horse, either
to ride or to take me in a light cart for the remaining six
miles of my way, the other cart still carrying my baggage.
I succeeded in engaging a vehicle, and while it was getting
ready, went to dry myself at the stove as well as I could, for it
had rained hard almost all the way. The mistress of the house,
a decent, well-mannered French-Acadian matron, prepared for
me a cleanly breakfast, of which, having walked about nine
miles after being up in the schooner all night, I was thankful
to partake. With all gratitude I profess my conviction,

especially as my duties often subject me to some fatigue and exposure, that forty years ago I should have been more exhausted by the privations and exertions (though I do not mean to call them severe) which I have here detailed, than I was upon the present occasion, and I felt that, if necessary, I could have undertaken, without any sort of distressing effort, to walk the remaining six miles, perhaps having been considerably invigorated by the sea-air upon my voyage."

The Bishop proceeded to the residence of Mr. Muncey, agent of the proprietor of the islands, Captain Coffin, R.N., at House Harbour, to obtain information which should guide him as to the course to be pursued in visiting the different settlements. Mr. Muncey was away from home, and the Bishop experienced great delay in prosecuting the objects of his visit, from the difficulty of obtaining a boat to go from island to island. He was detained three or four days at House Harbour, where he held services and baptized children among the few residents, but he was anxious to reach Grosse Isle and Entry Island, where the largest settlements are to be found. But " there was nothing left but submission and patience." At length, after many disappointments, a good Swede, who had been accustomed in his youth to episcopal ministrations, and had been confirmed by the Archbishop of Upsal, and who rejoiced at an opportunity of being of service to a Bishop, procured a boat and two men, with whom he conveyed the Bishop to Grosse Isle, a distance of about twenty-five miles. This man's father was a clergyman of the Church of Sweden, and he had been himself designed for the ministry, and had received a classical education at Upsal, but " owing to an inveterate habit of stammering, he had been obliged to abandon this prospect, and with his father's consent had gone to sea, and finally, after a variety of adventures, had settled in these islands as a boat-builder. He declared that he was cured of stammering by practising the new articulation required in learning the English language."

Grosse Isle was reached in safety, and " my friend Isaac,"
the Bishop says—

" Conducted me to a house where I was to take up my quarters. The
master was away for the summer, fishing on the Labrador coast, but his
wife did her best to lodge and entertain me. The poor woman had four
young children, and the whole house consisted of only one room ; there was,
however, a partition across nearly half of it, which served to screen each
of the beds from the view of the persons occupying the other. Every thing
bespoke poverty, with a total absence of all approach to comfort or attempt
at orderly arrangement. My hostess, however, soon busied herself in heaping upon the embers of the hearth some fragments of dry fir trees with the
branches left upon them, of which there was a deposit on one side of the
room ; and having first kneaded her flour, proceeded to bake a large flat
loaf, which she gave me hot, with pretty good butter and a cup of tea,
apologizing for having neither sugar or molasses to sweeten it. * * *
Means were soon found of inviting the attendance of the whole settlement
at divine service at seven o'clock the next morning. By about half-past
seven the people were all assembled, and numbered, children included,
upwards of fifty. The first who came in had made arrangements for seating
the congregation upon boards resting upon boxes or other articles in the
house. If there were two prayer-books in the settlement, I do not think
there was a third, and nobody was prepared to make the responses. All
seemed well-affected and thankful to see me. After the prayers I preached
to them. * * * I felt a great and anxious desire to set the seal of the
covenant upon the children, but the cases of those who were upon the verge
of being youths I directed to be reserved for the future opportunity of adult
baptism by another hand, explaining that they would be previously subjected to a course of instruction and examination. One woman would
gladly have brought me some subjects for the rite, but in despair of our
ministrations, she had taken her three children, born since her removal to
the islands, to be baptized by the Romish priest at House Harbour. Seven
children were presented to me, of whom four were infants in arms. I then
proceeded to distribute the books and tracts which I had selected and
arranged for the purpose. There was only one family in the settlement
without a Bible, and I supplied, besides this, two others whose Bibles were
worn out ; so far a pleasing fact, as it was an evidence of their having been
used. I distributed five prayer-books, being half of what I had left from
the supply brought from Quebec. I could not be otherwise than full of
thankfulness, for it was a happy and interesting day to me and to these
poor people. Never since their first establishment in this rude, sequestered,
and isolated corner,—never once in the twenty-two years which had
elapsed, had any religious service been performed among them,—never had
the children seen a protestant minister, or witnessed any form of public

worship, or even any kind of religious ministrations, unless those of a Romish priest who came up from House Harbour to bury the dead from a wreck which occurred at East Cape. It has been my lot, in not a few instances, to visit places where no Bishop had ever been before, but I remember only one or two instances in which it was permitted to me to be the first herald of the Gospel of any kind who had appeared in a settlement; and here was one where years had rolled away and infants had grown up to legal years of discretion, and not only the sound of the church-going bell, but the sound of the preacher's voice, had never been heard among the people. The wreck to which I have adverted took place in 1847, the same sadly memorable year in which such scenes of horror were to be witnessed at the quarantine station below Quebec, from the raging fever which was the consequence of the Irish famine. In the vessel wrecked at East Cape there were four hundred Irish emigrants, and disease and death were doing their work among them before the catastrophe occurred. Many bodies which had been thrown overboard were washed ashore in the storm, and many survivors landed only to die. A man who is a sort of patriarch in the settlement received into his house, barns, and out-buildings as many as they could possibly contain. He fed them, as far as his means would go, with his seed-potatoes and his stock of herring. He and his family caught the fever, and his wife fell a victim to it. About one hundred of the emigrants were drowned in attempting to land."

It was the 11th July before the Bishop was able to reach Entry Island. Immediately on his landing, he sent round notice of service to be held at seven o'clock, P.M., but it was eight o'clock before all the people could be assembled.

"There was a little question about lights. There was in the house neither candle nor oil for the kind of lamp which is in more common use than candles. Three candles, however, were procured from neighbours, not all from the same house. One was set in a candlestick, one forced into the lamp, and one stuck in the neck of a bottle. By means of these lights Mr. Muncey," (who had accompanied the Bishop from his own house, to which he had returned from Grosse Isle) "and one of the settlers who undertook to assist him in singing, were accommodated as well as myself. The arrangements for the congregation were the same as those at Grosse Isle. Forty-two persons were present, children included. Mr Muncey made the responses. The people all knelt in prayer, and the twenty-third psalm was sung. Five infants were baptized. Mr. Short had baptized nineteen children, of different ages, in 1848. I had laid out eleven packets of tracts, corresponding to the number of families in the island, and I gave them out after the sermon. A separate packet of address to godfathers and godmothers I divided among those who had acted in that capacity, and also distributed the remainder of my stock of Bibles and prayer-books. There was only one house, I believe, without a Bible. It was within an hour, or less, of midnight when all was closed. It was past midnight when, having retired to my little apartment, I heard through the partition a young child whom the parents had taken over with them to the service, answering a string of short, plain, elementary questions upon scriptural truths, and then saying the Lord's prayer. Friday, 12th July. I breakfasted with the family at whose house I had slept, and had morning prayers with them, with some exposition of part of a chapter, which I rather lengthened for the sake of an aged woman, the great-grandmother of the children, who had not been over to the service of the night before, and who was extremely deaf. I placed her close to myself, and raised my voice so that she distinctly heard me. An infant child was brought to me here for baptism by its parents, who had been unable to attend the public service."

From Entry Island the Bishop went to Amherst Harbour, to make arrangements for crossing to the main land of Gaspé. This was no easy matter, but he at last succeeded in chartering a schooner, in which, on Sunday morning, 14th July, he sailed back to Entry Island, where he held service and preached twice, and baptized one child, being the sixteenth whom he had baptized in the islands. The mothers were all churched, after receiving an explanation of the meaning and object of the observance. He completed here an exact list of all the protestant families in the islands.

Not having foreseen his detention in the islands, the Bishop had made appointments on the Gaspé coast which made it necessary for him to endeavour to reach it without loss of time, and he embarked therefore in his schooner after the second service. The owner of the vessel had laid in his sea-stock, but some of the women of Entry Island insisted on contributing loaves, home-made cheese, etc., and the farmer at whose house the services were held could hardly be prevented, though he avowed a scruple himself on account of the Sunday which he could only overcome for the special occasion, from killing a lamb to add to the store. Nothing could possibly exceed the civility and attention of the master of the schooner, but nothing certainly could have been more miser-

able than the voyage. The vessel was an old one, just about
to be replaced by another which was on the stocks. It
rained the whole night, and the Bishop was soaked through
as he lay sick in his berth. The voyage, however, was not
of long duration, for the mainland was reached on the forenoon of Tuesday, the 16th.

I have given many little details of this visit, as exhibiting,
not only some characteristic features of the work of a Bishop
in a diocese like that of Quebec, but also some incidental
proofs of the manner in which that work was performed,—
the carefulness in attending to little points which might serve
to make his ministrations effectual, and the considerate kindness shewn towards those with whom he came in contact, and
which would not suffer him to overlook the wants or infirmities
of any.

Having visited all the missions on the Gaspé coast, and
held confirmations in them (at one station for the first time)
the Bishop returned to Quebec by land, travelling up the
Bay of Chaleurs, and by the Kempt road to Metis, and
thence along the shore of the St. Lawrence to Quebec. It
was six hard days', and a good part of six nights', work to
accomplish this journey, which is performed by the mail in
nine. The Kempt road was scarcely ever used, and the
trees had so much grown up on its borders that a horseman
was wet through to his hips by the dew which he brushed
from them in passing between them in the early morning.
There were no houses on this part of the route, except one
or two where men were paid by the Government for remaining to afford shelter to travellers at the end of a day's journey. One night the Bishop and his companions slept on
straw in a ruined log hut by the road-side.

Three weeks after his return to Quebec, the triennial
circuit was completed by a visit to the missions of East and
West Frampton, where fifty-seven persons were confirmed.
One hundred and eleven had received the ordinance in Gaspé,

and the whole number in the diocese was one thousand eight hundred and thirty-eight, of whom eight hundred and ninety-three were confirmed at forty confirmations in the diocese of Quebec, and nine hundred and forty-five at thirty-seven in that of Montreal.*

At this marked period in the history of the diocese of Quebec, which from this date comprised only the districts of Quebec, Three Rivers, St. Francis and Gaspé, it may be interesting to give a summary of the increase of the Church in Lower Canada, during the fourteen years which had elapsed since the Bishop's consecration. It is taken from the Canadian Ecclesiastical Gazette, which was first published in this year at Quebec, having been prepared for that paper by the Bishop himself.

1836–1850. Clergymen ordained for Lower Canada, seventy-seven.

Clergymen adopted or introduced, ten.

Number of clergy in new diocese of Montreal: Seventeen in 1836; forty-eight in 1850.

Number of clergy in new diocese of Quebec: Seventeen in 1836; thirty-eight in 1850.

Increase in Lower Canada, fifty-two.

Number of churches in new diocese of Quebec: 1836, twenty-one; 1850, fifty-six.

Number of churches in new diocese of Montreal: 1836, twenty-one; 1850, sixty.

Increase, eighty-three, of which nine were built to replace old ones.

Number of places at which confirmations were held in 1836, thirty-six, of which nineteen were in the new diocese of Quebec: In 1850, ninety-five, of which forty-seven were in the new diocese of Quebec. Increase, fifty-nine.

---

* The numbers confirmed at two different places are omitted, but were probably rather more than thirty, making the total about nine hundred and eighty.

Thirty-four students had been admitted to Bishop's College since its opening in September, 1845, of whom eighteen had been ordained.

Two new sees had been erected in Canada since 1836, and one in Rupert's Land, to which Bishop Mountain carried the first episcopal ministrations.

In transmitting a statement of this increase to the S. P. G., he said : " The praise be to God above, whatever is done ; and may His grace and blessing go with us, and the light of His countenance be manifested to us in all the difficult work which is before us still, and amidst all the discouragements by which, for the trial of our faith, we are beset. Amen."

CHAPTER XIX.

Fifth visitation of the Clergy—Meeting of **Clergy and Lay** delegates—
Conference of Bishops **at Quebec.**

In the summer of 1851 the Bishop had the happiness of
opening a mission at the Magdalen Islands, and in July of
the same year the triennial visitation of the clergy was held
at the cathedral.   Thirty-six were present, out of forty then
serving in the diocese.   After the visitation, a meeting of
clergy and of lay delegates, whom the Bishop had invited
the different congregations of the diocese to send, was held
to consider the steps necessary to be taken with reference to
the threatened spoliation of the Clergy Reserves.   All the
parishes and missions of the diocese had elected delegates,
except the distant places in the district of Gaspé, and three
others; and forty-one delegates were present out of fifty-
seven who had been chosen, many of whom attended at
great inconvenience to themselves.   The proceedings were
unanimous and conducted with great spirit, and it was
resolved that petitions should be presented to the Imperial
and local legislatures, which were afterwards most numerously signed throughout the diocese.

In his charge delivered on this occasion, the Bishop again
adverted to the injustice done to the Church by—

"The State still pertinaciously refusing, after nearly a century and a
half for which this grievance has galled the neck of the Church, to permit
to her the exercise of her inherent privilege, indulged to every other religious body under the whole circle of the heavens, of holding her own formal

and deliberative conventions for the regulation of her internal affairs; and this the more signalized to view, because the General Assembly of the neighbouring religious establishment of North Britain sits, year by year, in solemn and dignified deliberations, under the sanction of the Crown, while again, the Romish hierarchy in Ireland has been permitted, without molestation, to hold, with all pomp and ceremony, a conclave in which the presiding influences are those of a foreign power radically and essentially antagonistic to the constitution of England in Church and State. • • •
A remarkable exemplification of the manner in which the Church is hampered when she is called upon to make provision for any exigency which may arise, or to devise any adaptation of her existing regulations which unforeseen circumstances may require, is found in the case of the arrangements put in train for facilitating the attendance of foreign protestants upon her worship, during the great exhibition in London of the present year. Here is an occasion on which it is eminently desirable, for the credit of the British name, for the interests of religion upon earth, for the benefit of souls, and for the honour of God, that the national Church at the seat of empire should sustain the glory of the country in religion, the first concern of man, and should conspicuously sanctify the whole scene, by throwing wide open her stately sanctuaries, with every ample opportunity afforded to the men of other tongues who throng the proud metropolis for uniting, each in his own tongue wherein he was born, in her pure and beautiful services, and receiving edification from her appointed teachers. Even to create a favourable impression of the national system of religion, in so unprecedented a gathering of strangers, and one which may be regarded as pregnant with consequences to the human family, is a point of much importance. But there are laws of the Church, framed without the contemplation of any such conjuncture as this, which forbid the performance of the liturgy in a foreign language within any consecrated edifice. And the Church, not being suffered to meet in convocation, has no power, no opportunity granted, to make so small an alteration as would be requisite for effecting the object in question, as the consequence of which inability on her part recourse is unavoidably had to the shift of opening service for foreigners within certain proprietary chapels and unconsecrated buildings alone.

" An incidental effect such as this upon the estimation and efficiency of the Church is certainly to be lamented. Worse, however, far worse than this is the want at which I have glanced, not of any infallible tribunal, which, we well know, does not exist, and is not to be looked for, upon earth, but of some tribunal which can inspire confidence and comfort in the bosom of the Church, when questions of a spiritual character and points of ecclesiastical obligation are to be decided. Waiving here the attempt, which might be obnoxious to the charge of presumption, to examine, as to its own proper and legal correctness or incorrectness, the verdict rendered by the Judicial Committee of the Privy Council in the celebrated Gorham case, and forbearing to speak otherwise than with all due respect of a body comprehending some of the highest functionaries in Church and State, we cannot fail to see that in its mixed and anomalous composition (anomalous with regard to the purposes which are here in question) it is liable to be such as can never command the reverence and loving acquiescence of devout and consistent churchmen. And one very undesirable consequence which has followed from the recent memorable decision is that there are many parties willing to embrace and eager to propagate the wholly false idea of its having been a decision favourable to the particular opinions, the maintenance of which had originally caused the appellant in the case to be excluded from institution to his benefice, and, in a manner, a triumph of those opinions; whereas it was, in point of fact,—and this distinction ought on no account to be lost sight of—simply a decision that the maintenance of such opinions by a minister of the Church of England was legally permissible, was capable, in the eye of the law, of a construction suffering it to pass according to the latitude which, more or less largely in different quarters, is considered to be indulged to the clergy of that Church, upon some nicer points of controverted doctrine.

The Bishop entered, at some length, into the question which gave rise to this judgment, as well as into some others respecting the claims and constitution of the Church which were stirred at the time, and referring to the hope which was then expressed in many quarters, and to which he had again and again himself given utterance, of a comprehension which might bring into the unity of the Church many who were separated from her by very small differences, he says,—

"There would be an evident necessity, *in limine*, of providing for the revival of convocation, in order to deliberate upon the question; and it must be quite needless to say, that the Imperial parliament, as now constituted, could never be recognized as the authority to deal with the subject. • • • It is plain that it must be taken as an indispensable basis of the whole negociation to retain intact the three Orders of the ministry, and to restrict the conveyance of title to the ministry to the channel through which it has passed to ourselves, and by which we shall continue to pass it on. • • • It is true, I speak as an Hebrew of the Hebrews; trained from infancy by one who held and eminently adorned the office which I have been called to hold myself, and linked in many associations of life, and by many powerful and endearing ties, with our own venerable Church, whose whole constitution, system and ritual, as well as her peculiar influence in the formation of the Christian character, as seen in her true-hearted sons and daughters, I regard with an attachment and an admiration, and a feeling of gratitude to God for the special blessing which I believe that He has vouchsafed to her, still deepening as I advance in life. Yet if any man could really convince me that I am wrong in all this, and that these feelings and sentiments are mere prejudices of inheritance, or mere fruits of education and habit which stand in the way of a consummation so devoutly to be wished as that here in question, and might bear to be sacrificed without sacrifice of principle, then I would cheerfully abandon them, and what things were gain to me, those I would count loss for Christ."

Having given expression, in the opening of his charge, to his feelings of thankfulness for the division of the diocese, and the appointment of Bishop Fulford to Montreal, the Bishop added:

"The vine which the right hand of the Lord hath planted, we may well hope, is deepening her roots from day to day, while she is stretching out her branches and will bear fruit upwards, more and more, to the glory of that Lord and the good of His people. Yet in the worldly aspect of the case, we have little to lift us up in heart, and much to abase us. Reserving here the consideration of some special circumstances which painfully affect the Church of the empire at large, or which affect it in the same manner within the province of Canada in particular, we see ourselves here, in this diocese, a straggling, and in many points of view, a feeble band. We may fix, in one instance, upon a missionary, with a handful of followers and some little detached outposts of duty to be occupied upon occasion, who has to look more than a hundred miles in one direction, and something approaching to three times that distance in another, for the nearest fellow-labourers of his own faith; and although this is a peculiar case, we know that it may be described, not indeed as the invariable condition, but yet as a characteristic condition, of our clergy, to be scattered, often at wide intervals, over a vast extent of country, and to minister to flocks of slender resources. The people, content, or, if not content, compelled, to worship in wooden churches, perhaps standing, for years together, unfinished, unfurnished, and unconsecrated, although in use; with no adequate provision for the education of their children, who are filling up the settlements, and to whom we must look as the hope of the Church, the means of communication and the accommodations of life all miserably backward, and the opportunities of intercourse with more favoured portions of the population infrequent or impeded. We stand, at best, in disparaging contrast with the splendid endowments, the substantial provisions, the imposing institutions and the multiplied engines both of religious and political influence, which distinguish the hierarchy of the Church of Rome. And yet we believe that all that proudly and wonderfully constructed fabric and all its peculiar apparatus, either of power or of fascination, are but (in an allowable variation from the original meaning and connection of the words*) 'res Romanæ perituraque regna.' And we know the utter fallacy, as we cannot fail to see the secular character, of that test of the true Church which has been put forward by a celebrated Romish champion, that amplitude, duration, and worldly prosperity should be found to concur as its characteristics. Let us, then, take courage, whatever be our comparative local insignificance, in the recollection of the question, 'Who hath despised the day of small things?' 'Fear not, little flock, for it is your Father's good pleasure to give you the kingdom.' The advances which we have been permitted to make are pledges to us that if we keep our holy faith unimpaired and our lamp burning in the brightness of unalloyed scriptural truth, our God has purposes of mercy to us, and to His people by our ministry. Our dioceses, we see, are multiplying; our own number of missions has increased considerably since we last met in visitation; and our college, poorly as it is endowed, and destitute up to this day, among other wants, of the appendage of a chapel, is most fortunate in its establishment of professors, and has proved itself an efficient nursery for the Church, having sent forth since it was opened, not six years ago, twenty-one young men, who went through their course of preparation for the ministry, in whole or in part, within its walls, and who, collectively regarded, are labouring in the field of the Gospel with decided fidelity and effect."

The year 1851 was made memorable by the meeting of the North American Bishops held at Quebec in the autumn, for the purpose of consulting together on the steps which it might be possible to take with a view to the removal of the difficulties, so far at least as they affected the colonial Church, which the Bishop of Quebec had recently described in his charge. The Bishops of Toronto, Newfoundland, Fredericton and Montreal, arrived at Quebec on the 23rd September. Until the last-mentioned prelate had visited Quebec a few months earlier, no Bishop of the Anglican communion of any other diocese than Quebec had ever been seen there since the erection of the diocese, with the exception of Bishop J. Inglis, of Nova Scotia, who had spent a few days there in 1827, and whose father, then the only

---

* It will be remembered that the " res Romanæ" are set by Virgil in the original passage in opposition to the " peritura regna."

colonial Bishop, had paid an episcopal visit to Canada in 1789. The meeting of five prelates was therefore a matter of universal interest to the members of the Church, as well as of deep thankfulness and the highest enjoyment to themselves. One of their number was personally a stranger to the Bishop of Quebec, but he had not been long in his house before he said of him : "That man is a real saint." Nothing could be more delightful than to witness the comfort and hearty refreshment which this opportunity of mutual intercourse and consultation afforded to them all, or the entire unity and sympathy that prevailed among them. Referring to this visit, the Bishop of Fredericton afterwards wrote : "I never left a house with more regret." The Bishop of Nova Scotia was unable to leave his diocese on account of his very recent arrival in it ; and the Bishop of Rupert's Land was separated from his brethren by too great a distance to make it possible to communicate with him in time. Both afterwards signified their general concurrence in the views put forth by their brethren. The Bishops remained at Quebec for a week, closely engaged in conference, the result of which was subsequently communicated to the clergy of the diocese of Quebec, in the following circular :

QUEBEC, 1st March, 1852.

REV. AND DEAR SIR,

I send herewith, for your information, a copy of the Minutes of the Conference of Bishops held in this city in September last. It was agreed among the Bishops not to divulge in other quarters the results of the Conference, till they should have been submitted to the Archbishop of Canterbury and time should have been given for his Grace's reply. This reply I received while upon my recent visit to the Eastern townships.

His Grace, who expresses himself with much kindness upon the subject, is of opinion that, as matters now stand in England, very great difficulties would be found to lie in the way of our attaining the objects of convocation or synodical action ; but that the appointment of a Metropolitan would be more readily practicable.

Upon this point, I have ventured to intimate to his Grace, in acknowledging his communication, my own opinion that there would be no advantage worth pressing upon **Her** Majesty's Government in the **appoint-ment of a Metropolitan at all, apart** from the object of his presiding in the councils of this branch of the colonial Church; and that, **till there is a hope of effecting this latter object, it is** quite as well for **us to remain, as at present, simply under his own archiepiscopal jurisdiction or that of his successors.**

The opinions and recommendations contained in the Minutes, although comprehending points which individual Bishops may, in their respective dioceses, make matter of official injunction, will not of course, as emanating from the assembled body, be understood, under existing circumstances, as having any legal or properly authoritative force.

I am, Dear Sir,

Your affectionate brother,

G. J. Quebec.

MINUTES OF A CONFERENCE

OF THE

BISHOPS OF QUEBEC, TORONTO, NEWFOUNDLAND, FREDERICTON
AND MONTREAL,

HOLDEN AT QUEBEC, FROM SEPTEMBER 23RD TO OCTOBER 1ST, 1851.

ORDER OF SUBJECTS.

1. General Declaration.
2. Convocation.
3. Church-membership.
4. Canons.
5. Articles and Formularies.
6. Division of Services.
7. Psalms and Hymns.
8. Offertory.
9. Holy Communion.
10. Marriages.
11. Registers.
12. Inter-communion with other re- [formed Churches.
13. Education.
14. Deacons.
15. Maintenance of the Clergy.
16. Conclusion.

I. GENERAL DECLARATION.

WE, the undersigned Bishops of the North American colonies, in the Province of Canterbury, having had opportunity granted to us of meeting together, have thereupon conferred with each other respecting the trust and charge committed to our hands and certain peculiar difficulties of a local nature which attach to the same.

We desire, therefore, in the first place, to record our thankfulness that we have been so permitted to assemble, and our sense of the responsibility lying upon us, before God and the world, to promote the glory of His great name, to advance the kingdom of His Son, to seek the salvation of immortal souls, and, what we feel to be inseparably united with those objects, to establish and extend, wherever there is a demand for her services, the system, the teaching, the worship and the ordinances of the United Church of England and Ireland.

We feel that, in the prosecution of this great work, we are surrounded by many discouragements, embarrassments and hindrances which, by the grace of God, we are prepared patiently to encounter, and, while they may be appointed to continue, to endure—but for which, nevertheless, it is our duty to seek all lawful remedy, if such remedy is to be found.

We have, therefore, prepared the statement which follows, of our views in relation to these subjects of our care and solicitude, and we desire to commend it to the favourable consideration of our Metropolitan, his Grace the Lord Archbishop of Canterbury, in the hope that he may be moved to assist us in obtaining relief from those evils of which we have to complain, as well as to counsel us in the disposal of questions which come before us in the exercise of our episcopal duties.

II. CONVOCATION.

In consequence of the anomalous state of the Church of England in these colonies, with reference to its general government, and the doubts entertained as to the validity of any code of ecclesiastical law, the Bishops of these dioceses experience great difficulty in acting in accordance with their episcopal commission and prerogatives, and their decisions are liable to misconstruction, as if emanating from their individual will, and not from the general body of the Church. We therefore consider it desirable, in the first place, that the Bishop, Clergy and Laity of the Church of England in each diocese should meet together in synod, at such times and in such manner as may be agreed on. Secondly, that the Laity in such synod should meet by representation, and that their representatives should be communicants. Thirdly, it is our opinion that as questions will arise, from time to time, which will affect the welfare of the Church in these colonies, it is desirable that the Bishops, Clergy and Laity should meet in council under a Provincial Metropolitan, with power to frame such rules and regulations for the better conduct of our ecclesiastical affairs as by the said council may be deemed expedient. Fourthly, that the said council should be divided into two houses: the one consisting of the Bishops of these several dioceses, under their Metropolitan, and the other of the Presbyters and Lay members of the Church, assembled as before-mentioned by representation.

Upon these grounds it appears to us necessary that a Metropolitan should be appointed for the North American dioceses.

III. CHURCH-MEMBERSHIP.

Doubts being entertained who are to be regarded as members of the Church of England in these colonies, and as such, what are their special duties and rights; we are of opinion that Church-membership requires (1) admission into the Christian covenant by holy baptism, as our Lord commanded, in the name of the Father, and of the Son, and of the Holy Ghost. (2) That all Church-members are bound, according to their knowledge and opportunities, to consent and conform to the rules and ordinances of the Church; and, (3) according to their ability, and as God hath blessed them, to contribute to the support of the Church, and specially of those who minister to them in holy things. Upon the fulfilment of these duties, they may, as Church-members, claim at our hands, and at the hands of our clergy generally, all customary services and ministrations. We cheerfully recognize the duty and privilege of preaching the Gospel to the poor, and of allowing to those who can make us no worldly recompense, the same claim upon our services, in public and in private, which we grant to the more wealthy members of our flocks.

We are farther of opinion that the Church-members in full communion are those only who receive, with their brethren, the sacrament of the Lord's Supper at the hands of their lawful ministers, as directed and enjoined by the canons and the rubrics of our prayer-book. Persons chosen as representatives of any parish or mission to attend any synod or convocation should, in every case, be members of the Church in full communion.

IV. CANONS OF 1603-4.

Although it is confessedly impossible, under existing circumstances, to observe all these canons, yet we are of opinion that they should be complied with so far as is lawful and practicable. But inasmuch as the retention of rules which cannot be obeyed is manifestly inexpedient and tends to lessen the respect due to all laws, we hold that a revision of the canons is highly desirable, provided it be done by competent authority.

V. ARTICLES AND FORMULARIES.

Whereas the multiplication of sects among those who profess and call themselves Christians, appealing to the same Scriptures in support of divers and conflicting doctrines, renders a fixed and uniform standard and interpretation of Scripture more than ever necessary, we desire to express our thankfulness to Almighty God for the preservation of the book of common prayer; our entire and cordial agreement with the articles and formularies of our Church, taken in their literal sense, and our earnest wish, as far as in us lies, faithfully to teach the doctrines, and to use the offices of our Church in the manner prescribed in the said book. And we desire that all the members of our Church should accept the teaching of the prayer-book, as, under the guidance of the Holy Spirit, their best help in the understanding of holy Scripture, and as the groundwork of the religious education of their children.

VI. DIVISION OF SERVICES.

We are of opinion that the Bishop, as ordinary, may authorize the division of the morning service, by the use of the morning prayer, litany, or communion-service separately, as may be required, but that no private clergyman has authority, at his own discretion, to abridge or alter the services or offices, or to change the lessons of the Church.

VII. PSALMS AND HYMNS.

Whereas the multiplication in churches of different hymn-books, published without authority, is irregular in itself, and has a tendency to promote division among us, we are of opinion that a judicious selection of psalms and hymns, by competent authority, would tend much to the furtherance of devotion and to the edification of pious churchmen.

VIII. OFFERTORY.

We are of opinion that it is desirable and seemly, and would tend to a uniformity of practice among us, that whenever a collection is made after sermon, in time of morning prayer, the Offertory sentences should be read, and the prayer for the Church militant should be used.

IX. HOLY COMMUNION.

We hold it to be of great importance that the clergy should attend to the directions of the rubric which precede the administration of the holy communion, respecting "open and notorious evil livers, and those who have done wrong to their neighbours, by word or deed, and those also betwixt whom they perceive malice and hatred to reign;" and that the members of the Church should signify to the minister their intention to present themselves at the holy table,—especially when they arrive in any place as strangers,—or when, being residents in such place, they are purposing to communicate for the first time. We conceive that it would greatly promote the welfare of the Church, if all our members, who may be travelling from one place to another, were furnished with a certificate of their membership, and of their standing in the Church.

X. MARRIAGES.

We hold that a clergyman, knowingly celebrating marriage between persons who are related to each other within the prohibited degrees set forth in a table of degrees published by our Church in the year of our Lord God 1563, is acting in violation of the laws of God and of the Church, and is liable to censure and punishment; and that persons who contract such marriages should not be admitted to the holy Communion, except upon repentance and putting away their sin. And we recommend that the aforesaid " Table of prohibited degrees" should be put up in every church in our dioceses. We are farther of opinion that injustice is done to our Church, in withholding from our Bishops the power of granting marriage licenses, which is exercised by the Bishops of the Roman catholic Church; and that in several dioceses great irregularities and grievous evils prevail, in consequence of the defective state of the marriage law. We also hold that the clergy of our Church should abstain from celebrating a marriage between persons, both of whom professedly belong to another communion, except in cases where the services of no other minister can be procured.

XI. REGISTERS.

We would earnestly recommend to the clergy of our dioceses (even though it should not be required by the civil law) to keep accurate registers of marriages, baptisms, and burials in their several parishes or missions.

XII. INTER-COMMUNION WITH OTHER REFORMED CHURCHES.

We are of opinion that it is much to be desired that there should be no let or hindrance to a full and free communion between ourselves and other reformed episcopal Churches; and therefore that where we derive our Orders from the same source, hold the same doctrines, and are virtually united as members of the same body of Christ, those impediments, which (as we are advised) are now in force, through the operation of the civil law, ought to be removed.

XIII. EDUCATION.

(a) General.

Whereas systems of education are very generally introduced and supported in these colonies, either (1) excluding religious instruction altogether from the schools, or (2) recognizing no distinction except between Roman catholics and protestants; whereby no opportunity is afforded us of bringing up the children of our communion in the special doctrines and duties of our faith, to the manifest depravation of their religious principles, and with crying injustice to the Church of England, we desire to express our decided conviction,

(1) That all education for the members of our Church should be distinctly based on the revealed religion of the Old and New Testaments, with special reference to their duties and privileges as by baptism regenerate and made God's children by adoption and grace.

(2) That all lawful and honourable methods should be adopted, to move the colonial legislatures to make grants to the Church of England, as well

as to the Roman catholics, and other religious bodies as they require it, and according to their numbers respectively, for the education of the members of their own communion.

(b) Sunday Schools.

(1) We desire to express our sense of the importance, in the existing state of the Church, of Sunday-schools, especially in large towns ; and we thankfully acknowledge the benefits which have resulted from the labours of pious teachers, both to themselves and their scholars, under proper direction and superintendence. In every possible case the Sunday-schools should be under the personal direction and superintendence of the minister of the parish or district ; or otherwise, the minister should appoint the teachers, choose the books, and regulate the course of instruction, that there be no contradiction between the teaching of the school and the Church. All Sunday-scholars should be instructed in the Church catechism, and regularly taken to church.

(2) We would carefully guard against the assumption that instruction in the Sunday-school, even by the minister of the parish, may be allowed to supersede the directions of the rubrics and canons on the duty of catechising in church ; for we distinctly recognize and affirm as well the great importance as the sacred obligation of those directions.

(c) Schools for the higher classes.

Schools for the higher classes of both sexes are much required, with particular reference to assisting the clergy in the education of their own children.

(d) Collegiate Institutions.

Although we consider it of great importance that each Bishop should connect with his diocese some college or a like institution for the special training and preparation of young men for the ministry of the Church, we believe that an University for the North American provinces, with foundations for each diocese, on the model of the two great universities, will be required to complete an educational system, as well for lay students in every department of literature and science, as for the students in theology, and candidates for the sacred ministry.

(e) Training for the Ministry.

In addition to the general studies pursued in the college or university, we deem it highly desirable that candidates for the ministry should apply themselves, under competent direction, to a systematic course of reading in theology, for at least one whole year, or longer if possible, previous to their taking holy Orders ; and that they should likewise be instructed in the duties of the pastoral office, in correct reading and delivery of sermons, in Church music, architecture, etc.

U

(f) Diocesan and parochial Libraries.

We deem it very desirable also, that libraries should be formed in every diocese under the direction of the clergy, both for the clergy themselves and for their parishioners.

XIV. THE ORDER OF DEACONS.

We would wish to discontinue the practice which the necessities of the Church have sometimes forced upon us of entrusting large independent spheres of duty to young and inexperienced men in deacons' Orders, deeming it desirable that every deacon should, if possible, be placed under the direction of an experienced priest.

XV. MAINTENANCE OF THE CLERGY.

While we hold it to be the duty of Christian Governments to maintain inviolate whatever endowments have been lawfully and religiously made for the establishment, support or extension of the Christian religion ; and while we acknowledge with heartfelt gratitude the aid given to our missions by the venerable Society for the Propagation of the Gospel in foreign parts, to whose fostering care and bounty the Church in these colonies owes under God its existence and means of usefulness, we desire to record our conviction, that the ordinances of the Church will never be rightly valued, nor its strength fully developed, until the people for whose benefit the clergy minister in holy things furnish a more adequate support to the institutions and to the clergy of their Church.

Farther, as the society, in consequence of numerous and increasing claims in all parts of the world, is compelled gradually to withdraw its aid, we desire to impress on all our flocks the duty of fulfilling their obligations in respect of the payment of their ministers, and with a view to this object, we recommend that the churchwardens in each parish or mission should furnish every year to the Bishop a written return, duly certified by themselves and by the clergyman, of the sums paid towards his support for the current year.

XVI. CONCLUSION.

Lastly, while we acknowledge it to be the bounden duty of ourselves and our clergy, by God's grace assisting us, in our several stations, to do the work of good evangelists, yet we desire to remember that we have most solemnly pledged ourselves to fulfil this work of our ministry according to the doctrine and discipline of the Church of England, and as faithful subjects of Her Most Gracious Majesty Queen Victoria—"unto whom the chief government of all estates of this realm, whether they be ecclesiastical or civil, in all causes doth appertain, and is not, nor ought to be, subject to any foreign jurisdiction." And we cannot forbear expressing our unfeigned thankfulness to Almighty God, that He has preserved to us, in this branch of Christ's holy Church, the assurance of an apostolic commission for our ministerial calling; and, together with it, a confession of pure and catholic truth, and the fulness of sacramental grace. May He graciously be pleased to direct and guide us all in the use of these precious gifts, enable us to serve Him "in unity of spirit, in the bond of peace, and in righteousness of life," and finally bring us to His heavenly kingdom, through Jesus Christ our Lord.

G. J. QUEBEC,
JOHN TORONTO,
EDWARD NEWFOUNDLAND,
JOHN FREDERICTON,
F. MONTREAL.

QUEBEC, 1st October, 1851.

CHAPTER XX.

IMMEDIATELY after the conclusion of the episcopal confer-ence, the Bishop of Quebec addressed a circular to his clergy on another subject affecting the Church at large, in order to recommend the participation of the diocese in the observance of the jubilee of the S. P. G. In accordance with a request made to him by the central board of the diocesan Church Society, it was now suggested to the clergy that sermons should be preached and collections made on Advent Sunday throughout the diocese on behalf of one or more of the objects specially indicated by the S. P. G., in order to shew the sense entertained of the blessings which that body had been the instrument of affording to the diocese. A good example was set at Quebec, where the Bishop preached in the cathedral; the holy communion was adminis-tered, and £51 2s. 6d. were collected at the offertory. A collection was afterwards made from house to house, in every part of Quebec, by clergymen and laymen appointed for that purpose at a public meeting held in aid of the objects of the jubilee and presided over by the Bishop. The meeting was most numerously attended, and an excellent spirit was dis-played, which exhibited itself in very large contributions. The Bishop headed the list with a donation of £50, to be given to St. Augustine's College, Canterbury. The whole sum raised in the diocese amounted to £500 sterling, which was remitted to the S. P. G., and was more than one-fifth of the whole amount contributed out of the British Isles.

The Bishop began the year 1852 by preaching in the cathedral on the festival of the Circumcision on behalf of the Canada Military Asylum, and on the following Sunday confirmed two hundred and twenty-four persons in the same church.* The collections for charitable purposes made within its walls from Advent Sunday to the second Sunday after Christmas (both included) amounted to £141 17s. 10d.

On the 19th January the Bishop left Quebec on a confirmation-tour through the district of St. Francis, confirming one hundred and eighty-six persons, at fourteen places. In one instance, a candidate, who had come twenty-four miles for the purpose, was baptized by the Bishop before being confirmed, and "his father, who stood by him, was greatly moved, and melted into tears, when the Bishop took his son by the hand and poured the sacramental water on his head." Besides holding confirmations, the Bishop visited and preached at several places more or less destitute of the ministrations of the Church. In one place the service was held in an unfinished house, where, though three different rooms and the staircase besides were occupied by the congregation, the Bishop was audible to all, and visible to most of them. His time was also engaged with meetings at Bishop's College, and in many places with visiting aged or infirm Churchpeople at their houses. A confirmation was held for the first time at Dudswell, and this ordinance, as well as the Lord's Supper, was also administered for the first time in the diminutive school-house of the township of Ham. "Some of the recipients of both were touched in their feelings in a manner

---

* At a supplementary confirmation held in St. Matthew's chapel, on the following Whit-Sunday, twenty-nine persons were confirmed, making the whole number for Quebec, including three confirmed elsewhere, two hundred and fifty-six.

which they could not conceal." It was the 23rd February
before the Bishop reached Quebec, and in the following month
he was again travelling and confirming south of the St. Lawrence, as well as attending district meetings of the Church
society. In June, July and August, he was similarly engaged
on the north shore; held two ordinations, consecrated two
churches and three burial-grounds, and twice visited Bishop's
college, after the last of which visits he made a short tour
among some destitute settlements in the St. Francis district.
On the 1st September he held a confirmation and consecrated
the little church at Rivière du Loup en haut, and a week
later confirmed at Rivière du Loup en bas, to which place
" some of the candidates had come a distance of forty miles,
and had to make a journey of three days to reach the place
and return." These two missions, lying among the Roman
catholic parishes on the St. Lawrence, are two hundred and
twenty-six miles apart, and between the latter and Point
Levi, opposite Quebec, a distance of one hundred and fourteen miles, there is no protestant place of worship. From
Rivière du Loup en bas the Bishop crossed to Murray Bay
to spend Sunday with the few church-people there, and
returned to Quebec by land. At the eight scattered confirmations held during the summer, the number of persons
confirmed was eighty-four. During part of his August journeyings the Bishop had the happiness of being accompanied
by his nephew, the Rev. J. G. Mountain, who had obtained
a short leave of absence from his self-denying labours in Newfoundland, for the first time since he had entered on them in
1847. One more visit, late in the autumn, to the Eastern
townships for the settlement of a local difficulty, completed
the journeyings of 1852 within the diocese.

In November, the Bishop addressed a circular to the
missionaries of the S. P. G. and their church-wardens in his
diocese, urging the necessity of sustained and increasing
exertions on the part of their congregations in order to relieve

that body, as far as possible, from the support of the Canadian Church. In the following month, another circular announced that he had been summoned to England to meet the Bishop of Sydney, who had undertaken a voyage from Australia in the hope of procuring at the hands of the Imperial Government some relief from the disabilities which imperial statutes were conceived to place in the way of synodical action in the colonies. Neither of these Bishóps had visited England since they left it after their consecration, together, in 1836, and it was felt that the senior prelates of Australia and British North America were the fitting persons to represent the wants which had been acknowledged by the councils of Bishops held in both countries. The Bishop of Quebec, however, shrank from the task, and hoped to the very last that he might be spared the necessity of leaving his diocese. But when it appeared that neither of the other Canadian Bishops could go at that particular time, and that the presence of one of their number was urgently desired, the Bishop of Quebec left his home, within about an hour after receiving the letter which fixed his decision, on the 30th December, and a few days afterwards, having paid a brief visit to Bishop's College, embarked at Boston for Liverpool. At Halifax he had the great and unexpected happiness of being joined by the Bishop of Newfoundland, who was his fellow-passenger across the Atlantic.

A few days only were allowed for a very hasty greeting of his nearest relatives before the Bishop was fairly engaged in the work which had called him from his diocese. He lost no time in putting himself into communication with the Bishop of Sydney and such other colonial prelates as happened to be in England, as well as with other persons in authority and friends of the Church, respecting the measures to be taken for facilitating the administration of colonial dioceses and procuring the cooperation of clergy and laity in Church affairs. Arrangements were made for holding conferences of the colonial Bishops in London, the first of which met on the 28th January, and was presided over by the Bishop of Sydney, who was never able to attend again. The Bishops of Sydney and Quebec met on this occasion for the first time since their consecration, and before they could do so again, one of them was called upon to act as a pall-bearer at the funeral of his brother. The presidency of the conferences, which were attended, at different times, by the Bishops of Newfoundland, Antigua, Capetown, and Nova Scotia, then devolved on the Bishop of Quebec. The Archbishop of Canterbury entered warmly into the question, and summoned meetings of the English Bishops at Lambeth, over which his grace presided, to confer with their colonial brethren on the steps which it was proposed to take in relation to it. Eighteen English prelates took part in these deliberations, and it was agreed that a bill, in its main features resembling that which had already been passed in the legislature of Victoria, (Australia,) should be introduced into the House of Lords by the Archbishop, for the removal of the disabilities which were supposed to hinder the free action of the colonial Church in the matter of synodical action. The Right Honourable W. E. Gladstone took charge of the bill in the House of Commons. The bill, however, did not pass, and it was reserved for the Canadian legislature to perform this act of simple justice, so far as the Canadian Church was concerned.

In order to exhibit the anomaly of their position as Bishops of the Church of England within the Province of Canterbury, and the necessity for the application of some remedy for the existing state of things, the Bishops of Quebec, Antigua, and Capetown addressed a memorial to the Upper House of Convocation praying to have that position defined. A question had been raised whether they had not a right to seats in that house, and though they did not for a moment affect to claim them, they believed that the consideration of it would tend to the advancement of their general object.

The labours of correspondence and of interviews with different persons in authority, ecclesiastical as well as civil, which the promotion of this measure involved was by no means slight. But there was another which added very seriously to the weight of care and the toil which already pressed upon the Bishop, particularly as he had left Canada unprepared for it. The petition of the Canadian legislature to be entrusted with the control of the Clergy Reserves had been sent home some time before; but when the Bishop left Quebec no danger was apprehended to the Church on that score, the ministry then in power being known to be unfriendly to its prayer. When he reached England, however, he found that a change of ministry had taken place, involving a corresponding change in the aspect of this question. It became his duty, therefore, (in conjunction with Archdeacon Bethune, of the diocese of Toronto, who was in England at the time) to use his utmost efforts to prevent what he regarded as a spoliation of the Church. He addressed strong and earnest remonstrances to the Duke of Newcastle, Secretary of State for the colonies, as well as a circular to the Bishops having seats in the House of Lords, of which a copy was sent also to several lay peers and other influential persons. The task of preparing and circulating this letter (which is here subjoined, having never been before published) together with that of communicating with no fewer than five hundred local secretaries of the S. P. G., and supplying them with a form of petition against the bill, demanded an amount of labour which almost left him " no leisure, so much as to eat." He was obliged, not only, as in 1825, to forego the pleasure of seeing many of his friends, and visiting other objects of interest, but even to decline meeting them on many occasions at the house which was his home during the greater part of his stay in England, the rectory of St. George's, Hanover Square. In his hurried letters to Quebec, he used to say that he had never been so driven for time, or so unable

to meet engagements, which it was an object, for the sake of
the Church, that he should not have given up.

BLUNHAM RECTORY, BEDS,

21st March, 1853.

MY LORD BISHOP,

It has pleased God that I should occupy in His Church, although in a
remote colony, and in a poor diocese struggling with multiplied discouragements and difficulties, the same office which is held by yourself in the
Church establishment at home ; and that poor diocese forms part and
parcel of the Church of England, and is within the metropolitan jurisdiction of the see of Canterbury. I am, therefore (being accidentally in
England,) impelled, in a crisis which threatens our religion throughout all
the three dioceses of Canada, to invoke the protection of your Lordship,
in that place, which, as becomes a Christian country, is assigned in the
great council of the realm to the fathers of the Church. (I address in the
same manner all the Bishops of the Bench in England.)

Your Lordship will very readily have apprehended that I refer to the
measure now in progress in the Imperial parliament, for enabling the
Canadian legislature to dispose, at its will, of the clergy reserves in the
colony. I am only discharging what, according to my unalterable convictions, is my plain duty before God and the world, in denouncing this
measure. Nor could I ever, holding the charge which I do, stand acquitted
to my own conscience, if, let the result be what it may, I should have
failed to use to the utmost any poor efforts of mine, to avert what I regard
as so disastrous, and, at the same time, so utterly unjustifiable a proceeding. I have been permitted, by the mercy of God, to go through some
lengthened labour,—perhaps to render some small service,—within my
sphere, in the cause of His Church ; but my memory would pass down
dishonoured to those who will come after me, were I to lift no voice
against this meditated wrong.

My Lord, with all the high respect which is due to some of the supporters
of this measure, who have every advantage of superiority over me, except
that which is founded in the merits of the case, or that which results from
immediate local experience, I am constrained to profess that I have not
heard one argument in favour of the measure, or in answer to the reasons
urged against it, which is capable of being sustained, or does not involve
some fallacy or some mistake.

I proceed, then, in the endeavour to maintain the following points :—

1. That the proposed measure is an interference with property which
ought to be held inviolably sacred.

2. That it involves a compromise of public faith.

3. That for these reasons it cannot be justifiable to put the issue to risk.

4. That, even if the risk could be justified, the arguments for hoping well of the issue are fallacious.

5. That the voluntary system would not provide for the deficiency to be created by the confiscation of the reserves.

6. That the clause which is relied upon, in the Act 31 Geo. III. cap 31, in justification of the measure, is misunderstood when so applied.

1. I advert, first, then, to what I have already declared to Her Majesty's Secretary of State for the colonies, that I do not see how this measure can be regarded otherwise than as partaking of a sacrilegious character. The clergy reserves have been set apart for the maintenance of the faith and worship of God. They have, in fact, been given to Him. And there has been no religious crisis or convulsion, no change of masters in the land, no extinction or failure of the object itself to which they were devoted, to give any sort of fair colour to the proceeding ; the reserves are wanted, and far more is wanted than they yield, for the maintenance and perpetuation of the same faith among the same people as at first contemplated. " It is well worthy of remembrance," to quote the words which I have used in addressing his Grace the Duke of Newcastle, " that in republican America the endowments of the Church of England have been held sacred ; they were preserved to her, in one noted instance, through the very convulsions of that revolution which separated the colonies from the mother country (and the circumstance was the more marked because the Church was exposed to particular odium, on account of the characteristic loyalty of her members) ; they were restored to her in another instance, by the decision of the courts of the United States, after a long space of years, in which they had been taken possession of, and held as town lands, in the absence at the time of any episcopalian claimants of the property." And although there may have been instances in which a tax or rate has been removed in that country, which had been imposed upon the population at large for the maintenance of a particular system of religion, there is none, I believe, to be produced in which the alienation has been permitted of endowments in land for religious uses. These endowments have been regarded as inviolable.

2. I must also recur again to the ground which I have taken, in writing to his Grace, respecting the engagement to the Church of the public faith. The settlement of 3 and 4 Vict. cap. 78, respecting the clergy reserves, was proposed and accepted as a FINAL settlement: it was under that pledge that consent to the act in high quarters in England was obtained : it is in that character that it has been recognised in formal documents printed under the sanction and for the use of the colonial legislature ; and even if these were considerations which could be made to yield to the claims of "responsible government," it would in itself be unfair in the

extreme, as well as untenable in **principle,** that the **effect of this** new system of Government **should be** carried back **to a point anterior** to its introduction **into** the colony, and thence take injurious **effect** upon **interests for which a definitive arrangement** had been provided by law. **And, in writing to your Lordship, I must feel** quite safe in saying that **the** pledge which is held out to our **expectations to** maintain " existing **interests,"** must never silence the remonstrances of **parties** whose personal **interests** would be so assured to them, against any scheme which endangers **the patrimony of the Church.** No, my Lord,—to strip the clergy **now** living in Canada of their slender compensation for labours sufficiently **severe in their holy calling would, beyond doubt, be an unjust and** cruel **thing ; but it would be a trifle compared with the confiscation of** the **Church endowments.** The case of a poor clergy made still poorer, and with actual starvation, in many instances, before them, might be expected to appeal with advantage to the compassion of the Church in England : and they might thus rely at least upon some sensible palliation of their condition : but the alienation in perpetuity of the means for supporting and extending the ministry of the Church, abstractedly from any present hardship inflicted upon individuals, would threaten almost the extinction, in many places, of the lamp of the Gospel, and the denial to the children of the Church of the bread of life.

3. If, then, in such a case as that which is here in question, the religious endowments given to a body of people ought, as a general principle, to be held sacred, it never can be right to put them in jeopardy. It never can be right, for an object of seeming political expediency, or under a plea of carrying out a new system of government, to throw the disposal of those endowments into the hands of another party, and to rely upon supposed probabilities for their being safe in those hands against any diversion from their original and legitimate object. A guardian in charge of the estate of a minor might, according to this reasoning, be justified in risking the interests of his ward, by a transaction which, according to his own calculation of probabilities, would afford a fair promise or a reasonable chance of leaving those interests undamaged.

4. But even if it could be granted that such a risk could be warrantably taken, and the property set apart for the Church be made the stakes for a game of chance, suffer me, my Lord, to put before you the real value, in the present case, of these arguments from probability, in themselves.

And, in the first place, let us examine the grounds of anticipating favour from the provincial legislature. Give up the principle, it is said— surrender the control—and that is all which is wanted on the part of colonial politicians. What favour, my Lord, what friendship, what protection, has the Church of England been taught by experience to look for, at the hands of the local authorities in Canada ? Look at the demands of the louder and more restless parties in that country, and the concessions

made to them by the policy of the Government.* Look at the University
which had been planted under Church auspices (but with open benefit, in
the departments of secular education, to the whole population, and with
the most promising auguries) in Toronto, violently wrested from the
Church, and despoiled of all religious character whatever. Look at the
refusal to grant the issue of marriage licences for our own people (beyond
this the privilege was never asked,) to the Bishops of the Church of England, and licences issued by the civil power, stamped, be it observed, with
the episcopal mitre; while the corresponding privilege is freely enjoyed
by the Romish prelates. My Lord, I should be carried to a length which
would be here quite out of place, if I were to accumulate the instances of
what I do conceive to be the hardships and grievances of the Church of
England in Canada. The history of the Church in that country (and it
will all one day come out) is, in a manner, made up of them; but if we
look only at the management of the clergy reserves themselves, it would
be easy to shew that, in repeated instances, the interests of religion have
been sacrificed to some passing political object, and the property has been
made subservient, in its administration, to secular ends. I forbear from
going here into the details; but, although I came home to England unprepared for this question (the news of the resignation of the late ministry,
whose dispositions upon the subject are well known, not having been
received at the time of my departure from Quebec,) and I have scarcely
any of the documents at command which would arm me for my purpose, I
am able to sustain what I say. And what regard was paid in the colony
to the expression of Lord Grey's "regret," when he was Secretary for the
colonies, that the question of the clergy reserves should be re-opened?
My Lord, we are told to rely upon the generosity of the Canadian people;
and truly we have claim upon it; for the country whose national Church
we represent among them has been most largely, and in many ways,
generous towards them; and in the day of public calamity of the province,
when it pleased God that the city of Quebec should be devastated, eight
years ago, by dreadful conflagrations, the relief freely rendered under the
Queen's letter, from within the very walls of the churches in England was

* It ought not to be forgotten that, if concession to parties who make
strong demonstration of feeling upon this or that subject is held to be a
necessary feature of colonial policy, there is a large body, commanding no
mean influence, of the Churchmen of Canada, who most keenly and deeply
feel the wrong which would be done to them in the confiscation of their
Church patrimony; and among whom the sentiment has been even known
to be uttered, in the vexation of their hearts, notwithstanding their attachment to British rule, that it would be better for them to be annexed to the
United States, for that then their patrimony would be safe.

beyond all expectation. And it was mainly for those of another tongue and another faith that it was bestowed.

But these things are not remembered by politicians and partizans, although they may be men by no means incapable of generous feeling. There is an eager party at this moment in the colony, who are vehemently opposed to the whole principle of religious endowments; and there are elections to certain seats in the provincial parliament, which turn greatly upon the favour of this party. Jealousies and alarms, of which the Church is the object, utterly unfounded in any reality, are studiously kindled, and the flame is sedulously kept up. Some men are afraid of facing this excitement; others find it convenient to adapt themselves to the changes of the times; others still are carried away by sounding and plausible, but empty, theories respecting the benefits of the voluntary system; very many are hurried on, without knowing the depths of the question to which they commit themselves. In all this turmoil and agitation, the sentiment of generosity towards the Church of England is too faint and feeble a breath to produce any effect; and, avoiding all personal allusions, I may venture to say generally that, in the incipient stages of the working of responsible government, it is not anywhere, I believe, a nicely measured policy, or a scrupulous recourse to the means of influence, which particularly characterizes the exercise of these new powers in the hands of new men. It is unnecessary, perhaps, to specify examples; but, apart from all considerations of this nature, the simple fact presents itself at once, when we are counting upon local probabilities to save the patrimony of the Church, that the Canadian ministry stand actually pledged to its secularization; and the subjoined extract from a paper which is considered the organ of the Government, of the 16th February last, may suffice to shew the justice of expectations which are built upon the dispositions, in Canada, of the party now in power:—

"The next great question now will be, What is to be done with the reserves? This question must be answered by reformers. Never before have they had the cup so near their lips: let them take care that, by quarrels among themselves, by miserable bickerings resulting in a great measure from personal spleen, it be not rudely dashed away. Let reformers be united among themselves, and they have nothing to fear. Let them count their strength in the present House; and if they should deem it inexpedient to risk a vote on the question of secularization, let them then push through the representation bill, increase and equalize the representation, and then let them go to the country as one man on this question, and success will be theirs. We sincerely trust that nothing will be done in this matter without careful forethought: one false step would furnish subject for years of regret."

It is important here to observe that, whereas many of the arguments in this question are based upon the assumption of an analogy between the

Imperial executive and legislature on the one hand, and the executive and legislature of the colony on the other, the analogy, as it does not hold in a single point, so does it especially fail when it is attempted to apply it to the Ministry. There are very obvious causes, which inspire an incomparably stronger tenacity of place in the minds of gentlemen composing the administration in the colony, than in the case of such parties as fill the corresponding posts at home ; and proportionable weight is to be attached to the fact just stated, respecting the pledges of the existing ministry in Canada.

My Lord, in these remarks upon the working of the system, whether in theory or in fact, I am neither pointing at individuals, nor passing whole-sale reflections upon the Canadian people. I believe that there are prominent individuals known to take part against us in Canada, who, in their hearts, wish well to the cause of the Church ; and, having spent all my ecclesiastical life in that country, I have found no difficulty in pre-serving a peaceable, friendly, and agreeable intercourse throughout, with men of other race and other creed than my own. I have never, in the most distant manner, been mixed up with the politics of the country or its party irritations ;* and if it be true, in this behalf, that *Principibus placuisse viris non ultima laus est*, I could shew that I have had some pretensions of such a nature. I think it hard, then,—very hard, and most signally unfair,—that odium should be thrown upon us of the Church of England for not surrendering our claim at once, and trusting the issue, under the circum-stances which I have indicated, to the mere good feeling of the Canadian parliament and people. The parties to whom we are to look as actively engaged in the question upon the spot, and having the power in their hands, and the influences acting upon those parties, I have in some measure described. These, then, are the parties with reference to whose dealings with our Church property we are told by British statesmen that we, the sworn guardians of the Church of God, ought to sit quiet and let them handle us as they please. We are charged with provoking the dispositions of which we stand in dread, and with bringing upon ourselves the very danger which we seek to avert. If the reserves should be lost to us, the loss is to lie at our own door. My Lord, by you, at least, it will be felt, and by the Right Rev. Bench in England at large, that we could not possibly be discharging our duty in passively letting this question take its course ; and that it is not kind nor just to suggest it to the mind of the local legislature, that they may confiscate the patrimony of the Church,

---

* Unless the publication of a pamphlet against the Annexation Movement, treating the question calmly upon religious grounds, can be called an exception ; or the fact of petitioning against the alienation of Church property can be so classed.

and then tell us that, because we expostulated beforehand, we are the authors of the mischief ourselves.

The real cause of the mischief, in the meantime, if we go to the original root of the matter, is to be found purely and simply in the management of the question by the Government from the first. It was at last thought to be closed by the 3 and 4 Vict. cap. 78 :—it might have been closed long before : it ought to be closed, without a compromise of Church interests, once and for ever, now.

We should, in point of fact, be in a far worse position by a seeming acquiescence in the proceedings of those who are known to be hostile to our endowments, than by our earnest, although not disrespectful remonstrance, and, *pro virili*, our vigorous, although not intemperate, opposition. There will be very much the less scruple in disturbing our rights, if it is left to be supposed that we have nothing to say in support of them ; and in my own humble judgment, utterly averse as I am to public noise and excitement, we ought to make England itself ring with our complaints, before we submit to the irrecoverable loss of this endowment.

But again, my Lord, we are told, under this head of probabilities to be counted upon in our favour, that we may rely upon the fears of the Roman catholic hierarchy and their supporters in the colony, respecting the precedent of confiscation. It might be a sufficient answer to this argument, that the facts stand as they are known to stand, respecting the action taken by the ministry and the majority of the provincial parliament in Canada, in the matter of the reserves—a ministry and a parliament composed of mixed religious elements, with so large an infusion of Romanism, as, at the very least, to balance the protestant interest ; and whether we look at parties individually or collectively, the answer would hold good. It may be conceded, however, that, in certain quarters, and to a certain extent, these apprehensions do actually operate. But the wealth, the varied resources, the numerical strength, the political ascendancy of the Romish Church in Canada—above all, the system of policy pursued by the British Government, by which that ascendancy has been nursed, can hardly have failed to inspire the breasts of the Romish hierarchy and their followers with a feeling of lofty and confident security, some evidences of which have very unequivocally been manifested ; and if the sympathy of the Church of Rome, upon grounds such as are here supposed, is to be indicated to us as our protection, and to furnish a reason to the Home Government for our being abandoned to our fate, it is a strange, and will be likely to prove a hollow, reliance.

5. But, farther, it is argued that if the Church were stripped of her State endowment, the development of the voluntary principle within her bosom might be calculated upon for enabling her to do her sacred work. In all the compass of the question, I do not know, on the side of our opponents, a weaker point than this. That it is the duty of the members of the Church

to contribute voluntarily and freely to the support of religion, is an acknowledged and prominent principle of the Christian faith, which your lordship will not suspect me of any disposition to impugn; and that among our own people in Canada their duty in this behalf will always be recognized, is what I have the comfort to believe. But that the voluntary system (passing wholly by the question of its liability to envelope certain vicious influences in its operation, as the received and settled system of a Church,) can possibly, in such a country as Canada, and specially in such a diocese as my own, provide for all the wants of all the people, or effectually minister the means of carrying out the Gospel principle that "to the poor the Gospel is preached," this is what I emphatically deny. An appeal is made to the case of the Church in the United States of America. Unfortunately for the authors of that appeal, it is where the endowments of the Church have been held sacred, and have become, in the progress of things, exceedingly ample, that the Church in that country is seen most to flourish and advance; and thence, eminently, that an impulse has been given to the Church throughout the Union. In general, it is for the paying classes that the voluntary system is found to provide: the classes who cannot pay, and the people who do not sufficiently value religion to be prompted to pay for it, and who can only be brought to a sense of its value by the actual ministrations of the Gospel,—these parties must shift as they can without such ministrations, or be left to the precarious efforts of casual charity and zeal.

Nothing can be more fallacious than the statistical exhibition, in this behalf, of the provisions for public worship in the United States, the number of places of worship furnishing there no sort of correct criterion of the number of stated services performed. Buildings are run up here and there, where services afterwards prove exceedingly scanty, or perhaps drop altogether. And it appears in a striking manner, from recent annual reports of the American Tract society, that in that rapidly advancing and wonderfully prosperous country, there are districts after districts, visited by the colporteurs of the society, of which the spiritual destitution is perfectly appalling. In the portions of Canada occupied by settlers of the Church of England, it is by extraneous help—the help of the great Church societies at home, specially the society for the Propagation of the Gospel, which cannot, of course, be a permanent provision—that the worship of God has been maintained; and if the Church of England has, in many instances, carried her ministrations for the benefit of emigrants in the forest, and of fishermen along the rude shores of the Gulf of St. Lawrence, to places where no other protestant ministry has penetrated; if she has, alone among protestant bodies, met the call of the forlorn and suffering strangers poured out by thousands, and literally dying by thousands in one summer, at the quarantine station below Quebec, and has sacrificed the lives of her clergy in the cause; if she has been ever ready with the succours of religion in prisons and pest-houses, and among the hovels of the poor (all which could be easily shewn in a detail of facts), it is not by the voluntary system that all this has been, or could have been done; it has been done, as I have said, in consequence of extraneous help, partly in the shape of bounty from the society above mentioned, and partly in that of certain limited allowances from Government which are fast dying out. In my own diocese, there is no wealth anywhere in the hands of the Church of England, except in Quebec itself, and nothing there which would be called wealth in England; in very many of the settlements occupied by our people there is extreme poverty and a total absence of cash. At this moment there are calls for clergymen which cannot be answered. The supplies once withdrawn which come from a distance, the help which the city can give abroad in the diocese, after providing for its own wants, will scarcely produce even an alleviation of the spiritual exigencies of helpless flocks. The country will, no doubt, advance; but new settlements will also spread themselves; and if the small revenue derivable from the reserves should be turned into other channels, the settlers who thirst in vain for the waters of life will have to charge their privations upon the authors and abettors of such a measure. It is with an ill grace, in my humble apprehension, that the Home Government would become a party to this alienation of our endowments, while the British Isles, year after year, are still emptying upon our shores a distressed population, for whom we are called upon to build churches and maintain ministers. Poor churches enough! and in a worldly sense, poor ministers they necessarily are.

6. I now come, in the last place, to the act 31 George III. cap. 31, known by the name of the Quebec act, and the notice which I have to take of it will be found, in one point of view, closely connected with the observations last made. What was the real intention of the clause which leaves it open, under certain guarding conditions, to the local legislature, to vary or repeal the provisions of the act affecting the Church? Simply, in all fair and reasonable construction, that everything being then new in the British establishment of the country, and it being impossible to foresee with what population it might be filled up, or what might be the wants of the Church within its limits, a margin was left for adaptation to unforeseen contingencies. And what is the state of things now? A quarter of a million of souls of the Church of England in the country, the germ of an enormous future population of the same faith, and now receiving its ceaseless augmentation from the influx of emigrants, many of whom bring hands to work with, and nothing more; few, very few indeed, of whom are persons of any substance in the world; and this in a climate of which the rigours create many additional wants, and abridge, at the same time, the season open to the toils of husbandry.

It is a mistake, therefore, unless I am grievously mistaken in saying so, to argue in favour of the contemplated spoliation from the clauses in question of the act of 1791. And if we are thrown back upon the wisdom of our fathers in framing, at that day, the constitutions which were to govern the ecclesiastical affairs of Canada, it would be well to consider, at least, to what we should stand committed by this retrospective proceeding. The Church of Rome would be declared not to possess the character of establishment, that being, by royal declaration, a privilege reserved only to our protestant Church of England. The clergy of this same protestant Church would, under the act here in view (31 Geo. III. cap 31), in which act the royal instructions, containing the declaration just mentioned, are referred to and in part recited, be sufficiently indicated as THE protestant clergy contemplated in the said act, by having rectories, all over the land, endowed out of the clergy reserves, *according to the establishment of the Church of England.* The Bishops of the Church of Rome would, with all tolerance of their functions among their own people, be officially recognized simply as Superintendents of the Roman catholic Church in Canada.[*] The convents would be subject to stated inspection by officers of the protestant Government: the male Orders of monastics would be suppressed.[†] It cannot be supposed, for one moment, that I am invoking the revival now of this order of things ;—that idea, if there were nothing else to forbid it, would present a plain and glaring impossibility ; but if we have recourse to the intentions of our fathers to guide us in the arrangements affecting ecclesiastical bodies in Canada, we ought, as I have said, to see all to which we stand committed.

My Lord, I will not say that I have trespassed upon you too long, for they are great and sacred interests which are at stake. And I might say much more. I might shew, in opposition to remarks which are still heard in different quarters, that the reserves present no obstruction to settlement, and entail no inconvenience upon any portion of the population. I might repel the statement, erroneous alike in principle and in fact, and repugnant to the spirit in which foreign America has acted towards the Church, that the present value of the reserves has been created by the labour of the Canadian people, and that, therefore, they have become a sort of popular property. But I will now close these poor observations, which I commend to your best indulgence, as I commend, in full confidence, the cause for which I plead to your protection, and I close them by a remark which must not expose me to a charge of meddling with political questions, for I

* The head of the Roman catholic Church in Canada is now acknowledged by the Government as His Grace the Lord Archbishop of Quebec ; and his coadjutor assumes the style, in a public document—being a formal ratification by a court of law in a transaction of business, published in the Government Gazette—of His Highness the Most Illustrious.

† By the terms of capitulation they were to die out.

make it with a much **higher import:** If the introduction of the system of responsible government into our colonial dependencies is to be understood as establishing the principle that this great Christian empire abandons, without exception or reservation, all check and control whatever over the internal proceedings of those dependencies, then what, in the first place, is the meaning of its being called an Empire?—an empire within which those dependencies are comprehended? And if parties aggrieved by colonial legislation, or other acts of colonial authority, can have no recourse, no redress, under any circumstances whatever, by means of an appeal to the mother country, then what, to suppose a case, is to be done, if, as matters proceed step by step, it should be judged proper in any colony to establish the Inquisition?

I am, My Lord Bishop,

Your lordship's faithful humble servant,

and brother in the Gospel,

G. J. Quebec.

The efforts of the Bishop and his friends were unavailing.* A great number of persons, who were quite ready to admit the justice of his cause and the force of his arguments, felt themselves, nevertheless, obliged to vote for the bill on the ground that it was unconstitutional for the Imperial Government to retain any control over colonial property in a country which had received responsible government. They expressed, at the same time, their conviction that it was only a question of principle on the part of the Canadian Legislature, and that if this principle were conceded, there could be no doubt of their "dealing generously by the Church." The Bishop however (as appears from the foregoing letter,) was unable to see that the principle could be held to reach a question which had received a "final" settlement before the intro-

---

* I have abstained from any thing like a history of the Clergy Reserve question, which had for many years been a fruitful source of occupation and anxiety, because it may be gathered from public documents, and my object has been chiefly to preserve what might otherwise be lost. Again and again had the Bishop issued circulars, and drawn up petitions to the legislature on the subject. With reference to one of these, he says, in 1852, "Our voice is feebly heard in the tumult, but it does not become us to be silent, and we must leave the issue to Him in Whose hands are the hearts of men and the course of events."

duction of responsible government into the colony; and though the Executive Government of Canada proved to be fully disposed to meet the claims which the act reserved of life interests in the most liberal manner, the action of the legislature very speedily verified the Bishop's anticipations by secularizing the reserves.

With all the occupation that these two great subjects entailed, the Bishop made time to advocate the cause of the S. P. G. and also that of the National Society at a great many places in England, both by preaching and addressing public meetings. The first meeting which he attended was at Bath, where he was the guest of Mr. Markland, who had been for many years one of the treasurers of the S. P. G. In a note written soon afterwards, Mr. Markland speaks of his " too short visit as a bright gleam" in his life. He was particularly interested by another short visit to St. Augustine's College, when he went to Canterbury to attend the funeral of Bishop Broughton. He delivered an address to the students, and " gave to each of them the right hand of fellowship, and, among them, to a negro from the West Indies, a copper-coloured Hindoo, and an Esquimaux from the North Pole." On another occasion, he assisted the Bishop of Oxford at the consecration of a church and preached at his ordination. The evening before, he had been requested to address the candidates on the subject of the Canadian Church; and they all, " without the most distant hint on his part," offered a sovereign each towards the completion of the chapel of Bishop's College, Lennoxville. On one of his journeys he had a most merciful escape; the express train in which he was travelling having been completely overturned, and the carriage in which he sat so crushed in that the only space left for the passengers was between the seats. Several persons were killed on the spot. As soon as he reached his journey's end, he went to the house of God to offer up public thanks for his deliverance, which was also done in his behalf

in the cathedral and St. Matthew's Chapel at Quebec, when
the news reached that city. Among the letters from Quebec
which he preserved at this time, is one which conveyed an
assurance which he deeply valued, that "many of the poor
people" prayed for him constantly. He had them ever in
his heart, and this feeling was thoroughly reciprocated. Referring to his taking part, for the first time in his life, in the
consecration of a Bishop (the Bishop of Lincoln), although
no one rejoiced more to see a decent solemnity attaching to
such ceremonials, or was more alive to the real interest which
belongs to them, he says that he had rather have been at St.
Matthew's, or the Magdalen Islands, for "they are the kind
of work for me." He frequently attended committee meetings of different religious societies, and it may be easily conceived that, altogether, he had not much time upon his hands.
After the decision of the two great questions which had chiefly
occupied him, he was ready to return at once to his diocese,
but the principal of Bishop's College having been deputed to
visit England for the purpose of making an appeal on behalf
of that institution, he was requested to await his arrival, that,
together with the Bishop of Montreal who had also come to
England, they might concert such measures as seemed to be
necessary for the furtherance of this object. He took the
opportunity of this enforced leisure to pay some very flying
visits to some of his oldest friends, whom he was never more
to meet on earth, and even then he was continually preaching. Just before leaving England he attended an annual
gathering at Windsor of the friends of the Bishop of New
Zealand, and went to Oxford by invitation, on the occasion of
the installation of the Earl of Derby, to receive the honorary
degree of D. C. L. He was there the guest of the Master of
University College, to whose kindness to his son, who was a
member of the college, as well as to himself and other members of his family, he felt deeply indebted. Wherever he went
he was surrounded by the "excellent of the earth," by per-

sons of tastes and feelings entirely congenial to his own, and by relatives and friends overflowing with kindness, who seemed to desire no greater happiness than the enjoyment of his society. The different scenes, too, and ceremonies in which he took part, were all occasions of deep interest. His early associations were revived with wonderful freshness. "Even the red cloaks of the old women" in country villages gave him an indescribable pleasure as something peculiarly English. It was a special happiness to him to visit, among others, his old tutor, Mr. Miller. The similarity of their tastes was as great as ever, though the part of the country where his lot was cast did not afford so great scope for their exercise as might have been found elsewhere ; yet though (as Mr. Miller had written long before, for during all that time he never had changed, nor wished to change, his place) " this scenery will not compensate perhaps, for that which we have seen and rejoiced in together, I trust there is a disposition in us both rather to make tastes and beauties where other and higher duties fix our lot, than to run daintily after a lot which shall minister to preconceived tastes. I trust I shall always love old houses, moats, walnut trees, and rookeries and avenues with peculiar feeling. But while we retain these sympathies inviolate, we shall, I am persuaded, prove the identity of our minds by more imperishable attachments which neither time nor the axe can reach. And, indeed, it is in confidence of this spiritual community that I look to the preservation of our affections in their freshness, with all the Atlantic between us." The lapse of upwards of thirty years from the date of this letter (it was more than forty since they had met), proved that their mutual affection had been built on a lasting foundation, for the Bishop was received with a love and veneration by Mr. Miller and all his family which were truly refreshing to his spirit.

CHAPTER XXI.

Return home—Visitation of Gaspé—Consecration of Fredericton cathedral—Opposition to measures for procuring synodical action—Pastoral letter—Diocesan assembly—Visitation of the clergy.

THE last meeting of colonial Bishops which the Bishop of Quebec attended was held on the 20th June, and on the 25th he embarked at Liverpool for Boston, en route to Quebec. Notwithstanding the happiness that he could not fail to derive from his visit to England, he was impatient to be again at his own proper work. His home was reached on the morning of Sunday, 10th July, and he preached the same day in his cathedral, as well as at St. Matthew's chapel. In a brief notice of his visit which was added to his sermon in the cathedral, he gave hearty expression to the feelings of thankfulness which had been stirred within him by the manifold improvements which he had been permitted to witness in the condition and prospects of the Church in his native land. As soon as he had been able to set in order the things that were wanting by reason of his absence in the general administration of the diocese, he began to make arrangements for completing the visitation which his voyage had interrupted. His first mark was the district of Gaspé, including the Magdalen Islands to which his first visit after the establishment of a resident missionary was now to be paid. He embarked at Quebec on the 8th August in a small trading schooner, and after visiting all the churches (of which three were consecrated as well as four burial-grounds), and confirming one hundred and thirty-two persons, crossed over to the islands in Her Majesty's steamsloop Basilisk, which had been ordered by the admiral of the station (Sir G. Seymour) to afford him every facility in his movements consistent with the duty of protecting the fisheries. The Admiral's orders were most effectually and obligingly carried out by the commander of the Basilisk, (Captain the Hon. Francis Egerton), who, though personally a stranger to the Bishop, shewed him "no little kindness," and every way "courteously entreated him." The Bishop was glad to be able to render some return for this kindness by repeatedly performing service on board the Basilisk, as well as in a smaller vessel in which he spent one night. The contrast between the vessel, as well as the society, in which he now reached the islands, and those in which he had approached them for the first time three years before was sufficiently marked, and a similar contrast was presented when he proceeded directly to the lonely dwellings of the islanders to celebrate in them the offices of the Church, from taking his part in the consecration of the cathedral at Fredericton, for which purpose he interposed a short visit to New Brunswick between the visitation of the mainland of Gaspé and that of the islands. His visit to Fredericton was a source of high and varied enjoyment, and his sermon preached on the day of consecration evinced the lively interest with which he had witnessed the wonderful advantages bestowed upon his own early flock. He was greeted with no less warmth and affection by his new-found friends at the Magdalen Islands than by his old ones at Fredericton. Three confirmations were held, and sixty-one persons confirmed; and one church was found sufficiently advanced to admit of its use, where three years before no protestant minister had ever trodden. His heart was full of thankfulness and joy, and he was enabled to sustain some considerable degree of bodily exertion and exposure. For though the Basilisk conveyed him to and from the islands, he shared, in his progress from island to island, the accommodation of the boat of the intrepid missionary upon the spot, in whose company he spent one night upon a sand-bank, on which they were cast by the violence of a squall, sleeping peacefully on the sand, protected from the falling rain by an umbrella held over him. He was obliged to return to New Brunswick in order to reach Quebec, which he did after an absence of seven weeks. It was a subject of great regret that his absence had deprived him of the pleasure of welcoming the deputation sent out by the S. P. G. to attend the triennial convention of the Church in the United States; Bishop Spencer (late of Madras), Archdeacon Sinclair, and the Rev. Ernest Hawkins. But some compensation for this disappointment was afforded by a brief visit paid to him soon after his return by his brother of Fredericton. The happiness which such intercourse as he then enjoyed and that which had refreshed his spirit in England, and the thankful remembrance of his visit to the Magdalen Islands, served as means to strengthen him to bear what nevertheless was a bitter trial to his sensitive nature, the malignant attacks which were at this time anonymously poured upon him in the columns of a local paper by parties hostile to the inauguration of synodical action within the Church. This opposition, which was by no means confined to Canada, but was fostered by so-called religious periodicals at home, increased more and more, and was a source of continual perplexity and distress, till it was quelled by the final triumph of the cause of synodical action in the diocese in 1859. It pleased God, in His mercy, to carry His servant through it all, though he suffered deeply in spirit from the strife: yet, conscious of the singleness of his aim, he never shrank for one moment, so far as his public acts were concerned, from maintaining with all boldness the principles which he believed to be those of the Church of England, and the justice of the measures to which he had been a party for the restoration of her synodical powers. While still engaged on his visitation in the gulf, he found time to begin a pastoral letter to the clergy and laity of the diocese giving an account of the object of his visit to England, and inviting them to meet him for the purpose of conferring on the steps to be taken in consequence of the failure of the Colonial Churches bill in the imperial parliament. The pastoral was put forth soon after his return to Quebec, and towards its close he thus alludes to local difficulties :

"If I apprehended that the anti-church spirit which, to whatever confined extent among ourselves, has manifested itself in the agitation of these questions would be infused, in any prevailing degree, into our deliberations, I should feel satisfied that it would be happier for us not to meet at all ; as, again, if I anticipated that the same effect would be largely developed by our being authorized to engage formally and legally in synodical action, I should feel that it would be more advantageous for us to go without it till we can be better taught in the school of Jesus Christ. But I bless God that I think I know the temper of my diocese at large, of which, among many other proofs, one eminently conspicuous was afforded in the earnest and cordial dispositions of the meeting of our clergy and lay delegates upon the subject of the clergy reserves in 1851 ; and as I am conscious to myself that I shall meet these two bodies in no magisterial spirit, and with the fullest sense of needing help and counsel at their hands, I am not without an encouraging hope that some persons who have made a grievance of the course taken in this matter, only because they have misunderstood it, may be brought, by the character and the result of our approaching proceedings, to a different estimate of that course, and that others may learn from us a new and happier spirit than that which before reigned within their bosoms.

" A great many misapprehensions of our local church matters, a great many false, and some most injurious, constructions of my own proceedings have latterly been anonymously put about in this community, of which I have not seen, I suppose, a tenth, perhaps not a twentieth, part, and of which I should have seen none if they had not, in some special instances, been brought under my eye by friends. I pray God to forgive the authors of them, and to turn their hearts ; but I shall take no other notice of them here than by applying to the case between these masked assailants and myself, the words of an ancient Roman, which came lately in my way : ' Varius ait Marcum, regiâ pecuniâ corruptum, rempublicam tradere* voluisse. M. Scaurus hinc culpæ affinem esse negat ; utri magis credendum putatis ?'

---

* One of the anonymous charges brought against the Bishop was that of "betraying his diocese."

" To those, however, who are accessible to the voice of their Bishop, I
would most earnestly and affectionately address the paternal charge that,
in all that now seems to be before us in the proceedings of the Church,
they will endeavour ' to keep the unity of the spirit in the bond of peace ;'
and ' O pray for the peace of Jerusalem ; they shall prosper that love thee.'
For myself—let other parties do what they will, and assail the Church and
her guardians as they please—none of these things shall move me from my
course ; through evil report and good report I shall, by the help of God,
go on, so long as I may be yet spared in the administration of the diocese
and the instruction of the fold, acting upon the same principles by
which I have been guided from the first, and which are in harmony with
those of my two venerated predecessors in the see. But whatever be my
attachment to Church principles, I am identified with no party, properly so
called ; and I do know, within myself, that I breathe a spirit of peace
towards all, and hope the day may come when we shall be all united. I
pray, then, that in the present crisis of our affairs, we may, both among
ourselves and to all men, manifest, as the disciples of Christ, such a temper
of heavenly love as may tend to disarm the adversary and to heal the hurts
of Zion. We shall never cease to misunderstand one another, more or less,
so long as we are encompassed with the infirmities of the flesh ; we see but
darkly now with reference to things human, as well as to things divine ;
let it be our aim to prepare for that day when we shall see face to face ;
and let each of us, for himself, so prepare his own heart by the grace of
Christ, and so fulfil his own task, as remembering that ' every man's work
shall be made manifest, for the day shall declare it.'"

On the 11th January, 1854, the clergy of the diocese
were assembled in visitation at the cathedral, accompanied by
a large number of lay delegates, of whom two had, at the
suggestion of the Bishop, been elected by all the congregations
of the diocese, except those in the district of Gaspé who are
cut off, during the winter, from communication with Quebec.
After the visitation, a meeting of Bishop, clergy, and delegates was held, at which the utmost unanimity and harmony
prevailed, and it was resolved to petition the imperial parliament for the passage of a measure to remove doubts as to the
legality of holding diocesan and provincial synods in the
colonies, and to endeavour to obtain the sanction of the local
legislature to the action of such synods.   Other resolutions,
relating to the secularization of the clergy reserves, and the
evils resulting from the operation of the laws relating to

education and the solemnization of marriage were also passed. Thirty-seven lay delegates were present, out of fifty-seven who had been elected.

One or two extracts from the Bishop's charge are here subjoined, as serving to shew the temper as well as the principles with which he exhorted his clergy to meet the difficulties of the times:

* * * "Men should be something more than men of the world—something more than men of acute parts, established character, and extensive information—to treat correctly and safely of matters involving the right exercise of a divine commission, and the right application of spiritual truths to the hearts of sinners. A heavenly discipline of the mind, a carefully cherished light within the bosom, which has been kindled from off the altars of the living God, an experimental knowledge of the wants of fallen nature before God and the relief of those wants in Christ, are what we shall all feel, I believe, to be necessary to a just discrimination and an adequate appreciation of doctrinal differences relating to the mystery of godliness. There is a certain tone of assumed superiority, a certain self-satisfied spirit of sarcasm, pronouncing, as from a seat of elevation, with an easy scorn and an ironical pleasantry upon the questions under review, whether religious, political, or more general in their character, which has become very fashionable among the writers, on whatever side, for the periodical press, but which is often very shallow and ill-sustained in its pretensions, usually in vicious taste, and always irreconcileable with the spirit of Christian humility and love. * * * In genuine charity, however, of spirit and of judgment towards our brethren of mankind, God grant that we may be 'as *broad** and general as the casing air.' And I do trust that we are not chargeable with party-spirit and prejudice, because we may feel ourselves compelled to stand aloof, when endeavours are made to carry on the cause of the Gospel under the banner of what is called 'our common protestantism.' * * * One prime, one prominent duty of the Christian ministry is to watch jealously, constantly, and closely over the soundness of the faith, as 'once delivered to the saints,' and its transmission, in its unimpaired integrity as well as its unsullied purity, from age to age. If this be true, it is evident that we cannot discharge our duty without being exposed to the imputation of exclusiveness. * * * What we are doing ourselves for Christ, and what we are teaching with the effect of bringing sinners to Him, these are the grand, the awful questions which we

---

* Reference had been just made to the use of the term " broad " then recently introduced as describing a party in the Church.

must invariably bring home to our bosoms. O! it will be to little purpose that we boast an apostolic ministry—to little purpose that we glory in the beauty and primitive character of our liturgy, in the orderly and chastened solemnity of all our venerable forms—to little purpose that we are found straining, after our ability, to clothe with all due and reverential effect the material sanctuary of our worship—to little purpose that we exhibit ever so dutiful and, in itself, laudable conformity to rubrics and rules—to little, little purpose if, in the meantime, we are not faithfully feeding the sheep of Christ, watching and praying, hour by hour, for the souls committed to us, working, in humble imitation of our Divine Master, ‘while it is day,’ in remembrance that ‘ the night cometh when no man can work,’ the night of that grave in which there is neither ‘ work, nor device, nor knowledge, nor wisdom,’ and our small distance from which, at best, prescribes the lesson with special solemnity to us who are engaged in the ministry of the Gospel, ‘ whatsoever thy hand findeth to do, do it with thy might.’ • • • We ought to correct the prevalent ideas that preaching consists only in the delivery of sermons, and that preaching, in this exclusive sense, is the sum and substance of the purposes of attendance upon the house of God. And yet how important, how tremendously important, and how gloriously too, is the task of preaching in this popularly-received acceptation of the word. We stand in the pulpit, ‘the legates of the skies,’ the messengers of the Most High, the ambassadors for Christ, pleading with men, in Christ's stead, to be reconciled to God. We have before us, for example, in all congregations, stray members of the Saviour's flock, prodigal sons of the Father of all, thoughtless beings unprepared for the eternity which is advancing upon them, the good seed choked within them by the cares and riches and pleasures of this passing life, their hearts and affections alienated from God, and we stand there to awaken them from their fatal lethargy by returning the echo of that voice which speaks from heaven, warning them, on the one hand, that ‘ it is a fearful thing to fall into the hands of the living God,’ winning them, on the other, by the accents of divine compassion and the overtures of Gospel love. How ought we, in the execution of such a task, while we keenly feel our own utter unworthiness and incompetency in ourselves, how ought we to rise above the torpor of worldly influences, and the laggardness of the flesh! What earnestness, what fervent unction, ought to be infused into the delivery of the Christian preacher, and how immeasurably ought he to be removed, at the same time, from all feelings which minister to the gratification or glory of self, from all the dangerously ensnaring love of human praise, from all pandering to itching ears, from all adaptation of himself to the predilections of this or that party in religion, of this or that favouring or flattering circle. • • • There are men who, with a purified eye to the glory of God alone, and in a severe repudiation of all meretricious ornament, ambitious effort, or popular trick, contract and even systematically cultivate a certain coldness and dryness both of language and delivery—one of the pre-eminent faults of our Church, and one which has contributed to her losing not a few of her children—which, constituted as human beings are, will always be a hindrance to the appeal which they have to carry to their hearers' hearts. The gravity and dignity of the pulpit ought indeed to be never compromised, and the arts of the actor or the demagogue can only profane the place; but if it would please God to gift us all for our work like Apollos, who was 'an eloquent man and mighty in the Scriptures,' we should combine two chief requisites for effectually preaching the Gospel. * * * Restriction to written discourses is apt to have a bad effect upon the *manner*—the restriction to extemporaneous delivery (which is much worse) upon the *matter* of men, and bodies of men, who discharge their part in the pulpit."

CHAPTER XXII.

Re-appearance of cholera at Quebec in 1854—Visit to New York—Completion of triennial circuit—St. Michael's chapel—Death of Colonel Mountain—Lieutenant J. G. Mountain.

THE summer of 1854 was marked by a fresh visitation of the cholera at Quebec, which served as before to call forth the self-denying zeal of the Bishop, who for some time, during the disablement of the chaplain of the marine and emigrant hospital, took the charge of that institution. It was also marked by one of those opportunities which always gave him so much pleasure, of intercommunion with the Episcopal Church in the United States. At the invitation of the Provisional Bishop of New York, he paid a visit to that city for the purpose of preaching at a large ordination in Trinity Church, and on his return was accompanied by Bishop Wainwright as far as Montreal, where they both officiated and preached. It was the first time that the Bishop of Quebec had done so in Montreal since the division of the diocese, four years before, and he had not visited New York for nearly thirty years. It was arranged that Bishop Wainwright should pay a visit to Quebec to plead the cause of the Church Society in the autumn, but very shortly before the time appointed for it, his unlooked-for and lamented decease deprived his brother of the opportunity of farther intercourse on earth.

The triennial visitation of the diocese, which had been partially interrupted by the Bishop's visit to England in

1853, was completed, by extensive journeyings both in summer and winter, and its statistical results are given as follows : Ordinations, five ; (priests, six; deacons, four ;*) confirmations, forty-two ; persons confirmed, nine hundred and eighty-seven ; churches consecrated, twelve ; burying-grounds, seven. There is also a note of four hundred and thirty-two sermons preached, of which one hundred and sixteen were written, and three hundred and sixteen extemporaneous addresses of a more familiar kind. Three were preached in Atlantic steamers, twenty-nine in England, three in vessels of war, four in New Brunswick, and two in Montreal.

Within his own parish of Quebec a new chapel was opened at the close of 1854, the chancel of which was built at the expense of the Bishop, as a memorial of his younger son, Lieutenant Jacob George Mountain, of the twenty-sixth Cameronians, who had died at Gibraltar in 1850, in the twenty-fifth year of his age. The Bishop's brother, Colonel Armine S. H. Mountain, who had commanded the same regiment, was a sharer in this work, but before the foundation-stone was laid, he had himself been laid to rest at a still greater distance from the birthplace of his nephew and himself. The names of both, as well as of the only other child of the first Bishop of Quebec (with the exception of one who died in infancy) who was a native of Canada, and who was also a most liberal contributor towards the erection of this chapel, have since been inscribed under stained windows in the chancel. The death of Colonel Mountain was a heavy affliction to the Bishop, (though more than lightened by the knowledge of his happy and peaceful end,) particularly as it came upon him at a time of unusual perplexity and distress of mind, and of bodily indisposition. And yet, even at the first, he thought more of his sister than of himself. Just after hearing of his loss he wrote :

---

* Two deacons were ordained for the diocese of Quebec by other Bishops.

"Two brothers never loved each other better than your uncle A. and I. It has pleased God to cut off my hope of ever seeing him again in this world. I copy what your uncle J. says: 'Our dear brother Armine is with his Saviour. He died of fever, after a few days' illness, on the 8th February. He suffered no pain, and was tranquil and conscious to the last. His expiring words were,—' peace, pardon, salvation.' My poor sister C., weak and shattered as she is, and bound up in him, and constantly familiar with the proofs of his tender affection, cannot, humanly speaking, long survive this blow, but God can strengthen her, if He see good, according to her need. The three of my father's children who have gone in years of maturity were all younger than myself. In the few years, at best, remaining to me, I must only pray and hope that I be not unfaithful. My work grows very complicated, and the different offices which I hold embarrass me by their united claims. At this moment I do not see my way through all the arrangements to be made either for diocese or parish. But if we conscientiously do the best we can with the means at our disposal, and decide all questions which perplex us with a single eye, we must leave the issue to God Himself. • • • Your mother is of course in sorrow, but she has a disciplined Christian mind."

I may here fitly introduce some fuller notice of the event referred to in connection with the foundation of the chapel at Sillery, though it carries us back to the year 1850. I was unwilling to interrupt my narrative of the important public events of that year by any details of private history, which I have accordingly reserved for this place. And perhaps I cannot here more appropriately recur to the loss of the only one of the Bishop's children* who grew up to manhood, and did not survive him, than by introducing a letter from his brother, written from India in reference to that event, in August, 1850:

"Little did I dream, my dearest brother, when I sent you, in reply to your kind letter of March, a long, gossiping epistle, that I was sending it to the house of mourning; little did I dream, when I complained of not hearing from our young soldier, that he was in that mysterious world from which no missive can reach us! Most truly and deeply do I sympathize with you and with the afflicted mother! Heavy is the hand of our God upon you. He alone can send you comfort, and He will! I feel for you in my inmost heart, and know that my loss, compared with yours, is light.

* Mentioned at the close of chapter xiv., p. 224.

Yet I mourn, too, for myself. Jacob has left but one other of our name and kindred in the British army. He was the only one in my branch of my profession; of all my nephews and nieces the only one with whom I corresponded; the only one with whom, since their childhood, I have been at all associated; one who was much attached to me. I was to him, poor fellow, for four years, a strict and exacting chief, but I believe he gave me credit for having his interest at heart, and I, vain worm, looked forward to the day when he should be again my companion in arms. I believe that you may look back upon his brief career with unmingled satisfaction. I never saw nor heard of any participation on his part in any of the vices or follies of his fellow-soldiers. His affection for his parents and brother and sisters was predominant in his breast, never absent from him, and I never saw nor heard of any departure on his part from the lessons of his home. I shall dwell a little on his professional career, as, although you live in a garrison town, you do not, perhaps, exactly feel as I do the importance of the situation which he held. His career embraced a period of about seven years and a half. He was actually serving with his regiment about six years and a half, out of which he was just four years adjutant, never absent from his duty, I may almost say, an hour. To pass through Dublin as an adjutant, to serve as such under three successive sharp commanders requires a thorough knowledge of professional details; the youngster possessed this; and though neither I nor Colonel —— are men to allow the adjutant to command the regiment, as too many colonels virtually do, an adjutant must always have greater power of good and evil, a more immediate influence over the mass of a regiment than any other officer except the commander, greater opportunities of giving pleasure and pain. How our poor boy acted under these circumstances shall appear. He devoted himself to the regiment; he did his duty, and did it well and strictly, but he never lost an occasion of doing an act of kindness, of working upon men by their better feelings, of extending charity to those in need. Had he been an A.D.C., and well spoken of, I should not value it a button. It might be that he carved a ham well, or was a favourite with his general's wife's lap-dog. Had he been a D. A. Adjutant or Quartermaster General, and much bepraised, I would not give a brass farthing for it. It might be that he wrote a good hand, and was obsequious to the head of his department. But when a lad, after four years' continued service as an adjutant under three commanders, dies repected by all, lamented by non-commissioned officers and men; when we find that his commanding officer was quite cast down, that his brother-officers mourned, that many of the soldiers cried like children, that poor women whom he had assisted grieve at the news of his death (this is what I hear from Gibraltar, from more than one undoubted source) we may believe, without fear of mistake, that he was a good and faithful soldier, and a right-minded and kind-hearted man. The staff is the post for show, for amusement, and in truth (though so it should not be) for advancement. The regimental career is the profession of arms, that in which a true reputation is earned, and the appointment of adjutant is that in which a young man is tried and called forth, and shews what is in him. I say not this, because I had any hand in his training * * * but it is my deliberate view of the profession in which my life has been passed, and I think it must be some consolation to you to feel, as without flattery you may, that through the power of the principles which you instilled into him and his own good disposition, a lad, naturally too sensitive and full of misgivings, succeeded in a difficult and prominent situation into which he was early thrown, holding his own with his superiors and equals, and obtaining, in no common degree, the attachment of his subordinates, at the same time that we may believe that he walked steadfastly with his God and Saviour. My friend Colonel —— of the Grenadier Guards says: 'I have rarely met with a young person who so much engaged one's regards as poor J. Mountain, so unassuming, yet so manly, so gentlemanlike.' A brother officer writing from Gibraltar, says 'He is now at rest, and many an older man would be glad at his last moment to be as ready to answer his last roll-call as he was. He was a thorough soldier, and at the same time, a thorough Christian.'" Colonel Mountain adds, "You must pardon my professional weakness. I aimed to make him a thorough soldier and I love to think he was so—though besides the other, nothing."

. I may, indeed, seem to have gone beyond the object of this memoir in giving this extract, but it serves to shew the effect of home-training, as well as the weight of the trial, though relieved by the highest comfort, which the Bishop was called upon to bear. And for the same reasons, I venture to add one or two briefer extracts. The Chief Justice of Gibraltar, in writing to announce the young officer's death, said:

"Your agonized hearts will be consoled, under God's blessing, by the assurance which your knowledge of your dear boy's character and conduct will afford of his fitness, through his Saviour's merits, for the great event which, though it has befallen him thus soon, has not, through God's mercy, found him unprepared: * * * the chaplain has assured me that he was in the best possible tone of mind. He said himself, what all the officers of his regiment bear testimony to, that he had always been a constant suppliant for grace at his Lord's table, *the whole merit of which he was always attributing to parental influence. Of the benefit which he derived from this cause he was always speaking to the chaplain.* * * * Lady C., who saw more of him than I did, was particularly struck with, and early remarked to me, the religious tone of his mind, as so different from that of most of his age."

The colonel in command of the regiment wrote:

"It is with profound and heartfelt sorrow I have to announce the melancholy intelligence of the death of your excellent and amiable son. • • • We followed him to the grave with sorrowing hearts, and it will be a consolation to you to know that he possessed the esteem and affection of every individual in the regiment. I cannot find words to express the depth of my own grief on this sorrowful occasion, suffice it to say, that I shall long deplore his loss. His merit as an officer was of the highest order, and his many virtuous and amiable qualities endeared him to all who had the happiness to know him, and to none more than to myself."

Another officer wrote, that he was known constantly to read the Bible and pray, and "was not ashamed to own it."

The loss of such a son, whose absence from home had specially endeared him to his parents, could not but be a sore trial to the Bishop, particularly as it came upon him without any preparation. The intelligence reached him just as he had landed on the coast of Gaspé from the Magdalen Islands, his only surviving son having gone to meet him for the purpose of carrying it to him. He was enabled, however, to carry on his work without interruption, though deeply anxious for those who were left in his afflicted household. But he had had sufficient experience of the manner in which she who shared his parental grief had been sustained under the deepest sorrows (experience abundantly confirmed by her most touching letters written at this very time), to be able to commit her and all belonging to him to the hands of a merciful Providence. The manner in which he was always able to do this in his long and often trying separations from his home was to the last most remarkable in one whose domestic ties and affections were so strong. This affliction seemed to serve only to strengthen those ties, while he cherished with the utmost tenderness the remembrance of his "precious boy," many most affecting instances of which might be here introduced, if they were not too sacred for public gaze. At the risk of seeming, perhaps, to violate this sacredness, I cannot forbear from adding an expression of

his feelings, because, in more ways than one, specially characteristic, from the beginning of a manuscript book in which his
beloved son had recorded some of his private thoughts :

"O my son J., my son, my son, my son J——! Would
God that I had died for thee! O J——, my son, my son'!
Yet I must not speak so! for it is more needful for others
that I than that he should abide in the flesh. And, blessed
be God, he was no Absalom, nor taken unprepared. When
I shall go to him, may I be as prepared as he was, whose
dear remains the rock of Gibraltar holds in deposit against
the last great day! His hand, before it was stiff in death,
traced the thoughts in this book, and his humble and contrite
spirit, which dictated them, has passed into Paradise, washed
from all its stains. And there is a Book in which his name
is written, even the Lamb's Book of Life."

CHAPTER XXIII.

Seventh triennial circuit—Illness—Visitation of the clergy—Visits of the
Bishop of Rupert's Land and of American Bishops—Commencement of
eighth triennial circuit—Obstacles to the advance of the Church—New
missions—Correspondence with S. P. G.

THE seventh triennial circuit of the diocese was begun early
in 1855, when, for the first time in his life, the Bishop had
recourse for that purpose to railway travelling. It did not
however, serve to expedite his movements, for he was detained
within sight of Quebec at the commencement of his journey,
for about twenty-seven hours, by a violent snow-storm which
entirely blocked up the line. A similar detention occurred
at the close of the journey, when he again took the train.
He was absent from Quebec, in the district of St. Francis,
exactly a month, during which twelve confirmations were
held and two hundred and thirteen persons confirmed, two
churches consecrated, nineteen sermons preached, and five
persons baptized, four of whom were adults and the fifth one
of his own grandchildren. The journeyings were renewed
in May, August, and September, when three more churches
were consecrated, and sixty-six persons were confirmed at six
places in the French part of the country. Two hundred and
twenty-six had been confirmed at Quebec at Easter. During
this summer, the Bishop was for some time disabled from
duty by a very severe attack of influenza, and spent some
time, for the sake of change of air which had been recommended to him, with his son who had taken charge of the qua-

rantine station.   He beguiled some sleepless nights by putting
his thoughts into verse, of which a specimen is here subjoined:

O hard and thankless heart of mine !
　How blest, if in these weary hours,
My soul could dwell on things divine,
　With all her concentrated powers !

How blest, if like the Psalmist king, (a)
　My waking thoughts I felt to rise,
And seek, with unencumbered wing,
　A cloudless region in the skies !

Vile earthly vapours, dull and dense,
　How long must I your torpor feel ?
O Saviour, to my darkened sense
　The fulness of Thy love reveal.

I know Thee, bright and morning star, (b)
　I own Thee for my only guide ;
But ah! I view Thee from afar,
　Between are waters rough and wide.

Hold up, hold on, thou laggard faith ;
　The Saviour walks the waters still ;
No phantom vain, no shadowy wraith, (c)
　Powerful in presence (d), prompt in will.

O no, I will not, will not say,
　From me, a sinful man, depart ; (e)
The sinner's hope, the sinner's stay,
　I claim Thee with believing heart.

Lost in myself, in Thee I live,
　Poor, wretched, helpless, naked, blind, (f)
Some largess to Thy suppliant give,
　Some salve, some covering let me find. (f)

O gold, which only makest rich ! (f)
　O pearl beyond all earthly price ! (g)
Say, shall the world their souls bewitch,
　Whose treasure hangs in Paradise ? (h)

(a) Ps. xlii. 8, lxiii. 6, cxix. 55, 147, 148, cxxx. 6; (b) Rev. xxii. 16;
(c) St. Matt. xiv. 26 ; (d) St. Luke v. 17; (e) St. Luke v. 8 ; (f) Rev. iii.
17, 18 ; cf. Is. lv. 1 ; (g) St. Matt. xiii. 46 ; (h) St. Matt. vi. 20.

Soon shall be closed this feverish dream,
  Worn through this *(a)* "mingled yarn" of life ;
Tried by stern test the things which **seem,**
  Fought out of good and ill the strife.

A rest remains, **a heavenly rest ;** *(b)*
  No death, no pain, **no** sorrowing sigh ; **(c)**
Chased every care from every breast,
  Wiped every tear from **every eye. (c)**

The day is near, far spent the **night ; (d)**
  Christ will His followers' place prepare ; **(e)**
The Lord our everlasting light,
  Our God shall be our glory there. (f)

Early **in 1856 he** was again journeying, and in the summer
of that year **paid his** seventh episcopal visit to Gaspé, accompanied by Professor Thompson, of Bishop's **College, who will**
forgive me for making public the impressions which **the intercourse he enjoyed** on this as **well as** other occasions **served
to fix in his mind :**

"My acquaintance with your beloved father commenced only a few years **back, yet beyond** the circle of my own immediate relations there is no **figure** which occupies so large a space in the field of memory as his. How many pleasant days of travel together ; how many lovely spots of Canadian scenery to which he first drew my attention ; how much cheerful conversation ; **how much valuable counsel ; what instances** of Christian gentleness and humility, and **of diligence in his great Master's** work come crowding on the mind when **I think of him that is gone!** Never, I may safely say, have I **felt for any one more thorough respect and reverence and love than** for him."

They journeyed **down the Kempt road,** which was still a matter of difficulty and fatigue, and were obliged to return through New Brunswick to insure their being in time for **the** convocation of Bishop's College in September. This afforded another opportunity for valued intercourse with the Bishop

---

(a) " **The** web of our life is of a mingled yarn, good and ill together ;" All's **well** that ends well—Act IV. s. 3 ; *b)* Heb. iv. 9 ; *(c)* Is. xxv. 8, xxxv. 10 ; **Rev. vii.** 17, xxi. **4** ; *(d)* Rom. xiii. 12 ; *(e)* St. John xiv. 2 ; *(f)* Is. lx. 19.

of Fredericton, who soon followed his brother to Quebec, to take part in the consecration of St. Michael's Chapel, mentioned in the foregoing chapter. As this was the last time that they were permitted to meet on earth, I may here properly give an extract from a letter of the Bishop of Fredericton, written early in 1863:

"I never saw one to whom I could more look up with veneration and respect and affection, and we shall ne'er look upon his like again. I shall never forget his visits to me, and each time have longed for a repetition of the blessing."

In the course of this journey the Bishop of Quebec experienced an attack which weakened him very much for some time afterwards, and in the following winter he was again visited with very severe suffering, from which, however, he gained sufficient relief to be enabled to visit the missions in the district of Quebec before the spring. He was naturally very sensitive to pain, and I well remember his reproaching himself by referring to the sufferings of the Cross, when tempted to shrink under a surgical operation. A renewed attack of the same kind in the early summer caused great uneasiness to his friends, and prevented his attendance and the delivery of his charge at the visitation of the clergy held on St. Barnabas' day, 1857. The clergy presented him with an affectionate address after they had met, by his desire, to confer together on the steps necessary to be taken under the Act of the provincial legislature, which had this year been obtained for the removal of the disabilities which were supposed to hinder the free synodical action of the Church. By the blessing of God on the means used, and a change of air (for he removed again to the house of his son, near St. Michael's chapel,) the Bishop was so far restored as to be able to hold an ordination at St. Michael's on St. Peter's day, and immediately afterwards to attend the convocation of Bishop's College. He was obliged, however, to abstain during the summer from nearly all public duties, and to spend some weeks in the neighbourhood of salt water, from whence he came up to his son's house, in the end of August, to welcome the Bishop of Rupert's Land, who visited Quebec on his way from England to his own diocese. Referring to this visit in a charge (dedicated to him " who was, in a manner, its first Bishop "), Bishop Anderson says:

"It was delightful to notice the warmth with which he made minute enquiry after many here, and the deep anxiety which he manifested for the progress of the Church in this land. The recollection of his wanderings in the western wilderness is, he seems to feel, a bright and sunny spot in the memory of the past."

And in a private letter written in 1863, he thus alludes to his intercourse with him :

"It was with deep feeling and emotion that I saw the account of the peaceful departure of your good and revered father. Very pleasant are my recollections of the hours spent in his society during my visits to Quebec in 1857 and 1860. Inclined even beforehand to look to him as a son to a father, from his former association with this country and the work in this diocese, I found this feeling only deepened by personal intercourse and the familiar friendship with which he favoured me. And now I think of his end, as of his life, as almost to be envied, if it were ours to appoint the manner of the approach of death. . . . Your sorrow is swallowed up in the thought of the honour and affection in which his name and memory will be embalmed throughout the Churches of Canada, even throughout the Church of Christ. I write with the portrait of his meek and gentle face on the wall by my side. You have that face and the lineaments of the soul and inner life more deeply imprinted on your hearts. . . . My sister shared in the deep reverence and affection which all felt in approaching your good father. Nor is this feeling limited to ourselves in this settlement. I alluded to it in preaching the Sunday after I received the tidings of his death, and all now recall their recollections of his tall figure, his engaging manner, his various sermons, and confirmation addresses. All speak of him with fond affection and regret."

The Bishop of Quebec had later in this year the pleasure of greeting two of his brother prelates of the sister Church in the United States, the Bishops of Massachusetts and Vermont, the latter of whom came to Quebec by invitation, to preach at the reöpening of the cathedral in November, which had been closed for several months for painting and repairs. The Bishop of Indiana had favoured him with a visit in 1856. His health was so far reëstablished as to admit of his holding an ordination in September, and undertaking a confirmation tour early in October, through some of the roughest parts of the county of Megantic, where he held eight confirmations, and consecrated two churches and four burial-grounds. His first sermon addressed to the cathedral congregation after his illness was preached from the text: "To me to live is Christ, and to die is gain." A sermon which he preached shortly afterwards to the same congregation on the fast-day for the Indian mutiny was published by desire. The journey just mentioned brought to a close the triennial circuit of the diocese, in which nine hundred and thirty-five persons had been confirmed on fifty-five occasions, twelve churches and seven burial-grounds consecrated, and five deacons and five priests ordained at six ordinations. The number of churches consecrated included the chapel of Bishop's College, in July, 1857. The erection of this chapel had been a long-cherished object with the Bishop, and its consecration was an occasion of great thankfulness. The Bishop of Maine preached the consecration sermon.

Early in 1858 he was again travelling, visiting the missions in the St. Francis district, and holding sixteen confirmations, three of which were in places where the rite had never before been administered. Part of the district of Quebec was visited for the same purpose in June, and the district of Three Rivers in August. Ordinations were held at Lennoxville on Trinity Sunday, and at Quebec at the ember-seasons in September and December. Another was held at Quebec on the feast of the Epiphany, 1859, when a deacon who had been prevented, by the effects of an injury he had received, from coming forward at Christmas was advanced to the priesthood. Towards the close of 1858, the present rector of Quebec succeeded the Rev. Official Mackie, who had for family reasons returned to England, as assistant minister of the cathedral, and the Bishop appointed his friend, Mr. Wood, examining chaplain. There is no record of the consecration of churches during this year, nor indeed during the triennial circuit which began with it, except of the chapel within the marine hospital at Quebec. The gradual withdrawal of aid from home was beginning to produce its effects. Not only had the S. P. G. been obliged altogether to discontinue the practice of making grants for churches, but the diminution of its missionary allowances created a local demand which was felt to be of paramount importance. The efforts of the Church were directed to the maintenance of the existing body of clergy, and new undertakings seemed to be beyond her reach. The Bishop, however, felt so urgently the need of opening some additional missions, that he proposed in 1858 to devote £200 a year, for five years, to that purpose, on condition that the Church Society should meet it with an equal amount. The mission of Danville was at once opened by this means, as well as that of Hopetown in the district of Gaspé; and mission-aries were afterwards placed at Barford, Acton, and Bourg Louis. The question of the maintenance of the clergy was daily becoming more important and sometimes distressing. The absolute determination of the S. P. G. to reduce its grants upon the occurrence of every vacancy created great difficulties in filling up such vacancies, and in effecting changes which were for the manifest advantage of the Church. The Bishop urged the claims of his diocese with all earnestness, and, at the same time, his desire for the completion of an arrangement which had been proposed in 1852, for committing the distribution of the society's missionary grant to some responsible body within the diocese, which he suggested should consist chiefly, if not exclusively, of laymen, by whom some mitigation of these difficulties might be secured. Several minor obstacles had, however, to be overcome, and details to be arranged in correspondence carried on across the Atlantic, so that it was not till 1862 that the plan was really carried into operation, by the establishment of a diocesan board composed of members of the synod and the Church Society, acting in concert with the Bishop.

The manner in which these difficulties weighed upon the Bishop's mind may be seen by the following little note referring to a letter drawn up by his desire to announce to the churchwardens of a certain mission the necessity for diminishing the supply of service, on account of the failure of the congregations to do what was required of them towards the maintenance of the clergyman.

"Dearest A.,—I have signed the letter, and feel something like King Charles when he signed the death-warrant of Strafford. Our people are not ripe for the self-supporting system, and we cannot—I am sure I cannot— carry on the Church upon that principle. I hope it may please God to look upon us and open some unlooked-for way of deliverance from our difficulties. Every thing at present looks very, very black, and synods, I am afraid, will do little to help us. But I must not forget my own maxim, 'Ora et labora.'"

But though he was thus reluctant to resort to measures of severity, and felt strongly the peculiar difficulties of his own poor and scattered diocese, he had all along maintained the principle on which the S. P. G. was acting as one which it was the plain duty of all concerned to adopt whenever circumstances should render it practicable. So long ago as in 1837,* he had himself suggested that no missionary allowance should exceed £100 sterling a year, and that it should be made

---

* In 1834 he had drawn up a circular for Bishop Stewart, on the occasion of the reduction of the grants of the S. P. G., caused by the withdrawal of the parliamentary vote. This circular "containing much wholesome counsel, and pointing out the sources from which the endowment of the Church must be ultimately derived, not only lays it down as a principle that the colonial Church must depend mainly upon its own resources, in the voluntary gifts and offerings of the people, but suggests a convenient mode of gathering those contributions." See Annals of the diocese of Quebec, Appendix B, p. 316.

conditional on the performance by the people, in each locality, of their part towards a proper maintenance for their minister. The difficulties of enforcing this rule, though it was never lost sight of, in the case of newly-formed settlements were almost insuperable, and the society had been always willing, " to its power, yea, and beyond its power," to provide them with the ministrations of religion. For many years no application for the establishment of new missions had been refused ; the great difficulty had been that of finding men for the work. In April, 1841, the Bishop submitted to the society a "plan for drawing out local contributions," one feature of which was that "the clergy should not be directly dependent upon the people," and proposed that, " in places where the congregations were decidedly able to do something in this way and fail to do so (if any such cases should occur) the missionary should be transferred to some unprovided settlement, till they should be brought to evince a more correct appreciation of their blessings." This he thought " would have a good effect, and yet it would be hard upon the poorer inhabitants upon the same spot." He urged, at the same time, the importance of securing, whenever possible, some moderate endowment, and the society for some few years made a grant of £1000 annually for this object, which was invested in the purchase of glebes. In the same letter he thus states the wants which pressed upon him on every side :

" Of eighteen new missions asked for in July, 1839, which the society unhesitatingly undertook, barely one-half are established, for want of men, while the demand still grows, the cry still swells from destitute settlements ; the applications and complaints (for the Church is supposed to have the means regularly at her command, as may be required) of the people still pour in upon us from new quarters or from old."

Soon after this date the increasing demands upon the society compelled it to restrain its liberality, though the wants of the diocese had not been met.

In April, 1845, the Bishop wrote, " I must not hope for the opening of new missions till it pleases God (and for the

sake, not only of Canada, but of all the dependencies of the
Empire, I fervently pray Him, for Christ's sake, to speed
the day) to enlarge the resources of the society." In the
following year, however, the clergy reserves having become
available, the society undertook to provide a reduced rate of
salary for ten additional missionaries. But a reduction in
its expenditure having become imperatively necessary, the
invariable rule was adopted, about six years later, of cutting
down the amount and limiting the duration of its grants on
the occurrence of every vacancy. This rule pressed very
severely on the poorer missions (where changes were naturally
the most frequent) while the wealthier were not compelled to
contribute towards the support of the ministry. The operation of this system presented so great a hindrance to the
growth of the Church, and made it so apparent that the diocese was not in a condition to meet great and indiscriminate
reductions, that the Bishop's strong remonstrances could not
be withheld. In December, 1853, he urged as a "plea for
not cutting down," the difference, which he conceived to be
too much lost sight of, in the material prosperity of Upper
and Lower Canada respectively, shewing that while, in 1851,
the wheat crop in the former yielded 15.33 bushels for each
inhabitant, in the latter the proportion was only 3.46 minots;"
and the settlers being, with scarcely an exception, dependent
for subsistence on their agricultural produce, this calculation
was a valid argument in his favour. A similar calculation as
to the relative value of the clergy reserves in the two provinces
exhibited a similar result. He described a visit which he had
recently paid to a backwoods mission, "a poverty-stricken
place," where he entered a log hut (and it may be presumed that the Bishop was not invited to one of the very
poorest) where the poultry raised for the Quebec market had
their share of accommodation in the single room of which the
building consisted. Some flat barley cakes were then put
before the missionary and himself, with a cup of tea lacking

all accompaniment of sugar or milk. He was careful to add that " every thing was clean and the people were kind."

Again, in January, 1856, in a letter (most of which was printed by the S. P. G.) written with reference to some particular reductions, he describes the general state of the diocese in the following terms :

Additional number of clergy required from extent of country. — I. In the first place, the enormous extent of country over which our Church population is scattered in this diocese,—the Magdalen Islands in the Gulph being nearly six hundred miles below Quebec, and the frontier townships in the St. Francis district about one hundred and fifty above it,—necessitates, unless our poor feeble flocks are to be left absolutely to the wolf, the maintenance of a body of clergy which may seem somewhat out of proportion to their mere numbers, while the same aspect of things at once tells the tale of their inability to find resources within themselves for such a purpose. And yet there has been a good beginning and a marked progress made ; and there is in those congregations the germ, and something more than the bare germ, of an important Church population, which to see crushed or blighted would indeed be a disheartening sight.

Poverty of the diocese.—II. But in addition to the fact that our people are, in many instances, not such a body as any man can slightingly regard, yet numerically too inconsiderable, as mere settlers, to support a clergyman upon the spot, and too isolated to command the stated visits of clergymen from more privileged places,—they have to contend with a rigorous climate, in which not one-half of the year is open to the toils of husbandry, and they occupy portions of country which from natural and other causes participate, if at all, to a very confined extent, in the advancing improvement and prosperity of the province. Most of the Church of England missions in this diocese are either in back-wood settlements, often with desperately bad summer-roads, or among the fishing-settlements of the Gulph. With reference to the former class of missions, the portion of the emigrants who remain in this part of Canada consists largely of those who are too poor to proceed farther. And it is notorious that if they become a little prosperous they are constantly prompted to move westward, and thus plant themselves out of the limits of the diocese.

In all particulars of the nature here considered, there is no part of Canada so disadvantageously situated, by many degrees, as the diocese of Quebec ; and in the whole of Lower Canada the benefit derived from a portion of the late Clergy Reserves fund, made available under the commutation system towards the support of the clergy, is strikingly contrasted with the corresponding case of the diocese of Toronto. In that diocese, I believe (not

X

speaking precisely,) that the commutation fund amounts about to £300,000 currency, or £2,000 for each clergyman of the present strength of the diocese (supposing them all chargeable to that fund). In the diocese of Quebec, it amounts to about £11,000 currency, or (making the same supposition) about £275 for each clergyman, and yet we have by far too few clergymen for our work. I suppose it would be hardly too much to say that the difference in favour of the diocese of Toronto is almost equally great, if we look to the general resources and advantages of the province, as thus far developed within the limits of either diocese respectively; and I could furnish, if it were necessary, a variety of distinct and pregnant details to sustain me in the supposition. Add to all which, that there are rectories in that diocese very richly endowed. Here we have no single instance of endowment beyond some little glebes of exceedingly trifling value.

I draw comparisons without the embarrassment of any delicacy or reserve between the diocese of Toronto and my own, because the Society having, as I understand, made conclusive arrangements with the former, which, after the grant in aid of the sustentation fund, is chargeable no longer to its bounty,—there is no possible competition or rivalry of claim between the two dioceses upon that bounty. Never, indeed, could I indulge in any unworthy jealousy of help given in other parts of Canada, or elsewhere,—it is all one cause, and that the cause of the Church of God upon earth. And I bless His name for all which, in any spot, can advance that sacred cause, "from the rising of the sun unto the going down of the same."

Claims of the diocese to help and to consideration.—III. I must press upon the venerable Society a consideration at which I have already incidentally glanced, that although the Church of England population of this diocese is, to a great extent, seated in backwood settlements which are, in a manner, struggling into life,—it has, under the nursing hand of the Society, been brought up to a hopeful condition, and has assumed, if I may so express it, an ecclesiastical consistency, which it would be grievous to think of breaking up by any severe and sudden check. That the see is comparatively old is evidently no argument for the discontinuance, or extensive and rapidly progressive diminution of supplies from home, if the state of the Church within the diocese, and the wants created by a new and continuous influx of emigration, are such as to fall, with exact propriety, within the objects of the Society's charter;—if all local resources at command are utterly inadequate even for the meagre and imperfect supply of those wants which is now provided; if the effect of what the Society has done and is doing yields encouragement for the future; and, finally, if the diocese stands now in a conjuncture of a critical kind, and any shock given to the progress of the Church would be charged with the most disastrous effects.

Now, all these suppositions may, I believe, be safely averred to correspond to the realities of our case. With reference, in particular, to the encouraging grounds which exist for protecting and cherishing the Church in the diocese, and the call which is presented in the insufficiency of its own resources, I would beg here to state 'some few details.

Statistics of the diocese.—We have a population of perhaps twenty-five thousand Church-people, of whom between four and five thousand are in Quebec. We have forty clergymen, of whom twenty-three are missionaries of the Society for the Propagation of the Gospel. We have sixty-one churches (including the chapels of the city). The number of clergy has been increased, since my own accession to the episcopate in 1836, from seventeen to forty; that of churches from twenty-one to sixty-one; and within the same period, we have gained the object of passing a Church Temporalities Act; formed our Church Society, and obtained for it the privilege of incorporation; established our college under a provincial charter, and procured for it a royal charter for conferring degrees; sent out from this college about thirty candidates for Orders, now labouring chiefly in this or the adjoining diocese of Montreal. About two thousand persons are confirmed in each of the triennial visitations, every church in the diocese being visited for the purpose. The proportion of communicants in our congregations is much larger than that which subsists in the mother-country. If we are enabled to keep our ground, we shall, by the blessing of God, lay a foundation in the country, firm and deep, upon which others, to enter hereafter upon our labours, may prosperously build up and enlarge the Church. We are now at a turning-point in our history, for the introduction of railroads, and the development of mineral and other resources not yet made available, cannot fail to give an impulse to the country; and its institutions and religious predilections, in connexion with the advances of the Anglo-Saxon race, will be moulded by the influences which can maintain the ascendant in supplying, intellectually and spiritually, the popular want. If we are in any measure ready to meet this demand, our pure apostolic Church and scriptural faith will establish their proper hold upon the people. If we are found in a paralyzed condition,—if it is seen that we have been compelled to leave the interests of religion to languish, and are exposed to the mortification—it is already most keenly felt—of rendering discouraging answers, and dealing out explanations and excuses to those who address their appeal to us,—we shall sink in their eyes to a character of inefficiency, and some of them will fall away to careless irreligion,—some will follow the teaching of unsound and fanatical sects,—many will be absorbed into the rich and powerful communion of Rome,—and others still, not drawn away in any of these directions, will at least be lost forever to ourselves. Alas! in different places which we could not supply, we have lost, and are now losing, some who would else have owned the bosom of their mother in the Church.

*　　*　　*　　*　　*　　*　　*　　*　　*　　*

Measures for reducing the charge upon the Society for the Propagation of the Gospel, and mutual understanding acted upon in all new arrangements for the missions.—V. I have been endeavouring, for a long time, to lessen the charge upon the Society for the Propagation of the Gospel, wherever it was possible; and have brought down, in several instances, the missionary allowance to a lower mark, by exacting the difference from the people. I have also been compelled, in carrying out what I knew the society had a right to expect, to leave here and there in the hands of one man a sadly unwieldy charge, and to forbear from attempting to subdivide great tracts of country into two or more missions, as was urgently required. One whole mission (Lower Inverness, with parts adjacent) I have struck off, and reannexed to the charge of a clergyman twenty miles away, who is loaded with other work, because the poor people could not, in the experiment, fulfil the part which was thrown upon themselves towards the support of a resident pastor.

*　　*　　*　　*　　*　　*　　*　　*　　*　　*

'My poor diocese—what is to become of the flocks? My poor clergy—what are they to do? Here, under all the difficulties which I have described, they must, for the simple exercise of their vocation, each keep his horse, each must provide saddle, bridle, a winter vehicle, harness, cariole-robes (or buffalo-skins for the sleigh), and winter equipments for his own person. With all the rigid self-denial which they can and do practice, they incur debt, which drags as a weight upon their minds. Their spirits are discouraged in the midst of a severity of labour which requires their unbroken energy of soul. I do not see, from any prospect now before me, or any calculations or auguries which I can now frame, how the missions of Ireland, Frampton, and Stoneham, and other such missions, are to be carried on at all if the allowance from home is to be cut down to £60 a year, and to undergo, at the end of three years, a farther reduction. The missions within themselves cannot make up the difference; Quebec alone cannot do for all. The parish of Quebec will, in a few short years at farthest—and it might happen tomorrow—have to provide for the payment of clergymen and some other objects within its own limits, for which the present rector, (holding other appointments also, and being obliged, for reasons known to you, to retain the rectory), is disbursing, in six separate payments, £670 currency a year. The whole annual income (apart from the special fund for widows and orphans of the clergy) of our Church society, raised not without much effort, is £850, of which, £500 is contributed in Quebec. It may be understood, therefore, that the approaching call for Church expenditure upon the spot is something which will be more or less sensibly felt, and will, so far, increase the difficulty of contributing to the support of the missions.

Commending all these observations to the favourable notice and candid consideration of the society,

I remain, Dear Sir,

Very faithfully yours,

G. J. QUEBEC.

He concluded a letter of about the same date as follows :

" I part with the subject, expressing on the one hand my deep and unalterable sense (to which I have again and again in all fervent sincerity given utterance) of the debt of gratitude due from the North American Church to the society, and the praise due to God above for the blessings which it has long and widely dispensed among us ; and recording, on the other, my solemn conviction that these measures of retrenchment, to the extent to which they are carried by the society, and so far as they are not the dictate of imperious and unavoidable necessity, are unseasonable and premature ; and that the actual and prospective state of settlements in this and certain other parts of the North American provinces constitutes a direct and legitimate claim upon the fostering help of that great and noble institution. If it be true that, in the language of Lord Bacon, ' it is the sinfullest thing in the world to forsake or destitute a plantation once in forwardness, for, besides the dishonor, it is the guiltiness of blood of many commiserable persons,' it is a great responsibility which lies upon the Church in England, if she would take her scattered children to record that she is pure from the blood of all men, to follow up to its needful mark the work which has been begun and thus far proceeded with in the spiritual plantation formed within these colonies."

CHAPTER XXIV.

Proceedings within the diocese for initiating synodical action — Difficulties encountered.

THE clergy who met at the visitation in 1857 passed a resolution to choose certain of their own body, and to request the Bishop to name an equal number of laymen, to act together, with the Bishop at their head, in preparing the draft of a constitution to be submitted to the first formal meeting of the diocesan synod. The Bishop, accordingly, appointed six gentlemen, representing the different opinions held on the subject, and after several meetings of the committee had been held, a draft was agreed upon. Early, however, in the following year, it became known that an unexpected interpretation was put, by some parties, upon the act of the provincial legislature for the removal of the doubts which had existed as to the power of the Bishop, clergy, and laity, to meet in synod. It was held that, as no distinct provision had been made for the representation of the laity, no diocesan synod could meet without first going through the form of summoning the whole of the laity to a preliminary meeting at which the principle of representation might be adopted. The Bishop of Huron had acted upon this view in organizing his new diocese, and it was represented to the Bishop of Quebec that it would be safer for him to follow this example, than to leave any room for doubts which might afterwards be found to affect the validity of the proceedings of the synod. It seemed so perfectly plain that neither the framers of the act nor the legislature which passed it could have intended such an impossibility as that of summoning to one place the whole laity of a diocese, and it was so well known that the act had been made as short and free from details as possible, being in fact only permissive and enabling, and not affecting to confer any new powers, or to prescribe any action whatever to the Church, that the Bishop of Quebec was disposed to adhere to the course which he had adopted of calling a synod to consider the proposed constitution on the 9th June, 1858. He yielded, however, to the views of others, and revoked the summons, calling instead, a meeting of the clergy and laity, to be held at Quebec on the Feast of the Nativity of St. John the Baptist. I forbear from attempting to describe what took place on that day, but let it suffice, in the words of a circular shortly afterwards addressed by the Bishop to the clergy, to say that it became " apparent that great confusion and multiplied mischiefs must ensue from the act as interpreted to require a meeting of the Church, otherwise than by representation, as well as that extraordinary prejudice must be done to the rights of the diocese at large." The Bishop was so wholly unprepared for any opposition, or for obstacles in the way of farther proceedings, that it was impossible, at the moment, and under the circumstances, to decide on any ulterior step, and the meeting was simply adjourned to the 1st September. He had caused resolutions to be prepared, similar to those adopted in the diocese of Huron, affirming the principles of representation and of voting by Orders, " pending the adoption of a constitution by the synod," thus much appearing to be necessary in order to put the machine in motion at all ; but an amendment was moved for the appointment of a committee, to report to another meeting similarly constituted, and when it was to be put to the meeting the question at once arose whether the clergy were to vote separately, or to be out-voted by those who claimed to represent the voice of the laity.

In order to be prepared for the adjourned meeting on the 1st September, the Bishop, after receiving many suggestions from different quarters as to the best course to be pursued, determined to seek the opinion of the law-officers of the Crown on the interpretation of the Act. He accordingly undertook a journey, in July, to Toronto, which was at that time the seat of Government. But on his arrival, he found that as the Act affected only the interests of the Church, they could not be called upon for their opinion, except in their private capacity as members of the Bar. It was, however, suggested by three or four laymen of high standing, connected with other dioceses, that the simplest remedy for the difficulties of the case would be found in an application to the legislature, then in session, for a short explanatory Act, which should provide for the representation of the laity. This course had indeed been suggested by a member of the committee, when the unexpected interpretation was first put forth, but no real inconvenience being then apprehended, it was thought that the legislature would be unwilling to take any farther action which might appear to be unnecessary, and the Bishop went to Toronto without this idea having been again presented to his mind, without the smallest possible expectation of any such unlooked-for relief, and with no other object than that of obtaining the opinion of the law-officers of the Crown, and governing his subsequent proceedings in accordance with it. The idea was now freshly presented to his mind again from totally different quarters, and it was conceived that there would be no difficulty in obtaining an explanatory Act, the intention of the original Act being sufficiently plain, while the obstacles to its working had arisen from an interpretation of which it had been accidentally left capable. The event happily justified this expectation, for when the bill was prepared it passed the Legislative Council without opposition, and the House of Assembly adopted it by a majority of seventy-two against seven. Not one member of the Church voted against it, notwithstanding that the party from whom the opposition had proceeded at Quebec used every effort to defeat it, holding a public meeting, and sending eminent counsel to Toronto for the purpose. The Act, however, having been assented to by the Governor-General, became law, and the meeting of the 1st September fell through. The Bishop then, not deeming it advisable to subject the clergy to the expense and inconvenience of another journey to Quebec in the same season, determined not to assemble the synod till the following year. He hoped also that time and reflection, and, above all, the gracious influence of the Spirit of purity and peace, which he earnestly besought them to seek, would have the effect of healing the sore which had been opened, and bringing those who had opposed themselves to a different view of their duty. He put forth a letter addressed to the clergy and laity of the diocese, explaining the course which had been adopted in the matter of synodical action, and endeavouring to prepare them for a right use of its privileges within the bounds now prescribed by law. Together with this letter were published some " Considerations relative to certain interruptions of the peace of the Church in the parish of Quebec," which had been previously prepared, but which he had withheld in the hope that the ill effects of those interruptions would pass away without his personal intervention. This hope appearing now to be groundless, he put them forth, not without much fear and trembling, " solemnly and affectionately charging it upon all into whose hands they might come, to resolve, by God's help, to read them without pre-possession." He entered at great length on certain points which had been publicly discussed, defending the Society for the Propagation of the Gospel, as well as the practices of some particular clergymen in Quebec, from charges which had been brought against them. I subjoin some extracts from the publication :

"It has been a just ground of thankfulness to God, which, in different ways and at different times, I have taken occasion publicly to acknowledge, that in all the eight North American dioceses of the Church of England, we have **been exempt** from the mischief of certain indiscreet proceedings relative to the minutiæ of ritual observance and of certain exaggerated and unsafe views upon doctrinal **points**, which have characterized an extreme party **in the** Church at home. **I am not** aware of any single instance **within the limits just specified of any such** objectionable doings, or of **the introduction and advance of any such** objectionable principles; nor has there **been a single instance of any apostasy of** the clergy to the ranks of Rome. And a **similar** happy verdict may **be rendered** respecting the character **at large of** the missions supported **by the Society** for the Propagation **of the Gospel, the mother and the nurse of the** Churches in the dependencies of the Empire throughout the world.

  *   *   *   *   *   *   *   *

"So **far then, of** the Anglican Church **in** the diocese, and its **connection with the Society for** the Propagation **of the** Gospel. Suffer **me to speak one** poor word of its present Bishop.

"It has pleased God, Who chooses His own instruments, unworthy in themselves, and puts the ' treasure' of His Gospel ' in earthen vessels,' that I should occupy in the Anglican Church the episcopal charge originally of the whole of Canada, and now, by successive subdivisions, of that portion of it which constitutes the reduced diocese of Quebec. I have held this charge (without speaking precisely as to the months), for twenty-three years, being exactly one-third of my life. Another third exactly was previously passed in the subordinate grades of the Christian ministry exercised, with the exception of three years, in Quebec. I have carried my episcopal ministrations (having volunteered, before the erection of Rupert's Land into a diocese, to visit that country) from the Red River in the Hudson's Bay Territory to the Magdalen Islands in the Gulf of St. Lawrence. I have, in one ecclesiastical capacity or another, ' gone in and out before this people '—my own people in Quebec—for forty-one years. For forty-one years I have watched and prayed and worked for them without ceasing—watched and prayed and worked. ' I am old and gray-headed, * * * and I have walked before you from my ' youth unto this day. ' Behold, here I am ; witness against me before the Lord.' With whatever errors of judgment, with whatever deficiencies in practice,—and I know that they have been many,—I have been chargeable, I challenge the world to shew that, over all this extent of space or of time, among ' high and low, rich and poor, one with another,' I have been unfaithful to the true interests of the reformed Church of England, or swerved from the proclamation, according to the doctrine of that Church, of Christ crucified as the only hope of fallen man, and the Word of the living God as the only basis of didactic theology. I appeal to the whole tenor of my public teaching;

and if ever (which, indeed, is not much to be anticipated,) that smaller portion of it were to see the light, which has been delivered in a written form, it would **be** seen whether I have failed to preach 'the unsearchable riches of Christ' **and to** 'testify the Gospel of the grace of God.' **And in** the regulation of worship or points of ecclesiastical observance, I have not **ventured even** upon manifest improvements, but with a wary hand and a **considerate eye to** the object **of avoiding** hurtful misconstruction, and have **abstained, in** different instances, **from the correction, however in** itself **desirable, of** practices with which **it might have created disturbance to interfere.** I have not been 'a' reed shaken with the wind.' **Whatever** influence may have been in the ascendant, whatever opinions accidentally most in fashion, whatever peculiarities most popular for their day, whatever shibboleths may **have been bandied** about by men who charge the lovers of the Church with exclusiveness, **being, in** their own way, without calling in question their zeal and **sincerity,** preeminently exclusive themselves, my principles have **never changed. I have trodden in** the steps of my two venerated **predecessors in the see, and with all the human** infirmities attaching **to each of** us, I have the **comfort of feeling** that I am, as they **were, 'pure from** the blood of all men,' in the aspect of the case here under consideration. And this consciousness I shall carry—thank God it is not far—to my grave.

"It might be thought, perhaps, that under **all the** circumstances which I have here described, the hope could have been left to me of being spared from such a task as **that of** defending my diocese and my own administration of it from the charge either of Romanizing tendencies or of deficiency **of concern** for the spiritual well-being of the children **of the** Church.
*   .   .   .   .

"**Of the** tenets and usages, then, which are here in **question, I proceed to** specify some examples,—being such as are associated in many minds which, in these points, are imperfectly informed, with ideas of assimilation to Rome, and such as, in instances known among us here, have exposed her ministers to misconstruction carried to its very extreme. For the present I merely state them. If unforeseen necessity should arise for shewing, by means of another address or a series of addresses like the present, that the Church does hold them, and that she is right in holding them, I shall not, by the help **of** God, be wanting **to my duty in this** behalf.

1. "The Church of England maintains the high and sacred importance of the two sacraments, and their living efficacy, **when** rightly applied, as direct vehicles of grace and privilege to man.

2. "The Church of England maintains, as **a** principle, assumed in various solemn acts and made the basis of legislative proceedings in her whole communion, both within and without the British dominions, the regular standing commission of the ministry—the power of providing for the preaching of the Word and administration of religious ordinances, and the

regulation of matters ecclesiastical, not being held to reside loosely in this or that body of believers who may agree upon this or that arrangement for the purpose, but to have been originally conveyed to the keeping and charge of an Order of men constituted for that end, and in the persons of those who occupy the chief grade in that Order (wherever the integrity of the primitive system is preserved,) invested with authority to transmit this commission from age to age.

3. "The Church of England holds it to be an appendage of this commission (however dormant in practice, and this partly in consequence of past abuses of ecclesiastical power), to preserve order and purity in the Church of God upon earth, by the authoritative exclusion of scandalous offenders from certain spiritual privileges, and their restoration to the same upon due evidences of their repentance.

4. "The Church of England, in common with other protestant bodies, maintains and precribes as a practice which she affirms to be founded upon scriptural authority, the duty of fasting, upon set occasions, in the literal and proper sense of the word.

5. "It is the genius of the Church of England, made conspicuous in many ways,—while she affirms in her thirty-fourth article, and elsewhere, the liberty which is left under the Gospel of adaptation in matters of ritual to 'the diversity of countries, times, and men's manners,' and while she avoids an overdone pageantry or an intricate and loaded ceremonial,—yet to clothe the exterior of her worship, the whole apparatus of public devotion in all its details, and the whole manner of its performance, with a certain grave, orderly and significant solemnity ; and, where it can be reached, to stamp upon it a certain grandeur of effect. She carefully preserves the associations of sacredness in 'all that is for the work of the service in the house of the Lord ;' and she surrounds with a peculiar and scrupulous reverence the holy memorials of the death of our adorable Redeemer.

6. "The Church of England takes order for the frequency as well as for the dignity and religious decorum of public prayer, and provides a digested series of commemorative observances through the ecclesiastical year, which bring in each instance specially before her members, either some grand feature of the Gospel history, or, according to the spirit of the apostolic charge, some eminent example from that 'cloud of witnesses' which is found in the first planters of the faith.

"All these are examples of characteristic points in the system of the Church of England ; plain, prominent features of that system so impossible to be mistaken that an attack upon any zeal shewn in the preservation of such principles or practices is not an attack upon Mr. A. or Mr. B.; it is simply an attack upon the Church of England. I am very far from maintaining that no minutiæ of observance can ever become obsolete or susceptible, under altered circumstances and with the tacit sanction of authority, of modification ; nor yet that we are forbidden to desire some lesser changes in this or that particular, when the time shall serve and such experiments can be safely tried; nor yet that indulgence may not be due to men who, under the influence of the times, are more or less lax in their church views, if only they would shew indulgence in return to those who love to keep the rule of their mother. But with reference to the foregoing general points, they are points which we must of necessity include in what we accept and assert, whenever in our approaching synodical proceedings we formally accept and assert the system and liturgy of that Church. Some of them are matters of faith; others lie in the province of ecclesiastical authority, according to the discretion committed to the Church, being conformable in their spirit and their object to the Word of God; all of them are to be practically carried out, *pro virili*, and according to the opportunities open to them, by the prelacy and clergy of the Church; all of them constitute a portion of the particular form and mode of carrying on the work of the Gospel, which that prelacy and clergy have in charge; all of them should be made instrumental in their hands, according to every just view of ministerial responsibility, to the edification of the flock, by the familiar iteration of endeavours to promote an intelligent use and appreciation of such observances,—endeavours which may in some instances be made unduly prominent, but the total omission of which is the very way to make men mere formalists in their public devotions; all of them are comprehended in the force of the question to which a clergyman assents, in rendering, when he receives the Order of priesthood, his solemn vows before God and man:

"'Will you, then, give your faithful diligence always so to minister the doctrine and sacraments and the discipline of Christ, as the Lord hath commanded and as this Church and Realm hath received the same, according to the commandments of God; so that you may teach the people committed to your care and charge with all diligence to keep and observe the same?'

"And is it fair, then, is it justifiable, is it of any possible good consequence that a clergyman, who, without any ill-feeling or breach of charity towards other Christians, or any want whatever of preparation to stand against the proselytism of those Christians who profess the Romish faith, conscientiously endeavours to act up to this solemn vow of his ordination, should be hunted down by a false, and in some instances an almost ferocious, cry of Popery, and that efforts should be made, as in very many places has been seen, to impair if not to destroy his usefulness, by undermining his influence and blowing an evil breath upon his name? I repeat it—I will make the utmost allowance even for the unfair prejudices and groundless alarms of persons who from sincere, simple attachment to the pure truth of the Gospel which they are made to believe in danger, and with instances in England of an unhappy apostasy before their eyes, may lend themselves too readily to such a cry—I will give credit for right motives to men who do very wrong things, (although they ought better to have examined what they are doing) but, whatever may be the dispositions of the party, such a proceeding is in itself both mischievous and cruel. Is it wise, is it safe, is it edifying to frighten the members of the Anglican Church with utterly imaginary phantoms of superstition in the simplest compliance with the rules of their communion, and to make them afraid—for I do suspect that even this has occurred—to use the privilege of uniting in humble prayer before their God, upon such occasions as that of a litany service twice a week! Such a litany as that in which the Church has enabled us to pour out our hearts before God!　　•　　•　　•　　•

"But now let it be asked, however really respectable for their day, however eminent may be some names which can be adduced in favour of low and latitudinarian views in the Church, however plain and willingly conceded a superiority may attach to them over the claims of him who is penning these humble remarks, let it be asked, so far as human authorities and examples are concerned, whether there are not names immeasurably higher—names which will stand when the names of any such living men shall have been long and totally forgotten—illustrious, imperishable names in the Church of England, the names of men of deep thought, of profound learning, of accomplished scholarship, of masterly eloquence, all sanctified by a holy spirit of love, and richly impregnated by the Word of the living God,—to which an appeal may be made on the other side—and these, observe, the names of men who have been specially distinguished as invincible champions of protestantism. What were the sentiments of Hooker upon the several points which have been above stated? Of Hooker, whose great work (and the words will apply to it in the parts which regard our controversy with Rome no less than in others) has been described by a distinguished scholar of the last century as the everlasting possession and the impregnable bulwark of all which the English nation holds most dear? Hooker might be quoted absolutely upon all the points in question—take him here only upon one, in contrast with certain views upon the subject of fasting. We are told in his life that 'he never failed, on the Sunday before Ember-week, to give notice thereof to his parishioners, persuading them both to fast and then to double their devotions for a learned and pious clergy, but especially for the last, saying often, that the life of a pious clergyman was visible rhetoric, and so convincing that the most godless men (though they would not deny themselves the enjoyment of their present lusts,) did yet secretly wish themselves like those of the strictest lives.'*

---

* See Acts xiii, 2, 3, as remarkably sustaining the observance prescribed by the Church in this particular behalf. I have no doubt in my own mind that Hooker derived assistance in achieving what he has left to posterity, by his habit of "keeping under his body and bringing it into subjection" in the observance of the prescribed fasts of the Church.

.   .   .   .

"I might fill a large book with similar examples, and I might have recourse to those of celebrated foreign divines, but let the above cited specimens suffice. I would only now ask, were Hooker, Hall, Chillingworth, Taylor, Andrews and Beveridge* men of Romanizing tendencies—by anticipation tractarians or Puseyites?

"I do not say that any of these men were infallible, or that in the sense of implicit acquiescence in what they have said, simply because they said it we are to call any of them our father or master upon earth. Whatever weight their opinions may justly claim, my own maxim, and that which I recommend to others, with respect to human authorities of this nature, is to be *nullius addictus jurare in verba magistri*. I refer to them as great, illustrious protestant champions of the Church of England; and if they, being such, confessedly and conspicuously such, held the views which have been exhibited by means of references or extracts here given, as views by which they were distinguished, I ask with what shadow of justice, I demand by what possible right, we can tax men with popish leanings because they hold the same or perhaps even more subdued, although similar, views upon the same points? I ask with what title to a just or generous or warrantable proceeding, we can resort to the common and easy artifice, in order to make them odious, of ringing the changes upon certain words such as semi-popery, Romanizing tendencies, the *opus operatum*, etc., etc., which have no particle of just application to the case, but which serve the purpose, with abundant readiness, of bringing suspicion and discredit upon a clergyman because he desires to preserve in their undamaged integrity the distinctive principles and usages of the Church of England, and which aid the object of introducing into favour, in substitution for the real system of that Church, a system which is stamped with the characteristics of dissent? Nobody attacks the Scottish presbyterians because they venerate the name and cling to the peculiarities of John Knox. Nobody quarrels with the methodists because they are fervently attached to the memory and cultivate some now traditionary practices of John Wesley; but if a minister or member of the Church of England would affectionately identify himself in faith and practice with all which has been handed down to us

---

The late Bishop Stewart, my honoured predecessor in the see, who never laboured under the imputation of popery, made it his ordinary practice, although not holding himself inviolably bound to it by any superstitious feeling, if circumstances occurred to suggest a deviation from it, to pass every Friday throughout the year in as much religious seclusion as was practicable, and to observe the day as a rigorous fast.

* Quotations from all these writers, or reference to their works had been given.—Ed.

by our martyr reformers and their venerable coadjutors in framing the standards of our faith and worship, such a man is not to be endured for an instant, and a movement must be made to put him down. The principles of toleration freely extended, right and left, to others holding all shapes or shades of opinion are to be refused in his exceptional case. And it is not for the most part an adversary who does him this dishonour, for then, per-adventure, he might have borne it, but it is done by those who ought to be his companions and his guides, his own familiar friends whom he could trust, with whom he could take sweet counsel together and walk in the house of God as friends. Well may we adapt to the case the prophetic words of our Divine Redeemer : 'A man's foes shall be they of his own household.'

"But how easy would it be in many of these unhappy cases of difference, to turn the tables upon those who make the attack, and to ask them how, in their own line of proceeding, they can reconcile it to themselves to repudiate the rules and provisions of their own prayer-book, and to put the force which they do, in particular instances, upon the plain, strong, unequivocal language of the forms of the Church which they use. More, much more than this. How easy to retort upon the assailants, the charge of helping forward the cause of Rome. Any reverential care in public worship, any strict attention to venerable rules, any solicitude whatever for that decorous ecclesiastical effect in the varied ministrations of the Church, which is eminently characteristic of the work of our reformers, creates an alarm in some quarters, and calls forth from others a torrent of unmeasured abuse or of ungodly ridicule. But there is no one thing more certain in the world than that a mean, cold, and denuded aspect of religious ceremonial, or a slovenly neglect of externals in the house of God, combin-ing with a meagre and inadequate, a clouded, uncertain, unsatisfactory estimate of the ritual ordinances of Christianity, as well as with a hasty disparagement of settled order and venerable authority, and a promiscuous recognition of new and multiplying forms of religious profession, have been the direct means of driving many well-disposed men into the arms of Rome, who under different auspices might have been won to spiritual views of their religion, and preserved in the profession of a pure and scriptural faith. The tractarian movement itself, which ran on to dangerous and unwarrant-able lengths, and wandered at last so far away from the Church of England, was urged to those very lengths, as it was in the first instance (and then, with wise and good intentions,) set on foot by the marked and wide-spread deviations, in another direction, both from the letter and the spirit of the Anglican standards which prevailed in the Church. Extremes beget opposite extremes.

"I will here illustrate my meaning by a familiar example in point. The laxity of observance which has crept over our own Church has produced the painful exhibition to be witnessed in our army and navy of bodies of men sitting in public **prayer.** That may now be said to have grown up into the rule of **the army and** navy, where the **Church of England is pro-** fessed,—at least **I never saw any** other practice **in either.*** Take an army of people belonging to the Romish or Greek Church. You may see ten or twenty thousand men during their public religious performances, all down. in humble reverence, upon their knees. An intelligent protestant will not be shaken in his principles **by this** spectacle **as contrasted with what he will see in** the corresponding case within the **Church of England.** He will understand very well that the prostrate awe **of superstition may exercise a power** over men which spiritual religion, **adopted nominally by the mass,** but actually influencing only **the true Israel of God, may fail to shew.** But if he is a truly intelligent **protestant, he will deplore the introduction of** that external irreverence **in this and other similar points which takes away** the aids to inward **reverence** provided by our own Church, and suggests the idea at once, with **all the heightening effect of contrast, to unsettled** minds, no less than **to the adherents of a superstitious system, that protest-** ants do not **care about their religion, and are ashamed to bow the knee to their God.** Our own people are chilled and impeded in their devotional **exercises; kept back in the moulding of the religious man;** the careless **among them are confirmed in their carelessness; those who are alienated from us as votaries themselves of an erroneous faith** are hardened in their **alienation; those who may be** described as standers-by and spectators in **religion receive** unfavourable **impressions,** of which they experience and communicate abroad the **bad effects; and** some, perhaps, are led to aposta- tize from their faith. It is therefore (since the train of natural causes and effects is assuredly not left **to be inoperative** among the influences which form religion within the heart), **the merest mistake** in the world, and the most complete misapprehension of the manner in which human beings are constituted and **are acted upon** in religion, to suppose that a care for exter- nals can be safely neglected, or that it is a dereliction of the preaching of Christ and Him crucified, to maintain the value of outward ordinances, and to cultivate a dutiful conformity to every prescribed observance. Nothing is more unfounded, nothing **can be more** shallow than such a charge. St. Paul tells us that he determined not to know anything among the believers save Jesus Christ and Him crucified. What did he mean by this? He meant, of course, that the great cardinal doctrine of salvation by the death of Christ should never, in any part of Christian teaching, be lost from sight—should inseparably be interwoven with every endeavour for the spiritual good of the flock—should constitute the grand, the absorbing object of Christian ministrations. But did he mean to be so literally taken

---

* I know an instance of one regiment in which the colonel succeeded in establishing the use of the proper posture in prayer, but this, so far as my opportunities of information have reached, was a solitary exception.

as that he would not teach anything, for example, about the operations of
the divine Spirit, or the resurrection from the dead, or other points of
christian belief, save the one here in question? Or did he mean that he
would never charge upon the believers the remembrance of their baptism
and of the obligations then contracted as well as of the privileges then
conveyed? Or did he mean that he would never descend to familiar
instruction respecting the details of duty in common life? Or did he
mean that he would not enjoin it upon the disciples to pay respectful
regard to the directions of those who were 'over them in the Lord'? Or
did he mean that it was impossible for him to afford a thought for the
decency and order to be observed in public worship, for the establishment
of rules which are to distinguish the sexes in the house of God, for the
reverence to be associated with the place where the holy communion was
celebrated, as distinguished from the houses which men have to eat and
to drink in? Certainly the holy Apostle did not mean all this or anything
resembling it, for if he did, he would most prodigiously contradict himself.

"The lessons of the past are apt to be lost upon the inconsiderate mortals
of any living generation. We might else deem it a marvellous thing that
the warnings should be forgotten which stand out in broad and awful
characters upon those memorable pages of the history of our own country
which record the demolition of the Church establishment by a religious
faction, in the civil war of the seventeenth century. *Delenda est Carthago*
was their war-cry. 'Down with it, down with it even to the ground,' was
the motto inscribed upon their banner. The ancient episcopacy, the venerable ritual, the solemn and spiritual liturgy, the grave and orderly observances of the Anglican Church were all to be exterminated, root and branch.
Then it was that the heavenly-minded, the evangelical Bishop Hall (among
thousands of similar examples), lifted that voice of lamentation of which
some notes are heard in an extract already given, over the dishonour done
to the Church which he loved, and in his 'Letter from the Tower' and his
'Hard Measure,' left a picture of her fanatical enemies which as it is touching in itself, so, in the agitations of our own time, it is curious and most
instructive to contemplate."

* * * * * * *

"And if a clergyman is seen to manifest any zeal for the correction of
neglects, irregularities and deviations in the things pertaining to the house
of God, which marked a drowsy day in the Church—if he does not look
with favour upon those happy times when the more convenient slop-basin
or pewter vessel displaced the ancient font, transferred, to serve as a flower-
pot, to the garden of the squire, and when the celebration itself of the rite
of baptism was passed from the house of God to the dwellings of men,—if
he does not sigh over the loss in some churches of high-partitioned pews
which snugly ensconced the more stately worshipper, and often shut off
the poor from public worship;—then *fænum habet in cornu, longe fuge*—this

man is a mad tractarian; he will toss you all if you let him come near you over the fences which divide us from Rome.

"There is, perhaps, no person living who has had more ample or more varied experience of public prayer and preaching conducted with the rudest appliances, or scarcely with any appliances at all, than myself. And the roughness and extreme bareness of the accessories of worship are felt sometimes to be aids to devotional feeling. You will hear persons who are inclined to deprecate, if not to denounce, every approach to pomp of ceremonial or ritual effect, describe with much zest, and in what, according to a hackneyed modern phrase, is called a 'graphic' manner, the touching simplicity of a scene where the preacher reminds them perhaps of the Baptist in the wilderness. Yet they are then owning the influence, developed in a different manner, of the very principle against which they are disposed to contend. They are recognizing the aid of circumstantials, the power of externals in the acts of devotion and the performances of the minister of God. Either way, these accidents of our worship are of course non-essentials; the grand points of the Gospel ministry may be gained, the heart may be lifted fervently in prayer and praise, the soul may be penetrated with the love of Christ, the Word of life may be carried with power to the heart of sinners within the walls of a very convenient and respectable building, whose architecture is most supremely unecclesiastical, and whose arrangements for the conduct of worship are utterly revolting to a correct and nicely formed taste. But where the bounty of God has placed the means at our command, I am well persuaded, and think I am sustained in this persuasion (as I have shewn elsewhere) by different passages to be found in the New Testament, that, as christian worshippers, we may adopt for our own, with reference to the exterior of our worship, to the order of its distribution, and to the solemnity of its effect, the language of the holy psalmist (according to the prayer-book translation): 'It is well seen, O God, how Thou goest, how Thou, my God and King, goest in the sanctuary.' It is, in fact, upon these principles, if we examine the philosophy of the thing, that music, sanctioned by the practice of the Redeemer,* is made an ingredient of devotion. The power of music, by a peculiar and mysterious kind of charm, by the touch of some hidden spring within us, moves and melts, subdues or elevates the soul of man; and this natural power, with the heightened effect of artificial culture, is made available in his religion. A remarkable exemplification of the principles laid down in some of the foregoing remarks is found in the following extract from the recent account given by Dr. Livingstone of his labours among the African tribes:

"'So long as we continue to hold services in the Kotla, the associations of the place are unfavourable to solemnity; hence it is always desirable to have a place of worship as soon as possible; and it is important, too, to

---

* St. Matthew xxvi. 30.

treat such place with reverence, as an aid to secure that serious attention which religious subjects demand. This will appear more evident when it is recollected that, in the very spot where we had been engaged in acts of devotion, half an hour after a dance would be got up.'—*Missionary Travels*, chap. ix., p. 206.

"'Stand ye in the ways and see and ask for the old paths, where is the good way, and walk therein, and ye shall find rest for your souls.' I do not know of any occasion within my own experience, which has afforded more room for such a charge as this, than the recent interruptions of our peace in this place. I do not mean, any more than the inspired prophet could have meant, that we are to check all advance, to disdain all suggestion of improvement, to resist all indication of progress. Every principle for which I am here contending is connected with genuine progress in the Church. The two things go on *pari passu* together, and of this, if we had room for them, many striking and satisfactory proofs might be stated, in the way of example, as seen throughout the Empire. But there are ideas often propagated and easily accepted among men, nay, caught at in many quarters with eagerness, of a necessity for substituting something new which seems to offer itself, or to be attainable in the management of affairs, for breaking up the old routine and brushing aside the inherited prejudices attaching to the received system—they have not yet got 'the real thing,'—nothing will effectually be done without this renovation; no life will be infused into the body till new influences are allowed to have their play and the channels of control and authority are changed.

" All this may be more or less true, or it may be more or less erroneous. Let us then, with reference to our own Church affairs, pass very briefly in review some principal historical facts of our case, and enquire under what particular auspices and in connection with what set of principles the work of the Church has been done among us, and how far it has, while thus conducted, earned a title to our confidence."

*   •   *   *   •   *   *   ♠

"The Society (the S. P. G.), since the formation of colonial sees, has carried on its work in an unswerving recognition of the principles received in the Anglican branch of the Church, and in concert uniformly with the local ecclesiastical authorities. It would take up space which cannot be spared here for the purpose, to trace its labours or those of the sister Society for Promoting Christian Knowledge, either in a review of the past or in a survey of what it has been recently doing and is doing now abroad over the world, in which latter aspect it has, among other benefits, provided, through a special department of its labours, for the multiplication of the colonial sees in all quarters of the globe, and has furnished a triumphant answer, in the conspicuous fruit of this enlargement of the episcopate, to those objectors who imagined that the means of augmenting the missionary force of the Church and other machinery of evangelization would be thence abridged. But not even looking at the adjoining portions of British North America, let us remember that if we can point here to recesses in the forest **where the rose** of Sharon has been planted by the hands of our labourers; **if we can indicate** remote and rude places of the Gulf untrodden by any minister of religion, till the ground was taken up by our own; if we can **shew the work of** the Gospel perseveringly carried on, by strained efforts and with meagre resources, among feeble flocks scattered over a prodigious **surface of** country, here buried in the woods, there in danger **of being** absorbed into one with the prior occupants of the country, proud **alike in** their numbers and ecclesiastical wealth, who profess the faith of Rome; **if** we can bless God for a race of clergy who, with all the faults attaching **to** them as 'men of like passions' with their brethren of the laity, have been ready, without worldly recompense, **to endure** privation, to encounter hardship in the service of Christ, to put their lives in jeopardy in **seasons** of pestilence, and have been known, in several instances, to fall as victims 'upon the sacrifice and service of the faith,'—men familiar with prisons, with hospitals, with all the haunts of squalid poverty; if we can boast of a college conducted by professors from English and Scotch Universities, and now constituted a University itself—a college often most ungenerously disparaged, often injuriously misrepresented as to its principles, in its present young and still struggling stage, which was at first set fairly in **operation by** an indomitable spirit of zeal and self-denial upon the spot, and has been the means of so moulding a great portion of the junior clergy in the two Lower Canadian dioceses, as not to be behind the race of men already described, and can shew many of its *alumni* ceaselessly devoting themselves to the labours of their ministry—never looking back after the hand has been once put to the plough—continually engaged, whether in cities or in the roughest scenes of missionary labour in the woods, in pastoral work; warning their people from **house to** house, assiduous in lengthened preparation of the youth for confirmation, **in the formation of** Bible classes, in the establishment of libraries for their people, and in other efforts for the spiritual **improvement of their** charge; if there has **been** recently engrafted upon our college a 'junior department' which affords advantages of education in its different branches, equal, as I believe, to those of any school in North America, and which preeminently excels in familiarizing the minds of boys with the Word of God; if the Church has been enabled to dispense the bread of life, not only to her own destitute children in the wilderness, but to many who had no claim upon her as **their mother;** to dot the back places of the **country** with decent though humble temples of the living God; to found permanent institutions for the general work of the diocese, or the wants temporal and spiritual of the poorer classes in the city, and all this in the face of disheartening difficulties and accumulated obstacles; if the Church of England has done all this, and more, in the country, then what, with the blessing of God, might she not hope to do—

                      " ' which honour bids her do,
Were all her children kind and natural ?'

and by what earthly agencies, by what human instruments has all this—**little, it** must be sorrowfully said, compared with what the ruling powers **of the empire ought to** have given (or to have left) her the means of **doing—by what earthly agencies,** by what human instruments has it been **done?** 'Stand ye in the ways and see and ask for the old paths.' It has **all, all been done ;**—and 'as the truth of Christ is in me, no man shall stop **me of this boasting'**;—**by the hands of those who love the** Church of their **fathers in the stable** integrity of her principles **and are linked in their religious** proceedings with the cause of ancient authority and **order."**

•   *   *   *   *   *   *

"**Under** the auspices, then, and by the agencies which have been here **pictured, the work of the protestant** Church of England, in this as in **other dependencies of the** empire, has been brought up to the point at which it **now stands.** The Church of this diocese is still mainly drawing its nutri-**ment from the bosom of the mother** Church at home and carried still in her **arms.** It is not time yet to turn round and say, 'We have done with you ; **we can walk alone now, and do** not want to be in leading-strings ; or what **help we want we will get from** other sources and manage upon a new plan **and upon new and more enlightened principles ; we will** discard all these **musty** prejudices which hinder the growth and vigour of the Church. We **will have a revolution.'** Alas! but what will be seen in the end thereof? **Where would the Church have been** now in the diocese, if both its support **and its administration had not been** provided for in connection with that **system, the plain, real, honest Church of England system, which some of us would desire to see superseded by what is new, and perhaps more popularly taking? Where is the hope, the strength, the reliance under God, of the protestant Church of England in Canada? Look** back upon the **past and tell.**

"**I am not, however, by profession or in principle or in feeling a mere** *laudator temporis acti.* I bless God for the marvellous improvements of the **age and believe them ordained to be gloriously instrumental in advancing the highest interests of the human family at large.** I bless God for the **revolution which has taken place within my own recollection in the Church ; but this is a revolution connected and indeed identified, in many of its most signal benefits, with the recovery, in practice,** of ancient and charac-**teristic principles of the Anglican system.** You then, who love the reformed **Church of England, know,** I beseech you, **who** are your friends. They are **not your friends, although some** among them, carried away by ill-examined impressions, may mean you well, who sound an alarm in this diocese about

Romanizing tendencies. That σκιαμαχια (for if ever there was a fighting with shadows, a 'beating of the air,' it is found in this instance) can only do hurt to the cause which is dear to your hearts. The interests of our Anglican protestantism in this diocese, I am bold to say it, are much safer in my hands and the hands of those who support me, than in the hands of men who would bring our fidelity into question. For my own, of course is brought into question, if I do not seek to put down those who are charged with dispositions to tamper with our protestant truth. I do not wish,— God forbid!—to extinguish a jealous watchfulness over that truth. I do not blame men who are so tremblingly and sensitively alive to the danger of covered advances on the part of Rome, that they start at the imaginary semblance where no reality exists, and are carried beyond themselves in their excitement. I do not impute bad motives to them simply because they may be prompted by these feelings not only to conceive but to propagate a groundless alarm. They may do this—I would to God, though, that we had seen a little more of such a spirit!—in a spirit of candour, of charity, of Christian forbearance. But I think, in the meantime,—nay, I am absolutely sure,—that by that propagation they are doing mischief to the cause which they mean to serve. Hard things have been said of tried and faithful ministers; hard constructions have been put upon their doings; sneers and taunts have been bandied about; much ridicule has been employed, and not exclusively on one side, a weapon which a well-known sceptical writer pronounces to be 'the test of truth,' and to which he would subject accordingly the pretensions of christianity; but though a playful sally, made in a kindly spirit, is not austerely to be condemned, it would be well to remember, when once religious discord begins, those beautiful words of Hooker: 'There will come a time when three words uttered with charity and meekness shall receive a far more blessed reward than three thousand volumes written with disdainful sharpness of wit.' 'Every idle word which men shall speak,' whether by tongue or by pen, 'they shall give account thereof' in that day. It will not look well then, and it will be wise to bear this in memory now, that men, in order to gratify malice, to weaken the force of truths to which they are opposed, to seize, without one thought of its fairness, the readiest engine for their purpose against their adversary, or possibly, 'as a madman casteth firebrands, arrows, and death, and saith, am I not in sport?' to indulge in mere wanton amusement,—fly at once to the press, the seeds of the mischief being thus blown throughout the province and beyond it, and bring disparagement upon the faithful servants of the Most High, weakening their hands in His work and wounding their hearts.

"The cause of the Church of England in this diocese has received a check. Rome and others who may have ill-will to her have had a triumph. The disturbance has been uncalled for; for I repeat it—let one instance be proved in which any of my clergy have outgone either the doctrinal teaching or the ritual directions of their Church. Let one instance be shewn in which they have even availed themselves of certain recent decisions in England under which decorations, and symbols, and appurtenances of worship are pronounced to be lawful, of which, nevertheless, from the sensation which they might excite, the introduction would not be expedient. But it has pleased God to humble us; and we cannot hope that the brand having been thrown in and the fire set running through combustible matter, with gusts of no gentle kind to fan it in its progress, we can speedily extinguish such a blaze. All that we can do is to hold fast to our duty in the sight of God, and 'through evil report and good report,' through rough or through smooth, to labour that we may approve ourselves to Him, and be prepared 'to stand before the Son of Man,' earnestly studying and striving at the same time, 'if it be possible, as much as lieth in' us, to 'live peaceably with all men.' To Him we must confide the issue. And He Who can bring good out of evil may perhaps, even in this world, though I do not anticipate any such result within the term of my own service, make the damage which we now suffer, not only to leave no hurtful trace, but to redound to the credit and prosperity of the Church. So shall it be seen that—

> ' Per damna, per cædes, ab ipso
> Ducit opes animumque ferro.' "

CHAPTER XXV.

THE first synod of the diocese of Quebec was held on the sixth of July, 1859, and two following days, and though three years had not elapsed since the last visitation of the clergy, the Bishop called them together for that purpose at the same time, partly because he had been unable to meet them in 1857, and partly because he was unwilling to place them under the necessity of travelling to Quebec again in the next year. The winter of 1858–9 and the following spring were times of very serious anxiety and distress to the diocese, which weighed most heavily on him who was entrusted with the care of all its Churches. But it pleased Him, Who is the author, not of confusion but of peace, to bring His Church safely and happily through the crisis, and to grant His servant, after the storms which had nearly overwhelmed him, a calm, for the few years for which he was yet to labour, such as he had not known before. The blessing of God rested upon the patience with which he had endured, and crowned his efforts with success far beyond what had been looked for. The two great points for which he was chiefly anxious in the constitution of the synod, and to which the greatest opposition had been made—recognition of its three distinct orders, and the communicant qualification for lay-delegates—were carried by overwhelming majorities, the first by one hundred and forty-three to thirty-seven votes, and the second by one hundred and twenty-five to twenty-two. The patience with which the Bishop sat for three days from early morning till late at night, during long and not always agreeable discussions, and the meekness which he displayed towards those that opposed themselves, had, in many instances, the effect of drawing over men who had differed from him. Their admiration of his personal character led them by degrees to look with more favour on the views which he maintained. At the close of the synod, a member who had taken a very active part in all the proceedings, which the Bishop had felt himself obliged to condemn, of a body styled "The Lay Association," proposed a vote of thanks for the address which he had delivered at its opening, and for his able and impartial conduct, of which he suggested that all present should mark their sense by escorting him in a body to the rectory. He declined the honour, and after dismissing the synod with the benediction, rode four miles on horseback, with a lightened and thankful heart, to his home.* It was nearly midnight when he reached it. But notwithstanding the close and trying nature of his occupations for the last few days, by nine o'clock the next morning he was on board a steamer (lying nearly five miles from his house) which was to convey him to the extreme point of his diocese.

The address to which reference has just been made relates to a crisis so important in the history of his administration of the diocese, that I think it right to insert the whole of it in this place:

ADDRESS.

"My brethren of the clergy and laity, we are met, by the permission of Almighty God, to discharge very solemn and important duties which are new to us all. And we must engage in them under a deep sense of our

---

* Bardfield, near Quebec, to which he removed in the spring of 1858, at the recommendation of his medical advisers, on account of his own health, and that of Mrs. Mountain.

responsibility before God and man. We have to regard our task, first, as to the christian spirit and religiously disciplined frame of mind in which it is to be fulfilled; and next, as to the preservation, in this portion of Canada, of the principles, constitution, and usages of the Church of England, for the better establishment and administration of all which, as well as for the perpetuation of them in their essential force and integrity, it devolves upon us, so far as depends upon human instruments, to provide.

"For the first point then. It is evident that in addressing ourselves to a task such as that which is before us, we undertake to deal with the interests of religion, the interests of the Gospel of Jesus Christ. We put ourselves forward in the community as men who are concerned for the kingdom of God upon earth, for His glory and the salvation of souls. These are views and aims which it is impossible to separate for a moment from the objects for which a Church is constituted and the affairs of a Church are conducted. It would be an utter mistake to regard our religious system merely as a certain method for the public worship of the Deity, which we have inherited, or from accident of situation have nominally adopted, and which it is left to us to mould after the prepossessions of the world. If we do not come here—with whatever sense of unworthiness, and this cannot, in any one of us, be too deep or too strong,— yet if we do not come here as religious men, as men who having assumed an active part in the promotion of objects just above enumerated are seeking guidance in the discharge of their duty from above, we cannot properly be considered as qualified for taking part in these deliberations at all. The eye of God is upon us at this moment and penetrates our hearts. It behoves us to consider whether we are about to engage in the affairs of His Church in a temper and preparation of mind which are fitted to endure that awful scrutiny. And again, it would be a very unhappy misconception of our case, and yet one into which, whatever side we espouse, we might be liable in a manner inadvertently to slide, to suppose that our proceedings in synod must be assimilated in all points to the proceedings of public bodies who manage the secular affairs of mankind. In the parliament, for example, of a free country, under a limited monarchy, it is, whether wrongly or rightly, a kind of recognized maxim that an organized opposition must be a standing feature of the system and a necessary element in the conduct of affairs. And there are certain parliamentary tactics, certain stratagems of party, certain engines of policy adroitly wielded by practised hands, certain appeals also ad captandum to popular prejudice and passion, certain artifices in getting up an agitation, certain catchwords scattered abroad to produce an effect, the truth of which, if it serve the purpose in hand, it is not conceived very necessary to examine; all which are understood in many quarters to be part of the routine of business in the body or familiar instruments employed in preparation for it. In an assembly convened for carrying on the work of the Church, any approach to such manœuvres as these, as well as any disposition to find matter for minute cavil and to produce embarrassment by ingenious niceties of law, is totally out of character and out of place. **I do not mean, of course, and** can hardly be understood to mean, that we **are not to desire the utmost** freedom of discussion; that we are not **to benefit, within the bounds imposed by pure religion and consistent orthodoxy, by** the unrestrained expression of opinion, and to work out, by what **may be** called a friendly **collision between** mind and mind, the best **digested** and most practically **useful plans which can** be brought under our **review.** I do not mean that we are not to exercise the utmost wisdom and prudence vouchsafed to us; that we are not to call in the aids of valuable experience; that we are **not to put carefully in train** the most orderly and efficient system in the management of our proceedings, **or not to** avail ourselves of the facility for working them, afforded by **forms received in** the conduct of public business. But I do mean that the synod is to be regarded not in the light of a parliament, or a political organization, but **in the light** of a family assembled under their earthly father, to deliberate in love **upon the interests of the house. These are the** right mutual relations **of the parties; and these, which, thank God,** do extensively prevail among **us,** are what I hope and pray that we may, in His good time, see everywhere established among ourselves. **I hope it will,** before long, be generally seen and felt that if anything is done calculated to sow feelings of distrust and suspicion towards the episcopal **office (the proper and reasonable** claims of which it will readily be **seen that I must not be withheld by** any false delicacy from maintaining), if anything is **done to** put men on their guard **against a presumed desire of encroachment on** the part of the person occupying that **office, it can only be compared—looking, however,** to things **done upon an enlarged scale and with far extended** consequences—to an **endeavour made in a family, who else would be** harmoniously and happily **bound together, to set the children, in the same way,** upon the watch against their father.

" The Bishops **of the colonial empire have some claim, if they had it upon** no other grounds, **to the confidence and good-will of their people, because the** whole movement **made to introduce synodical action has** been, from first to **last, purely and simply a movement of their own—an** unconstrained and spontaneous **movement to divide with the clergy and laity, because they trusted that it would** be **for the advantage of the Church to do so, the** powers which **were lodged exclusively in their own hands. There has been** nothing and there is nothing to **oblige them to do it, or to make it difficult** to them to avoid it. There **are dioceses now, here in** British North America, situated in all respects **like our** own, in which the system has not been put **in operation. And the Bishops, in** making **this effort,** had **in** the first instance to encounter great opposition and misconstruction, proceeding from what is considered (without meaning to use the word in an opprobrious **or offensive sense) the party leaning** to democracy in the Church, as persons here holding similar sentiments have since declared themselves opposed to the principle of representation, the only principle which can afford any voice to the rural districts. Of the interruptions of christian peace and the ill-omened appearance of any separation of the interests of the laity from those of their pastors, I wish to say but little. It is impossible, however, to refrain from saying that we might have indulged the hope of doing our work without disturbance. We might have imagined our way to be sufficiently smooth. We have precedents and patterns already before our eyes, and all uniform in their essential characteristics throughout the empire. We are now following in the wake of sixteen colonial dioceses, being the whole number in which synodical action has taken place; and in every one of them, without a single exception, that particular principle has been embodied and recognized as an indispensable feature of Church of England episcopacy, which is conceived in some quarters here to be a special grievance and which constitutes a main object of active and organized assault. But this opposition, we may well hope, will die away. We may well hope that the opponents will become reconciled in the actual working of the experiment to that from which, in theory, they have been prompted to anticipate ill consequences to the Church. And it cannot be doubted that gentlemen, who have been found hand to hand opposed to each other in the conflict of opinion upon points of the constitution, will afterwards cordially co-operate in all which they shall be alike persuaded to tend to the common good. In the meantime, we may challenge all parties to shew what special and local grounds have existed for attempting to make a difference in this point between the diocese of Quebec and all the other dioceses of the empire. Yes; the day will come when the excitement of the occasion having passed off and the clouds of some prevailing prejudice having cleared away, the objects upon which we fix our regards will be seen as they really are, leaving it only a subject for wonder that any such agitations should have existed at all, and a ground for true thankfulness of heart that all differences upon the subject may be forgotten. Upon this point I venture to say that we are strong; and as in the example of certain stories set afloat before the elections about particular clergymen, it will be found, by those who possess themselves of correct information, that they are pointedly opposed to the truth of the case; so with respect to our whole case at large, I feel safe in declaring, as I feel called upon to declare, that no plea has been afforded, either in the administration of the diocese, or the teaching, the proceedings or the practices of its clergy, for any alarm to be sounded, for any agitation to be put in train, for any organized opposition; still less, of course, for any movement liable to be regarded as having any revolutionary aspect.

"Most deeply is it, under these circumstances, to be deplored that any difficulties should have arisen from within, upon the invitation given to the laity to co-operate in the management of matters ecclesiastical, with those who are set over them in the Lord, and that the invitation should in any instance have been so misapprehended as to cause its being met in a spirit of unkindness. We have difficulties enough with which to struggle in planting and rearing up, in extending, directing, and upholding the provisions of the Church for the scattered and widely severed population who belong to her within the diocese; and a statistical exhibition of our progress which, together with a slight historical outline of the formation of our Church institutions within the diocese, I had intended, if I had not judged that I should trespass too far upon your time, to put before this meeting, would serve to shew that, with miserably meagre resources, and in the face of many disheartening obstacles, we have, by the good hand of our God upon us, and His blessing upon the help of our friends at home and upon the efforts of our labourers upon the spot, something more than kept our ground and laid some good foundation for those who will come after us. I had thought that a survey of such a nature (which I may possibly prepare at some future opportunity) might encourage and interest us farther in the work which we have now in hand, and aid us in appreciating, as well as—if anywhere it be imperfectly or incorrectly understood —in understanding our task. The whole subject is practically new among us, but we shall remember that we have not *champ libre*—we have not a clear stage for creating a new system or trying experiments in the way of remodelling the old one which we have received. We have to deal—and we are thus brought to the second part of our subject according to the distribution of it which I proposed in the outset of these remarks,—we have to deal, under the two provincial statutes which provide for the case, with the system of the Church of England.

"Now, here there are two postulates to be assumed. First, that if the legislature of a country or province concedes powers, of whatever kind, to a religious body, it must be understood, as a matter of course, that those powers are to be called into exercise according to the constitution, laws and usages of the body itself. And secondly, that if the body proceed to frame, under those powers, a representative constitution for certain deliberative, executive, and legislative purposes of its own, the enquiry presents itself, *in limine*, what that body is which is to be represented, and how its original, essential, and distinctive character is to be preserved.

"The body to be represented, in the present case, is the episcopal Church of England.

"What, then, is episcopacy?

"We need not to go to the schools of theology for an answer to this question, nor ransack the labours of learned divines. We have only to consult the most familiar repository of definitions in our own language.* We have only to look there for the word episcopacy, and we see it thus

---

* Johnson's Dictionary.

defined : 'The government of the Church **by Bishops, established by the Apostles.'**

"If we have to **frame** a synodical constitution **within the episcopal** Church of England, **it is** plain that we must frame it according to the principles of episcopacy. We are at liberty to repudiate episcopacy if, in **our consciences,** we cannot be persuaded of its primitive and apostolic **origin, but can** we, in that case, be qualified to bear our part in acting for **the Church of** England ? And **if we have never** fathomed the subject, —perhaps never looked into it at all,—ought we not to endeavour to **master** it before we refuse to acquiesce in the received principle of the **Church** here considered, or conceive ourselves prepared to deal with a practical question which involves the recognition or the rejection of episcopacy as above defined ? **For if the Order of Bishops in their distinctive** character could be ignored in the synod, and they could merge simply in the general order of the clergy, though with a complimentary precedence allowed to them, and the place of chairman reserved for their occupancy, this is not episcopacy. The system would cease to be properly an episcopal system.

"That the maintenance, as an inviolable principle, of such a transmitted **episcopacy is part and parcel of** the Church of England, is what it is most **abundantly easy to shew, but it is what I shall not take up your time by proving here ; nor** shall I labour to exhibit the **law of the case ; that latter** question has been recently treated amongst us by more competent hands. And with reference, in particular, to the construction, upon this point, of **the permissive statute (19, 20** Vict., c. 141,) I have had the benefit of an opinion rendered to me by an authority entirely unaffected by **our** immediate local influences and agitations—an authority which would **be** acknowledged by all parties whatever to be as high **as the province of** Canada can afford The act, according to this opinion, **expressly** recognizes the three distinct orders of Bishop, clergy, and laity, as three branches, the concurrence of each of which by **itself is necessary to give effect to** legislation within the body. **Each of** the three branches alike, therefore, has what, according to the popular rather than the correct phraseology of the day, is called, in the case of the Bishop, **a veto upon the other** two.

"There is, however, one point of enquiry upon which I shall, in **conclusion of this** whole subject, enter a little more at large, because **it is** one upon which great misapprehensions are seen to prevail and such as have great influence upon the judgments of men in the matters here considered. The remarks which I have to offer upon it, as well as a small portion of those already made, are not altogether new to some few members of the synod who **are** here present.

"The enquiry is this :

"What and where are the precedents to which we would have recourse if we **could** possibly establish a synod which, in making laws for the Church, could dispense **with** the episcopal concurrence ?

" I answer, my brethren, that we should be doing what has not yet, under the same circumstances, been seen in the Christian world. We should be inscribing a name upon this diocese of Quebec which would be new in the history of our religion upon earth. We should be seeking our pattern—not from the precedents of the pure primitive Church in her unchallenged and invariable practice in this behalf; not from the declared principles and settled system of the Church of England, or other reformed episcopal Churches; not from the proceedings of any one among all the colonial Churches of our own communion in different and far-divided quarters of the globe, who have thus far, whether upon a formally legalized basis or otherwise, adopted a synodical constitution; not from the action of public authority or the course taken in our own voluntary movement in Church matters within our own province (for look at the original constitution of our Church Society, subsequently incorporated by provincial statute, which makes the Bishop's consent necessary to all changes; or look at the charter of Bishop's College, in all which instances men have not been afraid to put large authority, within an episcopal institution, into episcopal hands); no, it would not be to any of these examples that we must have recourse, but to the semblance (as I shall shew) rather than the reality of a precedent in the introduction of the episcopate into the United States of America. And under what circumstances? With the wounds yet raw and bleeding, caused by the violent dismemberment of the territory from the monarchy of England; with prejudice raging all around in exasperated minds against those institutions of England in which the established Church is conspicuously prominent; with heightening effect added to this prejudice, as well by the notorious fact that the people of the Church had been characteristically loyal in the great struggle which had just been brought to its close, as by the circumstance that the constitution of the Church itself is of a monarchical aspect; and, finally, with utter local inexperience of any episcopal supervision whatever, and habits of mind remaining altogether to be formed with respect to the relations between this new order of men brought into the country under all these circumstances of difficulty, and the flocks who were to receive them.* In this conjuncture of affairs the original dioceses adopted a constitution in which the consent of the Bishop is not made essential in their ecclesiastical legislation, and the system once introduced into the republic, it has (with the exception of Vermont, the well-known defence of whose particular constitution, by the present Bishop of the diocese, I do think to be a victorious

---

* So little, in many quarters, was the Church then understood by her own people in America, that when the body at large was in process of organization in the country, the people professing to belong to her in one of the States applied to be received into convention, with the condition proposed that they should not be obliged to have any Bishop.

performance and one recent exception in a more qualified form) naturally been continued in the dioceses which have been since created. Is this feature, then, of the American Church convention the special precedent which any of us can desire to single out* for our own guidance?

"But here it is not unimportant to observe that this supposed American precedent does not after all (as I have intimated) go the length of divesting the Church of the episcopal control in legislation. For the Church in the United States provides, not only for the annual convention of each diocese, but for the supreme authority of a triennial convention of the whole Church throughout the Union. And in this general convention nothing can pass without the consent of the house of Bishops. It was not so originally; but it was made so, even in that land of democratic predominance, by subsequent legislation within the body, because in the working of the system its necessity was seen and felt. The case, therefore, of individual dioceses there, even if they could, under any circumstances, be made a warrantable pattern for ourselves in the point at issue, is not parallel to our own case here. We are proceeding to act in synod, not as one out of many dioceses which are all subject alike to the paramount authority of a general convention (or, according to older ecclesiastical language, of a Provincial synod) in which the ratification of the Bishops is required, but we are proceeding to act as a diocese, singly and independently; and we have no right to assume as a prospective certainty the formation of a Provincial synod in which we shall be comprehended. And therefore, it may safely be averred that, if the supposition of such a case could possibly be admitted as that of the disallowance of the episcopal privilege here in question, we should be doing what is unsustained by any single fair and full precedent in the whole world.

"It is farther to be observed, although at first sight we may receive exactly the opposite impression, that, in point of fact, any innovating surrender or diminution of the standing authority of the Church within our communion may with much less apprehension of dangerous consequences be ventured upon in the American republic than in our own colonies. For as there is in that country no Church-establishment or national religion, and nothing therefore in the way of prestige or association with the love of country or acquiescence in the transmitted system of privileged institutions, to bias or prepossess the minds of men in their adoption of one system of religion rather than another, the attachment of episcopalians to their own Church may generally be presumed to be founded upon their

---

* In the learned work of Judge Hoffman, of New York, on the law of the Church, it will be seen that it was by the surrender, from the force of circumstances, of an inherent right, that the Bishops became divested of what is called the veto.

distinct and intelligent preference for the system of episcopacy and the usages connected with that system. It is well known that the class of mind in that country which has a love for order, reverence, and stability, and which encounters a shock in the religious fluctuations and distractions and the many unwholesome excitements prevailing on this side and on that, is seen continually to fall in, as with something satisfactory and congenial, with the episcopal Church, to which there are very large and frequent accessions both of ministers and people from this very cause. And the self-evident consequence of all this is a powerful infusion of what is called the conservative element into the system. Whereas, among ourselves, it is a thing familiarly observable, that a vast proportion of our people throughout the empire are churchmen, not properly from holding episcopal principles, but simply from an inherited and too often an unexamined conformity to the received institutions of their country; and having so many loose adherents, we are as a body less prepared than our neighbours to admit with safety any sudden removal of checks of standing authority in the Church and to open the door for the agitation of questions, without any such balancing weight, in which the distinctive principles of the Church may be compromised.

"I might say a vast deal more upon many points which have been agitated among us. But I have said already more than I originally intended, and have felt it thrown upon me by circumstances to touch upon points—those especially connected with my own office—which it would have been far more agreeable to me to pass in silence. I do not want to bar the way, in any point, against freedom of argument here, but it never can be improper that, in presiding over an assembly met to frame a constitution for its future proceedings, I should indicate the necessity of our not violating the constitution of the very Church itself, of which that assembly avows that it is a part. It must be my duty to do what in me lies—I believe I have done too little—surmounting all reserve on account of considerations personally affecting myself, to make the real principles of the Church understood upon points to which the attention of her members is apt to be only called by some extraordinary occasion such as the present, and which in a multitude of instances are new to the habit of their thoughts. All which I have said, then, I commend to the candid acceptance and the serious consideration of minds—and I hope they are not few among us—which are accessible to arguments happening to jar against their own preconceived and perhaps very favourite impressions. Let it be seen that in entering upon the grave and important functions which are now before us, we 'do nothing against the truth but for the truth.' And let us be content if, among the principles to be now adopted for our guidance, we find one place reserved for the maxim of the wise King: 'Remove not the ancient landmark which thy fathers have set.'"

The visit of the Bishop to the district of Gaspé, in 1859, was marked by an occurrence new to that part of the diocese. An ordination was held at Paspébiac, when a deacon was advanced to the priesthood. The Bishop had heretofore ordained only at Quebec and Lennoxville, except, in one or two instances, at Three Rivers and Sherbrooke. But believing that the edification of the people would be promoted, and their interest in him who was to minister among them increased by witnessing and taking their share in the ceremony, he this year held ordinations in rural districts on two subsequent occasions, on each of which one deacon only was ordained. One of them, who had laboured for many years with exemplary zeal and fidelity as a lay-reader, was ordained as a permanent deacon. In the course of his Gaspé visitation, which occupied six weeks, besides holding the ordination above mentioned, he confirmed 181 persons at fourteen places, consecrated two burial-grounds, and preached eighteen times. Two Sundays were unfortunately lost, so far as public duties were concerned, in going to and from the Magdalen Islands, the landing there being effected on the first, at too great a distance from a settlement and too late an hour of the day to admit of any service being held, and the second being spent in the hold of the mail schooner, where he was glad to make his bed on the round stones that served for ballast, rather than continue to be drenched by the heavy rain which freely made its way into the berth which had been assigned to him. Other confirmations were held in the autumn in the neighbourhood of Quebec, as well as an ordination in the cathedral, at which the Bishop of Nova Scotia, who was on a visit (felt to be too short) to his brother-prelate, preached. Confirmations were held, in the places still remaining to complete the triennial circuit, in the earlier part, and some in the autumn, of 1860, making the whole number during the three years sixty-three, of which six were in Quebec, forty-four in country churches, eleven in school-houses or private dwellings, and two in dissenting places of worship lent for the purpose. At three churches no candidates were presented. Nine hundred and eighty persons in all were confirmed. On three occasions the service was held in French. The ordinations during the same period were eleven, of eight deacons and nine priests. This was the last triennial circuit which the Bishop was permitted to complete. Before the next had been gone through his work had passed to other hands. In this year (1860) he established an annual gathering in the cathedral on Whitsunday of the Sunday schools in Quebec. Four hundred children were present on the first occasion, whom he addressed in a simple and affectionate manner. In the summer of 1860 he had also another opportunity of exchanging friendly offices with the sister Church in the United States, having visited Burlington, on the invitation of the Bishop of Vermont, to take part in the consecration of the chapel of the diocesan Theological Institute. He had also, during this summer, the pleasure of receiving at his house the Bishops of Newfoundland, Montreal, Rupert's Land, and Victoria, besides enjoying a brief visit from the Bishop of Michigan.

The year 1860 was rendered memorable in Canadian history by the visit of the Prince of Wales. The Bishop, accompanied by a large proportion of the members of the diocesan synod, presented and read an address to His Royal Highness. The Prince presented the Bishop with a handsome Bible for the cathedral, in memory of having attended divine service there, as well as a donation to Bishop's College of two hundred pounds, being part of a larger sum given to the principal colleges in Canada. With this sum a scholarship was founded, called the Prince of Wales' scholarship.

CHAPTER XXVI.

THE second diocesan synod was held in July of this year. The deliberations of the first had been confined to the adoption of a constitution, and on this occasion, before entering upon the practical matters which seemed chiefly to demand attention, the Bishop thought it appropriate, at the marked period which had been reached in the history of the diocese, to give, in his opening address, a short sketch of that history, which it may be interesting to insert here in his own words, though the leading points of it have already been mentioned in these pages :—

"The first Anglican Bishop of Quebec, within the lifetime of the more aged men among us, began his task with nine clergymen for the whole of Canada, and after thirty-two years left the diocese, upon his decease, with sixty-one, having three archdeacons and two corporations of the clergy, in Upper and Lower Canada respectively, for the management of the clergy-reserves. His successor, whose diocese was also co-extensive with the whole of Canada, raised the number, in ten years of apostolic labour, to eighty-five. That was the state of the charge upon which I entered twenty-four years ago. Since that date Canada has been divided into four dioceses. Upper Canada or Canada West, now comprehending the two dioceses of Toronto and Huron, was under my episcopal supervision, as administering that of Quebec, for three years, during which I was enabled to add nineteen clergymen to the number of fifty-one which I had found within those limits. In that portion of Lower Canada which now constitutes the diocese of Montreal, the number was raised during its continuance under my direction for a space of fourteen years, from seventeen to forty-eight. From causes already indicated,* independently of the larger amount of Church population, the advances which I was permitted to make in this way in parts of Canada which are no longer within my jurisdiction were greater than I have made in that which now constitutes the diocese of Quebec, where the increase, in my hands, has been in twenty-four years from seventeen to fifty. The whole increase in Canada, within my own proper administration (not noticing what has occurred in any of its ecclesiastical divisions and subdivisions after their passing out of my hands), has been from eighty-five to one hundred and sixty-five. Since the meeting of the synod last year, I have admitted four gentlemen to the Order of Deacons and three to that of Priests. One clergyman has left the diocese, and one, besides the additions just named from ordinations, has come into it. Two new missions have been formed. Some more are in prospect and some more labourers to occupy the ground.

" My venerated predecessors in the see are too well remembered to make it necessary for me to disclaim any pretensions which, if I had the smallest disposition to advance them, would readily be open to repudiation, to equal myself in the discharge of my office with them. But it has been so ordained to befall, that the Church should not, till after my assumption of the episcopal charge, reach that stage in which she began to form her permanent institutions and provide her settled organizations within the diocese. I entered upon my charge in the latter half of the year 1836. The Church Society was established in 1842, and incorporated in 1844 : its objects and its operations are too well known to all who are present, to need any notice here from me. The Church Temporalities Act, having been reserved for the Royal Assent, finally became law in 1843. The corner-stone of the College was laid in 1844 : the College was opened in buildings temporarily occupied in 1845 : the royal charter conferring upon it the privileges of a University was procured in 1853 : the junior department, consisting of a first-rate school,† was opened in 1857 : the whole institution is still, in a manner, in its infancy, and will never be exempt from imperfections attaching to all things here below ; but it has now four efficient professorships (including that which is immediately connected with the junior department),—a library of between four and five thousand volumes, the promising commencement of a museum, and a chapel which may be cited as an architectural pattern. Of the fruits of the institution I forbear to speak, because I should speak before their faces of some men moulded within its walls ; and men who do best are least pleased to have their doings proclaimed. I will simply say, therefore, that the benefits of the College (speaking only, though I might give some farther extension to

* The local peculiarities of the diocese, climate, scattered population, &c.

† A school had been established long before under College auspices, and most successfully carried on for several years.

my remarks, of its supply afforded to the Church), have by no means been confined to the single diocese of Quebec. I might also refer to certain advantages reserved within the institution to the sons of the clergy. **And with help as well from this institution, as from other quarters, we have,** notwithstanding the meagreness of our resources and the diminution of extraneous aid to which I have adverted, been still taking up new ground, year by year, and have penetrated to remote and destitute quarters where **no other protestant ministrations have been known."**

This address, as originally **written, went back to an** earlier point in the history of **the Canadian Church, the reference** to which (omitted for the **sake of brevity) as it stands in the** manuscript, it **seems desirable to preserve :**

" In the **whole extent of the colonial Empire of Great Britain throughout** the world, **there was no Bishop of the Church of England before the** erection **of the diocese of Nova Scotia, to which the Rev. Dr. Charles Inglis was appointed in** 1787. **That prelate, acting under** powers **conferred upon him in his patent from the Crown, visited** Canada **and held confirmations* as well as a visitation of the clergy, some if not all of whom received licences at his hands, in** 1789. **The whole number of clergymen who could then be assembled from one end of the province to the other (Upper and Lower Canada having then constituted together the province of Quebec,) was eight. It appears that, in** 1774, **they had been four in number, including a chaplain to the garrison at Quebec.**

" In 1793 **the provinces of Upper and Lower Canada, of which the division had** taken **place two years before, were constituted a diocese of which the see was fixed at Quebec, and Dr. Jacob Mountain was appointed as the first Lord Bishop.**

---

* A printed account of this visit, taken from a periodical of the day, gives the following **interesting particulars, together with addresses pre**sented **to his lordship at Quebec and Montreal, and his replies :**

MONTREAL, July 9.

On Thursday evening last arrived here from **Quebec the Right** Reverend Father in God, CHARLES, Bishop **of** Nova Scotia. **The Bishop was** met at Pointe aux Trembles, and **conducted into** the **city, and has since** received the compliments **of many of the most** respectable **inhabitants both of** the Protestant and Romish persuasions. On Sunday **morning he** delivered to a numerous auditory an excellent discourse **on the** nature and end of confirmation, with a **view** to the administration **of** that ordinance **next** Sunday.

"During the greater part of his episcopate of thirty-two years,* the protestant population made very slow advances in Canada, and the difficulties
are almost inconceivable under which he had to labour in providing, even
in that slow advance, for the wants of the Church. He made great but
unsuccessful efforts for establishing efficient means of education in this
country. His visitations, in the then state of the country, were no less
arduous than they were extensive. He procured the erection of the cathedral at Quebec, which was consecrated in 1804, and was the first place of
worship belonging to the Church of England in that city.† Some years
afterwards he effected the incorporation, by separate charters for Upper and

QUEBEC, August 13.

On Wednesday, the 5th instant, the Right Reverend Father in God,
CHARLES, Bishop of Nova Scotia, held his primary visitation at the church
of the Récollets in this city. Divine service was performed to a crowded
audience, and a sermon was preached by the Rev. Philip Toosey, minister
of the parish; after divine service an excellent charge was delivered by
the Bishop to his clergy, upon the various and important duties of their
office, with great force and energy.

On Thursday divine service was performed and a sermon preached by
the Rev. Mr. Stuart, minister of Kingston.

And on Friday divine service was performed and a sermon preached by
the Rev. Mr. Doty, minister of William Henry; after which the Bishop
held a confirmation, at which upwards of 130 persons were confirmed.

On Saturday divine service was again performed and a sermon preached
by the Rev. Mr. Tunstall.

On the Sunday following the sacrament was administered by the Bishop
himself to a great number of communicants, several of whom had been
previously confirmed; and in the afternoon some persons expressing a
desire of participating in this ancient and salutary rite of the christian
Church, the Bishop indulged them with a private confirmation.

* In 1823, two years before his death, the whole number of protestants
of all denominations in Lower Canada was 34,400.

† The members of the Church of England had previously worshipped in
a chapel belonging to a Récollet monastery (which stood where the upper
town market now is), with the use of which they were accommodated.
The Bishop had maintained, while this building was occupied by the
Church of England, a surpliced choir at his own expense, which was afterwards transferred to the cathedral, where it was kept up for forty years.
The cathedral was opened with a full choral service, which, as I have heard,
was regularly maintained as long as a clergyman could be found qualified
to conduct it. The Rev. M. Feilde, mentioned at p. 14, had acted as pre-
centor.

Lower Canada respectively, of the Bishop and clergy for the management
of the clergy-reserves. He also succeeded in getting archdeaconries established, and left at his decease, in 1825, sixty-one clergymen in the
diocese."

An instance of the personal good feeling which prevailed in
many quarters through the troubles which had now been happily terminated, and one which was a cause of much gratification to the Bishop, was a proposal, emanating from a gentleman
who had taken a leading part in opposition to him on the
synodical question, that he should sit for his bust to be presented to his family. The gentleman referred to suggested
the idea to another who had been active on the other side, in
these words, " I think many who have often had the mis-
fortune to differ in opinion with our good Bishop, as well as
the many who have not, would be glad to unite in a testimony of affection to him who has spent so many years
amongst us." *

The last circuit of the diocese was begun in January, 1861,
in the district of St. Francis, where twenty-eight services
and twenty confirmations (being an increase of three) were
held, and one deacon was ordained at Richmond. Confirmations were now held, for the first time, in the new mission of
Hereford and Barford, and at Tingwick in the mission of
Danville. Several adult baptisms took place at the hands of
the Bishop. The extreme and unwonted severity of the
weather, and the accumulation of snow from a constant succession of storms, were such as the Bishop, in his long
experience, had never before encountered, and caused the
disappointment of several candidates for confirmation. One
storm in particular, on the 10th February, when the trains

* It would be an act of great injustice not to mention that while the
Bishop was supported by a large number of churchmen, whose devotion to
good works as well as their personal attachment to himself was a source
of comfort and strength to him, the same character in both points attached
in no less a degree to not a few of those who differed from him, as the
records of diocesan institutions abundantly testify.

were stopped for days together, deserves special notice, as it was found to have extended to Labrador, and to have raged even on the coasts of England and Ireland.* The number of persons confirmed on this tour was two hundred and ninety-seven, shewing, notwithstanding the disappointments just mentioned, a slight increase over the last occasion. Two hundred and twenty-nine were confirmed in the cathedral immediately before Easter, on which day most of them became communicants, making the whole number who partook on that day of the Lord's supper in the parish of Quebec eight hundred and eighty-nine, out of a population of about five thousand. In May, another confirmation was held at a place which had never before witnessed the ordinance, Montmorenci near Quebec, where a mission had been lately established. The diocesan synod was convened this year a month earlier than usual, in order to permit the Bishop to avail himself of a favourable opportunity of carrying out his long cherished desire of visiting the coast of Labrador. The few protestants settled there, whose number had increased now to about two hundred, scattered along a shore of about half as many miles in length, had been up to this time cared for, so far as was possible, by the missionary on that portion of the coast which belongs to the diocese of Newfoundland, whose parsonage is scarcely more than a dozen miles from the little stream which divides the two dioceses. But independently of the necessarily imperfect nature of this supply, the hands of the zealous missionaries being sufficiently full with their own proper work, the Bishop had felt for a long time that the Canadian Church should not leave the care of those few scattered sheep to pastors of another diocese, and had prevailed upon the S. P. G. to regard this as an exceptional case, and establish a new mission. Two years had passed by without the society having been able to find a man for the post, the wants of which the

* See Illustrated News, February 16th and 23rd, 1861.

Bishop was most anxious to ascertain by personal inspection. He had hoped to reach the coast in 1859 from the district of Gaspé, and had left Quebec with that expectation, but no opportunity was afforded. He had also endeavoured to make arrangements for visiting it in company with the Bishop of Newfoundland in his church-ship, but other engagements prevented this. The only means that remained of getting down were the small river craft, and a steamer which is sent down twice a year from Quebec with supplies to the lighthouses in the gulf. He would have been willing to encounter the hardships which a voyage in one of the smaller craft would have involved, but the uncertainty attaching to it might have caused an absence of many months from Quebec, which could not be spared from the other work of the diocese. The meeting of the synod had interfered with the first trip of the steamer in 1860, and the second was so long delayed that he could only have been landed from her, and left to find his way home again as best he might. The probability was that the opportunity of doing so might not occur till the following spring. At length, however, it pleased God both to open the door for his own visit, and to enable him to send a missionary who reached the coast from Gaspé a few days before him. Every accommodation was afforded on board the steamer, both by the commissioner of public works, and the captain of the vessel, and he remarked that he had never before been so comfortable at sea. He had the opportunity of visiting the solitary families at two lighthouses in Anticosti, and also at the Hudson's Bay Company's post at Mingan, where the steamer called, and ministering to their spiritual wants, a kind of work which he specially delighted in. Early on the morning of St. Peter's day (twelve days after leaving Quebec), he was landed at Blanc Sablon, and hospitably entertained at the establishment of Messrs. de Quetteville. This being, however, on the eastern side of the little river, he pushed on at once, being impatient to go to work in his own

diocese, proceeding on foot to the first settlement where an
English-speaking population was to be found. Settlement
there was none ; a solitary and poverty-stricken family occupied what had once been a large and flourishing establishment.
The comforts of the steamer seemed greater than ever when
contrasted with the misery that now surrounded him.   I
forbear from details ; suffice to say, that in all his varied
experience of roughing it in log-huts, in the woods, in open
boats, or on sand banks, he had never met with any thing
to compare with the wretchedness and discomfort which
he was now called upon to share.   But all was cheerfully borne, and he felt himself amply repaid for all his
privations by the comfort of being permitted to preach to
these poor destitute settlers the unsearchable riches of
Christ.   The missionary who had come from Gaspé was so
much discouraged by the aspect of things, that he asked permission to return there, and left the Bishop in order to seek
an opportunity of doing so.   The Bishop, meanwhile, pushed
on towards the west, encountering endless difficulties in
procuring the means of doing so.   He embarked in a *chaloupe*
(a small decked vessel), laden with salt, which was to convey him to the point which he wished next to reach in two or
three hours.   He had not been one hour on board before the
wind utterly failed, and he would fain have gone ashore again
to urge his way on foot.   The only means of reaching the
shore was by a small flat, and the captain was unwilling to risk
the possible loss of a breeze which might spring up during
the absence of his men if he spared them for the purpose of
putting him ashore.   The prospect of an indefinite detention
in the chaloupe, without bedding or provisions, and with rain
coming on, was not encouraging ; but more than thirty hours
were spent on board with cheerfulness, the cargo of salt furnishing a bed, and the sailors' fish-soup and biscuit serving
for breakfast and dinners.   Late in the evening of the second
day, when the prospect of passing another night on board

seemed certain, a boat was descried at a distance, which after many alternations between hope and fear, was found to have been attracted by the signals anxiously made from the chaloupe. On board this boat there was but one man, who willingly pulled the Bishop and his chaplain into the beautiful little harbour of Belles Amours, where they found a hospitable welcome, combined with cleanliness and comfort. And from this point there was less difficulty in every way. Eleven services were held in the Canadian part of the coast, and several children baptized. Everywhere the people manifested a kind and thankful spirit. The Bishop was depending on the steamer which had brought him down for the only sure opportunity of returning to Quebec. On this occasion she had carried down workmen to Belleisle for the completion of whose work she was to wait, and to call again at Forteau, where the Bishop was to be picked up. He was obliged, therefore, as the time fixed by the captain approached, to retrace his steps towards that place, where, however, he was detained more than a fortnight. He had made arrangements with the Montreal Ocean Steamship Co., for going on board one of their vessels if possible, at this point, and was in readiness day and night to embark whenever they were expected to pass the lighthouse where he was lodged. But one passed in a fog, another when it was blowing too hard for a boat to get out, and the signals of the third were not seen by the man who was paid to keep a look-out. Everything here was clean and comfortable, though the good woman of the house fancied herself so unequal to the task of entertaining a Bishop, that she positively refused at first to do so; and it was only when she learned the extreme discomfort he had endured when her door was closed against him, that she the next day relented. She soon found that she was waiting on no lordly prelate, but on one who remembered that he was the servant of Him Who had not so much as where to lay His head. The only ground of impatience or uneasiness was the anxiety to turn what seemed to be spare time to the benefit of his own diocese, though he did all that he could for that of those who were within his reach; and it was a satisfaction to him to do something in return for the services which the Newfoundland clergy had rendered to his own people. He could not however be withheld from making some farther effort; and after great difficulty in finding the means of conveyance (or rather the hands to guide it, for the missionary at Forteau, who shewed him every possible kindness and attention, placed his barge at his disposal), he again set his face westward, though it was blowing a gale in which he was strongly warned that such a vessel should not venture out.* He spent a Sunday at Isle à Bois, where he held two services, one of which was in French. The next day he had the great happiness of meeting the Bishop of Newfoundland. The comforts of the highest kind which were now enjoyed on board the church-ship, where he became an honoured guest, were sufficient to refresh him after what he had undergone on the shore. It was not long since no ministrations of the Church had been ever seen upon this desolate coast, and now, on the festival of St. James, her highest offices were celebrated in a pretty and well-appointed church by two Bishops, two priests, and a deacon. It is not easy to imagine the joy which such intercourse under these circumstances afforded. Before the church-ship left Forteau, the steamer arrived on her way to Quebec, and the two Bishops separated. She was detained however for two or three days, and they had the opportunity of once more joining in prayer and praise together in a store at L'Anse à Loup. The senior Bishop would not consent to deprive the people of the privilege of

* His fearlessness was very remarkable. I remember once, at the Magdalen Islands, his expression of regret, mingled with pity, when a brave crew, with the usually intrepid missionary at the helm, thought it prudent to turn the head of their boat towards the land because a squall was seen approaching.

listening to their own, who took occasion in preaching on
the second lesson (the epistle to Philemon,) to allude in a
most touching manner to the presence of " such an one as
Paul the aged " among them. They had just spent together
the birthday of the elder one, who entered then his seventy-
third year. The reverence and affection with which the
Bishop of Newfoundland always treated his brother were
most remarkable. The church-ship now went on her way,
and the two bishops parted, never to meet again on earth.
Eighteen months afterwards the Bishop of Newfoundland
wrote thus:

" I might almost say, *curæ leves loquuntur, ingentes* stupent, I am so
unable to express what I felt at the sudden and sad announcement of your
dear father's removal. He was to me more than an elder brother; I looked
up to him and revered him as a father. I look back, with deep gratitude
to God, on the advantage I have derived from his counsel and example, or,
I should perhaps say, may have derived if I could follow or profit by either
as I ought; particularly I shall ever remember the intercourse and communion I had with him and yourself on the Labrador, being, as indeed he was
then, 'such an one as Paul the aged and servant of Jesus Christ.' I shall
ever remember his patience, cheerfulness, and piety, with admiration and
thankfulness. I have hoped and earnestly desired to see him, and that he
might have been seen and heard by others, in Newfoundland, but it has
been ordered otherwise: better, surely, as we can all acknowledge, for
him; and that consideration must reconcile me to the disappointment. The
description which Mrs. M. received of the Bishop's last days and hours was
most touching and delightful, as it was, I am sure, faithful, for the end was
as holy and peaceful as his life had been laborious and useful, and the
blessings he gave to those who surrounded him must have been precious
indeed. I have never heard of any person's departure respecting which I
could more earnestly and sincerely say and pray, ' Let my last end be like
his.' As on the Labrador he might have addressed us ' being such an one
as Paul the aged,' so, I believe, he might have said, (though he, perhaps,
would have been the last to have said it,) in the same Apostle's words, ' I
have fought a good fight,' &c."

The Bishop reached Quebec after an absence of seven
weeks, on the 7th August. During the whole of that time
he had never been once able to hear from home, though he
had left Mrs. Mountain in a state of health which afforded

sufficient grounds for anxiety. When he had finished his work on the Labrador coast, he was desirous, therefore, of reaching home without unnecessary delay. But besides the disappointments already mentioned, he experienced another. The captain of the steamer, in which he had embarked at Forteau, kindly undertook to transfer him to another which was going direct to Quebec, and when she came in sight at two o'clock one morning, the Bishop was put off in an open boat for this purpose, but the steamer did not stop, though she had replied to the signals made from the other, and the Bishop was obliged to return to his own vessel. In the interval between this time and his reaching Quebec, the effect of his fatigues and privations began to shew itself in an attack resembling inflammatory rheumatism, and he was obliged to be carried on shore at Quebec. His patient trust in God's goodness was rewarded by finding all apparently well at his home ; and she for whom he might have been anxious, if he had not been always accustomed to cast all his care on Him Who cared for him, became his tender nurse. Before, however, her own anxiety on his account was relieved, she was removed beyond the reach of all trouble and care. On the 23rd August he lost the partner, for forty-seven years, of his life, the sharer of all his joys and sorrows, his help-meet in all his labours. And he bore it as one disciplined by trial only could have borne it. A few short hours of illness, during the whole of which she was unconscious, were all that were ordained for her at the last, and even to the very moment of separation he had not been able to realize to himself that it was so near. He had all his children and grandchildren around him in this hour of trial, and they never met together again afterwards till he was to see them so for the last time on earth.

CHAPTER XXVII.

Missionary sent to Labrador—First provincial synod—Appointment of
Metropolitan—Sermon before the synod—Triennial circuit continued—
Last visitation—Meeting of diocesan synod—Jubilee—Bishop Williams
of Connecticut—Finlay asylum.

Even this heavy sorrow and his own continued illness did
not hinder him from exerting himself for the supply of the
spiritual wants of the few sheep over whom his heart yearned
on the coast of Labrador. There was, indeed, no time to be
lost before the closing of the navigation, and the Bishop went
to Lennoxville on the 6th September, to confer Priests' Orders
on a young Augustinian who had accepted his call to tend the
straggling flock. He sent him forth with great thankfulness
and comfort, being well persuaded, particularly from the
manner in which the call had been received, that he was
prepared to " endure hardness as a good soldier of Jesus
Christ." Another Augustinian was at the same time admitted
to the diaconate, to supply the place of him who was going
to Labrador, on whom and on one other the Bishop laid
hands again at the last ordination which he held.* From
Lennoxville the Bishop proceeded to Montreal to attend
the first meeting of the Provincial Synod. He was still so
disabled that he could not take his place in the procession to the

---

* Three weeks after this the new-made priest was called upon to attend
the funeral of his Bishop, and this was the last public act in which he
himself took part in the diocese, if not on earth. He was obliged to leave
the ranks of the procession by illness, from which he never recovered.

cathedral, but he nevertheless preached with unusual power and energy before the Synod. The marks of sympathy and affection with which he was everywhere received were very soothing to him. In his address to the synod of his own diocese in the preceding June, he had thus referred to the appointment of a Metropolitan at Montreal :

"We are permitted to enter this day upon the business of our third synodical session in this diocese. If our proceedings have not yet produced any very marked effects, we must not suffer ourselves, on that account, to be discouraged. It must be the history, I apprehend, of synodical action, to work itself first, step by step, into a manageable shape and a capacity for practical benefit, and it is then that the engine is set freely in motion and so plays as to effect the purposes for which it is constructed. A great and important addition to the machinery by which these operations are to be conducted has been made, since we last met, by the appointment of a Metropolitan of the Church of England in Canada, binding together the several dioceses in order to their joint action in matters ecclesiastical, and at the same time leaving each diocese free to provide separately for its own local interests, and to regulate its own immediate affairs. I trust that we shall be blessed in all this. I trust that we shall always approach and carry through our task in a spirit of devout humility, and with firm faith in the promises of grace and guidance made to us in Christ. I trust that a religious, a christian character, a character different from that of mere political organizations, will always be impressed upon our proceedings : and that none of us will insensibly be drawn into a habit of immersion (with whatever aptitude for the purpose we may happen to be gifted,) in the forms and details of business, to the prejudice either of that spiritual frame of mind, or of that devotedness to pastoral labour, that close assiduity of attention to the flock, which ought (and with heightened effect in a missionary diocese like our own) to characterize the ministers of the Gospel.

"We have full reason, I think, to be satisfied with the location of the metropolitan see at Montreal. The situation of that city is central : its wealth and its population greatly surpass those of any other city in British North America ; and it is more marked than any other by a general spirit of progress and improvement. Nor is it a circumstance to be counted absolutely for nothing, that it has now a really creditable cathedral church, correct in design and beautiful in effect. As far as the person holding the office is concerned, all parties must be thoroughly satisfied : but, in point of fact, it is the place and not the person nor any personal considerations of whatever kind, which ought to determine the choice of the metropolitan see.

" As matters actually stand, the establishment of this chief see at Montreal would involve an arrangement of which the prospect has given rise to some jealousy, seeming not wholly unreasonable : for the diocese of Montreal alone, having the election of its own Bishop, would thus choose the man who is to have ecclesiastical authority over the whole Province. A movement, however, has been made to provide against objections conceived to attach to this feature of the arrangement, without disturbing the arrangement itself. Against any such remedial contrivances, however, as would invest the metropolitan see with an ambulatory character, making it shift about, upon the occurrence of vacancies, from diocese to diocese, I should most energetically and solemnly protest.

" We now expect very soon to have a fifth bishopric established in Canada. In our episcopal communion, the multiplication of bishoprics is the extension of the Church and of her service in the cause of the Gospel—a very natural and obvious consequence, and one which has been remarkably exemplified in our own day. We are rather backward, I think, here, as regards the interest which we take in the operations of the Church at a distance ; and the new task in which the Church of England has been permitted to engage in providing a local episcopate for the superintendence of missions among the heathen beyond the limits of the British dominions is an auspicious omen of great things to be achieved by her towards the gathering in of the Gentiles, which ought to stir within us more thankful emotion, more lively sympathy, more happy anticipation than is, I fear, likely to be actually witnessed. That hearty engagement in the affairs of our Church upon the spot, which is necessary to the effective character of synodical action, will never have life among us, unless we catch a glow of feeling reflected from abroad, and contract an animated sense of common interest in the advance of the cause of Christ over the world at large.

" In our own particular case in this province, the principle of elective Bishops has been introduced. Not that it has been made compulsory : we are left free to choose our own method in each diocese of providing for the occupation of the episcopate, and might leave the nomination, if we saw good, in the hands of the Sovereign. But we may consider it, in a manner, as a settled point, that all the bishoprics will be elective ; and the day cannot be very remote when occasion will be given to put this principle in exercise within the diocese of Quebec. I hope the clergy and laity will be prepared, when that day shall come, to act with a single eye to the glory of God, to the salvation of souls, and to the progress and consolidation of the Church ;—with an inviolate spirit of charity and forbearance ; with an utter repudiation of all worldly intrigue and partizanship, all recourse to the arts of canvassing and caballing,—everything, in short, which is described by the word *electioneering* in the transactions of popular government in the world. Without staying to examine the question respecting the preponderance of advantage in the system of election on the

one side, or nomination by authority on the other, it must be admitted that
there are evils and dangers incident, generally, (for these **remarks** are not
prompted by any suspicion of **our** particular local tendencies and dispositions,)—incident, generally, **to the** elective principle :—evils and dangers
against which it may be **for the wisdom of our synods to** provide some
adequate guard. The sentiment of Dr. Johnson, **with** reference to a
question similar in its nature, within another communion established in
one portion of the British Isles, without being adduced as condemnatory
of the principle of election here in our view, may serve to indicate some of
those incidental consequences, the prevention of which must, on all hands,
be desired. **Having had described to him, two parties,** ʻthose for supporting **the rights of patrons, independent of the people, and those** against
it,ʼ ʻIt should be settled,ʼ he said, ʻone way or the other.ʼ ʻI cannot wish
well,ʼ he continues, ʻto a popular election of the clergy when I consider
that it occasions such animosities, such unworthy courting of the people,
such slanders between the contending parties, and other disadvantages.
It is enough ʼ he concludes, ʻto allow the people to remonstrate against the
nomination of a minister, for solid reasons.ʼ ʼ •

The appointment of the Metropolitan had been in entire
accordance with the wishes of the Bishop of Quebec. It has
been stated that the office was offered to himself; but this is
not strictly true, though, if it had not been for his intervention, an arrangement for giving it to the senior bishop for the
time being, which had been actually agreed upon by the
authorities at home, and would have involved his acceptance
of it in the first instance,† would certainly have been carried
out. In the episcopal conferences held in London in 1853
on the subject of synodical action, it was understood that a
Metropolitan should be appointed for the whole of British

---

* I have inserted this passage, as well as that relating to the Metropolitan, as possessing a peculiar interest from the fact that the counsels which
it contains were so soon called for in his own diocese. The passage was
re-printed in a Quebec paper just before the election of the present Bishop,
and probably contributed to produce the right spirit with which that election
was conducted.

† His patent as Bishop of Quebec dating in 1850, some of the officials at
home who had not ascertained that the date of his consecration was 1836,
imagined the Bishop of Toronto to be senior in office as well as in years,
and this gave rise to a report that his lordship was to be the Metropolitan.

North America, **according** to the suggestion of the Bishops
who had met **at Quebec** in 1851, and that his seat should be
in that city. The Bishop of Quebec wrote privately, how-
ever, to the Archbishop of Canterbury, to decline the honor
for himself, and recommended, **at the same time,** the appointment **of the** Bishop **of Montreal. And when he was informed**
of the proposal just mentioned, which was supposed to be in
accordance with the prayer of **three of the four Canadian**
synods, he objected so strongly, not **only on personal grounds,**
but chiefly on account **of the principle which was involved,**
at the same **time recommending** Montreal as **the** best place,
that the present **arrangement** was **made.** Some disappointment was felt within **the diocese at his preference for** Montreal **over the mother-see,** particularly **as it carried a depar-**
ture **from the** practice which had **prevailed in all similar**
appointments **in the** colonies, and a feeling of the **same kind**
was more widely spread with regard to **his own non-acceptance**
of the office. But he justified his proceedings in **a protest***

---

  * The following is the protest:

*Reasons against those portions **of the** printed **draft** for the amendment of the
Letters Patent (**report of the** committee No. 3), of which the object is
to leave open **a** power **of transferring the** metropolitan jurisdiction to
other sees within the Province.*

  1. Because **the** office of Metropolitan, **according to the ancient and uni-**
versally (*) received **usage** of the Church and invariable practice of the
United Church of England and Ireland at home and abroad (there being
now five metropolitan **sees** in the colonial dependencies of the empire), is
attached permanently to a particular see.

  2. Because it is most highly inexpedient and undesirable to introduce
into any branch of the colonial Church any such marked deviation from
ancient ecclesiastical and Anglican usage, as would be involved in substituting for the office of Metropolitan, properly understood, a sort of ambula-
tory jurisdiction which would shift about from see to see.

  3. Because the very title of Metropolitan imports the designation of a
particular city as the permanent seat of the jurisdiction attaching to that

  (*) If any exception can be found, it is only such as to exemplify the
saying: *Exceptio probat regulam.*

which he entered on the journal of the first Provincial Synod, and which, when he caused it to be printed and circulated at the second session of that body, had no inconsiderable weight in producing the adoption of a measure accordant with his own views.

In his sermon preached before the Synod, he went back to the earliest times to shew the inherent right of the Church to express her voice by her synods, and referred to the measure of partial relief which had lately been accorded to the Church of England:

"I forbear also from expatiating upon such happily increased facilities for the work of the Church, and for the share assigned to her in the evangelization of the world, as are found, first, in the partial loosening of the rein

---

office; and the change now intended to be provided for would thus involve a contradiction in terms.

4. Because the endeavor to modify the Letters Patent in the manner proposed would, in the event of its being successful, nullify the professed object of the petitions for the creation of such an office, and virtually set aside the whole of the proceedings had in the case.

5. Because the appointment of Metropolitan having been made by Her Majesty, in compliance with petitions to that effect proceeding from three of the Canadian dioceses, it would be a plain inconsistency on the part of the petitioners to seek so to alter the provisions of the Letters Patent that there might by consequence be, in effect, no metropolitan see, and therefore no true Metropolitan.

6. Because the petitions for such appointment evidently implied and brought under the consideration of the Crown an appointment of the same nature with those previously made in other parts of the empire.

7. Because the only objection of any apparent weight against the provisions of the Letters Patent in this behalf being the seemingly undue preponderance of privilege assigned to the diocese of Montreal in electing the Metropolitan by the act of electing its own Bishop, that objection may be obviated by the transfer of such election (presuming the diocese of Montreal to agree to the same) to the hands of the Provincial Synod, or by other methods which that Synod, in its wisdom, may devise.

8. Because the city of Montreal is central in point of local situation, and is, of all the cities in the province, the most populous, the most considerable, the most prosperous, and the most increasing.

(Signed,)   G. J. QUEBEC.

by which convocation was so long and so rigorously held fast; and secondly, in the removal of all impediments to our sending missionary bishops into heathen lands beyond our own dominions. The Church must indeed be considered as in a hampered and crippled condition, if it be interdicted to her so to lengthen her cords and strengthen her stakes, that she can **freely** break forth on the right hand and on the left,* carrying **her ministry in its fulness into** any of the outlying highways and hedges of human society: Commissioned as she is by the voice of her Lord and Master to announce, wherever the sun illumines the habitable portions of the globe,† that all things are ready, and to **bring** in guests to His **table** from among the outcasts of the world. ' Go ye **into all** the world and preach the Gospel to every creature ; and lo! I am with you alway, even unto the end of the **world.**' Yes—blessed Lord—that is the lofty commission, and that the sustaining promise, which we have received from Thee ; and we will not have any rest in our spirits till we, till we of the Church of England, have done our part, trusting to Thyself to give the increase, **in** contributing to bring on the glorious consummation—how short, as **yet, of** its accomplishment!—when Thou shalt take to Thyself all ' the heathen for Thine inheritance, and the utmost parts of the earth for Thy possession,' **till ' the** earth shall be filled with the knowledge of the glory of the Lord as the waters cover the sea.'

" Within the British dominions in North America, and, to a certain extent, within our own province of Canada, we know that the Church has done labour, and has labour to do, for a race reclaimed, or remaining to be reclaimed from the darkness of heathenism and the wildness of savage life. But labour where we will, and in whatever advanced condition of civilized society, never, never will it cease to form part of our task that we should turn men ' from darkness to light, and from the power of Satan unto God.' And when we felicitate ourselves upon the enlargement of the Church at home from fetters long fastened upon her without relaxation, as well as upon the greater liberty and more open privilege which have been conceded to us in this behalf in the colonies, we shall none of us, I trust, forget, whether of the clergy or the laity who take part in our synods, that the *ultimate* objects of all ecclesiastical deliberations and proceedings are the glory of God and the salvation of the souls of men."

* * * * * * * * * *

" And here I would observe farther, with reference to a point not wholly without affinity to the remarks just made, that, as I do venture to think, there is a great mistake committed by some eminently pious and zealous

---

* Is. liv. 2, 3.

†—O qua Sol habitabiles
Illustrat oras.—*Hor.*

men who engage in the sacred work of extending the Gospel over the world,—a great mistake when they seem to confine their object simply and exclusively to the change to be operated upon individual souls, and to repudiate all idea of enlarging the kingdom of Christ in any other sense than as this effect is conceived to be produced—to measure, in short, the whole work, in all its parts, by this standard alone. For, granting most freely that we can never be too much in earnest in deprecating a mere formal adoption of Christianity, a name in religion without the reality of love, a mere carcase without life, it must be conceded, I think, on the other hand, that with respect to the evidences of grace in individual subjects, we are apt sometimes to pronounce upon them from tests which very insufficiently ascertain the case :—Men may be wrought upon, on the one side,—in fact it is a very common occurrence,—so as to exhibit what are accepted as decisive marks of conversion which may one day prove to have been fallacious ; and the power of religion may have sunk deeper into the hearts of others of a retiring character and a reserved temperament than we are ready to imagine or allow. The great day alone will bring all to light. I believe that, in this very point of view, as well as in others, the saying of the Saviour will be signally verified, that 'many that are first shall be last, and the last first.' It is a dangerous forgetfulness to lose sight of the maxim that we are to ' judge nothing before the time.' But this is not all. For supposing, *argumenti gratiâ*, such a case as that the ministry of the Church, from whatever cause, should be found, here or there, unsuccessful in the great work of turning sinners, whether Jew, Turk, Pagan, or nominally Christian, from darkness to light and from the power of Satan unto God,—are we to conclude from thence that nothing is done when a foundation is laid, among any body of people, for a scriptural and apostolic system of religion,—when the channels are opened, the machinery prepared, the provisions established for introducing and perpetuating a Church, which, in the lowest estimate of her performance, will distribute the Word and dispense the sacraments of Christ, with the sanctification of the seventh day ; and by her very worship, by her ordinances, by the cycle of her observances, will familiarize her people with the great and saving truths of the Gospel, of which these observances may, in their digested series, be well said to exhibit an epitome ? If we can imagine such a case as that all this can be done without any present return of fruit, or immediately satisfactory result in the spiritual condition of the worshippers,—upon which we ought never too hastily or without sure warrant to render our verdict—yet is nothing done when all is at least in fair train for carrying on the grand purposes of the christian ministry, and the instruments are ready by which Christ may, in God's good time, if it really has not been already done, be brought effectually home to the hearts of men ?

"Among these instruments, we indulge the hope and trust that our synods, now extensively introduced into the colonial dependencies of the empire, will, in the active exercise of their functions, sustain an important and beneficial part. Surveying all the provision and all the apparatus of the Church for executing the commission confided to her hands, we may contemplate, side by side with the delineations of our text, those glowing words of the psalmist, 'Walk about Zion, and go round about her, and tell the towers thereof. Mark well her bulwarks, set up (or consider) her palaces, that ye may tell them that come after'* and we may adapt, in the way of application to our synods, the words of another animated psalm, where the distinguished privileges of Zion are portrayed, that *there*, as one of those special privileges, is the seat of judgment.† We may look far back to the ancient Church of God in the wilderness, and we see there Moses sitting to judge ‡ the people—guiding their movements, regulating their proceedings, resolving difficulties, reconciling their differences, governing and administering their affairs at large. Yet though he acted under a direct commission from on high, enjoying "celestial colloquy sublime," § and was invested conspicuously by the hand of God with wonder-working powers, we observe that he availed himself at once of the suggestion offered by his father-in-law for his relief. Jethro had just witnessed the oppressive weight of his labours, as well as the inconvenience suffered by the people from his having to deal single-handed with them all; and recommended that, reserving for his own jurisdiction the disposal of the higher and harder causes, he should provide himself, out of all the people, with help. And the requisite qualifications of these proposed assistants are specified. They were to be 'able men, such as fear God, men of truth, hating covetousness.' Moses loved his people: he prayed, upon one occasion, in a strain similar to the sentiment expressed many centuries afterwards, on behalf of the same people, by St. Paul, rather to be himself blotted out of the book of life, than that the threatened doom should come upon them. And we see, in another instance, how far he was superior to any mere personal jealousy of power, such as would grudge to see others made participants of privileges vouchsafed to himself, 'Enviest thou for my sake? Would God all the Lord's people were prophets, and that the Lord would put His Spirit upon them!' ‖

"These words, we remember, were uttered upon the occasion of assembling, by Divine command, the seventy elders,—the same body, in the judgment of some divines, which had already been created, as just noticed, upon the recommendation of his father-in-law. And the origin is there supposed to be found of the Sanhedrim, or great council of

---

* Psalm xlviii. 11, 12, prayer-book translation.　　† Psalm cxxii. 5.
‡ Exodus xviii. 13.　　§ Paradise Lost.　　‖ Numbers xi. 29.

seventy, which subsisted so long as the nation had a home. The government and legislation of the State and the government and legislation of
the Church having been, under the system given to the Israelites, so
intertwined and incorporated together as to constitute, in a manner, one
and the same thing, this Sanhedrim may be considered as having been
alike an ecclesiastical synod and a feature in the political organization
of the country.

"The first Council of the christian Church of which we have record is
that held at Jerusalem upon the question, which had been agitated with
much heat, of imposing upon the Gentile converts the obligation to be
circumcised and to keep the law of Moses. The deputation from Antioch
were to address themselves to the Apostles and elders (or presbyters), and
the Apostles and elders came together, accordingly, to consider of this
matter. But we see that the multitude of believers were present, and that
after the address of James, who appears to have presided, a voice was
given, in the decision upon the course to be adopted, to the Church at
large. It pleased the Apostles and elders, *with the whole Church*, to send
chosen men to Antioch with written instructions for the believers there
upon the subject in dispute. The authors of these instructions announce
themselves, in the form of greeting by which the missive is headed, as the
Apostles, elders and brethren; and they proceed to say, it seemed good
unto us, *i. e.* to us the Apostles, elders and brethren just mentioned,
being assembled with one accord, to send chosen men.* It does appear,
therefore, that, while a distinctive place and character are preserved, in
terms sufficiently marked, to the Apostles and elders, the body of believers,
under the names of *the whole Church* and *the brethren*, were associated in
the transaction. To a similar effect is the testimony afforded in a passage
from the writings of St. Paul. St. Paul certainly never leads us to lose
sight of the estimation and reverent consideration of the christian
ministry. Yet we find that Apostle, where he refers to a judicial proceeding in the exercise of discipline within the infant Church of Corinth,
declaring the sufficiency of a punishment which he describes as having
been 'inflicted of many.'

"Some standing co-operation, therefore, of the laity in the conduct of
matters ecclesiastical appears to have been established, both under the
law and in apostolic days under the Gospel, as a sort of constitutional
feature of the Church."

    *   *   *   *   *   *   *   *   *   *

"Upon the whole, then, we have been doing nothing new, nothing
rashly experimental, nothing unsustained by ancient nor yet—for look
at the progress and successful working of the Church in the neighbouring

----

* Acts xv. 6, 22, 23, 25.

republic—by modern principles and practices, in enlisting the help of our lay-brethren and inviting their active interest in the management of our Church affairs. These affairs are their **own affairs; for** it is they who, with us, constitute the Church—and why should they not have a voice in the deliberations and the administrative functions of that **Church? They** will not, on their part, seek **to usurp more than their place. The** more familiar they are **made, by their practical share in it,** with the system of the Church, the more intelligent and the more lively will be their appreciation of it; the better they will understand the necessity of preserving an inviolable regularity and a well-balanced subordination in her associated proceedings. **As we, on our side, are taught** that we are not to lord it over the heritage nor to affect dominion over their faith; as we are ready, while 'we preach not ourselves but Christ Jesus our Lord,' to be their 'servants for Jesus' sake,'—so they, on theirs, will not fail to remember that their teachers are set over them in the Lord **and** that they are charged, with reference to the pastoral office of the clergy and the maintenance of conformity to the regulations of the Church, to obey them that have the rule over them and submit themselves to those who watch for their souls as they that must give account. Never **ought these principles to be lost sight** of, from any desire of popularity for **its own sake, or in accommodation to any** prevalent notions of the day; for there will always be some reigning and favourite error, and it will **always be part** of the duty of the Church of God to testify against it. What we have to do in our synodical proceedings is to carry on, ministers and people hand in hand, the system delivered down to us in the **episcopal Church** of England; and while we forbear from pronouncing upon the case of bodies differently constituted, or decrying their efficiency and zeal, none of us, whatever position we may occupy, ought, from any false personal delicacy, to suffer, without seeking to prevent it, the distinctive principle of our own system to be either assailed or undermined— the principle, linked inseparably as a safeguard with the preservation of order, unity, stability and soundness in the Church, that the supreme government of the Church and **the channel** for the conveyance of ministerial power are found in the Order of Bishops. Men among ourselves, and good men, too, may be found seeking to discredit this principle, and teach others to sneer at it as an exploded notion; but does any man seriously and deliberately believe that the ministry of the Church of England or any of her offshoots will ever, while the world lasts, be constituted and carried on upon any other principle than that which compelled the episcopalians of America, at the close of the revolutionary war, to procure consecration in England for the men who were to hold and pass on the episcopal office, and through that office to have the title transmitted for the other two Orders of the ministry? Would not the very men who cry down these principles, or who shrink from asserting them, be rather backward, if it came to the point, to accept a ministry which should be fabricated, *de novo*, at the will of this or that self-constituted authority, in order to provide for the demands of the Church ? No—look, in this very point of view, as well as in others, upon Zion, the city of our solemnities :—She is a tabernacle that shall not be taken down ; not one of the stakes thereof shall ever be removed, neither shall any of the cords thereof be broken.*

"Never, I trust, will the peculiar Anglican stamp, the genuine Anglican character and spirit, (with whatever necessity for some partial adaptation to local circumstances) be obliterated from our colonial institutions. They are dear and most justly dear to our hearts, and fervently may we hope, and fully may we trust, that the establishment of a metropolitan jurisdiction, in compliance with our own petitions, and in conformity with the Anglican system at home and abroad, will tend to confirm and to perpetuate our close identity with the honoured institutions which have been passed to us from our fathers. But while we are charged in our synodical capacity with the duty of carrying out the system of the Church of England in its integrity, we must remember that there may be such things as discipline to be improved, deflections in practice and usage to be corrected—neglects to be repaired—and the full original intention of ecclesiastical provisions and appointments to be recovered.

"And here I might enlarge upon a variety of points of this nature— but we should open a wide field upon which it is impossible now to enter, for these observations must be drawn to their close. I will barely enumerate, therefore, some two or three examples in point, which ought, in my apprehension, to be kept in view, as subjects for correction gradually to be effected as the time shall serve :—Such as the revival, in its proper efficiency, of the office of deacons and the employment perhaps of school-master deacons to continue in that grade ; but never the admission to holy Orders of men engaged in trades or callings purely secular. Or the restoration of rule and discipline in the admission of new or unknown comers to the holy communion, and of parties who present themselves to fill the office of sponsors, with reference to which last I presume that we are to have the advantage here of the action taken in convocation at home to adapt the 29th Canon to the altered circumstances of the Church :— And I think that we ought to take some steps to turn better to our own spiritual improvement and the effective condition of the Church certain particular observances provided for that end, such as the set seasons for special objects, and among others the neglected ember-days which suggest everywhere the prayers of the faithful at the times of ordination, that we may be furnished with godly and able ministers of Christ. I will say

---

* Isaiah xxxiii, 20, the text of the sermon.

nothing—for I must stop—respecting the recommendation of a closer attention wherever it is fairly practicable (and to such extent I may be pardoned, perhaps, for stating that I have long ago enforced that attention within my own diocese), to the law laid down for us by the Church that we should, for the more reverence of feeling and edifying solemnity of effect, celebrate the sacrament of baptism and the ordinance of marriage within consecrated walls."

On his way from Montreal to Quebec, after the close of the synod, the Bishop held confirmations at Three Rivers, Nicolet, Portneuf and Bourg Louis, where sixty-three persons were confirmed, making 592 at twenty-seven confirmations during the year. He reached home on the 20th September, and on the 2nd October set out on another journey to Lennoxville, to attend a meeting of the convocation of Bishop's College. He visited the college again in November, and this closed his journeyings for 1861. During this year he had the happiness of carrying out a project on which his heart had long been set, the appointment of a chaplain to serve the port of Quebec.

In March, 1862, he went to Kingston, to take part in the consecration of the Bishop of Ontario, and early in the following May set out for the visitation of the missions in the Gulf, choosing this season in the hope of being in time to afford the benefit of confirmation to the many young men who had missed it on previous occasions from being engaged in the whale fishery. He was so fortunate as again to procure a passage in the steamer which had conveyed him to Labrador, and his first mark was the Magdalen Islands, in approaching which the steamer was kept out a whole night in the ice. The Bishop was unfortunately so ill as to be unable to leave the steamer at House Harbour, and that place, as well as Grosse Isle, was consequently unvisited. By a great effort he held a confirmation at Amherst, and the day following at Entry Island, where he administered the rite as he sat on his chair, being too weak to stand, and afterwards addressed the candidates. It was with the greatest difficulty that he could be dissuaded from remaining at the Islands to complete his work, with recovered strength, after the steamer should have gone, and trusting to the mail schooner for a conveyance to the mainland. He was so ill, however, that he yielded the point, and bade a sorrowful adieu to his friends at Entry Island. A few days' rest at New Carlisle, with the care of kind friends, restored him, with God's blessing, so far as to enable him to resume the visitation of the district. The church at Port Daniel was used for the first time for any episcopal ministrations; and the new church at Percé, of which the interior arrangements and furniture elicited his special commendation, was consecrated. The Bishop reached Quebec on the 1st June, and at the end of the same month attended the annual convocation of Bishop's College, returning home to hold a visitation of the clergy, in the cathedral, on the 1st July, and to meet the synod on the same day. His charge to the clergy was chiefly occupied with a warning against the dangers of which the recent publication of Essays and Reviews afforded an example, and with some practical directions, especially with regard to pastoral visitation. It concluded with these words, the last he was permitted to address to his clergy collectively: "And oh! may God, in all our endeavours, in all our institutions, in all our difficulties and struggles, in all our ordinary labours, shed down upon us His abundant blessing, and give us grace, by the power of His Holy Spirit, never once to look back, never to fail in seeking the glory of our Master and the good of our brethren upon earth,—never to forget the solemn charge from the lips of the Lord, and the magnificent encouragement with which it is coupled, BE THOU FAITHFUL UNTO DEATH, AND I WILL GIVE THEE A CROWN OF LIFE." The same spirit breathed in his address to the synod, delivered the same day, of which the closing words were, "May God give grace to us to work together in wisdom and in love, and bless and prosper our work, that we may be effectually instrumental in promoting the great and sacred interests with which we are charged. The glory be all to Him, Father, Son and Holy Ghost, Whose we are and Whom we serve."

The attention of the synod was mainly engaged with the final arrangements for the constitution of the diocesan board, the first meeting of which was presided over by the Bishop on the 4th July, the day after the close of the session of the synod. But there was one resolution which must find a prominent place in this memoir, and which does credit to the kindness of heart of him who moved it, and with whom its idea originated. It was moved by W. G. Wurtele, Esq., and seconded by Rev. J. W. Williams, and "carried by acclamation, all the members of the synod rising up and remaining standing, while the Bishop, with much emotion, expressed his grateful sense of the kind feeling and affectionate attachment involved in the resolution and the manner of its adoption;

"That a committee be appointed, consisting of the Revds. Rural Dean Milne and E. W. Sewell, and Messrs. H. S. Scott and J. B. Forsyth, with the mover and seconder, to prepare an address of congratulation, to be presented, on behalf of the synod, to the Lord Bishop of the diocese, on the 2nd August next, being the day on which his lordship will (D.V.) complete the fiftieth year of his ministry, and that on that occasion as many of the clergy and lay delegates as can conveniently attend do make it a duty to be present; and farther, that divine service be celebrated in the cathedral church, with the administration of the holy communion, and that a sermon be preached on the morning of that day, and that the Right Rev. John Williams, D.D., Assistant Bishop of Connecticut, be requested to preach on the occasion."

"In accordance with the above resolution, on Saturday, 2nd August, 1862, the members of the Church of England in this diocese, celebrated the fiftieth anniversary of the admission to the sacred ministry of their venerable and beloved Bishop. During the half century through which his lordship has laboured in the fulfilment of his arduous duties, he has not only endeared himself to the members of the Church, but has also won the respect and esteem of the community at large. A general interest was therefore taken in the commemoration of the anniversary.

"Soon after nine o'clock a large number of ladies and gentlemen, including the clerical and lay delegates of the diocesan synod, assembled in the Lecture Hall, Ann-street, for the purpose of assisting at the presentation of an address to his lordship. At the appointed hour, the Bishop being seated at the head of the room with the Right Rev. John Williams, D.D., Assistant Bishop of Connecticut, and his chaplain, the Rev. H. DeKoven, on one side, and the Revds. J. H. Nicolls, D.D., and S. S. Wood,

M.A., chaplains to the Lord Bishop of Quebec, on the other, the committee entered the hall, preceded by the clergy and lay delegates; and advancing to his lordship, the Rev. A. Balfour, incumbent of Kingsey, read in a clear and distinct voice the following—

ADDRESS.

To the Right Reverend Father in God, GEORGE JEHOSHAPHAT, *by Divine permission, Lord Bishop of Quebec, D.D., D.C.L., &c., &c.*

MAY IT PLEASE YOUR LORDSHIP:

Half a century having this day elapsed since your lordship's entrance into holy Orders, we, the clergy and laity of the diocese of Quebec, beg to approach your lordship with the expression of our unfeigned affection and filial attachment, and at the same time to render our hearty thanks to Almighty God, Who has been pleased to prolong, beyond the ordinary period, a life and ministry which have been productive of so many blessings to the United Church of England and Ireland in Canada.

Many of us have been baptized, have been confirmed, have received the Lord's Supper at your hands; and many of us of the clergy have been admitted into the sacred ministry of the Church by your lordship; words must therefore fail adequately to convey all that is in our hearts this day.

Of your diligent labours as a parish priest at Fredericton and Quebec, of the privations and trials cheerfully borne by your lordship in your many and arduous missionary journeys, extending from Red River to Gaspé, both before and since your elevation to the episcopate, and at a time when, from the absence of the facilities now enjoyed, travelling involved hardships and dangers of no ordinary kind, we can, many of us, speak only from the grateful reports of others. Their memory, however, still lives, and will ever remain to the Church, the unconscious legacy of a devoted missionary, willing to spend and be spent in the service of his Lord.

For more than half the term of your ministry, your lordship has discharged the duties of a Bishop in the Church of God, how faithfully and how devotedly is known to all. For several years, sustained by indefatigable energy and unflagging zeal, your lordship was the Bishop of a diocese stretching from Lake Huron to the Atlantic; and now when, happily, that vast diocese has been subdivided into five, each of dimensions sufficiently ample to task the energies of a Bishop of its own, we cannot but congratulate ourselves that our lot has been cast in that portion of it which still remains under your lordship's personal supervision.

We trust that it may be neither presumptuous in us, nor unwelcome to your lordship, if now, when about to meet together in the house of God, and to partake in faith and love of the holy Eucharist, we first gladden our hearts with a brief and scanty retrospect of some of the many blessings which the great Head of the Church has vouchsafed to this diocese during your episcopate.

Inadequate as are in number the clergy in this portion of the Lord's vineyard, still would we lift up our hearts in solemn thanksgiving when we reflect that not a few of the poorest and most remote settlements in this province are this day cheered and blessed with the ministrations of our beloved Church.

May God, by His Holy Spirit, enable us, one and all, clergy as well as laity, to render, for the time to come, a truer and more active obedience to our crucified and risen Redeemer, and to be more self-denying in our labours in behalf of our brethren for whom He died!

Ample provision has been made for the maintenance of a successor in the see.

The clergy reserve fund forms a nucleus for the endowment of the diocese.

Ten separate endowments have been established, and are steadily increasing, and to these five others will be added in the course of the present year.

The management of the financial affairs of the rural missions has been recently confided to a board, under the direction of the diocesan, a measure from which we anticipate the happiest results.

The University of Bishop's College, founded and endowed chiefly by your lordship's exertions, has now been for seventeen years in successful operation. During this period the college has sent forth forty-five clergymen, to labour either in this or some other diocese of the province.

For twenty-one years the incorporated Church Society has conferred incalculable benefits upon the diocese.

The sagacity which moved your lordship so anxiously to desire, and so strenuously to promote, the inauguration of synodical action, has been evinced by the success which has already attended the periodical meetings of our diocesan synod.

When we look around and see the increasing brotherly love and christian toleration prevailing amongst us, truly would we take up the psalmist's words and say with him—'How pleasant and joyful a thing it is for brethren to dwell together in unity.'

And it is the heartfelt conviction of those who now address your lordship that for this real unity, peace, and concord, we are mainly indebted to the gentle wisdom, and the holy example of our beloved Bishop.

On the courteous and christian suavity which so eminently distinguishes your lordship, on your scholarly attainments and theological learning, of which we are justly proud, on the depth and delicacy of your kindness, on the single-mindedness with which you discharge the grave duties of your office, we would willingly enlarge, but for reasons which cannot and will not be misunderstood, we forbear.

That you may live long in the enjoyment of that intellectual vigour and bodily activity which you continue to manifest; that we may for many years yet to come reap the fruits of the wisdom of your counsels, of the excellence of your example, and of the paternal gentleness of your government, is, we beg once more to assure you, right reverend father in God, the heartfelt, unanimous prayer of the Church in your diocese."

Quebec, August 2, 1862.

On behalf of the Committee of Synod,

CHAS. HAMILTON, M.A.,   W. G. WURTELE,
     Clerical Secy. of Synod.   ·   Chairman.

J. BELL FORSYTH,
     Lay Secretary.

To which his lordship returned the following

REPLY.

" The address which has just been read to me from my dear brethren of the clergy and laity of this diocese cannot possibly be otherwise than acceptable to my feelings; and what is especially grateful to me and precious in my estimation is the affectionate tone by which it is marked. The only drawback from its value is the consciousness on my own part (a common thing perhaps to say, but it is said now in the utmost sincere conviction,) of the manner in which your good will towards me has prompted you to overcharge the picture both of my labours and of my qualifications. I am almost sorry for the effect, but I cannot quarrel with the cause. It is comforting to me more than tongue can tell or pen describe, to receive the assurance that my ministry in the Gospel of our Lord Jesus Christ has, by the blessing of Him Who giveth the increase, been productive, to whatever extent, of those fruits which constitute the end and object of the pastoral charge in its different grades. In my own retrospect of my ministry, if I may venture perhaps to hope that I have 'received mercy to be faithful,' and if thus I have enjoyed an exalted privilege, yet I cannot fail to be touched by a humbling sense of multiplied failures and deficiencies, and thence to need all the encouragement which may be afforded to me. I thank you, then, from my heart for the cheering effect of your present address: and I trust it will help to stimulate me, in the small remainder of my days upon earth, to a closer and closer preparation for the night which cometh, when no man can work.

" It is a happy thought that so many kind members of the Church, lay as well as clerical, have given their time, their counsel, and their constantly active help, in establishing and advancing those undertakings and institutions of the diocese, to which reference is made in your address. How large a proportion of credit is due in those quarters for the success of our

Church operations, how little, comparatively, would have been **effected but for the zeal, ability, and perseverance of those** friends, is what it needs **not to speak; but it is what I never, for my own share, can be so ungrateful as to forget.**

"**May God, of** His abundant mercy, give us grace always to cultivate such **mutual** relations, that in looking **to the** consummation of all things, **your Bishop may have warrant for applying** to our own case the words **of the Apostle, "For what is our** hope or joy or crown of rejoicing? **Are not even ye, in the presence of** our Lord Jesus Christ at His **coming?"**

At half-past ten **o'clock divine service was** celebrated in the **cathedral.** A very large congregation **was in attendance, including** his **Excellency** the Governor-General, **accompanied by Lady Monck and family. Upwards** of thirty-five **clergymen were present, among whom were** several from other dioceses. **An eloquent and most appropriate sermon** was preached by the Right Reverend **J. Williams, D.D., Assistant Bishop of Connecticut.** This noble **discourse, adorned as** it was **by the admirable** delivery of **the** eloquent prelate, **can never be** forgotten **by any one who** had the happiness of being **present on this interesting occasion.**

A full cathedral service was performed by **the** choir, **under the able** direction of Mr. **J. Pearce, Mus.** Bac. **Oxon,** organist of the cathedral.

The first part **of the** prayers **were said by** the Rev. **A.** J. Woolryche, incumbent of Pointe Levi, the psalms **for the day being** chanted **by the** choir. The first lesson. Jeremiah xxxi., was **read by** the Rev. J. **W.** Williams, M.A., Professor of Belles-Lettres **in the University** of Bishop's College, Lennoxville, and Rector **of the Junior Department;** and **the** second lesson, St. John xxi., by the **Rev. J. H. Jenkins, B.A.,** incumbent of Frampton. The remainder of **morning prayer was said** by the Rev. J. H. Thompson, **M.A., Canon** and Assistant **Minister of** Christ **Church** Cathedral, Montreal.

The anthem for **the occasion was from Psalm li. 9, 10, 11.**

After the Sanctus, **the Bishop of Quebec read** the ante-communion service, the epistle and gospel being read by Rev. H. DeKoven, of **the** Berkeley Divinity School, Middlebury, Connecticut.

The following hymn was then sung, in which the congregation **heartily** joined:

When all Thy mercies, O my God, &c.

The Rev. **J. H. Nicolls,** D.D., read the offertory sentences, and a collection was taken up on behalf of the Mountain Jubilee Scholarship.

The Holy Communion was administered to a large body of the clergy and laity, the Bishop of Quebec being the celebrant. He was assisted in the distribution of the elements by the Assistant Bishop of Connecticut.

the **Rev.** H. DeKoven, and the Revds. Rural Dean Wood, M.A., **G. V.** Housman, M.A., and J. H. Nicolls, D.D., chaplains to the Lord Bishop of Quebec. The benediction, by the Bishop of Quebec, closed this most interesting service.

At the close of the **service, the** Lord Bishop **of Quebec** was attended **by a large** number of the clergy **and** congregation **to** the Finlay Asylum, **on the St.** Foy Road, **when that institution, then recently** finished, **was formally** opened with **a special service, and an address by his lordship.** The ceremony had been purposely deferred until this auspicious day.

In connection with the celebration, the following circular had previously been issued :

" QUEBEC, 24th July, 1862.

" **DEAR SIR,**—It is proposed to mark in perpetuity the full **completion of** our venerable Bishop's service of half a century in the christian ministry, by **establishing a scholarship or a prize,** in the University of Bishop's **College, Lennoxville, to** be called the ' Mountain Jubilee Scholarship,' **or** ' **Prize,' as the case may** be.

" A sum of $1,000 would endow a scholarship with $80 a year. A sum of $500 would yield a revenue of $40, which might be spent on a medal or on books, to be given annually as a prize.

" If the sum (of $1,000) necessary to establish the scholarship be raised. it is proposed that the scholarship should be open to all candidates for holy Orders, and tenable for three years.

" If the sum of $500 only be raised, it is proposed that the prize shall be given to the divinity student who affords most satisfaction to the examiners in elocution—the reading of a chapter in the Bible and of a portion of the liturgy being included in the examination.

" The suggestion that the completion of the fiftieth year of our Bishop's service in the christian ministry should be marked in some enduring manner, in addition to the formal presentation of an address from the synod, and the solemn services to be held in the cathedral on the anniversary itself, has proceeded from so many quarters that the proposal is certain to recommend itself strongly to every member of the Church. Your co-operation is invited in making this proposal known in your n ighbourhood.

" In order to afford an opportunity to every member of the Church to join in this work, it should be understood that the smallest contributions will be admitted.

" In order that the proposal may become a fact before the 2nd August, it is evident there is no time to be lost in forwarding contributions.

" Our hope that others would have undertaken this matter must be our apology for the short notice which is now given ; and our unwillingness that such an excellent suggestion, proceeding simultaneously from so many, should not be carried into execution, our defence for putting ourselves forward.

> " Your obedient and humble servants,
>
> " JAS. BELL FORSYTH.
> " C. N. MONTIZAMBERT.
> " A. J. WOOLRYCHE.
> " C. HAMILTON.
> " HENRY ROE."

In answer to the above appeal, the sum of $950 was at once cheerfully subscribed, and many friends from abroad have promised donations, which, when received, will swell the amount considerably beyond the sum mentioned in the circular.   •

Quebec, August 30, 1862.   W. G. W.

The foregoing account was drawn up at the time, and published as an appendix to the sermon of the Bishop of Connecticut. That prelate displayed great good feeling and delicacy in accepting, and also in discharging, the task imposed upon him. He was anxious not to say too much, out of regard to the sensitiveness of one who, he knew, shrank from praise, but he said—

> " I will try not to make you feel uncomfortable, and to be as reticent, on points where your wishes would enjoin silence, as possible."

He discharged his task to the satisfaction of all who had invited him to undertake it ; and that the occasion was not without interest and pleasure to himself may be inferred not only from the sermon, but from his letters written a few months later :—

> " I can almost see the good Bishop, my truly honoured and beloved friend and brother, now, as I saw him last, on the evening of the 5th August, standing in his door, and waving his adieux to us as we drove away. If the thought crossed my mind that I might perhaps never see him on earth again, it only crossed it as it always does when one parts from friends whom one rarely meets. How little could I dream that in five months he was to gain the rest of Paradise! God's will be done! But I assure you there is a feeling of vacancy and sorrow in many hearts beyond the limits of his own family and diocese. Applied to him, the line on Berkeley was hardly an exaggeration, for he did really seem to have
>
> ' Every virtue under heaven.'

. . . My affectionate reverence for him as a godly and learned prelate, and truly holy man, has constantly been growing from the first time I was privileged to meet him—in 1845; and I am truly thankful that I was permitted to see him as I did during the last summer, and to be refreshed and strengthened by his kind words and wise counsels. It was in great mercy that God gave such a man to be a chief pastor in His Church, and we should not mourn that, in a good old age, He has given him, as one of his beloved, sleep. . . . May the good Lord comfort you all, my dear brother,* in this our bereavement, and in His own good time, send you one to walk in the steps of him whom He has taken from you. No one need ask more than that."

In connection with the mention of the Mountain Jubilee Scholarship, I may here give the testimony rendered, while he was still living, to the character of the Bishop of Quebec, by the Metropolitan of Canada. It is extracted from one of many most gratifying letters received from all sorts and conditions of men, with reference to the foundation of the scholarship, and enclosed a handsome contribution : †

" Few individuals, I feel sure, can appreciate more highly than I do the loveliness of his christian character, or the value of his labours, of which I have reaped so greatly the advantage in the foundation laid by him for the Church of Christ, upon which it has been my endeavour to carry on the work he had so well begun."

The feeling of him whom his diocese, and good men without its limits, thus delighted to honour, may be gathered from the following extracts from his own letters written at the time :

" The address is quite undesirably laudatory, for when we know ourselves, and remember ourselves, such language grates against our feelings. However, it is well that the effect should take in the Church, and among them that are without, of high appreciation of episcopal labours, &c. . . . I shrink from the thought of that day, and its bustle and praise,

---

* This is extracted from a letter addressed to a clergyman in Quebec, not one of the Bishop's family.

† Not the least gratifying among these letters was one from a young officer in India, a native of Canada, begging his father to add his name to the list of contributors to the scholarship, having learned the design from the newspapers.

of which I would fain escape from being the subject; and I feel the 2nd
August, upon another ground, to be a day upon which I should like to be
quiet; but, so far as the Church is concerned, it is probably desirable that
the celebration should take place. My fifty years in the ministry might
have been infinitely better filled up than they have been; things done and
things left undone alike suggest thoughts of self-humiliation.   .   .   .
What I like in the address is an affectionate tone which runs through it."

The other event, of which the 2nd August was the anniversary, was his marriage, and there were special reasons why
he should mark its recurrence this year.   It was the first
that had occurred since he had lost her who had witnessed
his ordination fifty years before, and his sense of solitude
could not fail thus to be sharpened.   And the double observance, too, must have brought her remembrance forcibly to
his mind.   For the three institutions which now found a
common shelter under the roof of the Finlay Asylum, the
Male and Female Orphan Asylums, and the Church Home
for widows and infirm persons, all reckoned her among their
originators.   The two former have been already mentioned
in these pages.   But after the orphans had been provided
with a home, she felt that a similar benefit should be conferred upon the widows of the parish, and in 1850 laid aside
a certain sum towards the building of such an institution,
which was designed to serve also a memorial of the son whom
they had lately lost.   In the meanwhile she hired part of
a house, where two or three widows were placed, whom she
constantly visited and cared for.   The plan, however, did
not answer her expectations, for it happened that most of the
persons whom she then befriended had children, and were
sufficiently young to be able to earn their own living, and it
became apparent that their comfort would be more promoted
by their living apart.   The memorial, therefore, took another
form, the money being applied towards the erection of the
chancel of St. Michael's chapel.   But the idea was not lost
sight of, and when a legacy, which came into the hands of
the Bishop in 1852, from Miss Finlay of Quebec, for the

benefit of the poor of the parish, had reached a sufficient sum, a house was purchased, to which some old and infirm men (who had before been gathered under a roof provided by another charitable lady) were removed, and the place was opened towards the close of the year 1857, under the name of the Finlay* Asylum.   About a year later, the Bishop (who had all along taken the greatest interest in the institution, and constantly visited the inmates,) received a note from a lady in Quebec (herself a widow,) enclosing a donation for the asylum, which he supposed might be of ten or twenty dollars, but when he opened the cheque he found it to be for two thousand.   With this help the corporation of the institution (consisting of himself and the cathedral church-wardens) resolved to remove it to a better site, and to endeavour to raise funds for the erection of a handsome building, the foundation-stone of which was laid by the donor of $2,000,† on the 10th May, 1860.   The formal opening took place, as above mentioned, on the 2nd August, 1862, with a special service, prepared by the Bishop, who afterwards delivered " a touching address."   The event was a subject of the deepest thankfulness to him.

---

* Miss Finlay also bequeathed $2,000 to the Bishop for the widows and orphans of the clergy.

† The same lady made a subsequent donation of $400, accompanied by one of $300 from one of her sons, who afterwards bequeathed $2,000 to the Church Home, and $2,000 to the Male Orphan Asylum.

CHAP. XXVIII.

Summer of 1862—Letters to his family—Latest acts of his life—Last illness and death.

It was perhaps **the peacefulness of** his diocese and parish which produced in **this** year (1862) an unwonted, or rather a more uniform, cheerfulness of mind, and apparently renewed strength **of body.*** **A clergyman in** Quebec wrote of him **in the summer of this year**—"**Our dear** Bishop seems **to have taken a new lease of his life."** **Alas** for human foresight! **God** was bringing him "peace at the last," to prepare him, in great mercy, **for** the blessed state, "where the wicked cease from troubling, and the weary are at rest." He gave him full strength of body and mind for His work so long as **He** willed that he should do it **here.** His letters to his children written **during this year are** overflowing, as ever, with affection and interest **in them,** and **all** that belonged to them, though generally written in great haste, from the pressure of business. I make one **or two extracts** from those **addressed** to myself:—

"It is really a **matter of** lively interest to follow **you in your** Norfolk wanderings and your **visit to Norwich.** * * * It is very delightful **to observe,** incidentally, in your **account of** things, the still growing recovery **of**

---

* He was never fond of walking, though an admirable horseman, yet **in** August he rose one morning soon after five (having been in bed less than five hours), and walked more than two miles and back before breakfast to refresh himself with a swim in the St. Lawrence. He never lost an opportunity of going into the water when he **had** time on his journeyings, but **this seldom presented itself at Quebec.**

ancient usages and helps to reverence in the worship of God, and **the
earnestness** of churchmen in making their worship really a thing of the
first interest and importance.* The advance of religion in every **other
way is** coupled with this, **and goes** on *pari passu.* * * * Your description
of your movements, and of the people, scenes, and objects with which you
meet, but particularly your mention of my dear relatives still remaining,
prompts a longing sigh **to see my own country** once more before I **die :
but it seems** scarcely **worth while for a** person who will **so soon** have done
forever with this **world to** undertake **such a visit, and perhaps** hardly
justifiable to leave my charge when I have no great **Church object to carry,**
and to incur an expense **of which the amount might** do very sensible good
for different objects **of religion or charity in this poor diocese.** I have
little to **do now in the way of planning journeys except to journey** about
among my clergy **and** people, **and to** prepare myself better (which there is,
ample room to do) for the last journey of all, seeking a better country, that is
an heavenly. I do not deny that I could find great delight now in visiting
the continent† as well as in re-visiting England, but I believe it will end in
my making up my mind **to** cross the Atlantic no more. * * * I hope and
trust that the present little interruption of your ordinary labours **will
refresh your** spirit and minister **to** your enjoyment and invigorate your
health."

The remainder of the year 1862 was spent at home, with
the exception of four short absences : one in August, to give
a Sunday to Murray Bay, ninety miles below Quebec ; the
second to attend the Provincial Synod at Montreal, on his

---

* In a letter written in 1844, he said, "O that we could see all **churches**
like that which you describe! O vile, vile disfigurements which have **over-**
spread the houses of God in the land."

† In a letter written nearly twenty years earlier, he said, "**It is good** to
get a glimpse (or more if we can) of foreign lands. * * * My early and continued longings after the continent I mentioned to you before. I have been
a great traveller, but other travels have been ordered for me than those for
which I once longed. In 1843 I travelled between 8,000 and 9,000 miles :
and my memorable journey to the Rubicon through the 'waste howling
wilderness,' affords more ground of thankfulness and satisfaction than if I
had been enabled to gratify my tastes by a continental tour. Even now
I should delight in going through the continental countries of Europe to
Jerusalem. But I indulge in no such vision : all that I hope for is that,
through the mercy of God, I may so pass through the journey of life, as
to reach at last the Jerusalem which is above."

return from which he spent a Sunday in the neighbourhood of the St. Francis river, where his presence seemed to be required ; the third to visit Bishop's College in October, and the last in December, to administer the holy communion at Portneuf, then served by a deacon.* In September he admitted a young Augustinian to deacon's Orders, who came to Canada for the purpose of serving at Labrador, where he relieved his fellow-collegian who had preceded him. The Bishop was greatly interested in this young man, both for his work's sake, and for his own. In his sermon at the ordination he referred specially to the wants of Labrador, which produced a response, among others, the next day, in the shape of a donation of $100 from a member of the same family already alluded to in connection with the Church Home. He wrote to me saying that he meant to put this and the other sums by as the beginning of a fund for church-building &c. on the coast, to which he thought of adding, if he were spared, four hundred dollars himself. He was not spared, however, long enough to do this, but his thoughts and prayers were with the missionary at Labrador to the last. In his last illness, when he could not speak without the greatest pain and difficulty, and did so only on subjects which he wished specially to remember, he said one day, " Poor little C———, God bless him and his work, and open the way for us there." And the very last word he uttered, when he saw his end closely approaching, before he turned to bless his children and dependents, was the single word " Labrador."

That end was drawing now much nearer than any one expected. One more ordination was held in Advent, when

---

* During this year he exhibited a proof of his desire for inter-communion with other branches of the Church, by permitting a clergyman in Swedish Orders, (with whom he was much pleased,) accredited by the Church in the United States, to officiate to his own countrymen among the emigrants at Quebec.

two others, who had been sent from St. Augustines,* **were**
advanced to the priesthood. On Christmas Day he preached
his last sermon, and celebrated the holy communion in the
cathedral. He attended divine service in the afternoon at St.
Michael's, and in the evening his children and grand-children,
with one or two other friends, were gathered round him. I
never saw him **more** happy and cheerful, or more animated
in conversation. Little did we know that we should never
so meet again. **On St. Stephen's day I was** surprised not
to see him at **church**, and hearing that **he had a** cold, I went
to Bardfield, but as he was asleep I would not disturb him.
The next day **he was** still in bed, a most unusual thing, and
though there was not supposed to be any ground for uneasiness, an indescribable feeling came over me, which told me
the end was **not far** off. On the following day (Sunday) I
did not see him till after morning service, but while I was at
the **Sunday school I received a little note from my sister,**
telling me that the doctor pronounced him to be suffering
from congestion of the lungs. I went to him as soon as
possible, **and found it** was indeed "the beginning **of the**
end." His medical adviser **told me that,** on account of his
age, it was a serious matter. On the evening of Monday, the
29th, **he insisted on my leaving** him to go to a Christmas tree,
which was to **be given to** my school-children, and which he
would not allow me **to postpone.** But the poor children were
in no mood for enjoyment, and it was a dull party, and soon
over. **On the** Saturday evening, before any one was alarmed,
he had been allowed to sit up for a little while, and he compelled all who were with him in the house to go to dinner.
In their absence he went into his study, where there was no
fire, to look for some books and papers which he wanted for his
gardener's children, whom he always taught and examined
himself on Saturday, and this greatly increased his cold.

* See page **393.**

His sufferings after Monday became very severe indeed, and no relief could be obtained, though all the best medical skill at command was employed. His chief care and first thoughts were still for his work and for others. When he found the doctor coming twice a day, he said, " I see this will be a tedious business, and I am thankful I have no visitation before me this winter, so I hope the diocese will not suffer much." And when a second physician was called in, he said to the first, " I see you think me very ill : if you think I am in danger, you ought to tell me so, for I am not afraid to die ; I know Whom I have believed." With reference to this he said to me a day or **two afterwards**, " I have been greatly humbled since I spoke to Dr. B. the other day. I spoke much too confidently, for though there is of course no limit to the efficacy of Christ's merits, there must be some to man's continuance in sin, and I have been a sinner for fifty years." I asked him how he would have answered me if I had spoken so, saying that his answer would apply with ten thousand times more force to himself. He was constantly engaged in silent prayer with uplifted eyes, and sometimes he told me to pray with him, directing me to use particular prayers from the liturgy, when he found "the constant pain made it difficult to keep the mind in one track of devotion." One night, as he lay awake (for he scarcely ever so much as dosed), he made me get a slate and write down his wishes on some points, delivered, a word at a time, with pain and difficulty, and not all even intelligible. They all related to some kindness which he wished to shew to persons whom we should have been least likely to think of, or matters of importance to the diocese which he feared might be lost sight of. On the morning of New Year's day he took the slate and wrote himself " cheques for clergy and bills of exchange," that I might get his signature at once, without the risk of subjecting them to any delay in payment. I told him all had been arranged without it. He desired me to give his special thanks to the

"churchwardens and the members of the board who had
helped him in the work of the Church," and gave special instructions respecting attention to the spiritual wants of some
young people who had formerly been in his service, with
many other touching remembrances. He spoke as little as
he could, and did not mention those who were nearest to him
on earth ; but there **was one, of** whom he said he could not
die without rendering his testimony to what she had been to
him and to her children.

The anxiety and sorrow which his illness caused **were not**
confined to his own house. The fervour of the amens of the
people, when he was prayed for in the different churches, was
most striking, and prayers were offered for his recovery even
in Roman catholic churches. A clergyman of great experience of life wrote to me that he had never seen " so universal
a demonstration of regard, respect, affection, hope and prayer
as that which **has been** elicited by the illness of your dear
father. That God **may speedily help and deliver** him is the
sincere prayer of *all* whom I meet." But that deliverance
was to come, not as they hoped. He said to one of his
children, " you know **my will is His** will, and even these
grey hairs are all numbered." On the evening of the 5th
January (the birthday of his youngest child, which he well
remembered,) he was lying on a sofa to which he had been
carried from his bed, in the hope of gaining some ease by
change of posture, with one of his children standing on each
side of him, when he suddenly looked up on us with a smile
such as I can never forget ; it was not of this earth. A few
moments afterwards, when I was alone with him, he called his
two daughters from the next room, but the exertion was too
great to admit of his speaking when they came. We saw the
end approaching, and knelt before him, while he laid his
hands on our head without speaking. God strengthened me
to say the commendatory prayer, and when I had finished
he said, " O Saviour," meaning me to use the short prayer
in the visitation office **beginning with those** words, which I

did. He then said, "I could not take sacrament, because I could not swallow, but I know God will be merciful to me a sinner," laying his hand upon his heart. After this he rallied a little, and when his daughter-in-law, who had been sent for, came in, he drew her to him, and kissed her repeatedly; and then, as she knelt, showered all blessings, spiritual and temporal, on her head. He did the same for her brother, adapting his words to the case of a young man; and then to his little grand-children, to whom he said, "My children, I am dying; I am going to the other world (pointing upwards): you know how tenderly I have always loved you here," and then laid his hands on the head of each. His servants next came in, but he was too much exhausted to speak to any but the first three, who had all lived very long with him. I am sure they will none of them ever forget that night. They all knelt for his blessing, and he spoke to all. To the first he said, "God bless you, and all your house; I wish it had pleased God that I could have seen all (the servants) before I die. I commend them all, and all the children, to God's blessing and guidance, through Christ." He was then moved back to his bed, and soon afterwards told me to read the twelfth chapter of Isaiah, after which he lay for several hours without speaking, with very little suffering, and engaged in peaceful meditation. About half-past one, A.M., on the feast of the Epiphany, the cold hand of death was laid upon him. He said, "Lift me up." We raised him in our arms, and I felt no more movement than if an infant had fallen asleep upon my shoulder, while those who were in front of him saw him gently close his own eyes. His family and diocese were fatherless. But they can still celebrate the feast of the Epiphany with sacred joy, for they believe that through the merits of Him Whom he knew here by faith, Whose he was, and Whom he served, his spirit then entered on so much of the fruition of His glorious Godhead as is permitted to the saints in paradise.

CHAPTER XXIX.

Funeral—Testimonies to his character.

ONE of his last wishes was that there should be " no super-
fluous expense at his funeral:" and it would have been in
accordance with our own feelings to have conducted it with
privacy. But we felt that he belonged to his diocese nearly as
much as to ourselves, and were willing therefore to yield to the
wishes of the many who expressed their desire to share with us
the privilege of doing honour to his remains. The wardens and
vestry of the cathedral charged themselves with the necessary
arrangements for the procession, which were left entirely in their
hands. We selected the six senior alumni of Bishop's College
for the mournful task of carrying him. I had indeed some
scruple in bringing some of them from a distance on account
of the expense to which they must be subjected: but I am
sure they all shared the feeling which one of them expressed
when he said, " The question of expense is nothing, for which
of the clergy would not deny himself almost anything, to
pay this last tribute of affection to him who was ever kind
and gentle, and loving as a father?" Thirty-eight clergymen walked in their surplices (besides four who followed
as private mourners), preceded by the male and female
orphans of the two asylums. The Governor General and
his staff, the Judges, members of the Executive and Legislative Councils, the Bar, the City Corporation, the delegates of the Synod, the wardens of the cathedral and
chapels, the Corporation of Bishops' College and of the Church

Society, the officers of the **garrison and the St. George's**
Society followed, as well as an immense concourse **of persons**
of all origins and denominations, many of whom **were** unable
to restrain their outward demonstrations of heartfelt sorrow.*
The procession moved on foot from the cathedral, where the
first **part of the service was** performed, to the cemetery, a
distance of three miles. Business was suspended in the city
at the suggestion of the mayor (a Roman catholic, though once
of the Church of England), **and scarcely** any one left the
ranks of the procession before the cemetery had been reached.
It had been the wish of some **persons** that he should be laid
with his father† under **the** altar in the cathedral, but we
knew he would **have preferred a** humbler resting-place in
his mother-earth, and we laid him to rest beside her who had
been dearest to him in life. The City Council had adjourned,
and unanimously resolved, **on** motion **of a** Roman catholic
member, seconded by another **of** the same persuasion, " **as
a** well-deserved mark of the deep respect of all denominations
and classes of citizens," to attend the funeral in a body. The
mayor, in his proclamation for the suspension **of** business, said :

" In requesting the citizens of Quebec to give expression, by outward
demonstration, to the profound sorrow and regret which they feel at the
great loss which the **entire community** has sustained by the lamented
demise of the universally revered and respected Lord Bishop of Quebec, I
am satisfied that I only anticipate their desire to evince another mark of
respect for the memory of **the distinguished deceased."**

In putting **the resolution** of the Corporation, he had said :

" The painful event is mourned by all **as** an irreparable loss to the **community,** and it will be difficult indeed to fill his place **by a successor who**
will approach **his** talents **and** his virtues."

---

* A clergyman who officiated at St. Michael's chapel on the feast of the
Epiphany was so overcome by his feelings that he was unable to go through
the service.

† It was erroneously stated in a Quebec paper that his mother had been
buried in the cathedral also.

The Bar of Quebec passed similar resolutions, one presbyterian and three Roman catholic gentlemen being among the movers and seconders, while among the bodies more immediately connected with him, the same marks of respect were overflowing. The Church Societies of Quebec, Montreal, and Toronto, the vestry of the cathedral of Quebec, the congregation of St. Matthew's chapel, the Corporation of Bishop's College, the St. George's Society of Quebec, have all placed on their records their strong sense of their loss. The cathedral vestry recommended the members of the Church to wear mourning for a month, which in Quebec, and probably in Montreal* also, was generally done by persons of all classes. There is one resolution which I must place on record here. When the diocesan synod met to elect his successor, before proceeding to business, it was,

"Moved by H. S. Scott, Esq., seconded by Rev. H. Roe, and carried by all the members of the synod standing in solemn silence, That this synod desires to express its sense of the great loss which this diocese has sustained by the removal of the late beloved and lamented Lord Bishop, whose patience and urbanity as its president, his devotion to the advancement of the interests of the Church and the personal sacrifices he was always ready to make in its cause, had secured for him the affectionate reverence of all who had the happiness to be placed under his charge."

Far, far better than any official pageant and ceremony were all these entirely spontaneous demonstrations. Many who took a leading part in them were personally unknown to him, but they prove how wide-spread is the effect of a holy life, though exhibited by one who never mixed in public or political affairs, except so far as they directly concerned the duties of that sacred calling to which his whole self was devoted. It had been proposed by some of the military authorities that the troops should line the streets on the day of the funeral, but some recent military rule was found to interfere with this,

---

* Many churches in the city and diocese of Montreal were hung in mourning.

and occasion was thus given for what was infinitely more gratifying, the volunteering of men of the Royal Artillery and 60th Rifles to keep the ground for the procession to the cathedral. The newspapers, in mourning, were full, from one end of Canada to the other, of expressions of veneration, affection and sorrow, as well as of long biographical notices. From these I make three brief extracts. The first is from a journal conducted under wesleyan auspices, which had often been made the vehicle for pouring out the complaints of discontented people in Church-matters, and had been regarded as strongly opposed to the Church, and not friendly to her chief pastor. Yet now it was

"Believed that it may be safely asserted that throughout the roll of existing Anglican bishops, whether metropolitan or provincial, * there are none who have surpassed him for untiring zeal in performing the duties of the episcopal office, or for the true christian urbanity which marked his intercourse with the people over whom he was placed. His loss is deeply regretted by our community generally. ● ● ● ● ● ●

" The ceremonies of yesterday were demonstrative of the extraordinary amount of respect entertained by our citizens of all classes and creeds, and must have been gratifying to his bereaved family as well as to the attached members of his flock."

Two French Canadian papers furnished similar testimony, the first (the organ of the R. C. clergy,) saying:

"He was universally esteemed by the catholics for his deeds of charity, as well as for the high tone and nobleness of his character. All catholics who had occasion to live in communication with him recognize these his eminent qualities."

The other:

"Mardi, les funérailles du vénérable Evêque Anglican de Québec avaient lieu avec grande pompe : le clergé Anglican, venu de loin et de près, entourait avec recueillement les restes mortels de son évêque. Le nombre des citoyens de toutes les classes et de toutes les croyances qui assistaient aux funérailles était immense. Le Lord Bishop Mountain avait

---

* These words are not used in an ecclesiastical sense, but denote British and colonial.

conquis par sa bienveillance, sa charité, et ses nombreuses vertus sociales et religieuses, le respect et l'estime de tous, et aussi cet homme de bien emporte avec lui dans la tombe le regret universel."

I abstain here from extracts from Canadian papers conducted by members of the Church of England, as they were more universally circulated among those who are likely to read these pages, and by many of them have been doubtless preserved. It shall suffice to quote the words of one of them :

"Independently of the loss which the Church has sustained by the removal of its chief pastor, every one feels that a father, a friend, a comforter and an adviser, has passed away from among us."

The New York *Church Journal* said :

"None who have enjoyed the privilege of knowing the Bishop personally will ever forget his tall and slender form, reverend with meek dignity ; his singular modesty and courtesy of demeanor, the gentleness of his voice, the kind considerateness of his thoughts for others, his ready and unaffected hospitality, and the ripe scholarly tone that was apparent in all that he said and all that he wrote. Unselfishness was never more strongly marked in any character, and those who know his life-long labours ..... in short, his faithful and quiet devotion to duty at all times—none who have known all this will ever cease to remember the departed Bishop as one of the rarest examples of the Christian, the scholar and the gentleman united, as they always ought to be, in the person of a Bishop."

The more private testimonies which I possess from Bishops, priests, and deacons in England, in the United States, and every part of British North America ; from officers in the army, and from men and women of every class, are almost without number. Some of them have already appeared in the course of this narrative, and I will not add here more than two or three, selecting them as proofs of the wonderful manner in which his light shone even upon short acquaintance. A lady who had never known anything of him till about fifteen months before his death, and had enjoyed but few opportunities of intercourse, thus writes :

"I was always so much struck by his wonderful energy in all his workings for God's cause. He seemed to me never for a moment to forget that ' the night cometh when no man can work,' and to consider this world as only a sphere for doing God's work. And how he did it! What an example he has left! May God assist those left behind to follow it! Though my acquaintance with him was but short, it had grown with me into a most sincere friendship. To me his loss is very great.....I pray that God will never let me forget his example, short as was the time it was before me. His ' virtuous and godly living' taught even more strongly than his words."

A clergyman of the diocese of Toronto, who had laboured but a few years in that of Quebec, expressed himself as follows :—

" That goodness, the constellation of so many excellences, which shone so brightly in your dear and blessed father, and which others beheld afar off with love and admiration, you felt, I know, in its most cheering warmth : and while never christian son had more cause to rejoice in the assurance of glory won by sainted father, you have, alas! in the loss of even his bodily presence, much to sadden you. But your father's God will strengthen and sustain you, and enable you to walk in his footsteps ; the best prayer of your best friends. You will be strengthened, too, in the remembrance of so great an example, and you cannot but be in some measure consoled by the universal affection in which the Bishop's memory is held everywhere ;—in these parts, I assure you, most strikingly...... I thank God most fervently that I have ever known him. My little knowledge and memory of him will be ever reckoned among my choicest treasures."

Another clergyman, of the diocese of Montreal, who had been for an exceedingly short time missionary of the Colonial Church Society at Stanstead, gave vent to his feelings in the following verses.* A short biographical sketch was subjoined to them in which he said,

" The author of these memorial lines will never forget the savour which this man of God left behind him after remaining a few days beneath his roof, on the occasion of a confirmation in his parish."

---

* Eleven years earlier a clergyman of the diocese of Quebec addressed his Bishop in the following lines :

To G. J. MOUNTAIN, BISHOP OF QUEBEC, OUR GOOD RULER IN CHRIST.

Prelate, who on Quebec's steep rock enthroned,
Rul'st o'er a land from savage hordes reclaimed,
With that "new law" of love which oft hath tamed

IN MEMORIAM.

THE **MEMORY OF THE** JUST IS BLEST.

Prov. x. 7.

Father of Bishops! ripe in years—
   Vacant the father see
Of this our land, and now with tears
The Church, 'mid many doubts and fears,
   Feels her deep debt to thee.

Now with the sainted Stewart, thou
   Art glorified, art blest:
All earthly care, all sorrow now,
Fled from sad heart, and furrowed brow,
   Thou art at peace, at rest.

Yes, thou art happy, happy there,
   Where oft thy soul did soar,
Thy cross, no lightsome one to bear,
Thy mitre, an unceasing care,
   Weary, oppress no more.

E'en in the rising fane of fame,
   In this yet infant land,
Thy name amid the wise and great,
Who shed a lustre on the State,
   In honoured niche shall stand.

But in that living temple reared
   By Him all-wise, divine,
Thy name, uncarved, unlimned by art,
On "fleshly tables of the heart,"
   Shall ever brightest shine.

Rebellious souls, under whose sway had groaned
The weak and helpless multitudes of earth ;
Now that the world is wild, and hearts grow cold,
Shaken by winds of doctrine manifold,
Bear living witness to thy heavenly birth !
Thy gentle tongue, dispensing rules of love,
Thy care-worn brow, and aspect mortified,
Give ample proof of what by faith we hear ;
—The voice of that mild Judge, Who does approve
His lowly servant; owns him close allied ;
Clasps to His heart His faithful shepherd dear !

21st January, 1852.   H. B.

Not thine the dignity alone
  By men all wiselygiven,
A mitre from the Church and throne,
And earthly honours thickly strown :—
  But thou wast owned of Heaven !

Thine were the vestments, graces, **He**
  Alone can give and shed :
That meekness, zeal, fidelity,
That tenderness, **that purity,**
  Which graced the Church's **head.**

And she, with mingled pride and pain,
  Shall mark where thou hast trod ;
Where **thou dids't** prayerful sow **the grain,**
She joyful reaps the fruitful plain,
  And binds rich sheaves for God.

Departed saint ! there need is none ,
  The grieving-Church should **raise**
Memorials of brass or stone,
Recording all thy triumphs won,
  In strains of fulsome praise.

Thy name is mirror'd on each lake,
  Stamped on each silent shore ;
Souls won to Christ have marked **thy way,**
From solemn shores of **Thunder Bay**
  To bounds of Labrador.

Where'er Canadian forests wave,
  Thy name shall honoured **be ;**
And many a convert Indian " brave,"
In light canoe, **or sounding cave,**
  Shall drop a tear for thee.

Safe shall thy fragrant memory
  Be held in faithful trust,
Till this fair land shall cease to be
Home of the true, the brave, and free,
  Her altars laid in dust.

I might fill another volume with similar testimonies, from
the sermon of his successor preached before the synod whose
proceedings resulted in his own election, or from his first address to that body ; from the sermon preached **at his conse-**

cration, or from a biographical notice, by the same hand, published in the Colonial Church Chronicle; * from the reports of the different institutions already mentioned; from the address of the Bishop of Montreal to his synod in 1863, or from the charge of the Bishop of Rupert's Land in the following year. Or I might refer to many casual instances of mention of his character, which have accidentally reached me, by persons unknown to myself. But I confine myself to one from the other side of the Atlantic. In the report of the S. P. G. for 1863, it is said,

> "The venerable Bishop of Quebec, who for a period of twenty-seven years presided over this diocese, and during the early portions of his episcopate over the whole province of Canada, was called to his rest on the morning of the Epiphany 'full of years and honours, bearing with him the esteem, the affection and the regret of all members of the community.' Never was there a Bishop of a more saintly life, of a gentler spirit, or of more self-denying habits. Like the first missionary Bishop of the Church, he was 'in labours more abundant;' and those who know how simply and how cheerfully he exposed himself to privations and perils of every sort, will not consider it an exaggeration to say that he counted not his life dear unto himself, so that he might finish his course with joy, and the ministry which he had received of the Lord Jesus."

It was proposed in the cathedral vestry to call a public meeting of churchmen, to consider what form the memorial, which all desired to raise, should take, and the meeting resolved to fill the large east window of the cathedral with stained glass, which has accordingly been done, and the subscription list left a balance of upwards of two hundred dollars to be added to the Labrador mission fund. This was scarcely six months after the foundation of the jubilee scholarship, and this, again, had followed at no long interval on the subscription for the execution of his bust. The following is the inscription on the cathedral window :—

> "To the glory of God and in grateful remembrance of G. J. Mountain, D.D., sometime Bishop of this diocese, whom the grace of Christ enabled

---

* The feelings of this writer are expressed in an extract already given in this volume.

to fulfil the duties of a long ministry to the advancement of His Church and the lasting benefit of many souls."

A similar project is on foot among the congregation and friends of St. Matthew's chapel, as well as one for an enlargement of the chapel of Bishop's College. His children erected, as a memorial of both their parents, a schoolhouse (the designs of which were taken from 'Instrumenta Ecclesiastica,') near St. Michael's chapel, where a simple brass plate in the chancel records his name. Close by are two graves, at the head of each of which, side by side, stands a plain stone, surmounted by a simple cross.

CHAPTER XXX.

Conclusion.

I HAVE finished the task imposed upon me, and I can have satisfied no one less than myself, in every way, with its execution. Those who have seen the accumulation of materials which I have left untouched will perhaps acknowledge that I could not have made the volume smaller, while not a few will regret the absence of much for which I thought I could not find a place. It has been indeed a most difficult task, for while I wished to " avoid those exaggerations into which the biographers of good men are tempted to fall," I am conscious that I may appear to have often failed in doing so, at least to those who did not know him : and for this reason I have inserted, in proof that the picture is, as I hope, not over-drawn, more of the testimony of others than might have otherwise been thought necessary.* For the same reason I have generally abstained from attempting anything like a description of his character, preferring to let it be judged of by his own words and deeds, and by the impression it made upon others. Yet, before I part with my reader, I cannot forbear from quoting Dean Goodwin's description of Bishop Mackenzie, which struck me, and I doubt not will strike others on reading it, as if it might almost have been written of him :

---

* I have to crave the indulgence of those whose private letters have been made use of for this purpose without their permission.

"Utter unselfishness and thoughtful kindness in small things, and imperturbable good temper, were perhaps the features which chiefly made it difficult or impossible to know without loving him. Then, too, he was thoroughly humble; he never put himself forward, and, even in giving up his home for foreign service, apologized as it were for his presumption by saying that nobody else would go, and therefore he would. I have said nothing respecting a point which suggests itself in these days very prominently to many minds, viz., the school of religious opinions to which he belonged. Was he High Church or Low Church, or what was his school? I shall be very glad if, after perusing this volume, the reader should declare himself unable thoroughly to answer this question. To say the truth, he could not be identified with any party: his doctrinal views were in loyal and affectionate conformity with the Book of Common Prayer; but I do not remember to have heard him discuss with earnestness any of the controversial questions of the day. The view of religion which commended itself to his mind was the practical application of the Gospel of our Lord Jesus Christ to the wants of men; and the best method of doing this was, in his opinion, a simple and faithful adherence to the principles and rules of the prayer-book. I never met with a more sincere Christian or one who had less of the spirit of party.* I never met with a man whose religious system seemed to be more completely within the four corners of the Book of Common Prayer. For religious speculation he had little taste—for religious eccentricities he had an utter abhorrence; but if there was any deed to be done, any work of mercy to be performed, either for the bodies or the souls of men, then his whole heart was engaged. To go about doing good was the only employment that he thoroughly and unreservedly loved."

The latter part of this extract is especially applicable. The text, "There is joy in the presence of the angels of God over one sinner that repenteth," was constantly in his thoughts, and he seldom transcribed it without writing the whole in capital letters. He made many efforts to establish a Magdalene asylum at Quebec, and almost the last words he ever

---

* In describing the proceedings of a successful meeting in aid of the objects of the Church Society, the Bishop of Quebec once wrote: "I did not quite like some portion of them; they jarred, at all events, against my taste; but it is not my business to be over-nice, and so to repress a zeal and activity exercised under the regular auspices of the Church, which, by God's blessing, may do good in an unobjectionable way, and set an encouraging example to the diocese."

spoke were expressive of a wish that such an institution might be established. And though he was never able to accomplish it, he defrayed, for upwards of ten years before his death, the cost of maintaining such subjects from Quebec as were found fit for it, in an asylum at Montreal. These, with scarcely an exception, were discovered and provided for through his own ministrations to the prisoners in the jail and house of correction. Preaching the Gospel to the poor was his delight. And he had a reward which he deeply valued, even in this world, in the love and gratitude of those who were the objects of his own love. In a letter written from Grosse Isle, in 1848, he said, in reference to the light nature of the work then to be performed there : " I have been thinking how wrong it would be to regard the hospital duty here as trifling or unimportant, because at present there are only about half a dozen patients. Half a dozen souls which will be saved or lost, and of which the welfare may be promoted,—not to speak of the present comfort given to them,—by the instrumental labours of the clergy."

Five and twenty years ago one of my sisters wrote out for me Southey's description of " the Doctor," ending with these words :

> His sweetest mind,
> 'Twixt mildness tempered and low courtesy,
> Could leave as soon to be as not be kind.
> Churlish despite ne'er looked from his calm eye,
> Much less commanded in his gentle heart,
> Nor could he cloak ill thoughts in complimented art.

My sister added, " You will be at no loss to apply this."

A few years later a friend, who then filled the post of organist of the cathedral at Quebec, sent me an extract, headed, " A picture, (the Bishop) "

" I have before my eyes at this moment his slender and spiritual figure, his calm but most subtle glance, and the incomparable expression of his smile. His face is classic, the ideal of thought. Where art thou, O Canova, that thou mightest transfer a portrait like this to marble ? it is so intensely pale, pure and profound."

The same friend, to whom, in an illness, I was reading one of his manuscript sermons, observing a few words introduced in the margin, remarked, " Whenever he dives, he brings up a pearl."

A writer in the *Quebec Mercury* (January, 1863), testified

" How completely the carrying out of the one idea of duty has been the sole purpose of his life ; how it shone through all his daily actions, through his courtesy, his charity, his mirth, his comfortings, his journeyings, the application of his vast literary attainments, his preaching and his praying ; indeed, if we may attribute the heavy blow which has fallen upon us to any worldly cause, we may, it is said, trace it to his resolute persistence in the discharge of a fatherly duty which he had undertaken towards some humble members of his own household."

And in the same paper a biographical sketch appeared, from which I make the following extract, though I had forborne from doing so,* as it seems wanting to make my work complete :

" The Bishop was most accessible, and consequently his time was very much broken in upon by persons calling continually upon all sorts of business, to whom he never refused a kind and courteous attention. His lordship's charities were very large, and well known to be so ; applications for relief, therefore, were unceasing ; but none was ever refused without the most apparent proof of its imposture. The writer of this notice remembers well how forcibly he was struck with the genuine christian kindness of the Bishop's own heart, when once, in speaking affectionately of an old and faithful servant whom the writer was enquiring after, the Bishop said, among other things, ' that he had noticed with admiration that W—— never spoke crossly nor impatiently but always gently and kindly to the poor, who were incessantly calling at the door.'

' The late Bishop of Quebec was universally known as a learned theologian, an elegant classical scholar, an able writer, an eloquent and, in the best sense, powerful preacher, and a most polished gentleman. Within the sanctities of his domestic life we ought not, perhaps, to enter ; suffice it to say that it was a life of great beauty ; and, notwithstanding several very severe domestic trials, of great happiness. Among his friends he loved to unbend, and he made all around him delighted with his playful sallies and his unbounded store of curious anecdotes. But in his most genial moments, you could never forget that he was a christian and a christian bishop, for

---

* See page 428.

there was a savour of piety and of genuine christian kindness about everything that proceeded out of his mouth. His sweetness and gentle tenderness,
so unusual in a man, were **wonderful**; his smile was enough to shew it;
hundreds of mourners can testify to it from his sympathy in the hour of
need.* Children were the objects of his regard and notice everywhere;
even the merest strangers, French Canadians for example, at whose houses
he had called but once casually in his 'journeyings often,' would years
afterwards speak of him, 'he was always so kind to the little children.'
The manner in which on his visitations he used to enquire after all the
members of every family, was constantly remarked upon.† His thoughtfulness and consideration for the feelings of others, the very poorest and
meanest, were only equalled by his forgetfulness of himself. In him
'patience had,' indeed, 'her perfect work.' In travelling he was continually subjected to the most vexatious detentions and difficulties, but was
always patient and cheerful. He could never bear to hear a loud word
spoken that seemed to betoken impatience. The only thing that seemed
to vex him was persons putting themselves or others out in the very least for
his personal comfort or convenience. His kindness and tenderness to his
servants no one could help remarking; never servants had such a master.
Such was the tenderness of his sympathy that the poorest and lowest could
feel towards him as a *friend*.

"The late Bishop of Quebec was what would be called in England an
evangelical High Churchman—such as have been all the great lights of
the English Church from the days of the Reformation. In the maintenance of the distinctive doctrines and observances of the Church he was
thoroughly uncompromising. He never gave way a single step to popular
clamour, nor did he ever hesitate to come forward in defence of his clergy
when unjustly assailed. He met with several very severe trials of his
principles as a Churchman, but in every instance he calmly stood his
ground, fought the battle and won it. Yet he shewed in his whole life, as
every one here knows, how those principles can be held consistently with
the truest universal christian charity.‡ * * *

---

* I possess very many written proofs of this, and I remember a lady, who
became a widow shortly after his death, saying to me, " This is the time
when I miss the Bishop."

† See page 339 (first extract from Bishop Anderson).

‡ A member of the Church Society, at a meeting held at Quebec early
in 1863, related an instance of this which had occurred some thirty years
before, when he had accompanied him, at the close of a Sunday's work, to
visit a poor family in the suburbs of Quebec who had solicited his help.
On his desiring them to come to his house for relief, his companion mentioned that they did not belong to the Church. "Never mind," he replied,
" they are God's creatures."

"Though methodical and exact to an extraordinary degree, he was not supposed very greatly to excel as a man of business, a financier, or a *manager* of other men—he dwelt too much in the higher regions of the christian life for that. But the writer of this notice is deeply persuaded that the diocese is now in a far more healthy condition, and that the episcopate of the late Bishop of Quebec has been far more successful, than if the ratio of these qualities had been reversed in his character, and he had been more of what the world calls an administrator and less of a saint." *

---

* With reference to this extract, see 2nd note at page 21.

APPENDIX.

~~~~~~~~~

𝔓rayers

COMPOSED FOR THE USE OF PARTICULAR PERSONS, OR ON PARTICULAR OCCASIONS.

FOR A SCHOOL OF YOUNG CHILDREN OF THE POORER CLASS.

Opening.—O gracious God and heavenly Father, bless us, we beseech Thee, in our task this day. Grant to us who teach, patience and skill in conveying knowledge; and to these little ones who learn, a willing, dutiful, humble and diligent spirit. Grant that the knowledge which they gain may be for their good in this world, and may help them in the knowledge which is above all price, even the knowledge of Thee and of Thy Son Jesus Christ, to Whom, with Thee and the Holy Ghost, be glory for evermore. Amen.

Close.—O God, Whose only Son, our Lord and Saviour Jesus Christ, did bless little children, and when He was a child Himself, sat in the temple to hear the doctors of the law, and to ask of them questions, and Who also has taught us by His holy Apostle St. Paul, that those who know the holy scriptures from childhood may thence be made wise unto salvation; bless the instruction which has been here given this day, set forward these children in the way of eternal life: let their souls be precious in Thy sight: keep them by Thine own power, and prosper them both here and hereafter, for the sake of the same, Thy Son Jesus Christ, our Lord. Amen.

DD

FOR OPENING A SUNDAY SCHOOL.

O Lord God, Who deignest to look down with favour upon the humblest efforts made in Thy service, and without Whose grace and blessing nothing can prosper that we do; vouchsafe, we beseech Thee, to bless the work in which our hands are here engaged : give to these children willing hearts and teachable minds : give to those who instruct them an affectionate concern for their spiritual good, and grant that the seed which is here sown may spring up unto life eternal. Thou, O Lord, out of the mouth of very babes and sucklings hast perfected praise : Thou hast caused it to be recorded in Thy holy word, that Thy servant Timothy from a child had known the holy scriptures which are able to make us wise unto salvation, and above all that Thy blessed Son, when He took our nature upon Him, was engaged, while yet a child, in the temple, both hearing and asking questions concerning Thy holy law ; grant that with these examples and encouragements before their eyes, both teachers and scholars may be diligent and persevering in their respective duties, and let Thy blessing more and more rest upon them, for the sake of Thy dear Son Jesus Christ. Amen.

Family Prayers.

1.—FOR PLAIN PEOPLE.

O God, we praise Thy name for the mercies of the past day, and we pray Thee to keep us in peace and safety through the night. Forgive all our sins : comfort our hearts : enable us to serve Thee in pureness of living and truth : to walk in love, and to keep always a conscience void of offence towards Thee and towards man. Bless and protect this house, O Lord, and preserve both us and all belonging to us in health and godliness, and grant that we may grow in grace and in the knowledge of our Lord and Saviour Jesus Christ. Bless this land and all the dominions of our Queen : prosper and extend the work of Thy Church upon earth, through the same Jesus Christ our Lord. Amen.

2.

O Lord God, Whose tender mercies are over all Thy works, we pray Thee to bless all the members of this family, present or absent, both spiritually and temporally; to sanctify to us all the dispensations of Thy fatherly hand; to relieve us in our sorrows, and teach us to trust always in Thy goodness. Keep us, O Lord, in body and in mind; do for us according to our several necessities; preserve us in all dangers; succour, comfort, and direct us in all our ways; make us happy, if it please Thee, in this world, and bring us to thine everlasting kingdom, through Jesus Christ our Lord. Amen.

3.—BEFORE THE HOLY COMMUNION.

O Lord Jesus Christ, the Saviour of sinners, Who didst command us to remember Thy body broken and Thy blood shed for our sins by the tokens of bread and wine, and Who by Thy holy Apostle hast taught us that we should examine ourselves before we eat of that bread and drink of that cup; give us grace so to cherish the remembrance of Thine unspeakable love, that we may always be prompted to partake thankfully of this instituted memorial and blessed means of union with Thyself; and so to prepare ourselves by devout meditation, serious consideration of our ways, and faithful inspection of our hearts, that we may come to Thy holy table with penitence and faith and love, feeling the wants of our perishing souls, and finding them supplied in Thee, Who livest and reignest with the Father and the Holy Ghost, ever one God, world without end. Amen.

4.—ANOTHER FOR THE SAME.

O God, who in Thy great mercy to sinners, didst give Thy Son Jesus Christ to die upon the cross, and thereby one offering to perfect for ever them that are sanctified, grant that we, being now invited to that holy sacrament in which we shew forth the Lord's death till He come, and partake of the bread which, being broken, is the communion of the body of Christ, and of the cup which, being blest, is the communion of His blood, may indeed spiritually eat His flesh and drink His blood. Give us a deep sense of our own sinfulness, with a full reliance upon the all-sufficiency of Him for our salvation, Who, knowing no sin, was made sin for us that we might be made the righteousness of God in Him. Penetrate us with a sense of His love: wash us from all our stains in the fountain opened for sin and for uncleanness; and impart to us both in this holy ordinance, and in every other method which is agreeable to Thy Divine wisdom, such a measure of Thy grace that we may walk worthy of the vocation wherewith we are called, and bring forth all the fruits of righteousness which are by Jesus Christ to the praise and glory of Thy holy name. Amen.

5.—IN TIME OF AFFLICTION.

O Lord God, Whose care is over all Thy works, and Who art able to bring good out of evil, and to turn sorrow into joy; we beseech Thee to make us deeply and constantly to feel that all which befalls us is directed by Thy hand and designed for our good. Give us under our trials grace to draw closer to Thyself; grant us a spirit of patience and faith and of conformity to the meek example of our suffering Lord. Protect this day and visit with Thy grace and favour all who belong to this family, far off or near: shew mercy to all according to their respective needs, and if it be Thy gracious will, grant that all may be blessed together in peace, health, and comfort, through Jesus Christ our Lord. Amen.

6.—FOR THE SAME.

O God, Who layest low and liftest up, and from Whose hand we receive both evil and good, we pray that Thou wouldst sanctify to us whatever affliction it is Thy will that we should suffer, and enable us to bear it with faith and resignation: remove it, if it please Thee, in Thine own good time, and where the stroke has fallen, there let Thy mercy restore; where Thou hast sorely smitten, there let Thy healing power be shewn, that the bones which Thou hast broken may rejoice, and that we may all be re-united to praise and magnify Thy blessed Name together, through Jesus Christ our Lord. Amen.

7.—FOR THE SAME.

O blessed and compassionate Saviour, merciful High Priest, Who canst be touched with the feeling of our infirmities, and Who, in the days of Thy flesh, didst relieve many sufferers in body and mind, and restore them whole and sound to their afflicted friends ; work the like mercy now for us : Thine arm is not shortened that it cannot save, nor Thine ear heavy that it cannot hear. Stretch forth Thine arm, then, to deliver, and open thine ear to our humble prayer. Lord, we believe; help Thou our unbelief. Speak the word, and Thy servant shall be healed. O heavenly Father, let not our faith or patience fail, though Thou shouldst seem long in granting our prayer ; but teach us in all things to tarry Thy leisure, and give us grace and wisdom, whatsoever Thou seest good to do, to say, it is the Lord, let Him do what seemeth Him good; though He slay me, yet will I trust in Him. Hear us, O Lord, for Thy dear Son Jesus Christ's sake. Amen.

FOR A PERSON IN AFFLICTION.

O God, Who art the God of the spirits of all flesh, and the Father of all the whole family in heaven and earth, look upon Thy poor sinful creature and give me grace to profit by all the dispensations of Thy hand. Thou, O God, makest all things to work together for the good of them that love Thee : O give me a thankful heart for all the earthly blessings and comforts which Thou hast heaped upon me, and wisdom to use them to Thy glory. And now in the hour of my affliction teach me to remember that Thou dost not afflict willingly nor grieve the children of men, but chastenest them in love and causest them often through much tribulation to enter into Thy heavenly kingdom. Grant to me, O Lord, a perfect submission of heart and an unreserved conformity to Thy holy will. Grant me grace to say, in the sincerity of my spirit, it is the Lord, let Him do what seemeth Him good. The Lord gave, and the Lord hath taken away, blessed be the Name of the Lord. Grant me grace, not only now, but in whatever sufferings or trials, however sharp, Thou mayest ordain for me, to conform myself to the example of my suffering Lord, and cheerfully to carry my appointed cross, remembering that the disciple is not above his master, nor the servant above his lord ; make me, O Lord, to turn this visitation to account by communing with my own heart, and in my chamber and in stillness , reviewing my past improvement of the talents committed to me, judging myself that I be not judged by Thee, and setting my house in order, that I may be ready also, not knowing when my soul shall be required of me. Extend the same mercy, gracious Lord, to all those dear relatives and connections who are now my fellow-mourners, that the living may lay to their hearts the lesson of death, and may be weaned more effectually from the world, and prompted more earnestly to lay up their treasure in heaven. And O Thou Who art the God of all consolation, comfort us, I beseech Thee, by the succors of Thy heavenly grace; kindle in us a more lively faith, and teach us to press forward more intently to the prize of our high calling in Christ Jesus; to look, as to a reality which is to be our own, to that blessed time when the Lord God shall wipe away all tears from all faces. Hear me, O Lord, for the sake of Thy Son Jesus Christ, that great High Priest Who can be touched with the feeling of our infirmities, and Whose own holy words which He has taught us to use we couple with all our feeble prayers, Our Father, &c.

FOR A SUNDAY SCHOOL TEACHER IN PRIVATE.

O Almighty God, Who, through Thy Son Jesus Christ, hast taught us to care one for another, and hast encouraged us by declaring that he which converteth a sinner from the error of his way shall save a soul from death; have compassion upon the poor and feeble endeavours of Thy most unworthy servant: give me a fervant concern for Thy glory and the spiritual welfare of my fellow-creatures; give me more zeal and wisdom, and a more patient and persevering spirit, that I may promote these ends in the task of instructing the children of the poor. Take away from me all indifference and languor, all hurtful distrust of the possibility of my success on account of the deficiency that is in me; enable me, through faith, to keep in my mind that Thy strength is made perfect in our weakness, and to hope that Thou wilt deign to use me as an instrument of good. Thou, O God, Who biddest us not despise the day of small things, bless the seed which is sown in this little field,* that it may bring forth fruit unto life eternal, for the sake of Thy dear Son Jesus Christ our Lord. Amen.

---

* This prayer was prepared for a teacher in a very small school.

FOR CHORISTERS.

(Partly adapted from a form drawn up by the Bishop of Newfoundland.)

I.

O Most merciful God, Who deignest to accept the homage of Thy poor servants upon earth, and hast taught us that we should pray and sing with the spirit and with the understanding, grant Thy grace, I beseech Thee, to us who are permitted to lead the songs of praise in the assembly of the faithful, that we may come with prepared minds and sanctified thoughts to our task. Teach us, O Lord, to reverence Thy sanctuary and the place where Thine honor dwelleth : remove from us all vain, worldly, wandering imaginations or concern for the applause of men : enable us, while we lift up our voices, to lift up also our hearts: and vouchsafe to us a spirit of fervor, faith and love, that, knowing ourselves to be temples of the Holy Ghost, we may duly set forth the glory of Thy great Name and help to edify our brethren, through Jesus Christ, Who with Thee and the same Spirit liveth and reigneth ever One God world without end. Amen.

II.

O gracious God, Whom the holy angels worship continually in heaven and Who deignest to accept the homage of Thy poor servants upon earth, grant Thy grace, I beseech Thee, to us who are here joined together in this blessed work, that we may sing Thy praises with the spirit and with the understanding : and so prepare our hearts that we may engage with all reverence in the services of Thy sanctuary, and duly set forth the glory of Thy great Name, to the edification of our brethren and the comfort of our own souls, through Jesus Christ our Lord. Amen.

III.

Grant, we beseech Thee, Almighty God, that we who are about to engage in singing Thy praises in the assembly of the faithful, being filled with all reverence, and preserved from worldly and wandering imaginations, and enabled to lift up our hearts in sincerity and love, may minister to the edification of Thy Church and the glory of Thy great Name, through Jesus Christ our Lord. Amen.

TEXTS FOR A BELIEVER SUBJECT TO DEPRESSION AND TIMIDITY IN HIS RELIGION.

Psalms xxx. 5, cxxvi. 5, 6, (6, 7, Prayer-book,) xxvii. 14, (16 p. b.) xxxvii. 5, li. 8, xlii. 11, (14, 15, p. b.) ciii. 11-14; Isaiah xl. 1, xxxv. 10, lxi. 1, 2, 3, xlix. 15, lxiii. 15, 16, lvii. 15, lxvi. 2, liv. 7, 8 ; Hosea, vi. 1, St. Matthew, v. 3, 4, xi. 28, xii. 20, xv. 21-28, xxvi. 41 ; Romans, x. 12 ; Heb. iv. 15, 16, xiii. 5 ; i. Peter v. 7, 10 ; Rev. xxi. 3, 4 ; cf. Isaiah, xxxv. 8 ; Ecclus, xxviii. 10.

MAXIMS AND MONITIONS DRAWN UP FOR HIS SON UPON HIS LEAVING CANADA TO PREPARE FOR THE UNIVERSITY.*

Aboard, aboard———,
The wind sits in the shoulder of your sail,
And you are staid for : There—my blessing with you,
And these few precepts in thy memory
See thou character.———

1. Never suffer any interruption of the habit of prayer, and always remember that special object of prayer which is intimated in St. Luke xi. 13.

2. Make it a point to read some portion of scripture every day.

3. Make it a rule to practice self-examination, comparing yourself with the Word of God and the example of Christ, in point of temper, sincerity, diligence, improvement of time, purity of thought, government of appetite, conformity to the divine will, thankfulness for mercies in providence and grace, kindness and (according to opportunity) beneficence to your fellow-creatures, as well as willingness to make sacrifices for them.

4. Particularly examine yourself thus before receiving the Lord's Supper, and avail yourself of all opportunities of doing this. And when the examination brings your deficiencies to light, make them matter of repentance before God.

5. Recur frequently to the nature and extent of your promises in confirmation.

6. Make yourself fully master of the distinctive principles of the Church, and you will not compromise them. While you would tremble at the idea of priding yourself upon your privileges as a Churchman, and while you cultivate the utmost charity of judgment

---

* See page 225.

and of feeling towards all the members of irregular bodies in religion, you **will understand at the same time the** inconsistency and ill-consequence of mixing the **Church with** those bodies in religious proceedings.

7. **Endeavour to keep constantly in mind a sense of the immediate presence of God.**

8. **In hard temptation pray the harder.**

9. **Let the distribution of your** time be as methodical as possible; **yet avoid being such a** slave to method, that **if you are put out of** your established time **you are unsettled** and incapable **of** acting to good purpose.

10. Where you **are a guest (and certainly with equal** care, where you are **a pupil,) conform with** readiness **to the** habits of the family; **observe their hours with unfailing punctuality; and never assume the liberty of judging anything to be** unworthy of **your** attention respecting which they are particular.

11. Never give a rough or short answer to any person in any class **of life.** Generous and obliging manners constitute a marked feature of the christian character, and promote to an incredible extent the happiness and comfort of human life. Remember that next to being good it is important to be agreeable; and to gain others to what is good being a great branch of christian duty, the christian is defective in a point of much consequence who does not recommend his religion by his deportment and address. Carry into the daily intercourse of life, domestic, social and civil, the spirit of **Gen.** xiii. 8, 9; St. Matth. v. 44; Rom. xii. 10; i. Pet. iii. 8.

12. Avoid in religion all approach to exhibition or **obtrusive-**ness, and repudiate all party-phraseology or party distinctions in things indifferent; but take heed that you do not, under this plea, appear to belong rather to the world **than** to God. Never dare to be ashamed of Christ. Never shrink from discountenancing irreligion. **Never** miss a fair opportunity (regard being had to age, station and other particulars) of being instrumental to promote a right knowledge of Him and advance the interests of true religion. —Ps. cxix. 51; Prov. xxix. 25; St. Mark, viii. 38; Rom. xii. 2.

13. Cultivate cheerfulness of mind and manner, and do not fear to indulge in a playfulness which may comport with the character of

a gentleman and a Christian ; but abominate buffoonery or noisy mirth.

14. Strictly preserve the refinement of a gentleman as well in your private habits as in all the varied usages of good society; but, of all things, avoid piquing yourself upon your gentility, being ostentatious in refinement, or contracting a dangerous fastidiousness which cannot accommodate itself to the varieties of human life.

15. In perplexity and difficulty, especially if conscience be concerned, go straight to God and try the question first of all by His Word ; but take counsel also, and that with all humility, from those upon whose advice you can wisely lean.

16. Avoid irresolution : but avoid also what some men are guilty of, a hasty adoption of your decision, or a determination to stick to your point from the fear of being thought or thinking yourself undecided.

17. Do not be satisfied with any christianity, nor think it safe or genuine, which would seek to stop short of the principles laid down in Gal. ii. 20, and ii. Cor. v. 14, 15.

18. In provocations, vexations, sufferings, and trials, have recourse to the lessons presented in i. Peter ii., 21, and Heb. xii. 3.

19. If you are familiarly in contact with youths of great worldly expectations, enjoying command of money, do not for an instant allow yourself to be mortified because you cannot do as they do, nor be ashamed to say plainly and decidedly that what may suit them will not suit you, because you cannot afford it. After doing this once or twice, you will probably have no occasion to do it again.

20. There is a vast gain, in many ways, in cultivating a habit of systematic early rising, and it saves the hurtful necessity of sitting up late. If ever you feel in the morning such a struggle between the love of bed and the desire of entering upon the proper work of the day, as is described in Persius, Sat. V., 132, 3, between the former propensity and the desire of wealth ; and if, so feeling, you suffer the worse desire to prevail, that defeat may lose more for you than the bare time which you lose upon the occasion itself.

21. Works of imagination should be sparingly read, and only *pour délassement d'esprit.* The moment that they engender a distaste for studies practically useful, the danger of them should be seen

and shunned. **But** you must have already drunk too deeply when **you have suffered your head to be thus affected.**

———

When his **younger son** left him in 1842 (see page 224) to **enter the army, the Bishop wrote out for** him the foregoing maxims, **from 1 to 19 inclusive, with some trifling** adaptations, adding **the following :**

—Hæc genitor digressu dicta supremo
Fundebat........

When your dear **brother left us, in 1840, I** gave him **a little book,** in which I had written **down certain** maxims and **rules for** his guidance in life. **They had relation to his** religion, his manners, his habits, **and his pursuits. The rough draft of** them being still in my possession, **I copy it for you, my equally dear son, making some few adaptations and additions, on account of the** difference **in the way of life which is before you.**

If you remember, as I believe you will, the foregoing rules, and sincerely endeavour to follow them, there will be no fear of your being enticed into any habits **of dissipation or excess, gambling, profaneness, or loose** conversation, **for your** mark **will be much higher than mere** abstinence from these destructive **vices, all** plausible **attempts to colour** which **may well be met by Ephesians v. 6. And when you are with** your **uncle, he,** who **will be a father and a pattern to you in all** things, will also **be a protection** against any **bad influence or** dangerous attraction. **But you are** very young, and you will be thrown **into** scenes **very** new **to you** before you can join **him ; and besides your recourse generally to** religious principles, motives, and means, **to keep** you from perilous deviations, **it** will be necessary for you to lay down certain fixed and invariable rules, among which are these :

Never to drink more than a specified and very moderate quantity of wine (which **I leave** it **to** yourself to prescribe,) and never to acquire the habit of drinking any mixtures **at** night. **I** recommend also a **" total** abstinence **" from** smoking.

Never **to play** for money at any games of chance, however small the sum.

Never to bet ; nor to **be** concerned directly or indirectly with horse-racing.

Never, if it can by possibility be avoided, to remain in company where obscene language or obscene songs are introduced.

It is matter of thankfulness that, in the **present** day, the **army will** everywhere, I apprehend, afford some choice of correct and desirable associates; and there are, **I** believe, many messes in **which** nothing offensive will be heard.

Respecting **the men, you will learn, I** hope, the art of combining with the inviolable maintenance of discipline and authority, the fullest exercise of kindness and consideration, and attaching those poor fellows **to you without suffering** them for an instant to take liberties inconsistent with the relation in which they stand to you. When your duty obliges you to cause them in any way to be punished, I am sure that you will be merciful to the utmost extent which that duty will permit. Opportunities will present themselves, and particularly after you rise to higher grades in the profession, of promoting the best and highest interests of them, their wives and their children.

I would say nothing upon those points if it were certain that your whole military training would be under the eye of your uncle, but nothing is certain in this world, except that we must go out of it, and that our preparation for the state beyond can only be made while we are in it, and only in the way indicated in the Book of God. And since a soldier, by his profession, may be called into danger of going out of it suddenly by the hand of man, he should, of all men, never allow himself to be unprepared for the summons. And so God keep you, in soul and body, through Christ Who died for you!

THE following are two or three passages from letters to his children, not referring always to his work, but characteristic of the tenderness of his affection, as well as of his cheerfulness of heart in his intercourse with them:

"RIVIÈRE DU LOUP en bas, 17th August, 1857.

"MY DEAREST A——,

"I am, thank God, quite well and strong now, with the exception of some slight remaining effects of the injury in the back,* which is growing daily

---

* Caused by a fall in trying to reach too great a distance to gather some flowers for an invalid child.

less. It would therefore be ridiculous, and something worse, that I should abstain altogether from the public duties of Sunday; and what a familiar lecture, to between thirty and forty people in a private room, is to do in the way of harming me, compared with some occupations of another kind, in the way of correspondence, which I have had to undergo here, *c'est ce que je voudrais bien savoir.* Yesterday I preached in the little Rivière du Loup church, and read the ante-communion service. • • • I went out the other day with all the N——s on a pic-nic to Cacouna, and we opened our baskets of provender not far from the Indian encampment, below the bank which is between the village and the St. Lawrence. We got near a little rill of water for convenience, and seats were arranged by means of the waggon-cushions, with the aid of large stones. As to myself, however, I was regularly enthroned or ensconced in a bushy cedar-tree, a horizontal branch affording me facility for sitting, and a perpendicular stem supporting my back, while I was completely " o'er canopied," not " with luscious woodbine," but with the verdant sides and head of the little tree. James and the horses were duly cared for, and the children gave the relics of the feast to the Indians.

"The learned and ingenious principal tried the experiment the other day (unwittingly, however,) of making tea with salt water for breakfast. The servants and children, from some hindrance of bathing, or other cause, were slack in appearing, and he undertook to go into the kitchen, where he laid hold of the first hot water which came to his hand, and this happened to be a provision of the marine tide, which was in process of heating, to temper the tub-full designed for little A——, who was to be dipped in the house. The mistake was only discovered after the milk and sugar had been put into the cups.

"On Saturday I took little K—— and G ——, by turns, before me on the mare, and rode down to the beach with them, through those beautiful fields which are at the back of Judge M——'s lodgings. The delight of the children was not small; and such delight, if anything in this world, has a reflecting power. . . . Thus I have given all that occurs to my recollection of incident worthy of note, and have scribbled it off as it came up before me. We shall, if it please God, meet this week, and I must shape myself for town-life, and buckle to for my work. I should, beyond all comparison, prefer travelling in September, to the arrangement for visiting Mr. King's mission in October; but the latter month will, as you say, be probably more convenient for the people, on account of harvest in the former, and so must be chosen. . . . (29th July, '57.) Mr. W—— lent me a number of the " Anglo-Saxon," in which Lord Napier's speech at Harvard University is given at length—really an extraordinarily clever performance. The speech of Mr. Dallas, the American Minister at home, at a meeting of the humane society, is given in the same paper—a clever and apposite speech enough.

Proximus illi **tamen** occupavit
Dallas honores.

But we must add a quotation from Virgil to that from Horace—
Proximus hinc—longo **sed proximus intervallo.**

"Last, but not least, as your dear K——'s birthday is registered, I believe, on the 28th, but she thinks she remembers being born on the 31st, the point at which we stand between the two may not be improperly chosen to wish her many happy returns of the day, and all blessings, earthly and heavenly, still growing, especially the latter, as she advances in her pilgrimage."

"QUEBEC, 5th Oct., 1854.

(In expectation of the return of two of his children from England.)

"O, the last time of writing! The next thing is to see you both. What a comfort in all our troubles, perplexities, vexations, exposures to misconstruction, and bad feeling, &c., to preserve true love and affection among members of the family and the circle of chosen friends, however far! After the hope of being accepted, for Christ's sake, before God, what is there like the confidence and love of those justly dear to our hearts on earth?"

"BISHOP'S COLLEGE, 3rd June, 1856.

. . . "My natural feelings, which circumstances have tended to deaden, have been unwontedly called into life by the baptism (of the first of his grand-children bearing his own name) of Sunday, and the sight of your sister and her children here. The blessing of God, I trust, will rest upon the heads of all my children, grand-children, and children by marriage."

I might give numerous other proofs, and stronger even than these, of the depth of his domestic affections, particularly such as are contained in birthday letters. But these must suffice. I add one extract, of a different kind, from a letter written in 1854.

"I hope you will not allow my letters to communicate any gloom to you. My whole heart is in the Church, and the work which I have to do for God upon earth, and I cannot fail to be anxious when difficulties and perplexities arise ; exigencies are to be provided for with inadequate means ; and declension to be seen in some departments of my charge. But in my settled and deliberate thoughts and feelings, I endeavour to separate myself from the Church; *i.e.*, that I know God will take care of His own cause, and if I do my part, however poorly, with a single eye, it matters little what may befall which affects myself."

A GOOD deal of what follows is taken from a packet of papers, on which was written—

"I have put together here a quantity of rubbish, the great proportion of which can only be food for the flames; but I have not found time to examine it, and there are some poor flowers to be preserved, when the weeds shall be doomed in which they are buried."

WRITTEN AT A TIME OF SEVERE DOMESTIC AFFLICTION, WHICH WAS ALSO ONE OF TROUBLE IN THE CHURCH:

O Saviour, they were bitter things
  Thou didst as man endure;
But ah! Thou knew'st no sinful stings;
  Work, work of mine the cure!

Yes! Saviour, yes! a sinner calls,
  Who, while beneath his woes,
Redoubling still, he prostrate falls,
  The sense of mercy knows.

Weak heart of man, if wounded deep,
  At once in home-felt joys,
And stabbed by those who hate the sleep
  Of envy, strife, and noise,

Turn thee to Him Whose power alone
  Can heal thy festering sore,
Can bid the sufferer cease to groan,
  The mourner weep no more.

THE MOURNER OF THE WILDS.
(Written about 1810.)

It was upon a wild and desolate shore,
While night, in her wide grasp, embraced the world,
A maid, whose inborn loveliness and grace,
Would not yield all, though much, to withering grief,
Strayed forth unsheltered, and exposed to all
The rudeness of the time, and thus she moaned—
(It would have grieved the veriest hardened heart
That ever lodged within a human breast,
To hear her plaints—) I know not what the cause
Of her deep sorrows was—but thus she moaned:

Alone ! I am alone upon the world,
There is not one to pity me, not one
That will be kind to my sore-wounded heart ;
And I shall know no more the interchange
Of love—no more the smile of tenderness—
The gentle and endearing offices
Of friend to friend ; O, I could bear to meet
The evils of man's lot, labour and pain,
And penury's freezing hour and drooping grief,*
Had I but one to stay me in the storm,
One on whose bosom I could lean my head,
One that would sooth me with the face of love,
And say, " thou'rt dear to me." I could bear all
If I had this,—but now !—I am not formed
To front the " hard unkindness" of the world
Alone and unsupported—I shall sink.
Little, ye prosperous ones, ye little know
The treasure of a friendly countenance ;
Nought while ye meet but smiles and gracious eyes
Responsive to your own, ye little think
What solace to my inmost soul would bring,
In this sad hour, one kind benignant look.

O, I have not deserved a fate like this.
Chastise me, Heaven, but let Thy chastisements
Be suited to my strength. I am but weak,
Thou know'st, and all unused to woes like these ;
I once had fairer hopes, and happier thoughts,
Happier indeed ! yet I must not repine.
Forgive the murmurings of a broken heart ;
And if it be Thy will inscrutable
My sins to visit with a hand severe,
Eternal Power ! support me with that hand,
And lead me to Thy peace, and heal my soul.

TO HIS BROTHER ROBERT, ON ENTERING THE ARMY, (1811):

Go, generous youth, an English heart is thine,
Go forth, and foremost in the battle shine ;
Go, deal to Gallia's sons the deadly blow,
And help to lay her proud oppressors low ;

---

* Man's feeble race what ills await,
Labour and penury, the racks of pain,
Disease, and sorrow's weeping train.—GRAY.

Go, and may He, Who that fair spirit gave, ⎫
Mild as the dove, yet as the eagle brave,* ⎬
In glory guide thee, and in danger save. ⎭
Awhile our tenderness may blame thy choice,
'Tis thou shalt quickly teach us to rejoice ;
O how our hearts shall glow some future day,
To learn thy courage in the dubious fray ;
While England hails each brave defender's name,
To find our Robert in the list of fame.
O how thy father's eye shall light with joy,
Thy mother yearn to clasp her gallant boy ;
Think, think on this, and let it cheer thy heart,
And mitigate the pang we feel to part.
Farewell, my brother, that I call thee so,
I count among my chiefest joys below ;
Farewell, my Robert, and whate'er betide,
Return unchanged, and we are satisfied.

———

TO THE SAME,

(With a copy of Anacreon, 1809) :

Accipe quem mitto, frater carissime, librum,
    Parvum non parvæ munus amicitiæ.
Vellem equidem majus donum et te dignius esset ;
    Sed quod amor jubet id sæpe crumena vetat.

———

TO HIS FATHER,

(1st January, 1813) ·

How shall the hand, benumbed with cold,
    Awake the warbling wire ?
What thoughts can scenes that but unfold
    One waste of snow inspire ?

---

* It was rather remarkable that a distinguished general officer, Sir F. Robinson, in whose division R. M. served in the Peninsular war, described him as an excellent young man, "very diffident, but as bold as a lion "

O where the circling snow-storm flies,
Or trackless plain wide-glittering lies,
Or where the solid stream along *
My steeds, impetuous, whirl the sleigh,
Some theme is there for fancy's play,
Some images of song.

Away! no outward aid I ask,
The heart shall prompt the easy task;
The chorus of your offspring hear,
For you they rend the frosty air
With song—for you, with early prayer,
Inaugurate the year.

AN ADAPTATION OF HORACE, ODE I. BOOK I.

(To describe the pursuits of a portion of the community at the University
of Cambridge: about 1809):

"Now blame we most the nurslings or the nurse?"—COWPER.

Miller, my tutor and my friend,
From northern names whose sires descend,
Of Granta's sons some take take their pride,
Tandem or curricle to guide,
To raise a smothering dust, and boast
Within a hair to pass a post.
They tell of racing victories,
And puff their merits to the skies;
One piques himself on social powers,
Pleased if the friends of festive hours
Enjoy his wit, and honour still,
With three times three, his toasting skill;
Another aims, with worthier toil,
Whate'er, on Granta's learned soil,
Of prize or honour may be reaped,
To feel on his own person heaped.

---

* Virgil's description of a Scythian winter (Georg. iii. 352,) is in some
of its points correctly applicable to Canada, though, by his account, the
Scythians used wheels upon the ice. His "cæduntque securibus humida
vina" may be matched by the solid milk sold in the Canadian markets.
The "solid stream" is introduced by Horace in his description even of
Italian winter in his day—"geluque Flumina constiterint acuto."

Yon Mopus, of his garden fond,
Its small square space ne'er goes beyond ;
Nor would he take a thousand pound
To run the risk of being drowned
In light canoe, where students gay,
Cleave Ely-ward the watery way ;
While others, skilled the boat to guide,
And not unused to wind and tide,
Who yet have somehow been such luck in,
As once or twice to get a ducking,
Vow, when they gain their rooms so snug,
And all their fireside comforts hug,
They'll waste no more their time and money
Upon an execrable funny ;*
But soon their art they ply again,
Nor from loved habit can refrain.

There are, it must be owned, a few
Who not dislike a glass or two,
Nor scorn long afternoons to spend
O'er the brisk bottle with a friend,
Whether in college-rooms reclining,
Or at some jovial tavern† dining.
While some to blow the horn delight, ⎫
Sonorous through the streets at night, ⎬
And with the fierce bargee to fight, ⎭
Or raise still wider rows, and greater,
Deaf to the prayers of Alma Mater.

Heedless of gentle admonition ⎫
For absence long, or imposition ⎬
From antie dealer in tuition, ⎭
The sportsman spends the wintry day
In following fox-hounds far away,

---

* The kind of small boat in vogue upon the river Cam.

† As the Bush and the Fountain are both among the customary ensigns of venal hospitality, it is peculiarly unfortunate that neither of these should have been adopted in Cambridge. (This refers to the corresponding lines in Horace :

Nunc viridi membra sub arbuto
Stratus, nunc ad aquæ lene caput sacræ.)

Or seeks, with gun across his shoulder,
The timid hare, and birds not bolder.
You,* whom those classic wreaths have crowned,
With which the learned head is bound,†
May sit by Honour's sacred side.   )
Me, with small cause alas! for pride, }
Yet from the coarser crew divide   )
Some social joys more choice of means,
Some taste, perhaps, for rural scenes;
While, now and then, the obliging nine
Encourage weak attempts of mine.
If really poet named by you,
I shall grow higher a yard or two;
Shall swell, my own importance feeling,
And strike my head against the ceiling.

EPIGRAMS.

(About 1809.)

Why do you, in this favoured nation,
Still rail at those who hold the helm?
Spit venom on exalted station,
Jeer at the pillars of the realm?
These once made cheap and vile to sight,
Society's a broken frame.
Sir, 'tis our country's free-born right,
Source of our pride and envied name;
Aye! that's indeed another story,
But do you not the thing misplace?
That you may do so is your glory,
And that you do so your disgrace.

"He that will pun will pick a pocket."

George, erst that fished at sea,
    Is turned a shepherd lad;
By hook or crook, says he,
    A living must be had.

---

* I have adopted the reading Te, instead of Me, because it suited my
purpose better.

† Miller obtained Sir W. Browne's medal for Greek and Latin epigrams
in 1805, and again in 1806. He took a wrangler's degree, was first
Chancellor's medallist, and became a fellow of Trinity college.

TRANSLATION OF **ENGLISH INTO** LATIN VERSE.

(Examination for Trinity college scholarship, 1808.)—See **page 18.**

Orpheus with his lute made trees
And the mountain-tops that freeze
  Bow themselves when he did sing ;
To his music plants and flowers
Ever rose, as sun and showers
  There had made a lasting spring.

Everything that heard him play,
E'en the billows of the sea,
  Hung their heads and then lay by ;
In sweet music is such art,
Killing care and grief of heart
  Fall asleep ; or, hearing, die.

            Shakspere, Henry **VIII**.

———

Arbores Orpheus sonitu canoræ
Flexit auritas* citharæ, geluque
Montium obstrictos apices amœno
    Carmine movit ;
Protinus flores varias videres
Crescere e terrâ viridesque plantas,
Præbet et sol haud alias et imbres
    Tempore verno.
Quicquid audivit stupuisse vocem
Dicitur vatis : neque non frementes
Ille pacavit maris aureâ tes-
    tudine† fluctus.

TRANSLATION OF GREEK INTO LATIN VERSE.

(On the same occasion.)

Οὐδὲν ἐν ἀνθρώποισι μένει χρῆμ' ἔμπεδον αἰεί.
Ἐν δὲ τὰ κάλλιστον Χῖος ἔειπεν ἀνήρ·
οἵη περ φύλλων γενεὴ, τοιήδε καὶ ἀνδρῶν.

———

  * Blandum et auritas fidibus canora
    Ducere quercus.

                     Hor.

  † O testudinis aureæ
  Dulcem quæ sonitum, Pieri, temperas !

                     Hor.

παῦροί μιν θνητῶν οἴασι δεξάμενοι
στέρνοις ἐγκατίθεντο. πάρεστι γὰρ ἐλπὶς ἑκάστῳ,
ἀνδρῶν ἥ τε νέων στίθεσιν ἐμφύεται.
θνητῶν δ' ὄφρα τις ἄνθος ἔχῃ πολυήρατον ἥβης,
κοῦφον ἔχων θυμὸν, πόλλ' ἀτέλεστα νοεῖ.
οὔτε γὰρ ἐλπίδ' ἔχει γηρασσέμεν, οὔτε θανεῖσθαι,
οὐδ' ὑγιὴς ὅταν ᾖ, φροντίδ' ἔχει καμάτου.
νήπιοι οἷς ταύτῃ κεῖται νόος, ἰνδέ τ' ἴσασιν
ὡς χρόνος ἐσθ' ἥβης καὶ βιότου ὀλίγος
θνητοῖς. ἀλλὰ σὺ ταῦτα μαθὼν βιότου ποτὶ τέρμα
ψυχῇ τῶν ἀγαθῶν τλῆθι χαριζόμενος.

Nil homines inter firmum manet atque perenne.
  Nec leviter Chii verba notanda viri;
"Haud secus ac frondes semper mutamur in annum."
  Auribus acceptum non tenuere diu
Mortales monitum: nam spes non deserit ullum,
  Spes adolescentis pectore blanda viget;
Dumque brevi fruitur mortalis flore juventæ
  Multa agitat nunquam perficienda sibi
Nec mortem exspectans obrepentemve senectam:
  Nec morbi sanus credit adesse malum.
Insipiunt tales, et quàm pede præterit ætas
  Veloci haud nôrunt, temporis immemores:
Tu tamen hæc animo digne præcepta recondens
  Supremum degas lætus ad usque diem.

ON THE EXAMINATION OF FRESHMEN AT TRINITY COLLEGE,
(1807.)

O verè miseros! novâ
Quos æstate furens exanimat metu
    Arcti rixa mathematos; *
Solvendos tibi Sphinx altera callide
    Nodos objicit Algebra,
Duræque insequitur calcibus Algebræ
    Vivâ voce Menexenus: †
Eheu quam tremulos dente‡ petit fero.
    Atqui hic, nescio quomodo,
Valde visus erat dissimilis sui

---

* Mathematics rather preponderate in the examination.
† Construing and questions vivâ voce in the Menexenus of Plato.
‡ This part of the examination was conducted by Mr Tooth.

Multo nempe minutias
Verborum studio, et **vel minimas quidem,**
  Sectabatur ineptias.

Post hunc Euripides in medium tibi
Phœnissas agit æquior.
   • • • • • •

Quis digno poterit carmine dicere
  Turmam quæ sequitur trucem?
Exercet miseris quæstio te modis;
  Per tres ah! miseros dies
Aut plumam geris **aut labra moves male.**
  Romæ non **aliter, ferunt,**
Pallentes **agitant hæreticos pii**
  Quæsitoris opuscula;
Nigrâ non aliter pontifices stolâ
  Vultuque incutiunt metum
Verborumque **dolos et laqueos** parum
  Vitandos **pariter struunt.**

CHARADE (about the same date.)

Cui primum dixit quivis **non optat ut hic sit;**
  (Quid sit mente capis si vel iota sapis)
Pauci per mundum ceperunt mente secundum,
  Miris res modis illa referta modis:
Credo magis duram tibi nodosamque futuram
  Volvas qui ista duo pectore juncta tuo.

ENIGMA (ditto.)

  Canis capillis, crede, candescens caput
  Canis carebat crinibus,

PROPOSITION VII. (ditto.)

Circuli in extremâ corpus se parte revolvat,
  Tendentis quærenda tibi est atque invenienda
Ad punctum quodcunque datum vis centripetæ lex.

ENIGMA (ditto.)

Primum arcere decet multis totidemque secundum
  Obicibus, cure cui bona sunt et opes,
Deque molâ totum, necnon **de** mole licebit
  Sumere, sed pecori si **sapis** abjicies.

EPITAPH ON PRIOR (ditto.)

Horatianus Stoicus hic credo jacet,
Regum ipse princeps atque sutorum fuit;
Quemvis enim si conferas mortalium,
Noster poeta semper evadet Prior.

PLAUTINI ET NUMERI ET SALES (ditto.)

Vos nomen olim quibus Hibernis inditum
Potius æstivi debuistis dicier,
Ita pol calente et fervidâ estis indole
Nisi à procellâ forte dicti et turbine.

GOOD ADVICE (ditto.)

My dear youth, I must blame that extravagant dress;
With fashion comply in a certain degree,
But yield not, I pray, to such foolish excess,
For *est modus in rebus* in Horace you'll see.

HOW THROWN AWAY.

In one's things there's a mode, that's the way to translate it,
Sir, I see we agree, let's no longer debate it.

To ——— ESQ., OF QUEBEC, (with a christening-fee returned.)

Old acquaintance works wonders, we well may agree,
When 'tis cause, who would ever believe it?,
That a lawyer insists upon giving a fee,
And a parson declines to receive it.

FOR HIS FATHER'S BIRTHDAY, 1824, (when his youngest brother was daily expected from New Brunswick, via Temiscouata.)

Le voilà mon jeune soldat,
—Ah qu'y penser le cœur me bat!
Qui, marchant d'une ardeur non feinte
De ses raquettes, à travers
Les lacs gelés, les bois déserts
En long sillage, laisse empreinte:
Mais il va toujours en chantant,
Et de ses chansons le refrain
De sa famille c'est le sein

O le bon père,
La tendre mère,
Mes sœurs, mon frère,
Famille chère,
Que d'y aller je suis content !

La nuit descend, pour tout couvert
D'un toit de neige l'on se sert,*
Dessous il n'y a point d'autres planches,
Pour lit, manteaux, fourrures, branches,
Aux pieds force bois fait chaleur :
Il dort—aucune dans son cœur
Crainte n'émeut ni ver le ronge,
" Je les connais,—c'est lui,—c'est elle,
    " O le bon père,
    La tendre mère,
    Mes sœurs, mon frère,
    Famille chère,
Heureuse maison paternelle."

Regarde sur l'amas de glace
Sa route ce canot qui trace :
Sautez dedans ! vite ! on reprend
Les avirons,—le fleuve on fend :
Parmi ce monde qui traverse
De le trouver l'espoir me berce :
Que de plaisir pour nous, pour lui,
S'il pouvait venir aujourd'hui !
Pendant que célébrant la fête
    De ce bon père,
    Famille entière,
    Avec la mère,
    Encore un frère
N'y mettrait pas de trop sa tête.

FOR THE 11TH MARCH, 1824; by Captain A. Mountain.
Alla Signora Mountain.

        Ecco quel di felice,
        Quel di si caro a noi !
        Madre, dei figlj tuoi
        Come 'l pensier spiegar ?

---

* This is a mistake, for in camping out there is no covering overhead
whatever, unless a snow-storm arrests the march of the party, in which
case a wigwam is constructed.

Pieno di affetto il core
Vorria parlar d'amore :
Ma non sa dirti il labbro
Quanto sappiamo amar.
Se tu de' pargoletti,
Gia tanta cura avesti,
Deh! soffri almen, che questi
Curia omai di te,
Soffri ch'a te d'intorno
Lodiamo sempre il giorno
Il qual, pel nostro bene,
La cara madre diè.

TO MRS. MOUNTAIN.

What in Italia's liquid tongue
Your soldier boy so well has sung,
Let his grave brother's priestly muse
More rudely to our own transfuse.

TRANSLATION.

This is the day,—the honoured day,
    But, mother, as they ought,
How shall thy grateful children say
    Each true and tender thought?
Our filial love I fain would speak,
    But speech, alas! is all too weak.

O if thy hand did gently rear
    A helpless infant set,
To them the task shall still be dear,
    To render back the debt ;
Forbid not then that still they press
    The day that gave them thee to bless.

WRITTEN IN BEATTIE'S MINSTREL, (given to his sister-in-law on her leaving Canada, 1824.)

Ainsi la maison paternelle,
Vous redemande, aimable sœur ;
Partez, mais portez dans le cœur
Qu'on ne vous cède ici qu'à elle :

Que Dieu vous conduise sur l'onde,
De vos souhaits vous guide au **but !**
Et par les flots de ce bas monde
Vous mène au havre du salut !

WRITTEN FOR ONE OF HIS CHILDREN as addressed from herself
to a cousin on leaving Canada, 1833 :

Cousin, we have not known you long,
  Till lately saw you never :
And here we sing our farewell song
  Farewell, perhaps, forever!
God bless you, cousin,—words are these
  Too oft but lightly spoken,
Yet can we, if the heart agrees,
  Exchange a dearer token ?
God bless you, then, and not for aye
  We part, if He shall guide us ;
No—to one Home we bend our way,
  Where nought shall more divide us.

TO THE REV. S. MOUNTAIN, WITH A GREEK TESTAMENT.

Moribus et linguâ pariter quo præcipis uti
Hunc a me librum tu precor accipias.

TO BISHOP STEWART, WITH A COPY OF BISHOP HALL'S WORKS. 1835.

Hic tibi quem mitto, præsul carissime, librum
  Fratris in officio est, corde itâ fratris opus :
Norvicensis opus : mente est Quebecensis eâdem,
  In Christum, haud scribens, ardet amore pari.
Unus utrique labor, gregis inservire saluti :
  Sors itidem **in** cœlis una duobus erit.

ON THE NOMINATION OF DR. FULFORD TO THE SEE OF MONTREAL.

Ecce vadum plenum : pons hic ut fiat, opinor,
  Plane opus est : opus est jam tibi pontifice :
Nonne vado e pleno res est jucunda, sodales,
  Ipsum si potero tingere pontificem ?

On sending the above to his brother, he received the following :

The Bishop of Montreal is reported to have replied to your admirable epigram by a very poor one :

Ecce vadum plenum, conclamant, siste viator !
Non ego : planitiem spernens celsum petam Montem.*

ANGLICE.

Here's a *full ford* : we can no farther go,
  Then stay below ;
I'll climb beyond that ford's o'erflowing fountain
  The lofty *mountain.*

ENIGMA.

Beginning of eternity,
  And end of time and space,
Beginning, too, of every end,
  And end of every place.

CHARADES.

My *first* is a bird,
  My *second* a fish,
An insect my *third*
  Whose destruction you wish.

---

* A similar play on the name of Mountain is found in the following epigram written by Archdeacon Lower, in 1835, (as well as in a well-known one in Camden's Remains, " Defensor Fidei," &c.)

In reverendissimum Patrem in Deo, G. J. M.

———

Monti olim montem audivi cumulare gigantes :
  Scandere regna adeo non potuere Jovis.
Complures capiant cœlorum regna fideles,
  Te duce, vi sacrâ, Mons Reverende, precor.

ANGLICE.

Mountain on mountain, poets tell, was piled by giant force,
  Nor even then could mortals scale the citadel of Jove.
More happy now, taught, Mountain, by thy words and faithful course,
  May thousands overcome, and gain the paradise above.

In the year 1836 the Bishop attended the consecration of a church, which was so crowded that he was obliged to sit on the pulpit steps. The preacher, immediately after passing him as he so sat, gave out as his text the words of Zech. iv, 7, " Who art thou, O great *mountain ?*"

First ornithology,
Next icthyology,
Then entomology,
Triple zoology :
—Range through philology
Where will be heard
So learned a word ?
Natural history
Dressed up in mystery,
Happy conjunction of sciences trine !
Never, O never,
Charade was so clever,
Never charade was so clever as mine.

———

A late charade touched, part by part,
Three orders scientific :
This, in three tongues, with noble art,
Proceeds from brain prolific.

My *first* shall be a Latin word,
And French shall be my *second*—
But, gentles, I will have a *third*
Among plain English reckoned

My Latin *first*, a little foe,
Delights in household spoils,
Remorselessly you doom his woe
If caught within your toils.

My next, in French, describes but ill
The lively sons of France,
It pictures what is sluggish still,
Unready to advance.

My English whole lies oft beside
Old England's roasted beef ;
In some disorders, too, applied,
It gives a sharp relief.

————

THE SPELLS OF IMAGINATION.

Unreal mockery hence !
Invent portum : spes et fortuna valete   (1833.)

The flowers of life are withered,
Its fire poetic dead,
Its fond romance for ever,
Like morning vapours, fled.

2.

Adieu, deceiving visions!
I loved you once so well,
E'en yet a sigh to lose you,
Will this weak bosom swell.

3.

I mean not of ambition,
The darkly thrilling game—
Vain chance of glittering riches—
Mad pleasure's lawless aim :

4.

No—though for things polluted
No sigh should stain the soul ;
Still, sorceress, all too slowly,
We break thy "soft control."

5.

Strange power of soothing fancies,
Thou yet cans't lead astray
The heart which godless passions
No longer make their prey.

6.

Tell how thy morbid musings,
Thy brilliant, shifting dreams,
Thy proud chivalric phantoms,
Can blend with Gospel themes.

7.

O Man of many sorrows !
And disciplined in grief—
Scourged, spit upon, insulted,
For our, for our relief !

8.

O sufferer in the garden,
And martyr on the tree !
Thy life was rudely taken—
And was it done for me ?

9.

It was—I read it written,
I feel it in my breast :
I know the pain which only
In Thee can find its rest.

10.

Then, if I cannot serve Thee,
  As should be man's delight:
If man can nothing render
  God's mercy to requite;

11.

If love, if best devotion,
  Ill do their bounden part,
Yet this, great God, vouchsafe me,
  To have a lowly heart.

12.

Chastised each wayward impulse,
  Each thought be captive led;
Quelled each vain fluttering fancy
  That revels round the head.

13.

What! would the worthless servant
  Be greater than his Lord?
And holds th' unskilled disciple
  His Master's lot abhorred?

14.

Like Him, indeed, Who bought thee,
  Thou art not called to grieve;
What share of earthly blessings
  Thy God has given, receive:

15.

Serene the charms of nature,
  Sooth are the joys of home;
Sweet oft the social converse
  That cheers **the way** we roam.

16.

Of taste, of fair refinement,
  The pleasures not refuse,—
Nor spurn the gentle solace
  Of her we call the muse.

17.

But oh! thy Master's glory
  Be still thy ceaseless aim:
Thy pearl of price His Kingdom,
  Thy hope His saving name.

18.

Yes, keep thy course, believer,
  Thy Saviour is thy strength;
And if the road be weary,
  Home, Home is reached at length.

MELANCHOLY MUSIC, (about 1836).

I'm never merry when I hear sweet music.—Shakspere.

How through the heart will sweep
With hidden spell and strong,
Those notes of sadness deep,
That swell of mournful song!
O still the charm prolong:
It touches on some tender string,
Akin to pain whence pleasures spring.

Stay, sweet vibration, stay,
To very soreness thrill:
Ah, has life's little day
Too small a share to fill
Our hearts, of real ill?
To quell its brightness must we borrow
A shade of artificial sorrow?

Oh no! in this lost world
Sad scenes and foul are rife;
Man from his glory hurled,
Breathes now a sickened life;
Lust reigns, with woe and strife:
And they who conquer in the Cross
Mourn still their sins and others' loss.

'Tis strange that so we love
Each melancholy air;
Sure in the choir above
No plaintive voice will share;
All is triumphant there:
The chants on high to joy are sung,
The harps of heaven to rapture strung

Seraph and saint around
Pour hallelujahs high,
The praise of God to sound

All with each other vie
The legions of the sky :
Rolls ever through the lengthened **throng**
The thunder of immortal song.

From rank to rank it rolls,
From side to side it rings,
And still from ransomed souls,
To God made priests and kings,
Redoubled tribute springs :
Glory to Him Who in the **flood**
Hath washed them **of** His blessed **blood.**

Before th' eternal throne
The prostrate orders cast
Their golden crowns, and own
Through present, future, past,
God ever first and last :
Lord God omnipotent, supreme,
Thrice holy, holy, holy theme.

ON A WATCH BEQUEATHED TO HIM BY BISHOP STEWART.
(1838.)

Golden gift bequeathed by one
Numbered **with the holy dead ;**
Marking still **the hours that run**
Swiftly by with noiseless tread.*

Precious gage, memorial dear,
Be **my** monitor and friend :
Moments make at last the year,
Warn me moments how to spend.

Wisely to redeem the **time**
He who wore thee once was skilled ;
So was **passed** his early prime,
So his closing hours were filled.

Moments lost and wasted **years,**
Ah! who now can call you back ?
Travellers through this vale of tears
Must not measure twice their track.

* The noiseless and inaudible foot of time
Steals on us unawares.

FF

Heed not, then, the things below,
　　Reach to those which lie before ;
Onward, onward press to find
　　Christ, alive for evermore.

ON BOWING AT THE NAME OF JESUS, (1841).

Prompt at the bidding of the soul,
　　Th' obedient body bends and plays :
Unseen, unheard, unfelt control
　　Which every spring and engine sways.

Unconscious of the power we ply,
　　Unskilled by deepest search to find
On senseless matter how and why
　　Can act this magic force of mind.

We rest, we move; we sit, we rise ;
　　We guide the pen, we touch the lute,
We feed the mouth, we turn the eyes,
　　We lift the flail, we drive the brute.

Nor thus alone ; for gestures mark
　　The movements of the soul within,
Paint thought or purpose bright or dark,
　　Impulse to seize or prayer to win.

We raise the brow, we wave the hand,
　　We bow the head, we bend the knee,
The bosom press, the arms expand,
　　'Tis language read by all who see.

'Tis this to forms and signs prepared
　　In social life has led the way ;
The palm is grasped, the hand is bared
　　Good will to speak or reverence pay.

Ah! if the flexion of the frame
　.　What stirs the inmost soul can shew,
How gladly at Thy glorious Name,
　　My Saviour, will I bow me low!

My Lord, my God, my life, my hope,
　　In darkness and in sin I lay,
With foes from hell unfit to cope,
　　And but for Thee their certain prey.

O didst Thou look on one like me,
　　King as Thou art of saints above,
And wert Thou lifted on the tree
　　To draw me by Thy boundless love ?

I yield me then—my heart is Thine,
　　(Would it were less a heart of stone !)
And still by each appointed sign
　　Thy sovereign claim I joy to own.

I thank the Church who early stamped
　　Her holy token on my brow :
Oh never be the memory damped
　　Of that my sacramental vow !

Taught by the Church, I duly kneel
　　To pour my prostrate soul in prayer ;
I rise when rising thoughts I feel,
　　And in the song of glory share.

I stand, with champions of the Cross,
　　Erect, aloud with one accord
To speak our faith : 'twere little loss
　　To lose our lives for Christ the Lord.

Thine is my soul, my body Thine,
　　My own I am not, would not be ;
I serve in all a Lord Divine,
　　I mark in all a homage free.

WRITTEN IN A CHILD'S ALBUM, (1836).

Sickness comes and sadness too,
Now to me and now to you ;
Praise the Name of God above,
Who afflicts us but in love.
Good, in time, from evil springs,
Blest effects from bitter things :
Those who suffer like their Lord
Gain, through Him, their high reward.
And the lesser ills of life
Fit the soul for sharper strife :
Sharper strife may be in store　⎫
Ere we reach the promised shore :　⎬
Grief and pain are *there* no more.　⎭

TO MRS. MOUNTAIN.

(Written in the canoe, on the return from Red River, **2nd August, 1844.**)

My Mary, we are growing old,
  And many a change have seen;
The world should have but slender hold
  On hearts like ours, I ween.

Yet not less truly knit than when
  We pledged our mutual vows;
Though years this day thrice numbered ten
  Have silvered since our brows.

Oh no! each added year but draws
  More close the hallowed bond,
And we for love have deeper cause
  Than youthful partners fond.

Long since the tribute I have paid,
  And bear thee record still;
Each blessing thou hast better made,
  And lightened every ill.

Mary, no poetry is here,
  If poetry be feigned;
'Tis language of conviction clear,
  And feeling unconstrained.

O varied track of thirty years!
  —Of small avail to count
Their tale of earthly smiles and tears;
  No—let our musings mount.

The Lord forgive our frailties past,
  And in the narrow space
Between this moment and our last,
  Bestow more ample grace!

Forget we all the things behind
  And press to those before;
Intent the glorious prize to find
  Through Christ reserved in store.*

---

* Phil. iii. 13, 14.

Yet not insensible our souls
  Of earthly good must prove,
Each year, each day, each hour that rolls
  Our thankfulness should move.

Of blessings here our children chief,
  Though some sweet babes we mourn ;
And sharp and sore domestic grief
  Our human hearts has torn.

Yet God Who gave with gracious hand *
  Has marked them all his own ;
O lead we still their faith to stand
  On that fast rock alone !

NUNC DIMITTIS.

(Composed while lying awake at night, in illness, 1857.)

When Simeon in his aged grasp,
The Christ is privileged to clasp,
His hope is crowned, he asks no more ;
And thus his thoughts their language pour :
  Lord, 'tis Thy pleasure to release
  Thy servant, and I part in peace :
  Thy word a faithful pledge has been,
  These eyes have Thy salvation seen.
  The gracious purpose long in train
  To every people shall be plain ;
  Make Gentile darkness gladly shine,
  And Israel boast in being Thine.

---

* Gen. xxxiii. 5.

www.ingramcontent.com/pod-product-compliance
Lightning Source LLC
Chambersburg PA
CBHW052338110726
47901CB00005B/1275